"ANYONE WHO LOVES ROMANCE MUST READ SABRINA JEFFRIES!"

—Lisa Kleypas, *New York Times* bestselling author

Praise for the Hellions of Halstead Hall

They are the scandalous Sharpes, five hell-raising siblings tainted by a shocking family legacy. Now each faces a daunting ultimatum: change their ways and marry soon, or kiss their inheritance goodbye.

THE TRUTH ABOUT LORD STONEVILLE

"Jeffries pulls out all the stops with a story combining her hallmark humor, poignancy, and sensuality to perfection."

—*RT Book Reviews* (4½ stars, Top Pick)

"Delectably witty dialogue . . . and scorching sexual chemistry between two perfectly matched protagonists."

—*Booklist*

"Launches a sparkling series by the always entertaining Sabrina Jeffries . . . Lively repartee, fast action, luscious sensuality, and an abundance of humor."

—*Library Journal*

"*The Truth About Lord Stoneville* has the special brand of wit and passion for which Sabrina Jeffries is recognized, where each enthralling scene will thoroughly capture your imagination."

—*Single Titles*

"Sabrina Jeffries . . . starts another excellent series, which will alternately have you laughing, crying, and running the gamut of emotions."

—*Romance Reviews Today*

A HELLION IN HER BED

"Jeffries's sense of humor and delightfully delicious sensuality spice things up!"

—*RT Book Reviews* (4½ stars)

"Rich with family interaction and overflowing with scintillating wit and heart-stopping sensuality, this addition to Jeffries's addictive series will keep readers eager for the next installment."

—*Library Journal*

"A perfectly matched pair of protagonists and a lively plot blending equal measures of steamy passion and sharp wit."

—*Booklist* (starred review)

HOW TO WOO A RELUCTANT LADY

"A delightful addition to the scandalous Sharpe family saga . . . Quick pacing, witty dialogue, and charmingly original characters set Jeffries's books apart."

—*Publishers Weekly* (starred review)

"Steamy passion, dangerous intrigue, and just the right amount of tart wit."

—*Booklist*

TO WED A WILD LORD

"Wonderfully witty, deliciously seductive, [and] graced with humor and charm."

—*Library Journal* (starred review)

"Marvelous characterization, lovely conversation, and drama perfectly leavened with humor make this a grand romantic adventure."

—*Publishers Weekly* (starred review)

A LADY NEVER SURRENDERS

"Jeffries pulls out all the stops. . . . Not to be missed."

—*RT Book Reviews* (4½ stars, Top Pick)

"Brimming with an abundance of simmering sensuality and a splendidly wicked wit."

—*Booklist*

'TWAS THE NIGHT AFTER CHRISTMAS

"Sharply witty, deliciously sexy, and infinitely endearing."

—*Library Journal*

"An enchanting holiday charmer with a complex and captivating plot; characters that interact with emotional authenticity; and a rich set of conflicted, heart-tugging obstacles . . . A satisfying happily-ever-after set against a fun holiday backdrop."

—*Kirkus Reviews*

"A moving Regency with heart, soul, and holiday spirit . . . Compelling, fast-paced, and lively . . . with several surprising, tear-jerking twists."

—*Publishers Weekly*

ALSO FROM SABRINA JEFFRIES AND POCKET BOOKS

The Hellions of Halstead Hall Series

'Twas the Night After Christmas

A Lady Never Surrenders

To Wed a Wild Lord

How to Woo a Reluctant Lady

A Hellion in Her Bed

The Truth About Lord Stoneville

The Sinful Suitors Series

A Talent for Temptation (enovella)

The Pleasures of Passion

The Danger of Desire

"The Heiress and the Hothead" in
What Happens Under the Mistletoe

The Study of Seduction

The Art of Sinning

The Duke's Men Series

If the Viscount Falls

How the Scoundrel Seduces

When the Rogue Returns

What the Duke Desires

The School for Heiresses Series

Wed Him Before You Bed Him

Don't Bargain with the Devil

Snowy Night with a Stranger
(with Jane Feather and Julia London)

Let Sleeping Rogues Lie

Beware a Scot's Revenge

Only a Duke Will Do

Never Seduce a Scoundrel

The School for Heiresses
(with Julia London, Liz Carlyle, and Renee Bernard)

The Royal Brotherhood Series

One Night with a Prince

To Pleasure a Prince

In the Prince's Bed

By Sabrina Jeffries Writing as Deborah Martin

Windswept

Stormswept

Silver Deceptions

By Love Unveiled

SABRINA JEFFRIES

The TRUTH ABOUT LORD STONEVILLE

POCKET BOOKS
New York London Toronto Sydney New Delhi

Pocket Books
An Imprint of Simon & Schuster, Inc.
1230 Avenue of the Americas
New York, NY 10020

This Pocket Books paperback edition December 2021

For information about special discounts for bulk purchases, please contact Simon & Schuster Special Sales at 1-866-506-1949 or business@simonandschuster.com.

The Simon & Schuster Speakers Bureau can bring authors to your live event. For more information or to book an event, contact the Simon & Schuster Speakers Bureau at 1-866-248-3049 or visit our website at www.simonspeakers.com.

Manufactured in the United States of America

10 9 8 7 6 5 4 3 2 1

ISBN 978-1-9821-8849-8
ISBN 978-1-4391-6756-4 (ebook)

To Jean Devlin, thanks for all you do.

And to all the readers who fell in love with Stoneville—here's your guy's book at last!

Dear Reader,

My name is Hester Plumtree, but most people call me Hetty. I've run the family brewery ever since my late husband died, and while there are people who give me grief over that, I always say if you have the time to complain about other people's lives, then someone needs to give you more to do.

Of course, when it comes to my grandchildren, I exclude myself from that. I have a right to tell them what to do, don't I? I did mostly raise them myself after their father, the marquess, and their mother, my daughter, died in a tragic accident. And that's all I'll say since people gossip enough about it as it is.

Truth be told, all I want is great-grandchildren. Is that too much to ask? Yet all my stubborn grandchildren give me is grief. Take Oliver, for example. I can understand a young buck on the town sowing his wild oats with an opera dancer or two, but Oliver has made a science of it! Between his drinking and his wenching, there isn't a gossip rag that hasn't written about him—more times than not in conjunction with some naughty incident involving a half-naked female and a tub of smuggled brandy. I blame it on his father, whose wild ways Oliver adopted after his parents' death.

And don't get me started on the other four: Jarret with his gambling; Minerva with her salacious Gothic novels; Gabriel with his racing; and Celia, who never met a target pistol she didn't want to shoot. There's a reason society calls them the

Hellions of Halstead Hall. Don't get me wrong—they're good grandchildren. They ask after my health and accompany me into society and make sure I don't work too hard. But they refuse to shed their scandalous habits, and I've had enough!

So I've contrived a way to force them into settling down and behaving like the heirs I deserve. They're not going to like it, but tough times call for tough measures. As God is my witness, I will have great-grandchildren . . . soon!

Sincerely yours,
Hetty Plumtree

Prologue

Ealing, England
1806

Oliver Sharpe, sixteen-year-old heir to the Marquess of Stoneville, left the stables at Halstead Hall with his heart in his throat. His mother had ridden off toward the hunting lodge in a fury, and Oliver rarely saw her like that. Mostly, she was just sad . . . unless something monumental set her off.

Like finding her son acting in the basest fashion imaginable.

Mortification swamped him.

You're a disgrace to this family! she'd cried in a voice of sickened betrayal. *You're behaving exactly like your father. And I'll be damned if I let him turn you into the same wicked, selfish creature as he is, sacrificing anyone to his pleasures!*

Oliver had never heard his mother curse, and the fact that he'd driven her to do so chilled him. Was she right about him? *Was* he becoming just like his careless and debauched sire? The very thought made his stomach roil.

Worse yet, she was now riding out to lay his sins at Father's door, and Oliver couldn't stop her since she'd ordered him to stay out of her sight.

But *someone* had to go after her. The only other time he'd seen her in a rage was when she'd first discovered his father's infidelity, when Oliver was seven. She'd set fire to Father's collection of erotic books in the courtyard.

God only knew what damage she would wreak now that she believed her son was following in his father's footsteps. Especially with the house party in full swing.

As Oliver rounded the walls of the semifortified manor that was their country home, he spotted a familiar carriage coming up the drive, and his heart leaped. Gran! Thank God she'd arrived; Mother might actually listen to her own mother.

Oliver reached the front of the house just as the carriage stopped. Hurrying forward, he opened the door for his grandmother.

"Well, now, isn't this a pleasant surprise," she said with a warm smile as she stepped down. "I am glad to see you have not lost your courtly manners like some young rascals your age."

Normally he'd make a witty retort and he and Gran would spar a little, all in good fun. But he couldn't manage it today, not with fear riding him.

"Mother is angry with Father." Offering his arm to escort her to the house, he kept his voice low. The servants mustn't hear. Half the world already gossiped about Father's infidelities—no need to feed the sharks more chum.

"That is nothing new, is it?" his grandmother said dryly.

"This time is different. She's in a rage. She and I quarreled, and she rode off toward the hunting lodge alone."

"Probably looking for him."

"That's what I'm afraid of. You know how he likes to bait her. If he's there, she's liable to do anything."

"Good." She flashed him an arch smile. "Perhaps she'll destroy that wretched lodge. Then Lewis will have nowhere to take his little whores."

"Blast it, Gran, I'm serious!" When she lifted an eyebrow at his language, he bit back an oath. "Forgive me, but this isn't like usual. You have to go after her, talk to her, calm her down. It's important. She won't listen to me."

Her eyes narrowed. "Is there something you're not telling me?"

He colored. "Of course not."

"Don't lie to your grandmother. What was your quarrel with your mother about?"

How could he tell her? He cringed every time he thought of it. "It doesn't matter. Just believe me when I say she needs you."

Gran snorted. "Your mother hasn't needed me from the day she was born."

"But Gran—"

"See here, Oliver," she said, patting his hand as if he were some child, "I know you're close to your mother, and it upsets you to see her angry. But if you give her time alone to let her anger run its course, she'll be fine, I swear."

"No, you've got to—"

"Enough!" she snapped. "It's been a long, hard trip, and I'm tired. I need a hot cup of tea and a good nap. I'm in no mood to involve myself in your parents' quarrels." At his look of desperation, she softened her tone. "If she hasn't returned by nightfall, I promise I'll go after her. You'll see—she'll be back long before then, full of apologies, and this will all be forgotten."

But his mother never returned. That night at the hunting lodge, she shot his father and then herself.

And Oliver's life was never the same.

Chapter One

Ealing
1825

Oliver stared out the window of the library at Halstead Hall. The dreary winter day further depressed his spirits as he fought to shove his painful memories back into the stout strongbox in which he kept them. It was so much harder here than in town, where he could lose himself in wenches and wine.

Not that he could lose himself for long. Though the scandal was nineteen years old, there were still whispers of it wherever he went.

Gran had told the guests that night that Mother had gone to the hunting lodge to be alone and had fallen asleep. Awakened by sounds of what she thought was an intruder, she'd panicked and shot him, only to discover that the man was her husband. Then, in her shock and grief, Mother had turned the pistol on herself.

It was a flimsy tale at best to cover up a murder and a suicide, and the whispers never quite subsided since the guests had been eager to speculate on the truth. Gran had ordered him and his siblings not to speak of it to anyone, even each other, from that day forward.

She'd said it was to stifle the gossip, but he'd often wondered if it was because she blamed him for what happened. Otherwise, why reverse her decree in recent months to question him about the quarrel between him and Mother that night? He hadn't answered, of course. The very thought of telling her turned his stomach.

Whirling away from the window, he paced beside the table where his siblings sat waiting for Gran. This was precisely why he avoided Halstead Hall—it always put him in a maudlin mood.

Why in God's name had Gran asked to have her blasted meeting out here? He'd kept the place shut up for years. It stank of must and rot, and was chilly as the Arctic besides. The only room lacking dust covers was the study where his steward did the work of running the estate. They'd had to remove the covers in here just to have this meeting, which Gran could have held perfectly well at her house in town.

Normally, he would refuse her request that they troop out to his neglected estate. But ever since his brother Gabriel's accident three days ago, he and his siblings had been skating on thin ice with her. That was made more than clear by Gran's uncharacteristic silence about it. Something was afoot, and Oliver suspected it wouldn't be to their liking.

"How's your shoulder?" his sister Minerva asked Gabe.

"How do you think?" Gabe grumbled. He wore a sling over

his rumpled black riding coat, and his ash-brown hair was mussed as usual. "Hurts like the devil."

"Don't snap at *me.* I'm not the one who nearly got myself killed."

At twenty-eight, Minerva was the middle sibling—four years younger than Jarret, the second oldest; two years older than Gabe; and four years older than Celia, the baby. But as the eldest girl, she tended to mother the others.

She even looked like their mother—all creamy skin and gold-streaked brown hair, with ivy-green eyes like Gabe's. There was virtually no resemblance between those two and Oliver, who'd inherited the coloring of their half-Italian father—dark eyes, dark hair, dark skin. And a dark heart to match.

"You're lucky Lieutenant Chetwin pulled back in time," Celia pointed out to Gabe. She was a slightly paler version of Oliver, as if someone had added a dollop of cream to her coloring, and her eyes were hazel. "He's rumored to have more bravery than sense."

"Then he and Gabe make a good pair," Oliver growled.

"Lay off of him, will you?" Jarret told Oliver. Closest to being a blend of their parents, he had black hair but blue-green eyes and no trace of Oliver's Italian features. "You've been ragging him ever since that stupid carriage race. He was drunk. It's a state you ought to be familiar with."

Oliver whirled on Jarret. "Yes, but *you* were not drunk, yet you let him—"

"Don't blame Jarret," Gabe put in. "Chetwin challenged me to it. He would have branded me a coward if I'd refused."

"Better a coward than dead." Oliver had no tolerance for

such idiocy. Nothing was worth risking one's life for—not a woman, not honor, and certainly not reputation. A pity that he hadn't yet impressed that upon his idiot brothers.

Gabe, of all people, ought to know better. The course he'd run was the most dangerous in London. Two large boulders flanked the path so closely that only one rig could pass between them, forcing a driver to fall back at the last minute to avoid being dashed on the rocks. Many was the time drivers pulled out too late.

The sporting set called it "threading the needle." Oliver called it madness. Chetwin had pulled back, yes. But Gabe's rig had caught the edge of one boulder, breaking off a wheel and subsequently turning the phaeton into a tangle of splintered wood, torn leather, and twisted metal. Thank God the horses had survived, and Gabe had been lucky to get out of it with just a broken collarbone.

"Chetwin insulted more than just me, you know." Gabe thrust out his chin. "He said I wouldn't race him because I was a coward like Mother, shooting at shadows." Anger tinged his voice. "He called her the Halstead Hall Murderess."

The familiar slur made the others stiffen and Oliver grit his teeth. "She's been dead for years. She doesn't need you to defend her honor."

A stony look crossed Gabe's face. "Someone's got to. You won't."

Damned right he wouldn't. She'd done the unthinkable. He could never forgive her for that. Or himself for letting it happen.

The door opened and their grandmother entered, followed

by the family solicitor, Elias Bogg. They collectively sucked in a breath. The presence of an attorney boded ill.

As Bogg took a seat, Gran stopped at the head of the table, a look of utter weariness etching lines in her already fully etched face. A new sort of guilt stabbed Oliver. She looked even older than her seventy-one years these days, as if the weight of her responsibilities had stooped her shoulders and shortened her height.

He'd tried persuading her to step down as head of the brewery that their grandfather had founded. She needed to hire a manager, but she refused. She liked the work, she said. What was she to do, stay in the country and embroider? Then she would laugh at the idea of a brewer's widow doing embroidery.

Perhaps she had reason to laugh. Hester "Hetty" Plumtree was what many would call "common." Her parents had kept the tavern where she'd met her husband, and the two of them had turned Plumtree Brewery into an empire big enough to afford the finest schools for Oliver's mother, Prudence. Big enough to enable Prudence to snare an impoverished marquess for a husband.

Gran always reveled in the fact that her daughter had managed an alliance with one of the oldest branches of English aristocracy. But she could never hide the taint of "trade" clinging to her own skirts. It crept out at odd moments—when she enjoyed a spot of ale with her dinner or laughed at a bawdy joke.

Still, she was determined that her grandchildren become what she could not: true aristocrats. Gran hated their tendency to outrage the society that regarded them as the ne'er-do-well spawn of a scandalous couple. Due to her struggle to move her family up in the world, she felt entitled to see the fruits of that labor in good marriages and fine great-grandchildren, and it angered her that none of her grandchildren were rushing to accommodate her.

Oliver supposed she had some right to feel that way. Though she'd often been absent during their youth, busy running Plumtree Brewery after her husband died, she was the closest thing to a mother the younger ones had ever had. That was why they adored her.

As did he, when he wasn't fighting with her over money.

"Sit down, Oliver." She fixed him with her sharp blue gaze. "Your pacing makes me nervous."

He stopped pacing, but didn't sit.

With a frown, she squared her shoulders. "I have made a decision about you children," she said, as if they were still in leading strings. She scanned the room, her voice growing steely as she said, "It is high time you settled down. So I am giving you a year, during which matters will remain as they are. Then I mean to cut you off—every single one of you. You will be cut out of my will, as well." She ignored their collective gasp. "Unless . . ." She paused for effect.

Oliver ground his teeth. "Unless what?"

Her gaze turned to him. "Unless you marry."

He should have expected this. At thirty-five, he was well past the age when most men of rank took wives. Gran often bemoaned the fact that there was still no heir to the title, but who in their right mind would want to see this benighted line continue? His parents had married for money, and the result had been disaster. No matter how low Oliver's finances sank, he wasn't about to repeat the error.

Gran knew how he felt, and for her to use his siblings to ensure that he danced to her tune was a painful betrayal.

"You would leave my brothers and sisters destitute just to get me leg-shackled?" he bit out.

"You misunderstand," she said coolly. "When I say 'you,' I mean the whole lot of you." She turned her gaze to include his brothers and sisters. "You must all marry before the year is out, or say good-bye to your inheritance. What is more, I will let my lease on the town house lapse, since I only stay there because the girls are there. There will be no dowries for them, and I will no longer foot the bill for Gabe and Jarret's bachelor quarters in London and the stabling of their horses. If you five do not marry, that is the end of my support. You will be Oliver's responsibility and Oliver's alone."

Oliver groaned. The cumbersome estate he'd inherited scraped by, but it was far from self-sufficient.

Gabe shot up from the table. "Gran, you can't do that! Where will the girls live? Where will Jarret and I live?"

"Here at Halstead Hall, I suppose," she said with no apparent remorse.

Oliver scowled at her. "You know perfectly well that's impossible. I would have to open the place up."

"And God forbid he do that," Jarret said, with a note of sarcasm. "Besides, he's got the income from the estate to support him. So even if the rest of us do as you ask, he doesn't have to, so we'll be penalized when he refuses."

"Those are my terms," she said coldly. "They are not negotiable, my boy."

No matter what Jarret thought, Gran had to know that Oliver wouldn't let his siblings suffer. She'd finally found a way to make them toe her line: use their affection for each other, the one constant in their lives.

It was brilliant. It was diabolical. And probably the only scheme that would work.

Jarret might tell her to go to hell if it were only him involved, but he wouldn't sentence his sisters to live as spinsters or governesses. Minerva, who made a bit of money from her books, might thumb her nose at Gran's terms and attempt to live off her earnings, but she also wouldn't sentence the others to poverty.

Each of them would worry about the others. Which meant they would all feel compelled to do as she commanded, even Oliver.

"You could make this place self-sufficient if you wanted," she pointed out. "Perhaps if the five of you split the duties of running it . . ." She paused to shoot Oliver an arch glance. "Or if your brother took more of an interest in it, instead of leaving it to his steward and spending his days wenching and drinking, it might bring in enough to keep you all comfortable."

Oliver suppressed a hot retort. She knew why he could barely stand the sight of the place. Father had married Mother for her money so he could save the precious family seat, and Oliver would be damned if he let this blasted estate and everything it represented destroy him as it had his parents.

"I happen to know," Gran went on, "that Oliver sold the

last unentailed piece of family property to pay off several debts that you gentlemen jointly accumulated, since I refused to cover them. There is little left to sell that is not entailed. You need what I can provide, if you are to continue to live comfortably."

Deuce take her for being right. With the town house and his brothers' lodgings gone, his siblings would have no choice but to move in here. Even Oliver was without a place at present—the property in Acton that she'd spoken of had been his home until recently. He'd been staying with his brothers while he figured out what to do. But he hadn't planned on having the estate support them all, as well as his brothers' future wives and children.

No wonder Gran had managed to run a brewery with such success for the past twenty-two years. She was a Machiavelli in skirts.

"So who would inherit Plumtree Brewery?" he asked. "Do you mean to say you wouldn't leave it to Jarret, as Grandfather wanted?"

"I'd leave it to your cousin Desmond."

As Jarret groaned, Minerva cried, "You can't leave it to Desmond. He'll run it into the ground!"

Gran shrugged. "What do I care? I will be dead. And if you won't take the necessary measures to make sure that it stays in your family, then it really doesn't matter where it goes, does it?"

Celia rose in protest. "Gran, you know what Desmond will do. He'll hire children and work them to death." Celia volunteered with a charity that fought to improve child labor laws—

it was her passion. "Look at how he runs his mills. You can't leave it to *him*."

"I can leave it to whomever I please," Gran said, her eyes cold as slate.

Surely she was bluffing. She hated Desmond as much as the rest of them.

Still, she'd never been the bluffing sort. "I suppose you've chosen our mates for us, too," Oliver said bitterly.

"No. I leave that to you. But you will not settle down unless I force your hand; I have indulged you all too long. It is time you do your part for the family, which means providing the next generation to carry on my legacy."

Celia dropped heavily into her seat. "It's not as if Minerva and I can just pick a husband at whim. A man has to propose marriage. What if no one does?"

Gran rolled her eyes. "You're both lovely ladies who turn heads wherever you go. If you, Celia, would stop trouncing your brothers' friends in shooting matches, one of them would probably offer for you in a trice. And if Minerva would stop writing those ghastly Gothic novels—"

"I won't do that," Minerva protested.

"At least take a pen name. I don't see *why* you must go about acknowledging the fact that you are the author of such disreputable stories, scandalizing everyone you meet."

Her gaze shifted to Jarret and Gabe. "As for you two, you could actually attend a ball occasionally. Jarret, you do not *have* to spend every night in the gaming hells, and Gabe . . ." She let out a weary sigh. "If you would only stop racing any fool who challenges you, you might have the time to seek out a bride. You lads are perfectly capable of enticing respectable women to marry you. You never seem to have trouble coaxing whores and actresses into your beds."

"Oh, God," Gabe muttered, his ears turning pink. It was one thing to bed a whore and quite another to have one's grandmother remark upon it.

She fixed Oliver with a steady look. "And we all know that your brother has a considerable advantage: his title."

"And the trade of title for money ended so well for our parents," Oliver said sarcastically. "I can see why you're eager for me to repeat the transaction."

When pain slashed over her face, he ignored the twinge of guilt in his chest. If she meant to force them into this, then she'd have to accept the consequences.

His mother's last words to him clamored in his brain. *You're a disgrace to this family . . . .*

A chill coursed down his spine. Abruptly he walked to the door and opened it. "May I have a private word with you in the hall, Gran?"

One gray brow flicked upward. "If you wish."

As soon as they were away from the others, Oliver faced her down. "Inflicting me as a husband on some hapless woman won't change anything."

"Are you sure?" Gran met his gaze steadily, her blue eyes softening. "You are better than this aimless life you lead, Oliver."

God, if she only knew. "This is what I am. It's time you accepted it. Mother did."

She paled. "I know you do not like to speak of what happened that day—"

"I don't," he cut in. "And I won't." Not to her or anyone.

"You will not speak of it because you blame me for it."

"That's not true, blast it!" He blamed himself alone. If only he'd ridden after Mother as soon as she'd gone missing. If only he'd pressed Gran harder. If only, if only, if only . . .

"I don't blame you for anything in the past. But I *will* blame you for this."

"Surely even you can see that something must be done."

"Why? Minerva and Celia will marry eventually, and Gabe and Jarret are just sowing their wild oats. Given time, they'll settle down."

"*You* have not."

"That's different."

"Why is it different?"

"Why are you suddenly so determined to push this matter of our marrying?"

"Answer my question, and I will answer yours."

So that's what she wanted—to force him into a confession of his sins. Well, she was never getting that from him.

"Someday, Oliver," she went on when he remained silent, "you will have to talk about what happened that day, if only so you can put it behind you."

"I *have* put it behind me." Turning on his heel, he strode for the door.

As he jerked it open, she called out, "I am not changing my mind about the inheritance or the rest of it. Marry or lose everything."

When he froze with his hand on the knob, she came up to stand in the doorway and sweep her gaze over his siblings inside the room. "I am tired of hearing you children called the Hellions of Halstead Hall in the scandal sheets. Of reading that my youngest granddaughter has once again horrified society by appearing at some shooting match." She leveled a glance on Gabe. "Or that my grandson nearly lost his life in a race. This will end now."

"What if we agree to behave more discreetly in the future?" Oliver snapped.

"Not good enough. Perhaps if you five have someone else depending on you—a spouse and children—you will finally learn the value of what you have."

"Damn it, Gran—"

"Stop cursing at me, Oliver. This is the end of the discussion. Mr. Bogg will explain the particulars of my demands and you may ask *him* your questions. I must attend a meeting at the brewery."

She walked off down the hall, her cane briskly tapping along.

The minute Oliver reentered the room, his siblings turned to Mr. Bogg. "She doesn't mean it, does she?" said one. "How could she do this?" said another. "You must talk her out of it," said a third.

Bogg sat back in the antique chair, which creaked in protest. "I'm sorry, but there's nothing I can do. After Lord Gabriel's injury, she became determined not to watch her grandchildren die before they do their duty to the family."

"You see what you've done, Gabe?" Celia cried. "You ruined everything!"

"It's not about Gabe," Oliver said wearily. "It's about me. She doesn't want to lose the title and position that she fought so hard to gain for her family. She means to make sure one of us chaps carries it on."

"Then why force me and Celia into it?" Minerva asked.

"Forgive me, your lordship," Bogg put in, "but you're wrong. She worries about all of you. She wants to make sure you're well settled before she dies."

Oliver's head snapped around. "Dies? Is Gran ill?" That possibility tied his insides into a knot. "Is there something she's not telling us?" It would explain the suddenness of her scheme.

Bogg paused before shaking his head. "She's merely tired of waiting for you five to provide her with great-grandchildren."

Now *that* Oliver could easily believe.

Bogg cleared his throat. "Have you any more questions?"

"Just one," Oliver said. "Did she really not stipulate *whom* we could marry?" He had an idea how to thwart her mad scheme.

"No stipulations on that score. But there are other rules."

Oliver listened as the man detailed those, one of which was that they must marry in England and not engage in a "havey-cavey Gretna Green elopement." Apparently she worried about such a marriage being disputed in court. Fortunately, none of what Bogg said would affect the plan forming in his mind.

After Bogg finished his duty and left them to their misery, Minerva appealed to Oliver. "You must convince Gran that this is insane. I don't see why I should put up with a husband when I'm perfectly content with my life as it is."

"I'm no more eager to marry than you are, Minerva," Jarret growled. "Next thing you know, she'll have me running the bloody brewery. And that is the last thing I wish to do."

"I say we move in here and show her that we don't need

her money," Celia exclaimed. "Do as she says, run the estate together—"

"Yes, because you know so much about running an estate," Gabe shot back.

"Celia has a point, though," Minerva put in. "If we show her we can manage perfectly well on our own, she might rethink her plans. Besides, if we're going to end up here eventually anyway, we should start getting used to it."

"God help us." Jarret shot Oliver a hard look. "You don't want us moving in here, do you?"

Oliver sighed. "I'd just as soon never see the place again. Unfortunately, Celia's idea is sound. If we live here, we'll call Gran's bluff. We can invite her to visit, let her see what fruit her nonsense will bear if she goes through with it."

He struggled to contain his revulsion at the thought of living at Halstead Hall again. But it would only last until he could bring his plan to fruition; then life could go back to normal.

"In the meantime, I have another trick up my sleeve," he went on. "It's risky, but it might force Gran's hand. She hasn't fully thought this through, and I mean to make her realize that. I still have money left from the sale of that last property, and here's what I propose. . . ."

Chapter Two

"For heaven's sake, Freddy, keep up," Maria Butterfield muttered at her spindly cousin as she strode down the muddy street. The clerk ahead of them was setting a rather brisk pace. Bad enough that they were forced to endure this miserable English weather; if they lost their quarry, they'd have no way to find Nathan Hyatt. She wasn't about to risk that after traveling all the way from Dartmouth, Massachusetts, to retrieve her fiancé.

"Are you sure that fellow's satchel belongs to Nathan?" Freddy wheezed.

"It has lettering on both sides, just like the one I had specially made for him. And the man carrying it was in the same area as London Maritime, where Nathan was last seen three months ago. I need only get a closer look at it to be sure."

"How're you supposed to do that? And don't think I'll do it—I'm not tangling with some English devil just at your say-so."

"I thought you were wearing that sword to protect me."

Freddy had donned Father's old sword and scabbard every day since they'd arrived in London. It drew attention wherever they went; no one carried a sword these days.

"It's to protect *me*," Freddy countered. "I hear tell that they duel for fun here. I didn't come all this way just to see my favorite sword nicked in a fight."

She snorted. "You came because your older brothers had families to look after, and Aunt Rose would have boxed your ears if you hadn't." When Freddy colored, she softened her tone. "Besides, there's no need for any dueling. We'll convince the fellow to let us look at the satchel peaceably—after we see where he's going. I'm hoping he leads us to Nathan."

"*I'm* hoping he leads us to a pie shop. It's been nigh on three hours since we ate." As if on cue, his stomach rumbled. "Didn't know you meant to starve me."

She sighed. Freddy lived in a perpetual state of starvation. Aunt Rose said that all young men of twenty-one ate like bulls, but right now, Maria would rather they ate like chickens and fought like bulls. Given how Freddy was eating up their funds, he was proving a rather costly protector.

How she wished Nathan had stayed in America, where he belonged. How she wished Papa hadn't died . . .

Grief stabbed her as she stepped over an ice-laced puddle. She still couldn't believe it. Papa hadn't been his usual robust self in some time, but she hadn't expected him to die in his office of sudden heart failure at age sixty-five.

A disturbing thought occurred to her. If Nathan hadn't received her most recent letters, then he didn't even know Papa was dead. He didn't know he was now sole owner of New Bedford Ships, assuming he married her as planned.

And what if he *didn't* marry her? Was that why she hadn't heard from him in months? Had he taken his chance to escape their betrothal?

Any man would have tired of Papa's incessant demands that Nathan prove himself worthy of running the company before he married the woman who would inherit half of it. Those demands had sent Nathan to England to negotiate a lucrative sale of clipper ships to London Maritime. Maybe once he'd arrived here, he'd reconsidered their engagement.

Tears welled in her eyes. No, he wouldn't do that. He was an honorable man. Their relationship might be less passionate than that of some betrothed couples, but surely he cared for her, as she did for him. Something dreadful must have happened—he would never shirk his responsibilities. She had to find him. She couldn't lose both him *and* Papa.

Yet that satchel in another man's hands didn't bode well for Nathan's being all right. Nathan would never have given it up. The man had to have stolen it.

Her heart pounded in time to her quickening steps. Nathan was probably lying dead in some field, done in by the treacherous English. And if he were . . .

She couldn't think of that right now or she'd surely shatter.

"Mopsy—" Freddy began in an undertone.

"Don't call me that. We're not children anymore." Besides, Nathan thought it unbecoming to a lady. He was particular about such things, having been raised in Baltimore high society before moving to tiny Dartmouth six years ago to partner with Papa.

"Sorry, Mop—Maria," Freddy mumbled. "I keep forgetting." He edged closer. "But I'm thinking we shouldn't stay out past dark. This part of town doesn't seem very nice. And those ladies up there look a little . . . well . . . naked."

She'd been so focused on not losing the man ahead that she hadn't noticed their surroundings. As she glanced about, her heart faltered. Scantily dressed women hung out of the windows above them, their bosoms spilling out of their bodices. They had to be freezing, but clearly that took second place to their purpose.

Memories of fetching Papa from such places when no one else could go after him made her stiffen.

"See here, sir," one of them called to Freddy, her breath a puff of mist, "I got a tuzzy-muzzy that'll bring you to a cockstand right quick."

"You can sample my quim for only half a quid, love," added another.

Maria didn't understand their words, but judging from the blushes darkening Freddy's freckled cheeks, they were rather . . . salacious.

"Let's go back to the lodging house," Freddy said.

"Not yet. Our quarry is stopping up ahead, and all we have to do is get a look at that satchel. We might not have another chance."

They hung back until the man entered the building. Then they approached the front. Raucous laughter spilled into the street, along with the gay tunes of a fiddle playing a jig.

Through the open door, she could see couples engaged in dancing and . . . naughty behavior.

While the lamplighters trudged by with their torches, Freddy's brown eyes studied the house. "You can't go in there. It's no place for respectable women."

"I can see that." She shivered in her black redingote as a cold gust of wind hit her. "It appears to be a brothel."

"Mopsy!" His cheeks shone as red as his wildly disordered hair. "You're not supposed to talk about such things."

"Why? We both know Papa went to one every Saturday night." She turned to him. "Why don't *you* enter? They won't notice another man in there. Just find the satchel, and see if it's Nathan's."

"And if it is? Then what?"

"Then lure the man out here so I can speak to him. Tell him that his mother is outside, and she'll come in if he doesn't come out. No young man wants that."

Freddy looked skeptical, and she sighed. "If you do as I say, I'll buy you as many pies as you want."

"All right." Drawing his sword, he handed it to her. "You'd best hold on to this. You shouldn't be standing on the street without protection."

That he'd give up his precious sword for even a moment touched her. "Thank you." She gave him a push. "Now go find out if that satchel is Nathan's."

With a heavy sigh, Freddy trudged up the steps. Trying not to look conspicuous, she slid into the shadows and stifled a laugh as he hesitated before going in. Any other male Freddy's age would be dying to enter a brothel, but as usual, all he could think about was food. Yet no matter what he stuffed in his mouth, he stayed thin as a toothpick. Meanwhile, if she so much as added sugar to her tea for a week, she started popping out of her stays. It wasn't fair.

But then, life generally wasn't fair for women. If she'd been a man, *she* would have inherited Papa's company. He would never have brought in an outsider.

Not that she didn't like Nathan. He was clever and quite handsome, the sort of husband most women would walk over coals to catch. And she had little chance of finding another good husband in Dartmouth. It was a small fishing town with only a handful of educated unmarried men, and Papa's colorful background made her ineligible to wed a true gentleman.

She sometimes wondered if Nathan would even have considered her as his wife if not for her connection to New Bedford Ships.

No, that wasn't fair. He'd always been perfectly lovely to her. It wasn't *his* fault that their few kisses had been underwhelming—she must have done something wrong. Or expected too much from them.

Maybe Papa was right. Maybe she *did* read too many of those Gothic novels by Minerva Sharpe. After all, no man could be as dashing as the Viscount Churchgrove, or as heroic as the Duke of Wolfplain. Or even as fascinating as the villainous Marquess of Rockton.

She scowled. How could she think of Rockton at such a time? Bad enough that she'd been secretly pleased when he'd escaped justice at the end of the novel. The intrusion of such a wicked villain in her thoughts when she should be thinking only of Nathan was most alarming.

Maybe she *wasn't* a normal woman. She was certainly more outspoken and opinionated than most women she met. And she did so love reading about murder and mayhem. Papa had called it unnatural.

A sigh escaped her. It was true that other ladies didn't seem to listen with avid interest to men's tales of fighting in the Revolution, or pore eagerly over every dark crime reported in the newspaper. They didn't pray to solve an enigmatical murder.

A sudden cry of "Stop! Thief! Stop him!" from inside the house jerked her up short. Oh no, surely Freddy had not . . . he wouldn't have . . .

But of course he would have. Freddy didn't think.

Racing up the steps with sword in hand, she hurtled inside just in time to see a man block Freddy's path on a staircase as Freddy clasped the satchel to his chest like a shield.

"We've got you now, thief," said the man.

Her heart plummeted into her stomach.

Several steps above Freddy stood their quarry, red-faced and half-dressed, and behind him other men crowded around the stairs to see what was happening. Meanwhile, women in various stages of undress emerged into the hall.

"Polly, go fetch the constable," the man called to one of the women.

Oh no! This was a disaster!

The two men closed in on Freddy, with him stammering that he just "wanted a look at it, is all."

Hefting Freddy's sword, she brandished it at the nearest fellow. "Let him go! Or I swear I'll spit you like an orange!"

To her right, a voice drawled, "An *orange*? That's your dire threat, my dear?"

Panic seized her as she caught sight of the tall man who'd emerged from the front room. He wore no coat, waistcoat, or cravat and his shirt was opened down to the middle of his chest, but his commanding air said he would be in control of any situation, regardless of his attire. And he stood much too close.

"Stay back!" She swung the sword at him, praying she could actually use the curst thing. She hadn't realized that swords were so heavy. "I merely want my cousin, sir, and then we'll leave."

"Her 'cousin' tried to steal my satchel, my lord," cried their quarry.

My lord? Her pulse faltered. The tall fellow didn't *look* like the elegant men she'd imagined from Miss Sharpe's novels, though he did seem to possess their arrogance. But his skin was darker than she would expect, and his eyes bore a deadly glint that shot a chill down her spine. If he was a lord, then she and Freddy were in even bigger trouble.

"You take the woman, Lord Stoneville," said the other fellow, "and we'll seize the man. We'll hold the thieves until the constable arrives."

"We're not thieves!" She swung the sword between the two men, her arm aching from its weight as she glared at the man at the top of the stairs. "You're the thief, sir. That satchel belongs to my fiancé. Doesn't it, Freddy?"

"I'm not sure," Freddy squeaked. "I had to bring it into the hall to get a look at it. Then this fellow started shouting, and I didn't know what to do but run."

"A likely tale," their quarry sneered.

"I tell you what, Tate," Lord Stoneville said, "if Miss . . ."

When he arched one raven eyebrow at her, she answered without thinking, "Butterfield. Maria Butterfield."

"If Miss Butterfield will hand me the sword, I promise to arbitrate this little dispute to everyone's satisfaction."

As if she could trust a half-dressed lord in a brothel to arbitrate anything fairly. The English lords in books fell into two categories—honorable gentlemen and debauched villains. This man seemed more of the villain variety, and she wasn't fool enough to put herself into that sort of man's power.

"I have a better plan." With her heart thundering in her chest, she darted forward to thrust the point of the sword at Lord Stoneville's neck. "Either you tell them to let my cousin go, or you'll be wearing this sword in your throat."

He didn't even flinch. An unholy amusement lit his face as he closed his hand around the blade. "There's no chance of that, my dear."

She froze, afraid to move for fear of slicing his fingers.

"Listen well, Miss Butterfield," he went on in a voice of frightening calm. "You're already guilty of attempted theft, not to mention assaulting a peer. Both crimes are punishable by hanging. I'm willing to be reasonable about the assault, but only if you release the sword. In exchange, I'll let you argue for yourself and your 'cousin' concerning the theft." He said the word "cousin" with skeptical sarcasm. "We'll sort this out, and if I'm satisfied you're blameless of theft, you and your companion will be free to go. Understand?"

He had her now, and clearly he knew it. If she hurt him, her life would be worth nothing among this crowd.

Trying not to let her fear show, she said, "Do you swear on your honor as a gentleman to let us go if we explain everything?" If he agreed to be reasonable, then perhaps he wasn't a villain. Besides, he gave her little choice.

A faint smile quirked up his lips. "I swear it. On my honor as a gentleman."

She glanced to Freddy, who looked as if he might faint. Then she met Lord Stoneville's gaze. "Very well. We have an agreement."

Chapter Three

"Excellent," Oliver said, releasing a breath. Until that moment, he hadn't been sure he would prevail. Any woman brave enough to thrust a blade at him was unpredictable at best, and dangerous at worst. "On the count of three, we both release the sword. All right?"

She nodded, her blue gaze dipping to where her hand gripped the hilt.

"One. Two. Three," he counted.

The sword clattered to the floor.

Instantly, Porter and Tate seized the stripling she'd called Freddy. When the chap let out a cry, she whirled toward them in alarm. Oliver bent to retrieve the sword, then handed it off to Polly, the brothel owner, who carried it to safety.

"Bring him in here," Oliver ordered, nodding toward the parlor as he caught hold of Miss Butterfield's arm and urged her in that direction.

"You needn't manhandle me," she hissed, though she didn't fight him.

"Trust me, Miss Butterfield, you'll know when I'm manhandling you." He stopped before a chair. "Sit," he commanded, pushing her into it. "And try to restrain your urge to attack people for half a moment, will you?"

"I was not—"

"As for you," he growled at her companion, "give me the satchel that caused all this furor."

"Yes, sir . . . I mean, my lord."

Oliver took the satchel from the young man, whose face was drained of all color. Clearly, he lacked his companion's fierceness.

The satchel appeared ordinary—made of decent leather, with the usual brass fittings. Though it contained a number of banknotes, that didn't necessarily mean the lad had been trying to steal it. Most thieves would have removed the money and left the satchel, if only to keep from alerting anyone.

"Where did you get this, Tate?" Oliver asked.

"At the pawnshop round the corner. I bought it months ago."

When Miss Butterfield snorted, Oliver shot her a dark glance. "You claim that it belongs to your fiancé?"

"If you'll check the lettering," she said loftily, "I daresay you'll find his initials, 'NJH,' stamped on one side, and the words 'New Bedford Ships' on the other. I had it specially made for him myself."

"Did you now?" Though she was right about the lettering, it didn't prove much. A couple of clever Newgate birds would have scouted the item before attempting to steal it. They would already know what was engraved on it.

Still, this pair didn't seem like Newgate birds. They dressed too well for that, in what looked like deep mourning. New Bedford was in America, and they were definitely American, judging from their accents.

That might account for the chit's boldness. He'd always heard that American women were saucy. But saucy was one thing; bold enough to brave a brothel and put a blade to a man's throat was quite another. They might merely be a higher class of thief. If so, wearing black was a nice touch. Who would suspect a woman in mourning of anything criminal?

Especially one who was so very pretty. Tendrils of strawberry-blond hair framed her lovely face beneath her bonnet of raven silk and crepe. She had a pert nose, freckled cheeks, and a mouth made for seduction. He skimmed his gaze down her form with the expert eye of a man long used to undressing women. Beneath the heavy fabric of her redingote, she clearly had a body made for seduction, too, with lush hips and lusher breasts. Exactly his sort.

Hmmm . . .

Perhaps he could use this situation to his advantage. He'd had little luck this week in finding a whore acceptable enough to further his plan.

He turned to Porter and Tate. "Release the lad, and leave us."

"Now see here, my lord, I don't think—" Porter began.

"They'll get their just deserts," Oliver asserted. "You won't have cause for complaint."

"And what about my satchel?" Tate pressed.

"*Your* satchel!" Miss Butterfield shot to her feet. "How dare—"

"Sit down, Miss Butterfield," Oliver ordered with a stern glance. "If I were you, I'd hold my tongue just now."

She colored, but did as he commanded.

Oliver tossed the satchel to Tate. "Take it and go. I'll let you know my decision about these two shortly."

Out of the corner of his eye, he could see the American woman bristle, but she remained silent until the two men had gone, closing the door behind them.

Then she exploded out of the chair to glare at him. "That satchel belongs to my fiancé, and you know it! Mr. Tate clearly stole—"

"I've been acquainted with Tate for years, madam. He has his faults, but he's no thief. If he said he bought it at a pawnshop, odds are that he did."

"You would take his word over the word of a lady?"

"A *lady.* Is that what you are?" He cast her a dismissive glance as he buttoned up his shirt. "You vault into a brothel with only this unlicked cub for a protector. You hold a sword to my throat and attempt to extract him from the place by force. And you expect me to accept your word about the situation simply because you're female?" He gestured at the hapless Freddy, who stood frozen in terror. "You must think me as stupid as your 'cousin' there."

She marched up to him, hands on her hips. "Stop sneering the word 'cousin.' Freddy is not some accomplice in crime."

"Then why is *he* with you, instead of your supposed fiancé?"

"My fiancé is missing!" She took a steadying breath. "His

name is Nathan Hyatt, and he's my father's business partner. We came to London to find him. Papa died after Nathan left, so he needs to return home and run New Bedford Ships. I wrote him several letters, but he hasn't answered in months. I recognized his satchel when I saw your friend carrying it near where Nathan was last seen, and we followed him, hoping he might lead us to Nathan."

"Ah." He strolled to where his cravat lay draped over a chair, then knotted it about his neck. "And I'm supposed to believe this Banbury tale because . . ."

"Because it's true! Ask the people at London Maritime! Nathan came here four months ago to negotiate with them for some ships, but they said that after negotiations fell through within a month, he left there and hasn't been seen since. They assumed he'd gone back to America. And the owner of the boardinghouse where he'd been staying said much the same."

She paced the room in clear agitation. "But there's no record of him traveling on a company ship. Worse yet, the boardinghouse owner still has all my letters—unopened."

Whirling around, she cast him a concerned glance. "Something dreadful has happened to him, and your friend likely knows it. Nathan would never pawn that satchel. I gave it to him for Christmas—he wouldn't have parted with it!"

Her distress was quite convincing. He'd lived in or near London all his life and had seen sharpers and schemers by the score. They could never quite hide the hardness beneath the smooth surface of their roles. Whereas she . . .

His gaze took in her agitated breaths, her worried expression. She seemed an innocent in every sense of the word. One advantage to having a black heart was that he could spot an innocent from a hundred feet off.

She was probably telling the truth. Indeed, it would be pointless for her to lie, since he could always hold her here while he confirmed her story. But he didn't intend to do that. Her tale of woe made her even more perfect for his plan.

Still, before he proposed his unorthodox arrangement, he should find out exactly what he might be getting into. "How old are you?"

She blinked. "I'm twenty-six. What has that got to do with anything?"

So, she was an innocent but not a child, thank God. Gran would be suspicious if he brought home some chit fresh from the schoolroom.

"And your father owns a ship company," he said as he donned his waistcoat. A rich man had connections. That could be a problem.

"Owned. Yes." She thrust out her chin. "His name is Adam Butterfield. Ask anyone in the shipping industry about him—they all knew him."

"But do they know *you* is the question, my dear."

"What's that supposed to mean?"

"So far you've given me no evidence that you're his daughter." He buttoned up his waistcoat. "Have you letters of introduction to smooth your way here?"

She thrust out her chin with a mutinous air. "I didn't expect to need such a thing. I expected to find Nathan at London Maritime."

"You can ask at the shipping office," the stripling put in helpfully. "They'll tell you what ship we came here on."

"They'll tell me what ship Miss Butterfield and Mister Frederick came on," Oliver interjected as he slid into his coat. "But unless the captain introduced you to them as such, that isn't much evidence."

"You think we're lying?" she said, outrage flaring in her face.

No, but he'd gain nothing by letting her realize it. "I'm merely pointing out that you've given me no reason to believe you. I imagine that America is little different from England in certain respects: ship company owners have a station to uphold. And since I assume that your father was wealthy—"

"Oh, yes," Freddy put in. "Uncle Adam had pots and pots of money."

"Yet his daughter could not send someone to find her fiancé, like any respectable female would do?"

"I was worried about him!" she cried. "And . . . well, right now Papa's money is all tied up in the estate, which can't be settled without Nathan."

Ah. Better and better. "So you're here virtually alone, with no money, despite your claim to have a rich father and a certain station in society." He fished for more information. "You expect me to believe that the daughter of a wealthy ship company owner—who would be taught to keep quiet, do as she is told, and respect the proprieties—would go sailing across the ocean in search of her fiancé, looking for him in a brothel, attacking the first gentleman who dares to question—"

"Oh, for pity's sake," she snapped. "I told you why I did all that."

"Besides," her companion put in, "Uncle Adam isn't . . . *wasn't* like other rich gentlemen. He started out a soldier in the Marine Corps. He never put on airs. Always said he was born the poor bastard of a servant, and he'd die the rich bastard of a servant, and that was better than being a rich ass."

She groaned. "Freddy, please, you're not helping."

"So you see, sir," Freddy went on, to Oliver's vast amusement, "Mop—Maria isn't like other women. She's like her father. She doesn't listen to those who tell her to sit still and keep quiet. Never has."

"I noticed," Oliver said dryly. It was a point in her favor. "And what of her mother? Did she not teach your cousin to behave?"

"I'll have you know, sir—" Miss Butterfield began.

"Oh, she died in childbirth," young Freddy explained. "And anyway, she was only a shopkeeper's daughter herself, like Ma, her sister. Uncle Adam took us in after Pa died, so Ma could raise Maria. That's why I came here with her." He puffed out his chest. "To protect her."

"You're doing a fine job, too," Oliver said sarcastically.

"Leave him be," Miss Butterfield said, her eyes alight. "Can't you tell he wasn't trying to steal anything? He went in for *me*, to check the satchel and see if it had the right lettering on it—that's all."

"And was caught running out of the place with it. That's why those men out there want him hanged."

"Then they're fools. Anyone can tell that Freddy is no thief."

"She's right about that," the dull-witted Freddy put in helpfully. "I've got two left feet—can't go anywhere without running into something. That's probably why they caught me."

"Ah, but in cases like this, the fools generally prevail. Those fellows out there don't care about the truth. They just want your cousin's blood."

Panic showed in her face. "You mustn't let them have it!"

He stifled a smile. "I *could* put in a good word for him, soothe their tempers, and get you two out of this with your necks attached. If . . ."

She instantly stiffened. "If what?"

"If you accept my proposition."

A fetching blush spread over her pretty cheeks. "I shan't give up my virtue, even to save my neck."

"Did I say anything about giving up your virtue?"

She blinked. "Well . . . no. But given the kind of man you are—"

"And what kind is that?" This should be amusing.

"You know." She tipped up her chin. "The kind who spends his time in brothels. I've heard all about you English lords and your debauchery."

"I don't want your virtue, my dear." He flicked his glance down her delectable body and suppressed a sigh. "Not that I don't find the idea tempting, but right now I have more urgent concerns."

And no man of rank was fool enough to seduce a virgin—that was the surest way to end up leg-shackled to a schemer. Besides, he preferred experienced women. They knew how to pleasure a man without plaguing him about his feelings.

"This may surprise you," he went on, "but I rarely have trouble finding women to join me willingly in bed. I've no need to force a pretty thief there."

"I'm not a thief!"

"Frankly, I don't care if you are. The important thing is that you suit my purpose perfectly."

She had the same brash temperament as his sisters, which Gran had always deplored. She had the sort of upbringing that Americans seemed to prize and Englishmen to despise. A mother who'd been a shopkeeper's daughter, and a father who'd been an illegitimate American of no consequence? Who'd fought in the very revolution that had cost Gran her only son? He couldn't ask for better.

Best of all, the chit was in trouble—which meant she wouldn't cost him a small fortune, unlike the whore he'd planned to hire. But since he'd met her in a brothel, he could still use that to thwart Gran.

He strode up to her. "You see, my grandmother and I are engaged in a battle that I intend to win. You can help me. So in exchange for my extracting you and Freddy from this delicate situation, I'll require that you do something for me."

A wary expression crossed her face. "What?"

He smiled at the thought of Gran's reaction when he brought her home. "Pretend to be my fiancée."

Chapter Four

Maria gaped at him. Surely she'd heard him wrong. "You want me to *what*?"

The secretive smile playing about Lord Stoneville's sensual mouth gave her pause. "Pretend to be my fiancée for a short time. As soon as I convince Gran that I seriously mean to marry you, the need for the pretense will end."

She felt as if she'd stumbled into one of her Gothic novels. "You're mad."

"No, I'm just plagued with a grandmother who thinks that forcing me and my siblings into marriage will settle her mind about our futures—an idea that I mean to show her is absurd."

"By pretending to be engaged to a perfect stranger?"

He shrugged. "I came here looking for a whore to do the job. But they're expensive, and why should I settle for a whore when you'll do nicely?"

His gaze traveled down her body with thorough insolence. "You're exactly the sort my grandmother would find unacceptable as a wife for me: an American of low birth, with an impudent manner and a reckless tongue. And you're just pretty enough to convince her that I might actually contemplate marriage to you."

Shock held her motionless. She didn't know which was worse—his nonchalant attitude toward hiring a *whore* to fool his poor grandmother, or the insults he'd lobbed at her with insufferable arrogance. "Now that you've offended me in every possible way, do you think I'd agree to this insanity?"

Amusement flickered in his black eyes. "Given that your other choice is to take your chances with the gentlemen in the hall . . . yes, I do. Of course, if you *want* to watch your cousin hang—" He headed for the door.

"Stop!"

He paused with his hand on the handle, one eyebrow arched in question.

The curst man had her trapped, and he knew it.

No one in London could vouch for her and Freddy. As he'd guessed, not a soul here knew them. Even the ship they'd traveled on had already set sail. If they were arrested, the English authorities might be willing to write to Aunt Rose and confirm their story. But until word came, she and Freddy would surely be imprisoned. She wasn't sure she could survive weeks in prison, and Freddy wouldn't survive a day.

What was she thinking? Freddy wouldn't survive an *hour*.

Still, she cringed at the idea of letting this aristocratic bully blackmail her into doing his bidding. "You know perfectly well we're not thieves. You could vouch for us if you wanted. They'd accept whatever you told them."

His eyes narrowed. "And why should I? What would it gain me?"

"The satisfaction of knowing that you've done the right thing."

"You really are quite fetchingly naïve," he drawled.

She bristled. "So you have no morals?"

"None."

He actually admitted it! And with an appalling lack of shame, too. Yet she pressed on. "You told me that if you were satisfied we were blameless of theft, you'd let us go. You swore it on your honor as a gentleman."

Leaning against the door, he crossed his arms over his rather impressive chest. "Unfortunately for you, I have no honor. And the term 'gentleman' doesn't suit me particularly well, either."

His blithe manner incensed her. "I should have thrust that sword through your neck when I had the chance!"

That only seemed to amuse him. "Ah, but then you'd almost certainly have been hanged. And that would be such a pity for a woman as pretty as you."

She ignored the feminine vanity that responded to his calling her pretty. He probably said such things to women all the time. "It's no wonder your grandmother despairs of you. God only knows what a trial you are to your poor parents."

The humor vanished abruptly from his face. "Sadly, my parents are too dead to be overly concerned about my behavior."

His words were flip, but the sudden glint of grief in his eyes told another tale. "Please forgive me," she said hastily, cursing her quick tongue. "It's awful to lose your parents. I know that better than anyone."

"No need for apologies." He pushed away from the door. "They despaired of me long before they died, so you weren't far off the mark."

"Still, it was very wrong of me to—"

"Come now, Miss Butterfield, this has naught to do with my proposal. Will you pretend to be my fiancée or not?" When she hesitated, he went on with a hint of anger, "I don't see why you make such a fuss over it. It's not as if I'm asking you to do anything wicked."

That ridiculous remark banished her brief moment of sympathy. "You're asking me to lie! To deceive a woman for the sake of your purpose, whatever that is. It goes against every moral principle—"

"And threatening to stab a man does not?" He cast her a thin smile. "Think of it as playing a role, like an actress. You and your cousin will be guests at my estate for a week or two, entirely at your leisure." A dark gleam shone in his eyes. "I can even set up an effigy of myself for you to stab at will."

"That does sound tempting," she shot back.

"As for Freddy there, he can ride and hunt and play cards with my brothers. It's better entertainment than he'd find in the gaol."

"As long as you feed me, sir," Freddy said, "I'll follow you anywhere."

"Freddy!" Maria cried.

"What? That blasted inn where we're staying is flea-ridden and cold as a witch's tit. Plus, you keep such tight hold on the purse strings that I'm famished all the time. What's wrong with helping this fellow if it means we finally sleep in decent beds?

And it's not a big thing, your pretending to be betrothed to him."

"I'm already betrothed, thank you very much," she shot back. "And what about Nathan? While we're off deceiving this man's poor grandmother, Nathan might be hurt or in trouble. You expect me just to give up searching for him so you can get a decent meal?"

"And keep from being hanged," Freddy pointed out. "Let's not forget that."

"Ah, the missing fiancé," Lord Stoneville said coldly. "I did wonder when you would bring him back into it."

She glowered at him. "I never let him out of it. He's the reason I'm here."

"So you say."

That inflamed her temper. "Now see here, you insufferable, arrogant—"

"Fine. If you insist on clinging to your wild story, how about this: while you pretend to be my fiancée, I'll hire someone to look for *your* fiancé. A simple trade of services. A Bow Street runner will still cost me less than hiring a whore for two weeks."

"For pity's sake, you doubt my identity because I don't fit your notion of a wealthy man's daughter, yet you quibble over the cost of hiring people? I thought you lofty lords had plenty of money."

He sighed. "Not all of us. But that situation will improve once my grandmother comes to her senses. You *are* going to help me with that, aren't you?"

Though he couched it as a question, his glittering gaze showed it was really an order from a man used to getting his way.

But he was offering to help her find Nathan. There was that. *If* she could believe him.

"You've made it abundantly clear that you have no honor and are no gentleman. So how can I trust anything you say? How can I be sure that when this is over, you won't just hand us over to the authorities?"

"You can't," he countered.

"Then I'll take my chances with the men in the hall." She headed for the door.

"Wait!" When she paused to glance at him, all trace of his smug smile and the insolent arch of his dark eyebrow were gone.

"What if I swear on my mother's grave to uphold my promise?" His gaze locked with hers, solemn as death. "That's a vow I'd take very seriously."

A shiver swept down her spine. Something haunted in that look called to her. As if sensing that, he stiffened and his expression returned to the one of bored nonchalance that she despised, making her wonder if she'd imagined that glimpse of vulnerability.

"Really, Miss Butterfield," he went on, "don't force me to go down to the magistrate's office and spend hours talking to the authorities. I lack the time or the patience for it. It would be such an inconvenience at this hour of the evening."

"We'll do it," Freddy said quickly.

"Great heavens, Freddy—" Maria began.

"We've got to, Mopsy. I'm not going to prison for your principles. Besides, he'll help us find Nathan. That's all you want, isn't it?"

A weary sigh escaped her. Freddy did have a point. She was tired of searching for Nathan, tired of being on her guard every moment in this curst city, tired of dealing with Freddy's complaints. Maybe it was time to get some help.

She glanced to Lord Stoneville. "How long would I have to play this role?"

"Two weeks at most, though I suspect it will take less."

She must be mad to even consider this. But he had her cornered, and he knew it. And if he *did* hire someone to look for Nathan . . .

"All right," she said. "Two weeks, no more." When he started to smile, she added, "But you must swear on your mother's grave to help me find Nathan, as you promised. And that when I've met your terms, you'll let us both go free and end this nonsense about having us arrested for thievery."

"Whatever you wish," he said blithely.

"Swear it!" Some instinct told her that he'd meant it when he said he would take such a vow seriously.

A muscle worked in his jaw. Then he nodded. "I swear on my mother's grave that I'll do everything in my power to find your fiancé. And that at the end of two weeks, you'll be free to go wherever you please."

She let out a long breath. "Very well. Then I accept your proposal."

"Good. Stay here." Opening the door, he called for someone, and a burly man she hadn't seen before came in. "Watch them until I return," Lord Stoneville ordered, then disappeared into the hall.

When their guard eyed her as if she were a particularly

choice piece of beef, Maria turned her back on him, trying not to dwell on what could happen to them now that they'd put themselves at the mercy of a lord with no morals. She tried not to remember the wicked scenes she'd read in novels, where villains kept women imprisoned in their houses and did shameful things to them.

The books had been rather vague about that part, but what they'd left out, Maria had made up from her imagination. Her down-to-earth aunt had told her quite a bit about how men and women joined in the bedchamber, and it didn't take much to envisage a villain like Lord Rockton lying between a woman's legs and having his way with her.

Or a villain like Lord Stoneville.

Freddy sidled up next to her, and with a furtive glance at their guard, lowered his voice. "Stoneville seems like a decent enough chap."

She stifled a hysterical laugh. "Oh, yes, quite decent. We met him in a brothel, and he's blackmailing us into deceiving his grandmother."

"At least he's not handing us over to the constable. And he did find out about the satchel for you. He could have had us tossed into gaol the moment my sword hit the floor."

True. He'd heard them out when he hadn't had to. But that was only because she "suited his purpose."

The door opened and Lord Stoneville walked in, carrying several items. He nodded to the burly man, who left.

Lord Stoneville tossed a vivid red gown and other pieces of clothing onto a settee. "You'll have to change clothes. You can't wear mourning when I present you to Gran. It'll rouse questions about your situation, and I don't want her guessing that this is a sham."

Warily, Maria examined what he'd brought. The white gloves, stockings, and cap of white crepe edged in red satin with matching satin ribbons looked presentable enough, but the gown was tawdry to say the least. Made of a very cheap silk, it was cut shamefully low. "You can't expect me to wear this."

"Polly tells me it should fit. You're about the size of one of her girls."

Her *girls*? Polly must own the brothel. No surprise then that he was so chummy with the woman, given what Maria had seen of his character.

"The rest is fine," she said, "but the gown is too scandalous."

"It's the only thing I could acquire on such short notice," he bit out. "We'll get other clothes for you tomorrow, but for now this is what you'll wear."

She bristled at his high-handedness, wanting to argue, but she dared not until she and Freddy escaped this place with their necks intact.

He stared at her expectantly. "Well? Put it on."

"Not until you and Freddy leave!" she exclaimed.

"Sorry, my dear. I can't have him stand out there where our friends can reconsider their decision to let him go. Nor shall I leave you two alone to escape through some window." He shot her a cursory glance. "Trust me, I've seen more women in their corsets and shifts than you've seen years."

"I can well believe that." She sniffed. "At least turn around."

"Fine." He turned his back to her, and Freddy followed suit.

"But be quick about it. I'd like to reach Halstead Hall in time for dinner."

"Do as he says, will you?" Freddy put in. "I'm about to faint from hunger."

"For once, Freddy," she grumbled, "would you stop thinking with your stomach?"

The stockings seemed to fit, and she managed to undo her own gown so she could slip the other one on. But she could never button it herself, especially since it was small in the waist. And the bust. Mercy, she would need help.

"Freddy, come fasten me up, will you?"

Her cousin's back stiffened. "I can't do that!"

"Oh, for God's sake." Lord Stoneville strode over. "I knew you Americans were prudish, but this is absurd."

Before she could even protest, he began fastening her gown. To her horror, the faint scent of his spicy cologne and his fingers working efficiently over the buttons made an odd sort of heat rise up from her belly. That couldn't be good.

"You seem to know how to do up a woman's gown very well." She struggled to sound nonchalant. "I take it you've had plenty of practice."

"You know us debauchers," he said dryly. "Practice, practice, practice."

That set her to wondering how many soiled doves he'd taken to his bed. Did he touch them everywhere, as her aunt said men did? When images filled her mind, she swallowed. It was hard not to imagine such things when his fingers brushed her back with every motion. Nor did it help that the process had slowed to a crawl as he struggled to fasten the lower part.

"The gown is too tight for me," she said, embarrassed.

"It's just these blasted small buttons." His breath wafted over her cheek, making a shiver sweep her skin. "They're too dainty for a man's fingers."

Skeptical, she sucked in a breath, which must have helped because he finally got the back done up. But now that he'd finished, she realized just how scandalous the gown was. It exposed a shameful amount of her chest. That became only more obvious when he circled around in front of her to rake her with a heated glance.

"That'll do nicely."

His husky words quickened her pulse, despite everything. And when his gaze lingered on her partially exposed bosom with particular interest, one of Aunt Rose's practical warnings about suitors sprang instantly to her mind: *Men will try to touch your breasts. Don't let them.*

A nervous giggle escaped her, and he arched one eyebrow. "Not the kind of gown you're accustomed to wearing, I suppose."

"Hardly. Most of my gowns fit. You won't be able to feed me, you know. One morsel of food, and I shall burst right through the cheap fabric of this bodice."

Turning around, Freddy snorted. "Wouldn't hurt you to take off a few pounds, Mopsy."

When she scowled at him, Lord Stoneville surprised her by saying, "Your cousin is perfect just as she is." His gaze raked her appreciatively. "Utterly perfect."

Her cheeks heated. She wasn't used to men giving her extravagant compliments. Papa was too practical for it, and Nathan too absorbed in his work at the company. It made it hard for her to trust Lord Stoneville's flatteries. "You mean I'm perfect for your purpose."

His mouth crooked up in what appeared to be a genuine smile. "That, too." He watched as she bundled up her gown and other things. Then he helped her into her redingote and offered her his arm in an oddly courtly gesture. "Shall we?"

For a second, she could only stare at it. Had she lost her mind, putting their lives in his hands? The man could do anything with them, carry them off anywhere, and they could do nothing to stop him.

But at least they wouldn't end up in the gaol.

When she took his arm, his dark eyes gleamed at her in triumph. "A wise decision, Miss Butterfield," he said as he led her to the door. "You won't regret it."

Unfortunately, she doubted that very much.

AS THE COACH set off, Oliver took out his watch and held it up to the window to catch the light of the gas lamps. A little after six p.m. Excellent—they should arrive in time for dinner. Gran never missed dinner.

He surveyed the pretty woman seated across from him. A pity that she wore her redingote, since the gown beneath it showed her figure off to greater effect. An even greater pity that he wasn't allowed to remove either one.

He'd had a devil of a time resisting the urge to run his lips down the sinuous curves of her neck while helping her dress. Odd sensation, that, being close enough to a female to touch her, yet not allowed to caress her body. He was used to taking what he wanted from women, something they generally encouraged.

Miss Butterfield's neck would make a delicious first course in a feast of delicacies. Her lips alone would keep a man happy for some time, not to mention her lovely plump breasts. For half a second, he indulged the fantasy of getting her alone in a corner, kissing her senseless, then slipping his hand inside the oh-so-accessible bodice of that gown to . . .

He stifled a curse as his cock stirred inside his trousers. There was to be no seduction of Miss Butterfield. Aside from the obvious problem of her virginity, her fiancé could show up at any moment to complicate matters.

And even if the chit was amenable—a very large "if"—she would regret it later. He couldn't afford to offend her "moral principles" and send her fleeing from Halstead Hall in a panic.

While her cousin gazed out the window in wide-eyed curiosity, she sat bristling with righteous indignation. Her soft bow of a mouth lacked any hint of a smile, and her shoulders were set for battle. She'd decided he was a wicked seducer, and even his rescuing her cousin from the hangman hadn't changed her opinion.

It rather intrigued him.

Women rarely voiced their true opinions about his character. The virginal ones were too terrified to do so, warned by their mamas about his being dangerous. The married ones were too eager to share his bed to chide him for his perfidy. Except when they talked about him behind his back, recounting with relish the particularly nasty rumors concerning his parents' deaths. A scowl knit his brow.

Please forgive me. It's awful to lose your parents. I know that better than anyone.

The sudden tightness in his chest made him stiffen. Why should he care if she were sorry? Or that her soft sympathy had slipped under his guard to warm a tiny corner of the dark place inside him?

Her sympathy meant nothing. She didn't know the gossip. Once she heard it, she would recoil from him in horror. She wasn't the sort of woman to find the rumors of his dangerous character intoxicating; she was too "moral" for that.

He shook off the depressing thought. He had only an hour to prepare her. "I should mention a few things before we reach my estate." When she turned a wary gaze on him, he told himself it was better if she despised him. It would make it easier to keep the pretty filly at arm's length. "Our agreement that I help you look for your fiancé must, for obvious reasons, remain between the three of us."

"I won't say a word," Freddy vowed from his seat next to Oliver.

"Nor will I, of course," she said.

"And you must appear willing to marry me," Oliver said.

"I understand."

"Do you? It means you'll have to act as if you enjoy my company."

To his surprise, a small smile curved her lips. "I believe I can manage that." Then, as if realizing she was softening, she wiped the smile from her face. "But you must behave responsibly, too."

"By not trying to seduce you, you mean."

She started. "No! I mean, yes . . . I mean, you already said you have more urgent concerns." Alarm rose in her cheeks. "Oh dear, I forgot that you also said you have no honor or morals."

He'd made similar assertions half his life, yet tonight he regretted making them. Shocking young ladies seemed to have lost some of its appeal.

"All the same, Miss Butterfield, I promise that your virtue is safe from me." When she looked skeptical, he added, "You're not the sort of woman I prefer." A respectable woman came with strings attached.

"Of course I'm not," she said with a roll of her eyes. "Anyone can see that."

That took him aback.

She went on. "A man with no morals isn't going to want a woman who *has* them. She'd never let him do anything wicked."

Freddy coughed, as if choking on something. Oliver understood why. Miss Butterfield had an unnerving way of cutting everything down to its essence.

"Yes," he said, for lack of a better response. "Quite." Then he narrowed his gaze on her. "So what did you mean when you said I had to 'behave responsibly'?"

"You promised to find my fiancé, and I expect you to hold to your word."

"Ah, right. Your fiancé." He kept forgetting about that. It was hard to imagine any woman sailing off across the ocean to hunt down her fiancé. No female would ever do such a thing for *him.*

Not that he'd want her to. That would mean someone cared for him more than was wise, given his character.

"Tell me about this Nathan," he remarked, an edge in his voice. "Why was it so deuced important to come yourself instead of sending someone from your father's company?"

"I told you—Papa's money is tied up in the estate. My trustees refused to do anything about Nathan, saying he was probably just busy negotiating the deal. And I couldn't afford to send anyone else."

"They could have sailed on the same company ship that you did. It wouldn't have cost any more."

"Yes, but once they were here, they would need money to live on while looking for him. Freddy and I are . . . more used to living on little."

"You can say that again," Freddy mumbled.

She glared at him.

"Well, it's true," the chap said stoutly. "When we were young, my uncle had a hard time feeding us all. At least until Nathan came along and joined up with Uncle Adam. Then things got better."

"Though he's only thirty, Nathan is brilliant with money," Maria said with pride. "Papa had the practical knowledge of shipbuilding, but Nathan knew how to make it work."

Oliver began to understand. "So your father offered his only daughter to Hyatt as a wife."

"It's not like that," she protested. "Nathan and I were already friends when Papa talked of us marrying. Since Papa had no son to pass his half on to, he said that once we married, he would leave his half to Nathan. Papa didn't force him to agree to me as a wife. He merely—"

"Sweetened the pot," Oliver said tersely.

A troubled frown touched her lovely brow. "It's not that cold-blooded."

"Isn't it? Hyatt gains the rest of the company, and you gain a husband. It's a common practice here, as well." And one that sickened him.

"It isn't . . . Papa didn't . . . Oh, how I can explain it to you? You see everything so cynically."

"Or perhaps," he said softly, "you don't see it cynically enough. Tell me, my dear, if Hyatt is so eager to marry, why hasn't he done so before now?"

She colored. "Because Papa insisted that he spend some years learning how to run the company before the wedding took place."

"And he didn't squawk at that?"

"He wanted to gain Papa's blessing, that's all."

The more he heard about this "betrothal," the more it angered him. "If I were in love with a woman, I'd waste no time in securing her, father or no father."

"Yes, but you don't live by the rules, do you?" she snapped.

She had him there. "What happens if Hyatt doesn't marry you?"

"Then he can buy my half from me. If he chooses not to, Papa's trustees will find a buyer to sell to. Either way, I will receive the proceeds."

"So it's very much to his advantage to marry you, isn't it?" For some reason, it infuriated him to think of her being bartered off. That never turned out well.

A shadow passed over her face. "I don't see what this has to do with anything."

"I find it interesting that you and I share similar situations. Your father tried to force his will on you from beyond the grave, while my grandmother is trying to do it on this side of the grave. And neither wants to give us any choice."

She swallowed. "You don't understand, that's all."

"I understand better than you think."

"Your situation is different." Her eyes narrowed. "Though I'm not sure I entirely grasp it."

"Then perhaps I should explain it to you."

"Yes. I wouldn't want to blunder as your pretend fiancée."

"Don't worry, you'll be fine. If this doesn't have my grandmother changing her demands overnight, nothing will. It's guaranteed to succeed."

Chapter Five

After hearing Lord Stoneville explain how his grandmother had dictated that her grandchildren marry within the year, Maria wasn't sure she agreed with his assessment of the matter. The woman sounded pretty formidable.

"Why are you all so reluctant to accommodate her, anyway?" she asked. "It's not as if your grandmother is trying to force you to marry any particular person you don't fancy. And everyone marries eventually."

"Not everyone." His voice softened. "Besides, it's not right that my siblings be forced into anything prematurely. What if they can't find someone who suits them in a year? Someone for whom they feel genuine affection? Marrying without that is more of a hell than never marrying at all." He gazed out the window, his eyes suddenly somber.

Had he been married before? Or was he speaking hypothetically? Maria wanted to know more, but she suspected he wouldn't tell her. Besides, it wasn't her concern. If he was bent on getting himself and his siblings out of marrying, so be it. As long as he held up his end of their bargain, she didn't care.

But it did annoy her that he'd been so cynical about her own prospects. Did he think no one would marry her unless Papa "sweetened the pot"?

All right, so sometimes she did wonder about Nathan's motives, but he'd always insisted that he would have married her without Papa's offer. He never spoke of love, but she'd never seen him flirt with other women, so he must have genuine feelings for her even if they weren't the passionate kind she read about in books.

She frowned. The trouble with Lord Stoneville was that he saw the whole world through a heavy black veil. He had no morals, so he assumed everyone else lacked them, too. No wonder his grandmother despaired of him.

"By Jiminy, will you look at that!" Freddy exclaimed.

Maria followed his gaze out the window to a well-lit group of buildings far back from the road. "What's the name of that village?" she asked Lord Stoneville.

"It's not a village," he bit out as the horse turned onto a long drive leading toward the lights. "That's Halstead Hall. My estate."

Her breath died in her throat. "But how . . . there are so many roofs—"

"Yes." For a moment, she thought he would say nothing more. Then he went on in an oddly detached voice. "It was built at a time when sprawling houses were common for the wealthy. Henry VIII gave it to the first Marquess of Stoneville in thanks for some service he rendered. It's been in the family ever since."

He didn't seem happy about it, which made no sense. How amazing to own such a spectacular house. And for his family to have inherited it from a king, too!

"If you don't mind my asking," she ventured, "how many rooms are there?"

"A few hundred or so."

"Or so?" she squeaked.

"No one's ever counted beyond three hundred. We take it on faith. By the fifth courtyard and the tenth building, you get a little muddled. It's fairly large."

Fairly large? It was a palace! She'd never imagined that anyone other than royalty lived in something so magnificent.

"Must cost you a fortune to keep it up," Freddy said.

"You have no idea," Lord Stoneville ground out. "This is the first time since my parents' death that I've seen it so well lit. The candles alone . . ." He frowned. "Now that Gran is visiting, someone is clearly doing it up brown for her, blast it."

Why on earth would that make him angry? This conversation grew more and more curious. "There's the answer to your financial woes," Maria said. "You just sell *that*, and your family will have enough to live on for another three centuries."

"I only wish that were an option," he said bitterly. "In England we have something called entailment. It means the property can't be sold by any of its heirs, including me. Even the contents are entailed."

"You could rent it out to a king or something," Freddy said.

"Only a king could afford it, I'm afraid. No one leases a pile like that unless they've got a serious fortune. And it's not the current fashion for the newly rich—it's too old, and the furnishings are ancient. Trust me, I've tried."

The way he spoke, as if his estate were nothing but a burden, surprised her. "I'm sure it's very difficult for you," she said dryly, "owning a palace and all."

He arched an eyebrow. "Isn't that the pot calling the kettle black, Miss Butterfield? If you can be believed, you're not exactly destitute. Your father owned a ship company, yet here you are without funds."

"True, but we never lived in a palace."

"Neither do I, most of the time." He gazed pensively out the window. "I rarely come here. It's been closed up until recently."

"Why?"

Silence followed, and she wasn't sure he'd heard her, until he said, "Some places are better left to rot."

The words shocked her. "What do you mean, my lord?"

He stiffened. "Nothing. And don't call me 'my lord.' That's what servants do. You're my fiancée, remember?" He sounded irritated. "I'll call you Maria, and you should probably call me by my Christian name—Oliver."

An unusual name for an English lord. "Were you named after the playwright, Oliver Goldsmith?"

"Alas, no. I was named after the Puritan, Oliver Cromwell."

"You're joking."

"Afraid not. My father thought it amusing, considering his own . . . er . . . tendency toward debauchery."

Lord help her, the man's very name was a jab at respectability. Meanwhile, his estate could probably hold the entire town of Dartmouth!

A sudden panic seized her. How could she pretend to be the fiancée of a man who owned a house like *that*?

"*I* was named after King Frederick," Freddy put in.

"Which one?" asked Lord Stoneville. Oliver.

"There's more than one?" Freddy asked.

"There's at least ten," the marquess said dryly.

Freddy knit his brow. "I'm not sure which one."

When humor glinted in Oliver's eyes, Maria said, "I think Aunt Rose was aiming for a generally royal-sounding name."

"That's it," Freddy put in. "Just a King Frederick in general."

"I see," Oliver said solemnly, though his lips had a decided twitch. His gaze flicked to her. "What about you? Which Maria are you named after?"

"The Virgin Mary, of course," Freddy said.

"Of course," Oliver said, eyes gleaming. "I should have known."

"We're Catholic," Freddy added.

"My mother was Catholic," Maria corrected him. "Papa wasn't, but since Freddy's mother is, too, we were both raised Catholic." Not that she'd ever taken any of it very seriously. Papa had always railed against the foolishness of religion.

A devious smile broke over Oliver's face. "A Catholic, too? Oh, this just gets better and better. Gran will have an apoplectic fit when she meets you."

Tired of his insulting comments about her background, she said, "Really, sir—"

"We're here," he announced as the coach pulled to a halt.

Maria glanced out, her stomach clenching. Halstead Hall seemed to go on forever on either side, glistening like a multifaceted jewel in the wintry moonlight. The front might be considered plain—no grand steps, no towering columns—if not for the crenellated stone façade and battlements at the corners. Not to mention the massive oak door, now opening for their arrival. It was as if she'd stumbled into King Arthur's court.

But the footmen and grooms in elaborate livery who came running were decidedly from *this* century.

Oliver tensed. "Apparently Gran brought her own servants, as well." A footman put down the step and Oliver climbed out, then helped her out, tucking her hand into the crook of his arm.

"Has my grandmother sat down to dinner yet?" he asked the footman in the same imperious tones he'd used at the brothel.

"No, milord."

"Good. Go tell Cook there will be three more for dinner."

Maria clung to Oliver's arm, feeling all at sea. It wasn't as if she'd never had servants. After Papa began doing well, he'd hired a few, but he hadn't dressed them in matching livery. These servants fluttered about them, taking her redingote and the men's coats and hats as if it were an honor to serve "his lordship." It unnerved her. Especially with Oliver glowering at them.

The archway she and Oliver walked through led them into a stone courtyard surrounded on four sides by walls punctuated with other doors. He took them across the cobblestones to yet another heavy oak door, which opened ahead of them. It made her feel like royalty being escorted through a palace.

Then they passed into a large room of such stunning aspect that she caught her breath. "This is the great hall," Oliver explained. "It's rather frighteningly medieval looking."

"I think it's beautiful."

"Gran loves it. It's her favorite room in the place."

Maria could well understand why. Two scarred marble fireplaces broke up the vast expanse of one oak-paneled wall, and well-worn benches ran along the other. But it was the Jacobean oak screen spanning the end of the room—twenty feet high and wide enough to accommodate two doors—that captured her attention. It was carved with fantastical creatures and coats of arms. At the top, near the plasterwork ceiling with its own intricate designs, was a breathtaking latticework.

She was so captivated by the screen that she didn't notice what lay at the other end of the room until a voice called out from behind them, "I see you managed to arrive in time for dinner, Oliver."

As she and Oliver turned toward the voice, she spotted the elaborately carved, painted, and gilded staircase that rose above the ancient entrance hall. With its paint rubbed off in places, it looked older than America itself, yet sturdy enough to easily hold the five people descending it.

At the head of them, clinging to the arm of a lovely young woman, was a gray-haired lady whose eyes surveyed Maria with sharp interest. Behind them descended two young men and another young lady, all of whom looked uneasy.

"Good evening, everyone," Oliver said, his voice cool. "May I introduce my fiancée? This is Miss Maria Butterfield and her cousin, Mr. Frederick . . ."

Maria realized he didn't know Freddy's surname. "Dunse," she murmured.

His startled gaze flew to her. "Seriously?"

She nodded.

"Mr. Frederick Dunse," he announced.

Behind them, she heard Freddy mutter a curse. She didn't have to look at him to know he was glaring at one and all as if daring them to laugh or make some joke.

"Maria," Oliver said, "these are my brothers, Lord Jarret and Lord Gabriel. My sisters, Lady Minerva and Lady Celia. And my grandmother, Mrs. Hester Plumtree."

His siblings murmured greetings. The older woman cast Maria a nod, though her eyes fixed on Maria's shamelessly cheap and low-cut gown. "How interesting to make your acquaintance, Miss Butterfield."

That was the understatement of all time. "I'm honored to meet you, madam." Maria hoped that was right. And why was his grandmother called "Mrs." when the rest were called "lord" and "lady"?

"Maria and her cousin are American," Oliver went on smoothly. "We only met recently—it's been something of a whirlwind courtship." He squeezed her hand. "Hasn't it, my dear?"

"Very whirlwind," she replied, not sure what he wanted her to say.

"Since her lodgings are less than adequate, I invited her and her cousin to stay here." He offered the words like a challenge. "She'll be living here after the wedding anyway, and we do have plenty of room."

Maria nearly choked on *that*, and it roused a chuckle from one of the other men that was swiftly quelled by a glance from Mrs. Plumtree.

When his grandmother returned her gaze to Maria, a strange light gleamed in her eyes, and Maria prepared herself for anything. This battle was being waged with weapons beyond her ken.

So she was surprised when the woman advanced down a few more steps and said, "I'll have the Royal Suite prepared for our guests, if that's acceptable."

"I don't know why you bother to ask my opinion," Oliver said, his voice steely. "You've clearly moved your entire household in here without my knowledge or approval."

"If you're all to marry in the next year, you can't look like paupers."

"And appearances are everything, aren't they?" he shot back.

She ignored his sarcastic tone. "Speaking of that, we'll need to send a notice to the papers about your wedding. Not to mention that the Foxmoor ball is next week. You'll want to announce your engagement there, as well. Or do you mean to have the marriage done before then?"

Oliver's fingers tensed on Maria's. "It depends. We may have trouble gaining a special license, since Maria is Catholic."

Had Mrs. Plumtree actually stumbled on the step?

If so, she recovered quickly, for her blue eyes sparked fire. "Yes, that might present a difficulty. But it can be surmounted."

"Of course it can," Oliver said with formidable calm. "A man of my rank can generally do as he pleases. You did say you wanted us married in all haste."

Mrs. Plumtree's eyes narrowed. "And Miss Butterfield's family? Won't they want to be here for the wedding?"

"Her parents are dead. That's fortunate for you, since I doubt you'd want a shopkeeper's daughter and the bastard son of a servant to appear at my wedding."

Maria squeezed his arm. Though her role was to horrify his grandmother into rescinding her demands, he made her family sound worse than they were. And of course he said nothing of New Bedford Ships, or how Papa had risen to a position of great importance.

Mrs. Plumtree fixed Oliver with a cold gaze and said, "I'm happy to welcome anyone in your future wife's family to your wedding."

Judging from his black scowl, that wasn't the answer he wanted.

"Tell me, Oliver," the dark-haired brother said. "Where did you meet your lovely fiancée?"

The calculating smile that curved Oliver's lips set off Maria's alarms. "Funny you should ask that, Jarret. As it happens, we met in a brothel."

Chapter Six

When Gran merely blinked, then steadied her shoulders and smoothed her features into nonchalance, it took all Oliver's self-control not to roar his frustration. Minerva and Celia looked more upset than she did, for God's sake!

And why were *they* upset, anyway? What had they thought he meant, when he'd said he would betroth himself to someone patently unsuitable in order to bring Gran to her senses? Subtlety never worked on Gran.

Suddenly he became aware of the fingers digging painfully into his arm.

"Excuse me," Maria bit out from beside him. "I need a word with my fiancé. Is there somewhere we can be private?"

Blast it to hell. He'd forgotten about Maria. Now he'd have to deal with her, too, and she wasn't going to take kindly to his pronouncement since she was decidedly *not* a whore.

When Minerva pointed toward the library, Maria stalked off, leaving Oliver no choice but to make his excuses and follow her.

The minute they were on the other side of the door, she whirled on him. "How dare you! You said nothing about making me out to be a whore. That was *not* our bargain."

"Would you rather I call you a thief?" he shot back, determined not to let her get the upper hand.

Her eyes blazed with indignation. "You know perfectly well I'm no thief. And I refuse to play a whore for you."

"Even if such a refusal means facing the authorities in London?"

Though she paled, she didn't waver. "Yes. Clap us in the gaol, if you wish, but I'm not playing your mad game one minute more."

To his shock, she headed for the door. Deuce take her, the chit actually meant to leave!

He swiftly blocked her exit, grabbing her by the arm to stay her. "We made a bargain, and you're not getting out of it that easily."

"This was your plan from the beginning, wasn't it? Dress *me* as a whore and use my situation for your own purposes. Did you think once you got me here, I would just go along because of your threats?" When he didn't answer immediately, she scowled. "That *is* what you intended. I knew it! You're a low, deceitful—"

A knock sounded on the door. "Oliver, is everything all right?" Gran asked.

"It's fine," he snapped, wanting Gran away from the door

before Maria got loud enough for her to hear. "We'll be there in a moment."

"I should be part of this discussion, I believe," Gran said.

At the sound of the heavy knob turning, he cursed under his breath. She was coming in, damn it!

To stop Maria before she ruined everything, he grabbed her about the waist, hauled her against him, and sealed his mouth to hers.

At first she seemed too stunned to do anything. When after a moment, he felt her trying to draw back from him, he caught her behind the neck with an iron grip.

"Oh," Gran said in a stiff voice. "Beg pardon."

Dimly he heard the door close and footsteps retreating, but before he could let Maria go, a searing pain shot through his groin, making him see stars. Blast her, the woman had kneed him in the ballocks!

As he doubled over, fighting to keep from passing out, she snapped, "*That* was for making me *look* like a whore, too!"

When she turned for the door, he choked out, "Wait!"

"Why should I?" she said, heading inexorably forward. "You've done nothing but insult and humiliate me before your family."

Still reeling, he presented his only ace in the hole. "If you return to town," he called after her, "what will you do about your Nathan?"

That halted her, thank God.

He forced himself to straighten, though the room spun a little. "You still need my help, you know."

Slowly, she faced him. "So far you haven't demonstrated any genuine intent to offer help," she said icily.

"But I will." He gulped down air, struggling for mastery over his pain. "Tomorrow we'll return to town and hire a runner. I know one who's very adept. You can tell him everything you've learned so far about your fiancé's disappearance, and I'll make sure he pursues it."

"And in exchange, all I have to do is pretend to be a *whore*."

He grimaced. Christ, she felt strongly about this. He should have known that any woman who would thrust a sword at him wouldn't be easily bullied.

"No."

"No, what?" she demanded.

"You needn't pretend to be a whore. Just don't leave. This can still work."

"I don't see how," she shot back. "You've already said we met in a brothel. Telling them we're thieves is no better. I won't have them thinking that we're about to steal you blind."

"I'll come up with some story, don't worry," he clipped out.

"Something else to make me sound like a low, grasping schemer?"

"No." She had him cornered, and she knew it. "Trust me, your background alone is enough to alarm Gran. She pretends not to mind it right now, but she won't let it go on. Just stay. I'll make it right, I swear."

She glanced away, her face troubled. "I don't know if I can believe you. How can I trust a man who has all this at his command?" She swept her hand to encompass the library. "You're used to demanding what you want, to ordering everyone around."

Sheer frustration caught him in the chest. Though that was true, the excesses of Halstead Hall or his title had never before been considered a deficit in his character. Any other woman would have thrown herself at his feet for them.

Any *English* woman. Americans were a different breed entirely. The irony was that the house and its trappings were nothing without the money to support it, and she was too unfamiliar with the workings of the aristocracy to realize it. She saw only its ancient charms.

"Look," he said, "we both know you don't want to travel back to London at this hour. Stay tonight. Eat dinner, sleep in a comfortable bed." When her pugnacious chin rose, he added swiftly, "Make a good try at playing my fiancée, and in the morning we'll go to town. If anything else happens tonight to displease you and you want to part ways tomorrow, we'll call everything even."

An uncertain look passed over her features. "You won't try to kiss me again?"

"Given your method for handling that problem? No. I don't particularly like pain."

She narrowed her gaze. "And if I say I don't want to keep up the masquerade tomorrow, you won't try to throw me and Freddy in the gaol?"

"No. But neither will I hire a runner to find your fiancé. It'll be your choice tomorrow." He hardened his voice. "Whereas if you try to leave tonight, I swear I'll have you both charged with theft."

He had half a mind to do it, too, if only to repay her for that knee in the groin. But even he had too much conscience for that.

If he could get her to stay tonight, the others would sway her. His siblings could be very charming when they wanted, especially once he told them she was not a whore. And once she realized that Gran expected Minerva and Celia to marry no matter what their wishes in the matter, she might sympathize with their situation enough to help him. Even if she couldn't sympathize with his.

"One night," she said. "That's all."

"Unless you decide that the bargain suits your needs after all."

She glanced toward the door, and he knew she was thinking of her hapless cousin. Then she crossed her arms over her chest. "Very well. We'll stay tonight. Then I'll see."

Thank God. He nodded, then moved rather stiffly to her side.

She hesitated. "I'm sorry I had to be so . . . firm."

"Liar," he grumbled. "You're not the least bit sorry."

A faint smile touched her lips. "All right, so I'm not."

He offered her his arm. "Where did you learn that, anyway?"

"One of my older male cousins showed me what to do if some man ever tried anything."

At least her zealousness in protecting herself would keep him from letting his attraction to her run away with him. Any woman who was willing to do *that* to a man was trouble, and he wasn't about to give her a second crack at the family jewels.

Outside the room they found his family standing in the Great Hall, discussing something in heated whispers as Freddy nervously paced the other end.

Oliver cleared his throat, and they all jumped. "My fiancée has made it clear that she doesn't appreciate my attempt at a joke."

"Oliver enjoys shocking people," Maria said calmly. When he looked at her, surprised that she had noticed, she arched one eyebrow at him. "I'm sure you know that about him by now. I find it a great flaw in his character."

She seemed to consider many things as flaws in his character. Not that he could blame her.

Gran glanced from Maria to him. "So the two of you *didn't* meet in a brothel?"

"We did," he said, "but only because poor Freddy got lost and wandered into one by mistake. I was trying to determine what he was looking for when Maria rushed in, mad with worry over where he might have gone off to. With two such Americans lost in the wicked city, hopelessly innocent of its dangers, I felt compelled to help them. I've been squiring them about town the last week. Isn't that right, sweetheart?"

She cast him a sugary and thoroughly false smile. "Oh, yes, dearest. And you were a *very* informative guide, too."

Jarret arched one eyebrow. "Astonishing that after finding you in a brothel, Oliver, Miss Butterfield wasn't put off of marrying you."

"I ought to have been," Maria said. "But he swore those days were behind him when he pledged his undying love to me on bended knee."

When Gabriel and Jarret barely managed to stifle their laughter, Oliver gritted his teeth. Bended knee, indeed. She was determined to prick his pride at every opportunity. She probably felt he deserved it. He could only pray that Gran backed down from the fight before he had to bring the chit around any of his friends, or Maria would have them taunting him unmercifully for the next decade.

"I'm afraid, my dear," he said tersely, "that my brothers have trouble envisioning me bending a knee to anyone."

She affected a look of wide-eyed shock. "Have they no idea what a romantic you are? I'll have to show them the sonnets you wrote praising my beauty. I believe I left them in my redingote pocket." The teasing wench actually looked back toward the entrance. "I could go fetch them if you like."

"Not now," he said, torn between a powerful urge to laugh and an equally powerful urge to strangle her. "It's time for dinner, and I'm starved."

"So am I," Freddy put in. At a frown from Maria, he mumbled, "Not that it matters, mind you."

"Of course it matters," Gran said graciously. "We don't like our guests to be uncomfortable. Come along then, Mr. Dunse. You may take me in to dinner, since my grandson is otherwise occupied."

As they trooped toward the dining room, Oliver bent his head to whisper, "I see you're enjoying making me out to be a besotted idiot."

A minxish smile tipped up her fetching lips. "Oh, yes. It's great fun."

"Then my explanation of how you ended up in a brothel met with your approval?"

"It'll do for now." She cast him a glance from beneath her long lashes. "You're by no means out of the woods yet, sir."

But I will be by the time the night is over. No matter what it took, he would get her to stay and do this, so help him God.

Chapter Seven

The minute Maria saw the regal dining room with its ornate plasterwork and walls of niches containing gorgeous marble statues, she had a fresh moment of panic. The long table was set with gold-chased goblets and fine china. The damask napkins might be frayed and the crystal finger bowls chipped, but there were pieces of silver on the table that she'd never even seen before, much less knew how to use. Meanwhile, several servants stood at the ready to do their master's bidding.

Freddy, too, looked as if someone had just dropped him into a mathematics equation. How were they to navigate among such sophisticated people?

Especially given what they must think of her. It still mortified Maria to remember his sisters' shocked looks when Oliver said they'd met in a brothel. She could *never* forgive him for that. She didn't like being made a fool of, especially by a man who seemed to think that women existed only for his pleasure.

A wave of heat rose in her face. He'd *kissed* her, for pity's sake! And for a moment, a very brief moment, it had done exactly what she'd always thought that a kiss was supposed to do—made her heart race and her pulse pound. That was the greatest indignity of all.

It had to be because of how Oliver had done it. Maybe Nathan just didn't know much about kissing. She'd assumed that her lack of feeling when Nathan had kissed her was *her* fault, but maybe it was his.

Or maybe the intensity of her anger at Oliver had caused her to feel something she normally wouldn't. Yes, that must be it. Her anger had merely riled up other passionate emotions.

At the moment he seemed angry himself, although clearly not at her. With a scowl, he left her at her chair, which thankfully was right next to Freddy's, and went to the head of the table. He didn't sit down.

"You may serve now," his grandmother told the nearest servant.

"Not yet." Oliver nodded to the servants. "Leave us."

"What on earth—" his grandmother began.

"This is a rather splendid dinner, wouldn't you say, Gran?" Waiting until after the servants were gone, Oliver strode to the sideboard and lifted the tops off the dishes one by one. "Fillet of veal. A sirloin of beef in wine sauce. Prawns and lobster . . ." He fixed his grandmother with a dark glance. "You brought your French chef with you. And apparently a goodly portion of the most expensive produce in London's markets."

"There's no reason I shouldn't eat well while I'm here," she said with a sniff.

"Except that it's *my* property." He strode to the head of the table. "You're in my house now, so while you're here, you'll eat what the estate can provide—venison and mutton and partridge—like the rest of us. There will be no more beeswax candles burning at all hours, and we'll keep open only the rooms we need."

"Come now, Oliver—"

"My own servants can accommodate you, so I want yours packed off to London in the morning. If these terms don't suit you, then I suggest you return to London as well."

His grandmother's eyes glittered at him. "I suppose this is your way of punishing me for the demands I'm making on the five of you."

"Not at all. For better or worse, this is my estate. You've never supported it before with your money, and you'll not begin doing so now. I take care of my own." His tone sharpened. "Think of it this way: it will demonstrate to my brothers and sisters exactly what they can expect if they don't do your bidding."

The elderly lady cast him a searching glance. "And make me feel sorry enough for them to relent in my plans, is that it?"

"You wanted me here showing an interest, and now I am. Those are my terms."

"Oh, very well," she said with a wave of her hand. "But the servants are here for tonight and the food is already laid out, so you might as well enjoy it."

He hesitated before conceding that point with a nod.

"Thank God," muttered the brother sitting on Maria's other side—the blonder one named Lord Gabriel. "I adore prawns."

"So do I," Freddy said.

Busy trying to understand Oliver, Maria paid them no mind. She watched as he called the servants back in, then took his seat stiffly at the head of the table. Apparently he was a prouder man than she would have expected after his cavalier remarks.

Until now she'd assumed he was just some spoiled rich lord, willing to go to any length to gain his creature comforts. But his anger at his grandmother didn't fit with that.

Nor did his seeming hatred of the place. She could tell from the musty smell pervading the rooms that he hadn't lied about its having been closed up, but why would a man choose to let such a glorious place rot? Was it just a matter of money? Or did it have something to do with the bleak look she'd seen in his eyes more than once since they'd first approached Halstead Hall?

One thing was certain—there was more to the Marquess of Stoneville than met the eye. And more to this battle with his grandmother than she'd expected.

Maria shot a furtive glance to where Mrs. Plumtree sat at the other end of the table. She was as stubborn as he, and just as bent on getting her way. Something simmered beneath the surface whenever the two sparred, and Mrs. Plumtree gave as good as she got. Even after the shocking way he'd presented Maria, his grandmother hadn't wavered. But was their conflict just about the woman's demands? Or was there some other, more ancient, grievance between them?

And did that grievance extend to the others, as well? She didn't think so. They seemed perfectly content to dine with her. Lord Jarret, the brother sitting directly across from Maria between his two sisters, had asked Mrs. Plumtree about her day. Lady Celia had made a joke that had her grandmother chuckling. Lady Minerva had observed the exchange with an indulgent smile.

Minerva. How odd that Oliver's sister should have the same Christian name as Miss Sharpe. It must be very popular for ladies in England. Never having heard it until discovering Miss Sharpe's books, she'd assumed that Minerva Sharpe was merely a pen name. But maybe not.

The footman coming around with a tureen asked if she wanted any eel soup, and Maria blinked, then nodded. People actually ate eels? Was it just an affectation of lords in England?

And how exactly was she to eat it? There were three spoons at her disposal: one that looked like a miniature spade, a lovely one with strange designs on it, and a plain one about the same size. Which was for the soup, curse it? The spade one didn't make sense, but she wasn't sure which of the other two to choose. Neither looked much like a soup spoon.

She was staring blindly at them, terrified she'd choose the wrong one, when Lady Minerva softly cleared her throat. Maria looked up to find the woman casting her a meaningful glance as she picked up the plain spoon and dipped it into the soup.

With a grateful smile, Maria did the same. The eel soup was actually quite good. She dipped her spoon again.

"So, Miss Butterfield," Mrs. Plumtree asked, "what brings you to England?"

Maria froze, her mind racing. What was she supposed to say to that?

"Came looking for Nathan," Freddy said blithely beside her.

"My cousin," Maria put in quickly as she pinched Freddy's arm beneath the table. "Freddy's brother. Nathan came here on business. My aunt needs him at home, but he hasn't answered her letters."

"And have you found him?" Mrs. Plumtree asked.

"Not yet," Maria said. "Oliver has promised to help us look, though."

"Least I could do," Oliver said smoothly.

A long silence ensued, during which she wondered how many more such slips Freddy would make before the night was over. When engrossed in eating, he tended to forget anything but that.

"Have you any brothers or sisters of your own, Miss Butterfield?" Lord Jarret asked.

"I'm afraid not," Maria said. "Just Freddy and his three brothers, all of whom grew up in the same house as I did."

"Four boys in the same house with you?" Lady Celia exclaimed. "You poor dear. I can hardly endure it when my brothers are staying at the town house. They're always causing some trouble or another."

"Oh, yes, and *you* never cause any trouble," Oliver teased. "Never mind the shooting match where you brought three men to blows over whose rifle you should deign to use. Or the spectacle you made of yourself when you dressed as a man to enter a match. Or—"

"You can shoot a rifle, Lady Celia?" Maria leaned forward. "How did you learn? I've always wanted to myself, but Papa and my cousins refused to show me how a rifle works. Could you teach me?"

"No!" Oliver and Freddy said in unison. Then Oliver added, "Absolutely not."

Lord Gabriel leaned close. "I'd be happy to teach you, Miss Butterfield."

"Stay out of this, Gabe," Oliver growled. "Bad enough you taught Celia. Maria already has enough weapons at her disposal."

His grandmother arched one eyebrow. "Pray tell, what sort of weapons do you mean?"

Oliver paused, then gave a lazy smile. "Why, her beauty, of course. That weapon is devastating enough."

"It won't stop a scoundrel from manhandling a woman," Lady Minerva put in.

"As if you know anything about *that*," Lord Jarret pointed out. "Just because the heroines in your books get manhandled with nauseating regularity doesn't mean the average woman does."

Maria stared at Lady Minerva, heart pounding. Had she actually stumbled into the presence of— "Are you by any chance the authoress, Minerva Sharpe?"

Lady Minerva smiled. "As a matter of fact, I am."

"Good God, Miss Butterfield," Lord Jarret said. "Don't tell me you read Minerva's Gothic horrors."

"They're not Gothic horrors!" Maria protested. "They're wonderful books! And yes, I've read every single one, more than once."

"Well, that explains a few things," Oliver remarked. "I suppose I have my sister to thank for your turning a sword on me at the brothel."

Lord Gabriel laughed. "You took a *sword* to old Oliver? Oh, God, that's rich!"

Lord Jarret sipped some wine. "At least the mystery of the 'weapons at her disposal' is now solved."

"He was misbehaving," Maria said, with a warning glance for Oliver. Did he *want* them to know everything, for pity's sake? "He left me no choice."

"Oh, Maria's always doing things like that," Freddy said through a mouth full of eel. "That's why we won't teach her to shoot. She always goes off half-cocked."

Maria thrust out her chin. "A woman has to stand up for herself."

"Hear, hear!" Lady Celia raised her goblet of wine to Maria. "Don't mind these clod-pates. What can you expect from a group of men? They would prefer we let them run roughshod over us."

"No, we wouldn't," Lord Gabriel protested. "I like a woman with a little fire. Of course, I can't speak for Oliver—"

"I assure you, I rarely feel the need to run roughshod over a woman," Oliver drawled. An arch smile touched his lips as his gaze locked with Maria's. "I've kissed one or two when they weren't prepared for it, but every man does that."

Lady Minerva snorted. "Yes, and most of them get slapped, but not you, I expect. Even when you misbehave, you have a talent for turning ladies up sweet. How else would you go from having a sword thrust at you to gaining Miss Butterfield's consent to be your bride—eh, Miss Butterfield?"

Maria didn't answer. Something was nagging at the back of her brain—a vaguely familiar line from one of Lady Minerva's books: "He had a talent for turning ladies up sweet, which both thrilled and alarmed her."

"Heavens alive." She stared at Oliver. "*You're* the Marquess of Rockton!"

She hardly realized she'd said it aloud until his brothers and sisters laughed.

A pained look crossed Oliver's face. "Don't remind me." Sparing a glare for his sister, Oliver muttered, "You have no idea how my friends revel in the fact that my sister made me a villain in her novel."

"They only revel because she made *them* into heroes," Lord Jarret pointed out, eyes twinkling. "Foxmoor got quite a big head over it, and Kirkwood's been strutting around ever since the last one came out. He loved that he got to trounce you."

"That's because he knows he couldn't trounce me in real life," Oliver remarked. "Though he keeps suggesting we should have a 'rapier duel' to prove whether he could."

Maria stared at them agape. "Do you mean that the Viscount Churchgrove is *real*? And Foxmoor . . . great heavens, that's Wolfplain!"

"Yes." Oliver rolled his eyes. "Churchgrove is my friend, the Viscount Kirkwood, and Wolfplain is another friend, the Duke of Foxmoor. Apparently Minerva has trouble coming up with original characters."

"You know perfectly well that I only used a version of their names," Lady Minerva said smoothly. "The characters are my own."

"Except for you, Oliver," Lord Jarret remarked. "You're clearly Rockton."

Oh yes. Like Lord Rockton, he had a dry wit, shrewd intelligence, and a face like a prince, albeit an Italian one. His blithe unconcern for gentlemanly honor mirrored Lord Rockton's, as did his ruthless determination to get whatever he wanted.

But she began to understand that he wasn't entirely a villain. For one thing, he cared for his family. The way he'd spoken of his siblings and their right not to marry showed he was carrying on this masquerade on behalf of them all, not just himself.

And though he'd obviously intended from the first to present her as a whore to shock his grandmother, he'd changed his mind with surprisingly little persuasion when Maria had opposed the idea. Considering how she'd kicked him—*where* she'd kicked him—he could have had them carted off in chains. Instead, he'd repeated his offer to find her fiancé. He'd given her an out, too, by saying that if she wished to leave tomorrow, he would accept her decision.

Of course, she wasn't sure if she believed him. He was abominably arrogant and annoying, and he possessed an appalling cynicism. But sometimes, when he got that bleak look in his eyes, she felt almost . . . sorry for him.

Which was ridiculous. Clearly there was something wrong with her to feel such a thing for the scoundrel.

"Rockton is no more Oliver than Churchgrove is Lord Kirkwood," Lady Minerva said stoutly.

"Then why did you steal my name for him?" Oliver asked.

"It's not quite your name, old chap," Lord Gabriel said.

"And you know perfectly well that Minerva likes to tweak your nose from time to time."

"Stop calling me 'old,' blast it," Oliver grumbled. "I'm not some doddering fool."

"How old are you, anyway?" Maria asked him, amused by his vanity.

"Thirty-five." Mrs. Plumtree had said little until now, but apparently the conversation had piqued her interest. "That's long past the age when a man should marry, don't you think, Miss Butterfield?"

Aware of Oliver's gaze on her, Maria chose her words carefully. "I suppose it depends on the man. Papa didn't marry until he was nearly that age. He was too busy fighting in the Revolutionary War to court anyone."

When the blood drained from Mrs. Plumtree's face, Oliver's eyes held a glint of triumph. "Ah, yes, the Revolutionary War. Did I forget to mention, Gran, that Mr. Butterfield was a soldier in the Continental Marines?"

The table got very quiet. Lady Minerva focused on eating her soup, Lady Celia took several sips of wine, one after another, and Lord Jarret stared into his soup bowl as if it contained the secret to life. The only real sound punctuating the silence was Lord Gabriel's muttered "bloody hell."

Clearly, there was some undercurrent here that Maria didn't understand. Oliver was watching his grandmother again like a wolf about to pounce, and Mrs. Plumtree was clearly contemplating which weapon would best hold the wolf at bay.

"Uncle Adam was a hero," Freddy put in, oblivious as usual to undercurrents of any kind. "At the Battle of Princeton, he held off ten of the British until help could arrive. It was just him and his bayonet, slashing and stabbing—"

"Freddy," Maria chided under her breath, "our hosts are British, remember?"

Freddy blinked. "Oh. Right." He waved his spoon. "But the war was a long time ago. Nobody cares about it now."

One look at Mrs. Plumtree's rigid face told Maria otherwise. "I daresay Oliver's grandmother cares."

Mrs. Plumtree drew herself up stiffly. "My only son was killed fighting the Colonials. He, too, was a hero. He just didn't get to live to tell the tale."

Maria's heart broke for the woman. How could Oliver do this to her? Maria glared at him, but he was staring at his grandmother with his jaw set. Why did she consistently bring out the devil in him?

Mrs. Plumtree glowered at him. "That is why I am forced to leave my business and my money to my daughter's children. To *this* lot of ingrates."

Oliver's eyes narrowed. "Ah, but you *aren't* leaving them to us, are you, Gran? Not without getting your pound of flesh."

Lips thinning, his grandmother rose abruptly. "Miss Butterfield, might I have a word with you in private?"

Maria glanced to Oliver, whose gaze was fixed on his grandmother.

"Why?" he bit out.

"If I wanted to tell you why," the woman said coldly, "I would ask you to join us, which I decidedly did not."

"Maria has barely had a chance to eat," he said. "Leave her be."

"It's all right," Maria put in. "I'd be happy to speak to your grandmother." She wanted to know what was going on, and with any luck she could find out from Mrs. Plumtree without giving away her role. Though it appeared that Mrs. Plumtree had already guessed what Maria's role was.

Oliver looked fit to be tied. "Maria, there's no reason—"

"I don't mind." She rose and laid her napkin on the table. "I'm not that hungry anyway."

"Do I have to go, too?" Freddy asked in a plaintive voice.

"No, Freddy," Maria said, stifling a hysterical laugh. "I imagine that's unnecessary."

Mrs. Plumtree walked out, and Maria followed. As soon as they passed into a nearby parlor and the woman shut the door, she whirled on Maria with a look of barely controlled anger. "How much money do you want to put an end to this farce?"

Maria blinked. "I beg your pardon?"

"Come now, Miss Butterfield," she said coldly. "I know that my grandson must have offered you money to pretend to be his fiancée until I come to my senses. I can double whatever he offered. Just tell me how much that is."

For a moment, Maria could only gape at her. Insulting as the woman's offer was, Maria briefly considered accepting it. With money, she could hire someone herself to find Nathan and wash her hands of this mad family. She didn't owe Oliver anything—he'd behaved abominably so far.

Well . . . he'd saved her and Freddy from that mob at the brothel. And though his grandmother would probably make sure he didn't follow through on his threats to have them arrested, Maria had promised to maintain the "farce" through tonight at least. She had no right to rail at him about morals if she couldn't keep her own word.

Besides, it annoyed her how his grandmother seemed to think everyone could be bought. Weren't the English gentry supposed to be too lofty to concern themselves with the exchange of filthy lucre? Mercy, they were worse than American captains of industry.

Mrs. Plumtree tapped her cane on the floor. "I need your answer."

"I beg your pardon." Maria lifted her chin. "I'm stunned by your assertion that this is a farce. Are you saying your grandson does *not* want to marry me?"

"Do not play me for a fool, girl." Mrs. Plumtree moved toward her with surprising agility for a woman of her age. "My grandson knows you are exactly the sort of woman who would not meet my requirements of a wife for him. That is the only reason he chose you." She stamped her cane on the floor. "And I will not tolerate it! So tell me how much money you want, damn you!"

Well! The woman had certainly made herself clear. But if Mrs. Plumtree thought Maria would turn tail and run simply because of some blustering, the lady didn't know whom she was dealing with.

"I don't want your money. I don't want anything from you. Oliver 'chose' me, as you put it, because he had feelings for me." Not the kind Mrs. Plumtree would think she meant, but at least it wasn't a lie. "I'm sorry if that grieves you, but since I have feelings for him as well, you'll have to endure it."

"So you *admit* that you aren't in love with him?" she pressed.

Even for her agreement with Oliver, she couldn't lie that blatantly. "I've hardly known him long enough to claim to be in love. But I do like him a great deal." When he was being genuine and not playing the bored and cynical villain. "He seems to find my liking for him sufficient and is rather eager to marry, so his feelings are the only things that matter."

Mrs. Plumtree stepped up close, her blue eyes ablaze in the pale ice of her face. "If you think to get a greater reward by marrying him, think again. He owns this house and its contents and little more. Without money from me, he will not be able to buy you fancy gowns or take you to Paris or whatever it is your grasping little heart has seized upon. And I promise you, if he marries so far beneath him just to spite me, I *will* cut him off."

Maria's gaze narrowed. "I thought you said that this was a farce. That he never intends to marry me."

"It is." A hard smile touched Mrs. Plumtree's face. "But men follow their cocks." While Maria was struck speechless to hear a woman using such a vulgarity, Mrs. Plumtree went on with no hint of shame. "A *clever* woman, as you appear to be, will use her beauty and her close proximity to ensnare even a wily gentleman like my grandson."

"Oliver? Ensnared? You clearly don't know him very well if you think he can be coaxed into doing anything against his will." That's what had brought about this whole mess in the first place—Mrs. Plumtree's foolish belief that she could force his hand.

"I know my grandson better than you. He has vulnerabilities that you cannot even begin to imagine."

The words echoed hollowly in her chest. "What sort of vulnerabilities?"

Mrs. Plumtree snorted. "Do you think I would tell you? So you could use them to get him in your clutches? Not on your life." She loomed closer. "For the last time, Miss Butterfield, will you reconsider my offer of money?"

Tired of being painted as a schemer, Maria stared her down. "I will not."

"Even though you won't ever get a penny—"

"I don't care." Though she wasn't marrying him, she was just willful enough to resent his grandmother's high-handedness and just compassionate enough to sympathize with his determination to thwart the woman. "I don't break my promises."

"Do not let Minerva and the others fool you. You would never be fully accepted in this family, never be accepted in good society, never—"

"If Oliver doesn't care, I certainly don't. This discussion is done, Mrs. Plumtree." Turning on her heel, she walked back the way she came, seething. And she had thought *Oliver* insulting! At least now she knew where he got it from. Heavens alive, what a family!

She almost felt sorry for him, having a grandmother that condescending. No wonder he had thought his plan would work.

In that moment, she decided to see this out. If he wanted to thwart his grandmother, she would help, as long as he held up his end of the bargain and hired someone to look for Nathan.

She was doing this for Nathan alone. And no amount of

nastiness from Oliver's grandmother was going to stop her from following through.

IT TOOK EVERY ounce of Hetty's will to hold her stern expression until she was certain Miss Butterfield was gone. Then she allowed a smile to break over her face.

Strolling to the brandy decanter, she poured herself a healthy amount. The girl was perfect. Perfect! Draw a sword on him? Take him to task for implying that she was a whore? Then refuse any amount of money that was offered to betray him?

Hetty sipped her brandy. She supposed the girl really could be some grasping wench hoping for a fortune in the end, but it was unlikely. Hetty hadn't risen in the world without learning how to read people, and she would swear that Miss Butterfield was a woman of character. The young lady hadn't claimed to be madly in love with Oliver, even though it would have been to her benefit to do so. And she had shown pride and backbone in standing up for herself.

Oliver had obviously manipulated the poor girl into playing out this farce—something havey-cavey was going on behind the scenes. But that did not mean it couldn't still work.

For one thing, Miss Butterfield was his preferred physical type—blond, buxom, and blue-eyed. And he was clearly attracted to her. While Oliver was attracted to many women, he generally avoided innocent young females, wary of being "ensnared." And this girl was definitely an innocent young female—her shock when Hetty used the word "cocks" clearly showed it.

Yet Oliver had chosen her over one of his opera dancers or

some whore, which would have been more typical of him. He clearly thought that the girl's flawed background would make Hetty admit defeat. Hah! He didn't know his Gran very well. She would marry him to a fishmonger's daughter if it meant getting the man settled.

But she was not about to let him know that, or Miss Butterfield, either. A little opposition from the scary matriarch whom Hetty so enjoyed playing was guaranteed to have those two joining forces against her. Joining forces meant private conversations, learning to trust each other . . . even falling in love, if she were lucky.

She owed Oliver that much. Thanks to her own mistakes, he had spent too long building his castle of wickedness, believing it was the sum total of who he was.

She knew better. He was capable of greatness, if only he allowed himself to find it within. Miss Butterfield would help him with that—Hetty just knew it.

And she was never wrong.

Chapter Eight

Oliver stood in King's Courtyard, so called because it had been Henry VIII's favorite when he'd owned the semi-fortified manor. It had been Oliver's favorite, too, growing up. Whenever his parents had argued he'd escaped here, to the expanse of paving tiles between the buildings of roughly hewn ragstone.

Staring up at the stars, he remembered how he used to stand here, wishing he could fly up and away to be consumed in a fiery blaze of glory. He'd leave everything earthly behind—the estate, his role as heir to a lofty title . . . the madness that had been his parents' marriage.

He uttered a bitter laugh. What an idiot he'd been. People couldn't fly, and they sure as the devil couldn't escape their mistakes by burning them up in stars.

A pity, because right now his biggest mistake was inviting Gran to come here. He hadn't counted on her spending money on the place, trying to make them even more reliant on her than they already were. Trying to lull them into acquiescence with her riches.

He gulped some wine from the golden goblet in his hand. Well, it wouldn't work. He'd be damned if he let her take over at Halstead Hall. He might hate the place, but it was still his. He would run it the way he saw fit.

"Your sister told me I would find you here," a soft voice said behind him.

He stiffened, then sipped some wine. "I thought you'd be headed to London by now."

"Why?" Maria asked.

A harsh breath escaped him. "Because if I know Gran, that little conversation in the parlor was an offer to buy you off."

Maria walked up next to him. He sensed rather than saw her. She had an unusual scent—roses and something he couldn't place.

"You expected me to take her money?" Maria asked.

He erected the armor of cynicism that always stood him in good stead. "Why shouldn't you? I would if I were you."

"And what good would that do me? You said if I didn't stay tonight, you'd have me and my cousin hauled off to the gaol."

"I'm sure you guessed that Gran has the influence to prevent that."

"Maybe I'm afraid to risk it."

He snorted. "Yes, because you're so timid."

A soft chuckle sounded beside him. "No one has ever accused me of that."

Slanting a glance at her, he tried to gauge her mood. "You should throw in your lot with Gran. With her money you could hunt for your fiancé, and you'd be well free of this place." *And of me.*

"Fortunately for you, I'm not that mercenary. I promised I'd stay tonight, and I will."

The swift surge of relief that her words provoked unsettled him. She was a means to an end, nothing more. He could find someone else if need be.

And yet . . .

In the starlight, her face held an angelic glow, and her hair, plaited to lie in a circle atop her head, bore a halo-ish look.

He groaned. Halos and angels and stars—what had come over him, spinning such fancies? "I wouldn't blame you if you left. You care only about finding Hyatt, so I could hardly be surprised if you took your chance to flee when Gran offered it."

"You have a very low opinion of people. But some of us do keep our promises. Some of us have integrity."

He'd long ago forgotten what *that* was. "Good for you, Miss Butterfield." He raised his goblet in a toast. "That was probably a first for Gran—finding someone she couldn't buy off."

"Oh? Whom has she bought off before?"

He flashed on a dark night when he'd sat shivering in horror while Gran hurried about, silencing servants, bribing whoever might gainsay her. "No one. Forget I said it."

"You do that a great deal, don't you?"

He swallowed the rest of his wine. "What?"

"Close up into yourself whenever someone tries to peer into your soul. Make a joke of it."

"If you came out here to lecture me," he snapped, "don't

bother. Gran has perfected that talent. You can't possibly compete."

"I only want to understand."

"I want to be consumed by a star, but we don't all get what we want."

"What?"

"Never mind." Turning for the nearest door into the house, he started to stalk off, but she caught his arm.

"Why are you so angry at your grandmother?" Maria asked.

"I told you—she's trying to ruin the lives of me and my siblings."

"By requiring you to marry so you can have children? I thought all lords and ladies were expected to do that. And the five of you are certainly old enough." Her tone turned teasing. "Some of you are beyond being old enough."

"Watch it, minx," he clipped out. "I'm not in the mood for having my nose tweaked tonight."

"Because of your grandmother, you mean. It's not just her demand that has you angry, is it? It goes back longer than that."

Oliver glared at her. "Why do you care? Has she got you fighting her battles for her now?"

"Hardly. She just informed me that I was, and I quote, 'exactly the sort of woman who would not meet my requirements of a wife.' "

A smile touched his lips at her accurate mimicking of Gran at her most haughty. "I told you she would think that."

"Yes," she said dryly. "You both excel at insulting people."

"One of my many talents."

"There you go again. Making a joke to avoid talking about what makes you uncomfortable."

"And what is that?"

"What did your grandmother do, besides giving you an ultimatum about marriage, that has you at daggers drawn?"

Blast it all, would she not leave off? "How do you know she did anything? Perhaps I'm just contrary."

"You are. But that's not what has you so angry at her."

"If you plan to spend the next two weeks asking ridiculous questions that have no answers, then *I* will pay you to return to London."

She smiled. "No, you won't. You need me."

"True. But since I'm paying for the service you're providing, I get some say in how it's rendered. Bedeviling me with questions isn't part of our bargain."

"You haven't paid me anything yet," she said lightly, "so I should think there's some leeway in the terms. Especially since I've been working hard all evening furthering your cause. I just finished telling your grandmother that I have 'feelings' for you, and that I know you have 'feelings' for me."

"You didn't choke on that lie?" he quipped.

"I do have feelings for you—probably not the sort she meant, though apparently she believed me. But she was suspicious. She's more astute than you give her credit for. First she accused us of acting a farce, and then, when I denied that, she accused me of thinking to marry you so I could gain a fortune from her down the line."

"And what did you say to that?"

"I told her she could keep her precious fortune."

"Did you, indeed? I would have given my right arm to see that." Maria was proving to be an endless source of amazement. No one ever stood up to Gran—except this American chit, with her naïve beliefs in justice and right and morality.

It amazed him that she'd done it, considering how he'd treated her. No one, not even his siblings, had ever defended him with so little reason. It stirred something that had long lain dead inside him.

His conscience? No, that wasn't dead; it was nonexistent.

"I now understand why you're determined to thwart her," Maria went on. "She does have a hateful side."

He stared down into the goblet. "I suppose you'd see it that way. She sees it as protective."

"Yet you're angry at her."

"Oh, for God's sake, will you stop harping on that? I'm not angry at Gran." He stepped closer to her. "And if you intend to stand out here all night and plague me with questions about it, I'll give you something better to do with your mouth."

She gazed up at him, perplexed. "I don't under—"

He cut her off with a kiss. Let her knee him in the groin. Let her slap him. Anything was better than having her ask him about things he didn't want to discuss. Ever.

But she didn't kick him. She stayed very, very still, but she didn't fight him.

He drew back to eye her suspiciously. "Well? Aren't you going to punch me in the kidney? Pull a knife on me?"

A smile curved her lips. "You'd like that, wouldn't you? I kick your shin and march off in a huff, and you don't have to answer me. But I'm wise to your tricks now, Oliver. I'm not going to stop asking just because—"

He kissed her again, dropping the goblet so he could drag her close and take advantage of her gasp to plunge his tongue into her mouth. Her sweet, silky mouth. So warm and innocent.

So dangerous.

Swiftly he retreated.

She did not. "What was that . . . you just did?" she asked in a breathless voice.

Such clear evidence of her arousal made something resonate deep in his chest. And that wasn't good. "It's another way of kissing." He ran his thumb over her lower lip, unable to stop himself. "A very intimate way."

Maria heard his explanation in a daze. Another way of kissing? There was more than one? Was it supposed to make her pulse jump and her heart thunder? And why had Nathan never done it to her?

Great heavens, Nathan. She had let the villainous Rockton himself kiss her, without a thought for her fiancé!

Still, she wanted to know why kissing was different with Oliver. Was it her? Or was it just that Oliver had experience that the respectable Nathan could never have?

"Do it again," she blurted out.

Oliver's eyes, black as the mouth of hell, glittered in the moonlight. "Why?"

"Don't you want to?" Her heart sank. It *was* her. She'd been so inept that even a debauched scoundrel like Oliver lacked any urge to kiss her again.

"Of course I want to," he growled. "But I don't fancy having your knee shoved in my groin."

"I won't hurt you. I just . . . want to see what it's like. That's all."

He narrowed his gaze on her. "Didn't your Nathan ever kiss you?"

"Not like that."

"Never?"

She tipped up her chin. "Not all men are as shamelessly wicked as you."

The faintest of smiles touched his lips. "True." Then he kissed her again, taking advantage of her slightly parted lips to thrust his tongue inside her mouth.

And it was glorious, a hundred times more thrilling than any kiss Nathan had ever given her. Her skin felt too tight to contain her body, and her body felt too tight to contain her stampeding heart. Every sense was heightened. The taste of tart-sweet wine on his breath intoxicated her, and the smell of his spicy cologne made her dizzy.

When he delved his tongue deep, again and again, all she could do was grab his coat and hold on, sure that she would disintegrate into a million pieces if she didn't. Tentatively she put her tongue into his mouth, curious as to how that would feel. Groaning low in his throat, he flattened her body against his hard one with the iron band of his arm. Then his mouth became more ravenous, bolder and hungrier, all-consuming.

She reminded herself that this was only a game to him, one of a thousand kisses he'd given a thousand women. But she kept hearing his grandmother say, *He has vulnerabilities that you cannot even begin to imagine.*

He tore his mouth free to whisper, "Your fiancé is clearly mad, to run off and leave you to the mercies of other men." He trailed open-mouthed kisses along her jaw to her neck. "He's not worthy of you."

"But you are?" she breathed as Oliver tongued the hollow of her throat.

"God, no. The difference is, I don't care."

"You don't care about . . . much, do you?"

"I care about this." His hand slid up to cover her breast, and to her shock, he kneaded it, making the nipple ache. "I care about making love to an angel in the starlight."

As his words trickled into her haze of desire, she froze. Making love? Oh, mercy, what was she doing? He had his hand on her breast!

She shoved him away. "You mean, making love to a *woman* in the starlight, don't you? Any woman will do. I just happen to be handy."

For a moment, the stark anger in his eyes gave her hope that he would protest her claim. Then he shuddered, and the anger gave way to a cynical arch of his brow. "You do know me well, I see."

"Yes," she choked out. "I have your sister to thank for that. I'm very familiar with Lord Rockton's habits." She fought to quell the violent beating of her heart. He mustn't guess how deeply he'd dragged her into fancying that he cared. He would use it against her. She was sure of it.

"Then you know Rockton never stops with kissing," he

drawled and reached for her again, but she shied away, crossing her arms protectively over her chest.

She'd poked a stick at a sleeping beast, and now she'd better run before he fully awakened. "That's enough practice for one night, sir."

He went still. "Practice?"

"In kissing, of course. Since I clearly have much to learn about it before I marry Nathan, I figured no one could show me the proper way to do it as well as you. Especially after your sister touted Lord Rockton's talent with women."

The muscle that ticked in his jaw told her she had struck a nerve. "And did I perform as advertised?"

"No one in life can ever match fiction. Surely even you know that."

"Yes," he said coldly. "I believe I do."

"But it was still a valuable lesson, and for that I thank you." She meant that: he'd taught her not to take him too seriously. Not if she wanted to leave with her virtue intact.

He'd made it clear that he had no desire to marry, and despite her uncertainty about Nathan, she wasn't ready to give up on her betrothed, either. So she must tread very, very lightly around his lordship from now on.

"I think we should rejoin the others, don't you?" she said.

"You go on," he ground out. "I'll be along in a moment."

Grateful for the reprieve, she fled.

Only after she'd reached the dining room did she remember that he'd never answered her question about his anger at his grandmother.

Chapter Nine

Oliver watched Maria hurry into the house, her round bottom swinging in a way that did nothing to quell his arousal. If she did stay beyond tonight, he'd have to get her some clothes that didn't make him long to lay her down and—

Damn her hide. His kiss generally had women leaping into his bed, and she'd regarded it merely as "practice" for marriage to her dull fiancé! Though apparently she found *him* equally dull.

No one in life can ever match fiction.

Impudent chit. Now he'd have to read one of Minerva's blasted books to find out what the devil she'd been writing about him.

Meanwhile, his cock was as hard as the tiles beneath his feet, with no hope of relief anytime soon. He had to pretend to be the doting fiancé until Gran gave in, and Gran was already suspicious of the scheme. She would never take it seriously if he rode off to London to visit the stews whenever the fetching Maria aroused him. So he was stuck.

Unless I seduce Maria.

His blood roared in his veins anew. It would serve the chit right if he did. *She* was the one who'd asked him to kiss her again. *She* was the one who'd opened her warm, tender mouth beneath his and made him burn and yearn.

He stiffened. Burn, yes. But yearn? He yearned for no woman. They were only playmates to while away the time until . . .

Until what?

In a flash, the future stretched before him. Years of drinking himself into oblivion to get through the nights. Years of keeping women in his bed and out of his life so they wouldn't muck around in his thoughts as women were wont to do.

What choice did he have? He wasn't well suited to marriage, and any woman with an ounce of sense would know it. He was a ne'er-do-well and a bounder.

You're behaving exactly like your father . . .

Except that Father wouldn't have balked at a flirtation with the likes of Maria Butterfield. Shortly after he'd secured the family estate with Mother's money, he'd returned to living like a bachelor, and none too discreetly.

It had humiliated Mother. Oliver had watched as she became more brittle, more jealous, more hurt with each instance of infidelity, until at the last they'd lived in two armed camps, their children stuck squarely between them.

Picking up the goblet, Oliver stared grimly into his reflection in its golden surface. *That* was the one difference between him and Father—having felt the effects of such an arrangement as a child, he wasn't keen to inflict them on anyone else. As far as he was concerned, marriage and children meant fidelity.

And since he had his father's appetites, he refused to bring some woman into his life. Not for Gran or anyone, and certainly not to secure the family dynasty and Halstead Hall. That's what Father should have done. At least he wouldn't have ruined Mother's life and the lives of his children.

So Gran was mad if she thought Oliver would follow in his father's footsteps in that respect. He was *not* going to marry some innocent chit just to please Gran. Which meant he'd best not think of seducing Miss Butterfield. If anything would shatter his plans to remain a bachelor, that would.

Especially since she had this uncanny and very dangerous ability to see beneath his defenses. *There you go again. Making a joke to avoid talking about what makes you uncomfortable.* Not even his friends had guessed that his outrageous remarks and flirtations were meant to hide how much he envied their easy contentment.

That must be why Maria tempted him so. She teased him with the promise of happiness. No matter how much he told himself it was elusive, that if she knew the truth about him she would shun him, he still buzzed after her like a bee to nectar. Her combination of innocence and curiosity, of determination and vulnerability, utterly bewitched him.

Then there was the fact that she'd turned down Gran's money. What woman did that? She'd had the chance to thumb her nose at him and walk out, but she hadn't. Instead, she'd let him kiss her.

He sucked in a ragged breath. Kissing her had been like tasting a forbidden fruit—the respectable woman. It had proved more intoxicating than any kiss he'd shared with a more experienced woman. Especially after she'd asked him to show her how. He'd not expected to find so much satisfaction in teaching her.

Imagine what it would be like to teach her other pleasures, other caresses. He could do that without being caught in any snare, couldn't he? He needn't seduce her to take advantage of her wish to "practice." Pleasuring women was his forte, after all. And the thought of watching her in the throes of passion, her body quivering with need, her sweet mouth begging him for more, made something tighten in his chest. He wanted to be the one to give her what she craved, the one to watch those blue eyes darken with desire as she found release in his arms, to hear her say his name in that throaty voice . . .

With a groan, he forced the thought of it from his mind. It was madness to consider it. He still didn't even know if she would stay beyond tonight. And if she did, he'd be a fool to risk scaring her off.

No, he'd better forget their kiss had ever happened. And he wasn't going to do that if he lingered out here, where it had taken place.

Determinedly he strode for the door. It was long past time he should rejoin the others, anyway. God only knows what Maria, or worse yet, Freddy, was telling them in there.

But when he entered the dining room, he found it empty except for Minerva, who seemed to be waiting for him.

He stopped short. "Where is everyone?"

"Jarret and Gabe went to the card room to have cigars and port. Gran went to bed. Miss Butterfield said she was tired, too, and insisted that her cousin retire as well, so Celia took them up to their rooms."

The quick stab of disappointment in his chest made him scowl. He was behaving like a fool. "Well then. I suppose I'll join the other chaps."

As he headed for the door, Minerva rose. "Oliver, wait."

"Yes?"

She came toward him, a frown darkening her brow. "What do you intend to do with Miss Butterfield?"

Strip her bare and kiss every inch of that lush, delectable body.

He bit back an oath. Hadn't he just decided he couldn't? "I'm not sure what you mean," he said, praying his sister couldn't read his thoughts.

"It's just that she seems to be a very nice, respectable woman, for all your hinting that she is not. I don't know where she got that ghastly gown, but—"

"Actually, that's my fault. She was wearing mourning for her father when I encountered her, and I couldn't have Gran asking why she was going against propriety by getting engaged to me while in mourning. So I . . . er . . . acquired a gown for her at the brothel."

"Because you wanted to portray her as a fallen woman," Minerva said with a measure of disapproval.

He bristled. "You asked me to handle this, so that's what I'm doing. If you don't like my methods, you can damned well come up with your own."

She cast him an assessing glance. "But I'm not the only one

to question your methods, am I? I gather that Miss Butterfield took issue with them as well."

He snorted. "That's putting it mildly."

His saucebox of a sister broke into a grin. "Ooh, what did she do while you were in that room alone? Do tell!"

"Not a chance. I don't need her teaching you any new tricks."

"You're no fun at all," she complained. "Well, I'm sure you deserved whatever she did. And that's my point: I rather like her. So it doesn't seem fair for her to be put in a situation where she could be—"

"Ruined by a scoundrel like me," he finished for her.

"Compromised," she corrected. "I know that you wouldn't deliberately ruin a respectable woman. But you must admit you have a talent for making women fall in love with you, and then breaking their hearts."

"Oh, for God's sake, I don't *make* women do anything." He set the goblet down hard on the table. "They just don't listen when I say I'm not interested in marriage."

"All the same, I'd hate to see Miss Butterfield harmed by her association with you, when she's being so kind as to help us with Gran. It was one thing when I thought you were going to hire someone who would understand the nature of the situation. But Miss Butterfield is unmarried and probably as susceptible to your flirtations as any other young lady. If she should misunderstand your intentions—"

"She won't," he broke in. "Nor does she have any romantic interest in me." Except as "practice," he thought sourly. "She has a real fiancé."

A startled expression crossed her face. "You're bamming me."

"I'm not. The Nathan she mentioned isn't her cousin. He's engaged to her, and he's gone missing somewhere in England. In exchange for her help with Gran, I'm hiring a runner to look for him. So you needn't worry about my breaking her heart or any of that rot. This is a business arrangement, nothing more."

His sister's eyes gleamed with interest. "Is it, indeed?"

He forced himself to meet her gaze steadily. "Of course it is. Surely you didn't think I would actually marry the chit."

"To be honest, I'm never sure what you might do."

"Well, I'm not marrying some sweet-faced innocent. But Gran clearly believes I would, which is why this might work. Gran has already tried paying Maria off to abandon the engagement."

An odd look crossed Minerva's face. "That doesn't sound like Gran."

"Why not?" He eyed his sister askance. "She always uses her money to get what she wants."

"But what she wants is to see us married. You, in particular."

"She wants to see us married *well.* It's not the same."

Minerva shrugged. "If you say so." She gave an exaggerated yawn. "I think I'll retire, too. It's been a long day."

As she turned for the door, he called out, "If I wanted to read one of your books, would you lend me a copy?"

With a chuckle, Minerva faced him again. "Curious to know what I said about Rockton?"

"What do you expect?" he said sullenly. "You made me out to be a villain."

"For three books now. You never wanted to read them before."

He shrugged off her curiosity. "I've been busy, that's all."

"Ah."

When she said nothing more, he snapped, "Can you lend me one or not?"

"I'll take one to your room after I leave here." She hesitated, then softened her tone. "I know we all joke about it, Oliver, but the truth is . . . well, Rockton isn't you, no matter what Jarret and Gabe claim. As with Foxmoor and Kirkwood, there are a few similarities, nothing more. I named him after you because I thought it might make you laugh." Her eyes twinkled. "And you do so adore being thought a wicked scoundrel."

"I *am* a wicked scoundrel," he drawled, "in case you hadn't noticed."

"Whatever you say." She turned for the door again. "But you really must get that poor woman some clothes. She can't keep wearing that dreadful gown."

"I know. I don't suppose she could wear some of yours?"

Minerva laughed. "Since I'm half a foot taller and not as buxom as her, that would be difficult. And Celia is far thinner than she." She mused a moment. "It will cost a fortune to dress her properly. Perhaps if you ask Gran—"

"Absolutely not."

"Then your only choice is the secondhand shops. The clothes will be outdated, but she's American. Everyone expects them to dress in older fashions."

"Excellent idea, thanks. I'll take care of it when we go into town tomorrow."

"You might want to visit a carpenter, too. The servants' stairs badly need repair, now that we're in residence again. Someone is sure to fall right through if it isn't done soon."

"I know. Ramsden mentioned it a week ago. I already told him to hire that fellow over in Richmond who repaired the pantry floor."

"And did our steward also tell you that the tenant farmers want to meet with you about the spring planting?"

"He wrote me about it, yes. I'll do it this week."

"Also, the windows in the drawing room—"

"Already taken care of, Minerva." He eyed her closely. "Since when do you care what happens to the house?"

"Since when do *you*?" she countered.

A scowl knit his brow. "Since I found myself forced to live here again." When her gaze turned speculative, he added bitterly, "But don't think it means anything. I merely don't like drafts, or servants falling and breaking their ankles, making them incapable of serving me."

"I understand completely." Her gaze held a decided glint of mischief. "You *are*, after all, an unrepentant and thoroughly irresponsible rogue."

"Something it would behoove you not to forget," he growled, unnerved by her refusal to take him seriously.

"How can I forget it when you work so hard to remind us of it?"

"Damn it, Minerva—"

"I know, I know. You're my scary big brother, and all that." She waggled her fingers. "I'm off to bed. Don't get into too much trouble before morning."

As she sauntered out laughing, he couldn't prevent the smile tugging at his lips. God help any man who tried to make Minerva submit to his will. She would eat him alive and lick her fingers afterward.

But what she'd said did remind him—he needed to go over the ledgers before he met with the tenants. He walked into the hall, then paused as laughter came from his brothers in the card room. His responsibilities tugged him the other way, toward his study and the waiting ledgers.

He tensed. This was how it began. First, he'd handle a few small matters, then he'd take on more and more, until one day the house and all it stood for would have him in its grip, and he would become like Father, willing to do anything, marry anyone, to keep the blasted estate going.

No, damn it! He wouldn't let the ghosts of Halstead Hall drag him where he didn't want to be. The ledgers could wait until tomorrow. A night of drinking and cards lay before him, and it was exactly what he needed.

Then Gran's words rose unbidden from his memory.

You are better than this aimless life you lead.

A strangled laugh erupted from him. Gran was wrong. He didn't know how to be better—not without sacrificing his soul to respectability.

And he would be damned before he ever did *that.*

Chapter Ten

On her first morning at Halstead Hall, Maria stood in front of the tarnished silver mirror in her bedchamber, tugging at the bodice of the ghastly red gown. "Is there nothing you can do to bring the neckline up, Betty?" she asked the maid who was plaiting her hair.

"Oh! I plumb forgot, miss." Betty scurried over to pick up something she'd laid on a chair when she'd first entered. "Lady Minerva said you could use her pelerine if you want." She draped the wide lace collar over Maria's bodice and fastened the little button. "She said to tell you how sorry she was that she had no clothes to fit you, but this might help."

"It's very kind of her." Maria gazed at her image and sighed. "A pity that it makes the gown only slightly less vulgar."

"Yes, miss." The girl colored. "I—I mean, no, miss."

Betty was awfully skittish for a servant. Ever since she'd come in early to find Maria making up the bed, she'd been anxious. She kept fluttering about, trying to help Maria do things she could do perfectly well on her own, getting even more agitated when Maria insisted on doing them.

"Say what you really think about the gown, Betty. It's fine."

"You look very pretty in it."

Maria snorted. "The only one who thinks that is your master." And that was only because the wicked devil clearly had a fondness for well-displayed bosoms.

She couldn't meet with an investigator dressed like this—he would never take her concerns seriously. Not to mention he would assume that she and Oliver were . . . intimate. Especially if Oliver kept casting her those heated glances.

She swallowed. Nathan had always given her brotherly looks, whereas Oliver made her feel naked whenever he raked those dark eyes down her body. How horrible was it that she didn't mind that nearly as much as she should?

Then there were his heady kisses. Her cheeks heated at the memory of his lips gliding over hers, of his warm mouth doing scandalous things that even now turned her knees wobbly. Heavens alive, why couldn't she stop thinking about it? She'd tossed and turned half the night, reliving every second in his arms. It was ridiculous! It meant nothing to him. And it *should* mean nothing to her; she had a fiancé!

A fiancé who'd never kissed her anything like that.

When she grimaced, Betty said, "It *is* a shame about your clothes, miss. Lady Minerva told us about the storm at sea that ruined even the gown you were wearing. I daresay the gown that the dressmaker loaned you isn't much better."

Maria had to bite back a laugh. Clearly Lady Minerva was adept at spinning all sorts of tales. Now she would have to find out what reason Oliver's sister had given for a dressmaker's loaning her a gown. She couldn't very well ask Betty.

"Lady Celia also said you could use her knit scarf with your redingote if you like. She said as how you looked cold when you came in yesterday."

Tears stung Maria's eyes. Oliver's sisters were so kind. She'd never had sisters and it touched her deeply that they were treating her like one. "Tell her thank you, if you will."

"Of course, miss." A long silence ensued as Betty concentrated on pinning her plait in place. After a while, she said, "I hope you slept well, miss."

"Yes, very well," she lied.

"The hard bed didn't bother you?"

Compared to her bed at home, it had been a cloud. "No."

"I know it's musty smelling, but we didn't have time to air out the bedchamber properly yesterday. Tonight will be better."

A laugh swelled in her throat. How could anyone possibly improve on a room fit for a princess?

Everything in it suffered from age. The linens were frayed, the chairs creaked when she sat on them, and the upholstery was quite worn. All the silver in the room was tarnished black.

But it was *silver*, for pity's sake—silver frames, silver sconces, a silver mirror with a matching dressing table also ornamented in real silver. The embroidered hangings on the massive canopied bed were red cut velvet held by rope ties of silver and gold thread, and every inch of wood had once been heavily gilded. Even the faded rug had an elaborate court scene woven into it. It must originally have been intended for a guest of far higher status than her.

Is that why Mrs. Plumtree had put her in this room? To intimidate her? Or had the woman thought it would reinforce what she'd already said about Oliver's difficult finances?

Little did Mrs. Plumtree know that Maria would happily live in the English version of a rundown house, if *this* is what it was. She loved the place already. It was pretty yet Gothic, crumbling yet stately, like a grand old dame whose fine bone structure and translucent skin never went out of fashion. She now understood how Lady Minerva managed to bring such places to life in her books. She lived in one.

"You must be very pleased to be marrying his lordship," Betty said.

It wasn't the first statement Betty had made in a clear attempt to learn more about the sudden betrothal. Heavens alive, the servants were curious about everything. It was distracting, especially since she didn't know which servants were Oliver's versus Mrs. Plumtree's.

"Yes. I'm very pleased," Maria said noncommittally.

"He's a handsome gentleman, our master."

Maria cast her a sharp glance, wondering if Oliver was one of those men who preyed on his servants. But the girl's expression showed nothing but idle interest.

"Have you worked for his lordship long?" Maria asked.

"Aye, miss, at the other house. After he sold it we were afraid we'd be a long time without work, but he got places in town for every one of us. So when he decided to open up this house and he let it be known that we could have our positions back if we wanted them, pretty near all of us came."

How odd that a man with no morals should take such care of his servants. "He's a good master, then."

Betty nodded. "Very good. Always treated us well. Don't you be listening to the nasty gossip about the Sharpe family. They're nice people, they are. If not for that old scandal, folks in society wouldn't be nearly so vicious about Lord Jarret's gambling and Lady Celia's shooting matches."

"Old scandal?" Maria asked, her curiosity thoroughly piqued.

Hot color flooded Betty's cheeks. "Beggin' your pardon, miss. I thought you knew. I spoke out of turn, I did."

"It's fine. But what—"

"There now, your hair looks very pretty," Betty said, practically jumping to put the last pin in place. "If you don't need nothing else, miss, I should go help the other ladies. There's only two of us for the four of you, now that Mrs. Plumtree's servants are gone."

"That's fine. I don't want to keep you."

"Thank you, miss." Betty bobbed a pretty curtsy and fled, leaving Maria staring after her.

An old scandal. Might that have anything to do with this strange scheme of their grandmother's? Did she dare ask Oliver about it? He'd probably just refuse to answer, as always.

With a sigh, she left the room to head down the hall, praying she could find her way to wherever breakfast was. She'd tried to pay attention to Lady Celia when the woman had led her through the warren of rooms, but the place was so oddly laid out that she wasn't sure where she would end up. Fortunately, she stumbled across a footman, who directed her to the breakfast room.

Upon entering, she was surprised to discover Oliver already having breakfast with his grandmother, his sisters, and Freddy. Lady Celia had given her the impression that Oliver was not an early riser. Of course, it wasn't that early anymore. It had taken Maria so long to tidy her room that it must be nearly nine.

"Ah, Miss Butterfield, there you are," Mrs. Plumtree said as Maria rounded the table. "Oliver was just telling me about the tragedy that befell your trunks. A pity that the dressmaker couldn't loan you a better gown."

She lifted her chin. "Indeed it is."

"I was explaining to Gran," Oliver put in, "that you ordered some new clothes made.You said those would be ready today, didn't you, sweetheart?"

She let out a breath. "Yes, today." The whole family seemed to have conspired on the subject of her clothes. She might as well go along, especially since Freddy was no help at all. He was too busy shoveling down shirred eggs to even hint at what tales they'd invented.

Oliver went on buttering his toast. "I thought we'd go into town to pick them up and perhaps shop for whatever else you need. If that's all right with you."

Mrs. Plumtree's eyebrows arched high at that, but she said nothing.

"Of course," Maria said cheerily.

Freddy's head snapped up. "I don't have to go, do I? I hate shopping."

"You have to chaperone," Maria chided him.

Inexplicably, Oliver tensed.

Freddy didn't seem to notice. "Oh. Right. Should I bring my sword?"

"I returned it to him last night," Oliver explained in a tight voice.

"I see," she said. Oliver seemed awfully upset about it. She glanced at Freddy. "Leave the sword here. I'm sure Oliver can protect us."

When Oliver let out a breath, she stared at him quizzically. The tension seemed to have drained out of him, and he looked relieved. It dawned on her that he'd been waiting to see if she meant to abandon ship this morning, as he'd promised she could if she was still unhappy.

The realization brought her up short. Ever since her conversation with his grandmother, she'd felt a fierce urge to help him thwart the woman. From that moment on, she'd acted as if the matter were settled, when in fact it still wasn't.

For half a second, she considered the possibility of backing out now. If she stayed, he would help her find Nathan. But he might also attempt to give her more of those incredible kisses. Did she dare risk it?

She had to. Without his help, she had no way to find Nathan. And surely she could resist a few kisses, no matter how amazing. No matter how the thought of them set her blood to pumping and her insides flipping crazily about.

Mercy, what did that say about her character? She had to get this foolish fascination under control.

Breakfast proved to be a tense affair. Oliver's grandmother peppered her with questions about her family, and she had no idea what to say to help Oliver's situation. She didn't like to lie, but she didn't think it wise to explain that they had a higher status than Oliver had implied.

She was so grateful to finally have it over that she didn't even protest when Oliver laid his hand in the small of her back as they strolled toward the front of the house. Even if it did send a delicious tremor through her.

When they reached the courtyard, he bent his head close. "Am I to understand that you've decided to continue our arrangement?"

"As long you keep your end of the bargain. I still need to find my fiancé, you know."

"Of course," he clipped out.

"Why did you tell your grandmother that I'm picking up gowns in town? She'll be suspicious when I don't return with any."

"After we meet with the Bow Street runner, you and I will go to the secondhand shops. Their clothing won't be in the first stare of fashion, but it'll be adequate."

"I don't think I can afford—"

"I'm paying for them. It's my masquerade, so it's my expense. If you don't want to keep them, I can always give them to the servants or resell them. If you do want to keep them, you can consider it a bonus for helping me."

"If I keep them, Nathan will repay you for them as soon as we are married," she said tightly.

He eyed her closely. "You mean, as soon as you find him. Have you thought about what you'll do if you *don't* find him?"

"No." The nightmare of legal entanglement that would ensue was more than she could bear to consider. She had to find him. There was no other choice.

But the gravity of the situation weighed even more heavily on her an hour later, when a clerk ushered them into the cramped and windowless office of Mr. Jackson Pinter. The clerk said that the Bow Street runner, recommended by one of Oliver's good friends, would return shortly. Then he left them to wait.

While Oliver settled into a chair, she paced the small room. Sketches of hard-faced men were pinned up on the walls, and an assortment of weapons hung in a glass-fronted cabinet beside them, reminding her that the runner's job was to hunt down criminals.

Things were desperate indeed if she had to resort to a man familiar with the seediest parts of London. Still, if Nathan were in any trouble, surely this runner fellow could get him out of it.

"Now *that* is a sword," Freddy said in awe as he went to look at an impressive saber hanging from the hat rack near the door.

"Stay away from it," she cautioned. "I'm sure it's sharper than yours."

As usual, Freddy ignored her. "Just think what I could do with this," he said as he lifted it off its hook.

"So far I haven't seen you do anything with a sword, my boy," Oliver remarked dryly. "Though I shudder to think what your cousin would attempt."

Maria glared at Oliver, which only made him laugh. Meanwhile, Freddy unsheathed the saber with a flourish.

"Curse it, Freddy, put it back," Maria ordered.

"What a fine piece of steel." Freddy swished it through the air. "Even the one Uncle Adam gave me isn't near so impressive."

Maria appealed to Oliver. "*Do* something, for pity's sake. Make him stop."

"And get myself skewered for the effort? No, thank you. Let the pup have his fun."

Freddy cast him a belligerent glance. "You wouldn't call me a pup if I came at you with *this*."

"No, I'd call you insane," Oliver drawled. "But you're welcome to try and see what happens."

"Don't encourage him," Maria told Oliver.

The door opened suddenly, and Freddy whirled with the sword in hand, knocking a lamp off the desk. As the glass chimney shattered, spilling oil in a wide arc, the wick lit the lot, and fire sprang to life.

Maria jumped back with a cry of alarm while Oliver leaped out of his chair to stamp it out, first with his boots and then with his coat. A string of curses filled the air, most of them Oliver's, though Freddy got in a few choice ones as the fire licked at his favorite trousers.

When at last Oliver put the flames out and nothing was left but a charred circle on the wood floor, dotted with shards of glass, the three of them turned to the door to find a dark-haired man observing the scene with an expression that gave nothing away.

"If you hoped to catch my attention," he remarked, "you've succeeded."

"Mr. Pinter, I presume?" Oliver said, tossing his now ruined coat and singed gloves into a nearby rubbish pail. "I hope you'll forgive us for the dramatic intrusion. I'm Stonevi—"

"I know who you are, my lord," he interrupted. "It's what you're doing here setting fire to my office that I'm not certain of."

"Mr. Pinter," Maria put in, too mortified to hold her tongue any longer, "I am so sorry for what my cousin did. I assure you I'll pay for having the floor and the lamp replaced, and whatever other damages there are."

"Nonsense." Mr. Pinter's gaze shifted to her. Though his eyes seemed to soften, the thick rasp of his voice sent a chill down her spine. "That lamp smoked like the very devil. I was about to buy a new one anyway. And that charred spot can be covered with a rug quite easily." He shot Oliver a veiled glance. "I'm sure his lordship won't mind offering one. He's bound to have an extra, now that he's sold his infamous bachelor quarters in Acton."

Oliver went rigid. "I see that my friends have been gossiping about me."

"I spend my days upholding the law," Mr. Pinter said with a shrug. "It behooves me to keep abreast of what men of rank are doing."

Oliver's eyebrow arched high. "Because we break the law?"

"Because most of you have little regard for it. Except when it suits you."

Something dark glittered in Oliver's eyes. "I see. Does my friend Lord Kirkwood know you're so cynical about men of rank? He's the one who recommended you."

That gave Mr. Pinter pause. "His lordship sent you to me?"

"He told me that if I should ever need investigative services, I could trust you to be discreet. Can I?"

"That rather depends on what it is that requires discretion."

"It's a matter that concerns me, not Lord Stoneville," Maria put in. For some reason, Mr. Pinter seemed less than keen to deal with Oliver. Perhaps he would be more inclined to help a woman with no rank at all.

"Forgive me for not introducing you at once, Mr. Pinter," Oliver said. "This is my fiancée, Miss Maria Butterfield."

That seemed to startle Mr. Pinter. "You have a fiancée?"

"She's not *really* his fiancée," Freddy put in. "You see, Lord Stoneville's grandmother—"

"Come, lad," Oliver said sharply, taking Freddy's arm in a firm grip and leading him forcefully toward the door. "Let's leave your cousin and Mr. Pinter to discuss their business, shall we?"

On their way to the door, Oliver extricated the sword neatly from Freddy's hand. Then he paused in the doorway to glance at Mr. Pinter. "Give her whatever she wants. I'll pay you well for your services."

"Rumor has it, my lord, that you're up to your neck in debt. Are you sure you can afford me?"

Maria sucked in a breath. Any other man would have been insulted, might even have called the man out. But though Oliver narrowed his gaze, he showed no other sign of outrage. "I sold my bachelor quarters in Acton, remember? I'm sure I can find a few pounds lying around."

"It will cost you more than a few pounds. *If* I take the case."

A sudden twinkle appeared in Oliver's eyes. "You will. Maria can be very persuasive." He hung the sword he'd taken from Freddy on the hat stand, then gave her a wink. "Though I'd keep your weapons well away from her, if I were you."

As Maria blushed furiously, he and Freddy left. Mr. Pinter strode to the door and called for his clerk to come sweep up the glass on the floor, which gave her time to survey the runner.

He looked to be about thirty, younger than she'd expected.

Tall and lanky, he wore a formfitting coat and straight trousers of black serge, a plain gray waistcoat, a white linen shirt, and a linen stock simply tied. His angular jaw and thick black brows lent him a hawkish appearance. Some women might even call him handsome . . . if they could get past the chill of his expressionless features.

Once the clerk had finished his task and scurried out, Mr. Pinter gestured her to a chair before his desk. When they were both seated, he leaned back and steepled his fingers. "So you're his lordship's fiancée, are you?"

Mr. Pinter's eyes, sharp and gray as slate, assessed her with a quick, thorough glance indicative of his profession. Thank heaven she wore her redingote. Who knew what he'd make of her gown?

"Actually, it's more complicated than that." During the drive into town that morning, she and Oliver had decided on what they would tell Mr. Pinter. They had to continue with their masquerade even while asking for Mr. Pinter's help with finding Nathan. Clearly, Freddy had *not* been paying attention to the plan. But then, he rarely did.

It took her a few minutes to detail the complex terms of her father's will. When she was done, Mr. Pinter's face showed nothing of what he might think. That was rather unnerving.

"So you see," she said, "until Mr. Hyatt is found, my future is up in the air."

"And where does the marquess fit in?"

Now came the difficult part. "We met while I was looking for Nathan. One thing led to another, and we became engaged." That was true, sort of. "I'm sure you can understand why it's essential that I find Mr. Hyatt as soon as possible to resolve this matter."

"In other words, you have *two* fiancées at the moment. And you're hoping that I'll rid you of one of them."

Heat rose in her cheeks. "In a manner of speaking."

"Now I comprehend why Lord Stoneville is willing to pay for my services. He can't get his hands on your father's money until I find your fiancé."

"That isn't how it is!" She hadn't realized he might put that face on it.

Mr. Pinter's eyes narrowed. "How long have you known his lordship?"

Unsure whether to repeat what Oliver had told his grandmother or to tell the truth, she opted for an evasion. "Not long."

"So you're unaware of his reputation with women."

She thrust out her chin. "Actually, I know a great deal about that. I just don't care."

"Ah." He leaned forward with a contemptuous stare. "You've found a way to gain a titled gentleman and inherit your fortune without having to marry the man your father chose for you. This Mr. Hyatt must be quite old and ugly indeed."

Outrage swelled her chest. "Certainly not! Nathan is a fine, upstanding young man whom any woman would be proud to marry!"

The minute the words left her mouth, she realized her error. Especially when Mr. Pinter sat back with a look of sly satisfaction. "You're not really engaged to Lord Stoneville, are you?"

Great heavens, she was terrible at this masquerading business. "I . . . well . . . you see, it's very . . . it's . . ."

"Complicated," he said dryly. "So I gather."

With a glance toward the open door behind her, she bent toward the desk and lowered her voice. "Please, you mustn't tell anyone the truth. It's important that you keep our secret until you find my fiancé."

"Important for you? Or for his lordship?"

"Both. I beg of you, sir—"

"Tell me about your fiancé," he said with a sigh as he took out a notepad. "The real one. I need to know where he's been, how you know he's missing, anything you've learned." His gaze sharpened on her. "And I want the truth this time. I don't take cases where the parties involved lie to me."

She dropped her gaze in embarrassment. "The truth. Yes, sir."

For the next half hour, she laid out all the avenues she and Freddy had pursued, answering each of his questions as thoroughly as she could. When he'd filled several pages with notes, he set down the pad.

"Now, I want you to explain what Lord Stoneville has to do with this."

Her hands grew clammy. "He's helping me."

"Why?"

Because my cousin is accused of stealing from his friends. "It has no bearing on your search for my fiancé," she said stoutly.

He gazed steadily at her. "It does if the price for his help is higher than a respectable young woman should have to pay."

She took his meaning at once, coloring deeply. "It isn't, I assure you."

"Tell me something, Miss Butterfield. Do you know anything about the character of the man you are relying on for help?"

"I know enough."

"Did you know that his mother murdered his father? And then shot herself?"

Pure shock kept Maria speechless.

What if I swear on my mother's grave to uphold my promise? That's a vow I'd take very seriously.

"Oh, poor Oliver," she whispered.

"I wouldn't be so quick to sympathize if I were you," Mr. Pinter snapped. "Ever since that day, he's lived a life of debauchery. The man you're trusting to help you is known for his many affairs with opera dancers and loose women. He plays in the fleshpots of London while letting Halstead Hall go to rack and ruin."

A sudden tightness in her chest made it hard for her to breathe. "Where did it happen?"

He blinked. "What?"

"The murder of his father and his mother's suicide. Where did it happen?"

"In the hunting lodge on his estate. Why?"

Some places are better left to rot.

His bitter words took on new meaning. "And how old was he?"

"Sixteen, I believe."

Her heart twisted in her chest. "He was only a boy, for pity's sake! Have you no compassion? He lost his parents in the most horrible way imaginable, then suddenly found himself, at a tender age, the head of a family of four young brothers and sisters. Don't you think if such a thing happened to you, you might strike out at the world? Or lose yourself in some den of iniquity?"

Mr. Pinter scowled. "No. I would learn from the tragedy by embracing a more sober way of life. Instead, he and his siblings spend their time scandalizing society with their reckless behavior."

She thought of the Sharpe family—how adorable they were together, and how kind the two sisters had been so far. Then she remembered what the servant had said about their treatment by society, and her temper ignited.

Rising to her feet, she fixed the runner with a blistering glance. "You judge them by your own standards without knowing them personally. How dare you?"

Clearly taken aback, Mr. Pinter rose as well. "I haven't told you the worst of it. After his parents died, he inherited everything. Some say he knew more about what happened than he admitted. That he might even have been there, if you take my meaning."

A chill coursed down her spine. "I do *not* take your meaning, sir. Surely you're not implying—"

"He's not *implying* anything," said a caustic voice from behind her.

Her stomach sank as she turned to see Oliver standing in the doorway. He wore his many-caped cloak of black wool to cover his lack of a coat. With his face a mask of nonchalance and his dark eyes hooded, he reminded her of the huge black gyrfalcon she'd seen once, swooping down to seize prey in its beak.

Oliver's cloak flapped as he strode into the room. "Mr. Pinter is stating his opinion of me quite decidedly. I'm a scoundrel and a debaucher. I'm untrustworthy. And most importantly, I probably murdered my own parents."

Chapter Eleven

When Pinter didn't deny the accusation, Oliver wanted to throttle him. Wasn't he allowed to have one person see him for what he was, without having it colored by a thousand versions of his past? Every time he thought the gossip was dead, it reared its ugly head again.

And to think that Pinter had suggested that his family should have "learned" from the "tragedy"! Damned arse had no idea what he was talking about.

He probably should have marched in to stop Pinter when he first heard him from the outer office. But if he hadn't stood there listening, he wouldn't have heard Maria defending him and his siblings so sweetly.

Have you no compassion?

The very words pried at the lid of the strongbox he kept so tightly closed. No one had ever defended him for anything, and certainly not with such deep conviction.

Then Pinter had gone and destroyed any sympathy she might

have had by telling her "the worst of it." Maria now wore a look of such horror, it made Oliver want to howl.

"Surely you can't really believe that his lordship had a part in his parents' tragic deaths," she charged Mr. Pinter.

Her sharp tone arrested him. Could she actually be questioning the rumors?

"For if you do, then you're clearly basing your opinions on gossip," she went on hotly. "If that's the case, I'm not sure I want to hire you."

A lump caught in Oliver's throat. She was standing with him, not with the gossipmongers. But why? Only his handful of friends had ever done so, and that was only because they'd known him long before that horrible night at Halstead Hall.

"I deal in facts, Miss Butterfield," Pinter said firmly. "I told you nothing but the truth."

Much as Oliver hated to admit it, that was accurate. Oliver had indeed lived a life of debauchery and let Halstead Hall fall to rack and ruin. There really had been speculation about his presence at the scene. It wasn't the facts that bothered him. It was Pinter's need to tell them to *her* that rankled.

"Yes," she countered, "but when you make conclusions based on so few facts, how can I even trust you to do your job properly?"

"Enough, Maria," Oliver put in.

He might not like Pinter or his urge to poison Maria against him, but he understood the man. And Pinter was considered a first-rate investigator. For Maria's sake, Oliver had to be practical and put his dislike of the runner aside.

Besides, every other investigator would know the rumors,

too. They just wouldn't be so forthright about them. Pinter could have attempted to twist the meaning of what Oliver had overheard, but he hadn't. And Oliver preferred a man of conviction to a sycophant any day.

"Like most gentlemen," Oliver went on, "Mr. Pinter wishes to save the damsel in distress from a known rakehell and rumored murderer. That's no reason to refrain from hiring him. Indeed, it means he'll probably do a more thorough job of finding Mr. Hyatt than the average fellow." He shifted his gaze to the Bow Street runner. "Am I right in assuming that you'll take the case?"

"You're right indeed, my lord." His gaze locked with Oliver's. "But I won't take your money for it. If I find Mr. Hyatt, *he* can pay me. If not, then I'll take no fee. I would prefer that Miss Butterfield not be obligated to you for it."

"You don't understand—" Maria began.

"Nonsense. Let the man be a hero," Oliver bit out to prevent her from explaining the nature of their bargain. He had to get her out of here before she revealed too much. If Pinter was ready to save her now, only think what he'd be like once he heard how Oliver was using her to thwart Gran.

Oliver held out his arm. "Come, sweetheart, we have shopping to do. And Mr. Pinter will want to get started on the search right away."

Pinter bristled at the thinly veiled command, but at least he nodded his assent. "Good day, my lord." The man's gaze softened as he glanced to Maria. "I'll give you my report as soon as I learn something, Miss Butterfield. And if you should need anything—"

"Thank you," she said with an upturned nose and ill grace. "I'm sure I'll be fine. You can reach me at Halstead Hall. I'm staying with his lordship's family."

God only knew what Pinter would make of that.

She took Oliver's arm and they walked to the door, but when they reached it Oliver paused, unable to resist one last word.

"You do realize, Mr. Pinter, that waiving your fee means that Miss Butterfield will now be obligated to *you.* Which begs the question—what price will she end up paying for *your* help?"

Without waiting for a response, he led her through the door.

"Deuced prig," Oliver muttered under his breath as they headed to the stairs.

"We didn't have to hire him."

"Of course we did. By all accounts, he's the best at what he does."

She clung to his arm as they descended the stairs. "But he said such . . . cruel things about you. I don't know how much you heard—"

"I heard enough," he clipped out, keeping his gaze averted, afraid he might see speculation in her eyes. Just because she'd defended him to Pinter didn't mean she wouldn't rethink her opinion later. Though he was used to shrugging off looks of morbid curiosity or outright disapproval, he couldn't bear to see hers. Not after all her sweet words.

"I'm sorry about your parents," she murmured.

The soft sympathy in her voice nearly shattered his control. "Why?" He kept his voice calm and unmoved, though it took every ounce of his will. "You had nothing to do with it."

"Neither did you, of course. I hope you don't think I believed his insinuation."

"Believe what you wish. It doesn't matter," he lied.

They'd reached the entrance to the building. As he held the door open for her, she paused to stare at him, forcing him to meet her gaze. "It matters. He shouldn't have said it."

For a moment, he couldn't look away. There was so much compassion in her eyes that he wanted to drown in it.

Then he wanted to run.

It wouldn't last. How could it?

Snapping his gaze from hers, he led her down the front steps. "Trust me, Maria, that's only a fraction of what he could have insinuated. He could have related the entirety of the rumor—that I shot Father so I could inherit, and then Mother when she tried to wrest the gun away from me."

Though her hand tightened painfully on his arm, he didn't relent. She might as well know the full extent of what was said about him and his family, if she meant to do such a foolish thing as go around defending them. "Then there's the rumors that Father was meeting a woman and that's why Mother shot him. Or that Gran paid to have Father killed because Mother had asked it of her, but something went wrong when it was done. Every one of those theories has been whispered about my family during the past nineteen years."

"That isn't right!" she protested.

"It's human nature," he said wearily. "If the truth is too boring, people create more interesting versions. No one knows what really happened that night, even me. As best Gran could tell, Mother mistook Father for an intruder and shot him, then shot herself in a moment of grief when she realized what she'd done."

"So their deaths were just a tragic accident."

"Yes."

It wasn't a lie. That *was* what Gran thought. But he knew perfectly well that it wasn't the truth, either. He just couldn't stand having Maria know the truth—that although he hadn't pulled the trigger, the result was the same. Because of him, his parents were dead. And nothing he could do would change that. Certainly, no amount of sympathy from an American chit with a soft heart would.

The carriage pulled up before him and the footman put down the step. But even as he handed her up into it, she asked, "Where's Freddy?"

God, he'd forgotten all about her cousin. "I took him round the corner to my club," he said as he climbed in after her. "I didn't want him giving away our subterfuge to Pinter, and he said he didn't want to shop with us anyway." It was true . . . except that he'd rid himself of her cousin because he had wanted to have her to himself for a while.

The minute he'd left Freddy, he'd known it was madness. She already got under his skin too damned much; time alone with her would only make it worse. He'd scarcely been able to sleep last night for his erotic dreams of having her beneath him in his bed, driving away the dark night with her tender mouth and soft sighs and brilliant smiles.

Ah, what a pleasure it would be to lose himself in the warm embrace of her body, to lay her down in the overgrown gardens surrounding Halstead Hall and make love to her as if she were a forest nymph and he a Greek god. Perhaps that would banish the curse on the place at last.

He ground his teeth together. Even if she would allow it, taking her to bed would only give her license to poke at his secrets, like a child digging out the currants in a plum pudding. And when she'd lined them up and seen how black they were, she would recoil from him. She would leave him naked and alone. Always alone.

Why the devil did he care if she left him alone? Damn her for tempting him so innocently. And damn him for being tempted.

He unbuttoned his cloak. It was suddenly very hot in the carriage, even without his coat and gloves. "We'll pick up Freddy after we finish with the secondhand shops. He can't do much harm at the club—"

"Are you serious? Freddy has the loosest tongue of any man in creation. By now, he's probably revealed the whole tale of our pretend engagement to every member of your club."

"Ah, but I took care of that. I told him he could order whatever he wished from the club's chef as long as he kept silent about our activities. Surely he can't say much with his mouth stuffed full of beefsteak."

"You'd be surprised. Freddy is adept at all the wrong things." She slanted a pretty glance at him. "You do realize that bribing him with food might end up costing you a fortune."

"What do I care? I'm saving money on Pinter's fee."

When her face fell, he cursed his quick tongue. The last thing he wanted was to remind her of Pinter.

"It's not Freddy you have to worry about, anyway," she said

in a low voice. "Thanks to something I said, Mr. Pinter guessed that our engagement is a sham. I'm sorry."

He'd already surmised as much from Pinter's demeanor. "No need to apologize. It would have been better if he hadn't figured it out, but Pinter is clever—he knows perfectly well what my reputation is. He was bound to be suspicious. I'm sure you didn't mean to give it away."

"I truly didn't. But he started insinuating things about you and me, and then me and Nathan and—"

"He manipulated you into revealing the truth. It's all right. That's what he does. It makes him a good investigator." He softened his voice. "And you aren't as practiced at playing a role as I am. It's not in your nature."

"No, but I promised you I'd keep the secret."

He shrugged. "He'll be discreet, now that he's determined to 'protect' you. As long as Gran doesn't get wind of it, we'll be fine."

The carriage slowed, momentarily snarled in some welter of carts and coaches, and he found himself grateful for any extra time it gave him alone with her.

"What did he say about his chances of finding Hyatt?" Oliver asked.

"Not much. But at least I'm closer to that than I was before, thanks to you."

He didn't want her thanks. As far as he was concerned, Nathan Hyatt could rot in hell. Oliver had probed Freddy for information on the way to the club. The more he heard, the more he despised the man. Hyatt clearly wanted her for practical reasons that had nothing to do with her generous heart and her fierce loyalty. It was like watching her repeat Mother's mistake. It could come to no good.

He had to make her see that. "Has it occurred to you that Hyatt might not want to be found?"

With a hard swallow, she stared out the window at the clamoring crowds. "Yes."

"And if that's the case? What will you do then?"

"I don't know." Her gaze shifted to his. "Why? Are you offering to marry me in his place?" When Oliver stiffened, she added hastily, "I'm joking, you fool. Can't you tell when a woman is teasing?"

No. Women rarely joked with him about matrimony. Worse yet, the idea wasn't as repulsive to him as it should be. Just the thought of having her in his bed to talk to on nights when he couldn't block out the memories . . .

"It's a shame you're so deplorably virginal," he quipped, trying to match her light tone so she wouldn't see how she'd unsettled him. "Otherwise, I'd make you a proposal of a less savory kind."

A teasing smile touched her lips. "Oh? Would you offer to ravish me?"

As soon as the words left her mouth, the air between them crackled. And suddenly he couldn't joke about it anymore. "Actually, no." He waited until her gaze met his. "I'd offer to make you my mistress."

Chapter Twelve

The air left Maria's lungs. Did he mean it? She was never sure with Oliver; he tended to say things just to shock her. Yesterday he'd succeeded, but she was rapidly coming to realize that it was his way of holding people off, keeping them from rejecting him first. If he swaggered about, proclaiming himself a devil before others could say it, then in his eyes he had won.

It was much the same way Papa had acted about his bastardy. He had never kept it a secret—he'd offered his pedigree to anyone who asked, as if daring them to look down on him for it. How odd that the two men were alike in that.

The difference was that Papa was always belligerent in his assertions, while Oliver delivered them in a coolly bored manner.

Except for now. He looked surprised by his words. Then his gaze steadied and started to smolder, igniting a heat within her, and she was suddenly aware of how very alone they were.

"Ah, but since I *am* deplorably virginal," she said, striving to keep her tone as casual as his, "the point is moot."

"Let's say you weren't," he persisted, his voice a rough rasp. "Just for conjecture's sake. You could stay here under my protection until we tired of each other, and then return to America. No one need know how you'd spent your time in England. Hypothetically speaking, of course."

Something stirred low in her belly at the idea that he might seriously be making her an indecent proposition. No man had ever done that to her, especially one so sinfully attractive. How did he manage to make something insulting sound so flattering?

Careful, Maria, she cautioned herself. *He came by his reputation honestly.* "Hypothetically speaking, you've known me only a day—surely you need longer than that to choose a mistress."

"I wanted you the first time I saw you."

His look held such primitive hunger that she knew there was nothing hypothetical about this discussion.

Fighting to hide how badly his words had thrown her off guard, she quipped, "And what would I be . . . fifteenth in your long line of mistresses?"

His breathing seemed as unsteady as hers. "The first, actually." The low rumble of his voice resonated in every nerve. "I've never had a mistress."

She choked out a laugh. "As if I would believe *that.*"

"It's true. I've always preferred less permanent connections with women."

That shouldn't surprise her, but it did. "Am I also supposed to believe that you'd alter that preference for me? Hypothetically, that is."

The carriage felt too small to contain them both. He didn't move from the seat opposite her, yet his very presence overpowered her. "Why not? People change." His gaze darkened to a fathomless black as it scanned her face. "I would treat you very well. You'd want for nothing, I swear."

She arched one eyebrow. "Except respectability."

"To hell with respectability," he ground out.

"That's easy for you to say. You lose nothing. I, on the other hand, would lose everything."

He looked ready to devour her whole. She shifted nervously on the seat.

"I'd make sure you were cared for," he said, his voice ragged and deep. "That you had a roof over your head. After Gran gives up her mad scheme, she'll return to supporting my siblings and I can live on my income. We wouldn't need much—a cottage in Chelsea. You could use as little of your inheritance as you wanted once you came into it. At least you wouldn't be bound to a bastard like Hyatt, who didn't even have the courtesy to send a letter to you when he changed his address."

That stung. "Perhaps he couldn't," she said, voicing the worst of her fears.

"He took his leave of London Maritime in person, according to Freddy. Freddy also told me that Hyatt's rent at the lodging house was paid up. That doesn't sound like a man who went missing after meeting with foul play."

Curse Freddy for his loose tongue. No telling what other secrets he'd revealed while Oliver had been shuffling him off to a club.

"You don't know Nathan. He wouldn't . . . he couldn't . . ."

"Abandon you without a word? Apparently he could, and did."

His blunt words drove a stake through her heart. "I'll have you know, Oliver, that I don't need him *or* you. If he really is running away from marrying me, I'll inherit Papa's money and I can do as I please with it."

"Once you get it. But until Hyatt shows up or can be declared dead, you'll be in a sad state financially. It could take years to have your estate untangled."

"I—I'm sure Papa made provisions for that."

"Yes—like the one he made for buying you a husband."

"He didn't buy me a husband!" Her voice dropped to a whisper. "He didn't."

The hurt in her voice seemed to spark something desperate in Oliver. He leaned forward, his eyes lit with an unholy fervor. "Even if he had made provisions and you got the money soon enough to beat the wolf from the door, what would it give you, except a life as a chaste and respectable spinster?"

"I could marry," she protested.

"And you'd never know if the men courting you wanted you for yourself or your money."

"That's no worse than being wanted for my body alone."

"It's not just your body that I—" He broke off, clearly agitated by what he'd almost revealed. "You can't imagine what it's like to have a passionless marriage. My parents had one. The only emotion in their marriage was resentment. Between arguments, they barely breathed the same air."

Slowly he peeled her gloves from her hands, his gaze immobilizing her. "And now I'm watching you head blithely for a marriage to some fellow who will set you up on a shelf with his other possessions, and take you down only when he has a use for you." Tossing her gloves onto the seat, he took her hands in his, kneading the backs with his thumbs. "*If* you even see him again."

The words struck at the very heart of her fears about Nathan—that he desired her only because of how she could serve his ambition. She didn't want to hear it. She didn't want Oliver so close, reminding her that he alone made her heart race and her blood rise, when Nathan should be the one to do so. She didn't want him touching her, making her want things, making her yearn.

Jerking her hands from his, she slid over to the window to look out. "How far is this dress shop, anyway?" she choked out.

Oliver reached past her to yank the curtains closed, then moved to sit beside her. She stiffened, but didn't resist as he looped one arm about her waist to pull her back against his hard body.

"You don't even know what you're giving up," he rasped, "what it's like to shatter beneath a man's touch. If you knew, you wouldn't be so eager to throw that away for the cold comfort of a respectable marriage."

She closed her eyes against his words, but they were designed to tempt her, and tempt her they did. Last night had only roused her curiosity. Now, with the spicy scent of his cologne in her nostrils and his breath warming her cheek, she wanted to know more, *feel* more.

His voice lowered to a whisper. "Let me at least show you what you'd be missing."

She felt rather than saw him shrug off his cloak, leaving him in his shirtsleeves. That sent a wayward thrill down her spine.

"Have you forgotten that I'm deplorably a virgin?" she said, attempting to regain control over the situation.

"No. And you'll still be one when I'm done." He pressed his lips against the bit of neck below her bonnet, making her shiver deliciously. Then he untied her bonnet and tossed it onto the opposite seat so he could press a kiss into her hair. "I only want to give you a taste of passion, sweetheart. Enough for you to see what it could be like between us."

"Oliver . . ." she protested, turning toward him.

That proved a mistake, for he caught her head in his hands and kissed her. Boldly. Deeply.

And she couldn't even bring herself to stop him. Mercy, how fiercely he kissed! He scarcely allowed her breath as his mouth plundered hers over and over, startling her pulse into a wild gallop. She curled her fingers into his shirt, not sure whether she was trying to hold him closer or push him away.

It didn't matter. He had full command of her, and he knew it. His large hands held her still as his tongue tangled with hers, and his thumbs slid down to caress her throat with a tenderness at odds with the wild abandon of his kisses.

He reached back to close the other curtain, then tugged her onto his lap.

She tore her mouth free. "Oliver, you really shouldn't—"

"Shh," he murmured against her lips, then dragged his mouth along her jaw, kissing a path down to her neck. "Let me do this. I swear I won't hurt you."

Maybe not physically, but he had the capacity to hurt her far worse in other ways. Before she'd known the horrible scandal plaguing his family, she could dismiss him as a scoundrel. But now she saw the angry boy inside the man, railing at the world for taking his parents from him, daring people to gossip about him.

It broke her heart. It made her ache for him as she hadn't ached before. And that was dangerous with a man who knew women only as vessels for his desire.

Yet even as he untied the ribbons of her redingote, she didn't stop him. He did it with a reverence she wouldn't have expected, his breath sweetly unsteady and his eyes haunted.

"It's not as if I'm entirely ignorant of . . . what happens between a man and a woman," she whispered to cover her embarrassment. "I do know a few things."

"Do you?" he said as he finished unfastening her redingote. His features sharpened. "Things that Hyatt taught you?"

"No." She spoke the word so quickly that Oliver's eyes locked with hers, a curious triumph shining in them. "My aunt . . . told me a bit."

"Ah." Flashing her a faint smile, he pushed her redingote off her shoulders, then dispensed with the pelerine, baring her low-cut gown to his dark gaze. "And what did she tell you?"

"She told me that . . ." She trailed off as he bent his head to press a kiss to the upper swell of one breast. Her heart seemed to leap beneath his mouth, beating more furiously with every caress of his lips. "She said . . . men would want to . . . touch me in . . . places they shouldn't."

"Like this?" Raising his hand, he covered one of her breasts.

Great heavens. A blush heated her cheeks as he kneaded her breast, slowly, sensually. When he thumbed the nipple through her gown, she thought she might die if he stopped.

"Yes," she breathed. "L-Like that." She shouldn't be letting him do this. But she yearned to know the things he meant to teach her. Besides, he'd promised not to take her innocence, and she trusted him. How odd was that?

His mouth moved lower now, down the slope of her other breast. "Did she tell you that a man might want to do more than touch?" he asked in a husky voice. He dragged down her bodice, then her corset cups.

She caught her breath as he untied her chemise.

"That he might want to do this?" he growled as he bared her breast. Then his mouth was covering her nipple, sucking it, teasing it.

Pure, unadulterated pleasure shot through her. Anything that felt this good had to be naughty. Yet when she closed her hands in his thick black hair to pull him away, she found herself holding him there instead, so his tongue could lick and flick over her nipple, and his teeth could tug at it in a most astonishing fashion.

No wonder women were always falling at rakehells' feet. Heavens alive, his mouth was teasing her in ways she'd never even dreamed of.

"Oliver, are you sure you should be—"

"Do you like it?" he murmured against her breast.

"It's . . . oh, mercy . . ."

"I'll take that as a yes." He laid her back in his arms until she was sprawled shamelessly across his lap, her breasts lifted for his devilish hands, her throat bared to his questing lips. "I've never done this with a virgin, did you know that?" he whispered against her throat. "I've never wanted to until now."

The words lodged in her heart, no matter how much she tried to block them. She drew his head back so she could stare into his eyes. They were slumberous, the lids heavy. He looked like a man just awakening from a deep sleep.

So why did it feel as if *she* were the one awakening?

"Why now?" she asked. "Why with me?"

His gaze turned a molten black. "I don't know." He kissed her again, ravenously, with a raw need that roused an answering need in her, especially when his fingers fondled her breast wantonly, smoothing the damp nipple, rolling it until he made her gasp.

Then his hand left her breast to slide down and lift her skirts.

She jerked her mouth from his. "What are you doing?"

"There are other places a man wishes to touch a woman." He slipped his hand beneath her skirts. "I take it your aunt never told you that."

"She told me. But she said only a husband should do so."

"Or a prospective lover," he said hoarsely. He cupped his hand between her legs, and she squeezed them together in shock. "Maria . . ." he breathed, her name like a prayer on his lips. "Open for me. Let me caress you, angel."

Angel? Angels didn't sit on the laps of wicked scoundrels—not unless they were the fallen kind.

"I just wish to caress you," he choked out, "nothing more."

A strangled laugh escaped her as she fought the sensual spell he was winding around her, the one that made her ache to have his hands wherever he wanted to put them. "I'd make you swear to that, except I know how little you can be trusted when you swear."

He looked torn between protest and laughter. "I tell you what." He drew his hand from between her legs and shifted her on his lap. Then he placed her own hand on the bulge in his tight trousers. "Since you clearly know how to make a man suffer, I give you leave to do what you must if I dare go further than caressing."

As he curved her hand around his thinly clad flesh, his voice grew thick. "Of course, given the choice, I'd prefer that you caress *me* while I'm caressing you."

"I don't know how," she whispered, fascinated by how his flesh seemed to leap beneath her hand.

"Just rub it." He released her hand so he could delve beneath her skirts once more. "Up and down along the length." When she did, he sucked in a harsh breath. "God, yes. Like that."

Meanwhile, he'd found the slit in her drawers and had slipped his hand inside. But this time he didn't only cup her, he rubbed her right on what her aunt had always called her "special place." When she released a moan, his eyes blazed hot. "That's it, angel. Open for me . . . let me feel your pleasure . . ."

Heavens alive, what he was doing to her . . . there were no

words. He dipped his head to nuzzle her temple as his palm pressed her down there in a motion that made her want to squirm, then push against it.

"You like that, do you?" he rasped, moving his mouth over her hair in a series of featherlight kisses.

She buried her hot face in his shirt.

"It's nothing to be ashamed of," he whispered. "Women were made to have the same pleasures as men, no matter what the prudish in society say." His clever fingers combed through her damp curls as if in search of a prize.

When had she become damp there? Aunt Rose had said naught about that, just that her "special place" would grow ready for a man, and then the man would put his "thing" inside her.

Only it wasn't his thing that Oliver was putting there now. It was his finger, teasing, taunting, stroking her so silkily she wanted to cry. Who knew that a finger could feel so . . . very . . . amazing . . .

"My God, angel," he murmured, "you're like hot velvet to the touch." His breath grew labored, and he thrust his flesh against her hand in much the same way as she undulated against his palm.

It reminded her that she'd meant to stroke him, too.

When she did, he seized her mouth in a fierce, heady kiss that sent her head spinning. Now there were two fingers thrusting inside her, and his thumb was pressing her in a way that made her absolutely insane. The strokes of his thumb grew rhythmic, insistent, pulling at her, dragging her from the heavens down toward the black waters that called to her from below, that had always called to her, always fascinated her.

Before she knew it, she was falling, spiraling, her wings riding the wind as her body swooped and twisted and rushed toward the dark, secretive water. And as she plunged into its churning depths, a wild joy like nothing she'd ever known shattered her apart.

She tore her mouth from his, gasping, straining against his hand, her knees shaking and her body shuddering as wave after wave of pleasure rocked her.

"Oh, God, yes . . ." he murmured, "yes . . . keep doing that . . ."

Doing what? Oh. Right. She was still pressing the bulge in his trousers, except that for the last few minutes, she'd been using the same rhythmic motion he'd used on her. Suddenly a hoarse cry escaped his throat, and his flesh spasmed beneath her fingers. Within seconds the fabric grew wet, dampening her hand.

She jerked her hand away, not sure what she'd done. But when he threw his head back, a ragged sigh escaping him, she realized that it had pleased him. A smile hovered on his lips, and his features wore a look of utter bliss.

"Angel . . ." His eyes were heavy-lidded as he stared down at her. "You're . . . amazing."

I'm fallen, she thought.

Not literally. He hadn't ruined her, but she'd still fallen. Because he'd been right. Now that she'd tasted passion, she didn't know how she'd bear never tasting it again.

The coach abruptly halted, and the coachman above called out, "Mrs. Tweedy's Fine Dresses, milord."

Maria froze, then jerked upright in a panic. Heavens alive! Her bodice was undone, she was sprawled across his lap like some doxy, and the footman would be opening the door any moment!

"It's all right," he said soothingly as he helped her scramble from his lap. "There's no need to rush. The footmen know not to open my carriage door if the curtains are closed."

It took a second for the words to sink in, then her blood ran cold. He did this all the time—she was just one of many. The words he'd said about showing her passion, the offer to make her his mistress—they were calculated to soften her for his seduction. If not for their arrival at the dress shop, what might have happened?

He reached to help her with her bodice, and she pushed his hand away. "Don't you dare! I can do it myself."

A stricken look crossed his face, making her briefly doubt her conclusions. Then she saw the closed curtains, and any doubts fled.

"Maria," he said in a low, aching voice, "what's wrong?"

Tears sprang to her eyes and she ruthlessly squelched them. She might have behaved like a fool, but she wasn't about to let him see her cry. Not here, not now . . . not *ever*. "Nothing's wrong," she lied.

Thank heavens her hair had stayed pinned. As she tied on her bonnet and looped the pelerine about her shoulders, she gave a silent thanks to Betty, who'd stuck enough pins in her hair to keep it in place for an eternity.

But when she tried to struggle into her redingote alone, Oliver cursed and grabbed it from her, insisting on helping her into it.

As she fumbled with the ties, he laid his hand over her fingers. "Come now, my angel, tell me what's wrong."

"Don't call me that." She shrugged off his hand so she could finish fastening her ties. "I'm not an angel. I'm certainly not *your* angel. Though I thank you for the lesson in passion, it isn't something we should repeat."

Turning the handle, she pushed open the door before he could stop her.

"Deuce take it, Maria—" he growled, but caught himself as the footman came running to put down the step.

Only then did she venture a glance at him. He was watching her with something dangerously feral in his eyes.

She forced herself to ignore the tiny swell of regret that rose in her. "I think it's best if you go to fetch Freddy. By the time you've returned, I should be done shopping. It won't take me long to select a few dresses, and you'll find it boring."

"I doubt that very much," he bit out.

She had to get him out of here! She wouldn't survive another tête-à-tête ride in the carriage with him. She forced an imploring note into her voice. "Please, my lord? If you stay, you'll make me nervous."

That seemed to give him pause. "It's dangerous for a woman alone."

"I'll stay," the footman surprised her by saying. When Oliver turned a scowl on him, he squeaked, "But only if you wish it, milord."

Oliver shifted his gaze back to Maria, then sighed. "Very well, John," he told the footman. "If that's what she wants. Tell the shopkeeper I'll pay for the gowns on my return."

She stiffened. The closed curtains . . . gowns he bought for her . . . That might be acceptable for a fiancé in English good society, but he wouldn't be her fiancé for long. If she kept letting him do these things, she'd be ruined in the eyes of the world by the time she could break off their engagement.

But she said nothing; right now, she just wanted him away.

"You're sure you'll be all right," he said, concern in his voice.

"Yes." She pasted a smile to her lips. "Really, my lord, there's no reason for you to stay."

The words "my lord" made him stiffen. "As you wish." He called up to the coachman, "Return me to the Blue Swan post-haste."

The coach drove off, and she released a breath. At least she'd escaped another ride alone with him, where he would tempt her into doing what she ought not.

She paused outside the shop to face the footman. "If you please, John, I'd rather you not mention the issue of payment to the shopkeeper. I want to deal with it myself."

"But his lordship said—"

"I know what he said." She steadied her shoulders. "This is what I want."

John nodded, a strange expression crossing his face. "Very well. But I should warn you, this shop ain't one of those low secondhand shops. Mrs. Tweedy prides herself on having clothing of the highest quality, so it might be costly."

She hoped it wasn't *too* costly.

The shop did look rather lofty. Jaunty bonnets of expensive satin and silk were perched on hat trees, while brocaded and heavily embroidered ball gowns were draped over bureaus and linen presses to show their fine qualities. The everyday attire sat folded neatly in open cupboards, and even the day dresses were made of fine muslin and wool. There were half-boots and dancing slippers, scarves and shifts—anything a woman might need to outfit herself for society. She'd seen nothing like that in Dartmouth, to be sure.

As she roamed the shop looking at the goods, the shopkeeper introduced herself. After a short chat in which Maria explained that she needed a few gowns, she added, "I happen to own some very fashionable mourning attire in a variety of fine designs and fabrics. Might you be interested in trading yours for mine?"

The woman looked at Maria's well-made redingote and said, "If it's good quality, miss, I certainly would. There's always those ladies who need mourning clothes, and fashionable ones are harder to come by than most."

Maria hated to part with them, but once this bargain with Oliver was done, she could dye the gowns she acquired here if she had to. She only had two more months of mourning—by the time she left England, she might not need mourning clothes anymore. And she still had the one gown she'd carried away with her from the brothel.

She made arrangements with the woman to have a clerk accompany John to the lodging house where she and Freddy had been staying, so the two young men could fetch her trunks. Before John left, she took him aside.

"I'd appreciate it very much if you'd keep quiet about my mourning gowns, especially with Mrs. Plumtree. I know his lordship would appreciate it as well. I have a ring I could offer you in payment—"

"No, miss, I won't take aught from you for my discretion. That's my job—to be discreet about his lordship's coming and goings. And his fiancée's as well."

She cast him a grateful smile. "Thank you."

Working the brim of his hat furiously, he looked toward the shop front, then back to her. "Tell me, miss, did his lordship do aught to upset you in the coach?"

"No," she lied.

John looked skeptical. "It ain't like him to harm a young lady, but perhaps he got carried away, with you being his fiancée and all. I just want you to know that if you wish . . . if I could help you in any way—"

"That's sweet of you," she said, truly touched. "But you have no reason for concern. Your master has been very kind."

"All right then." With a quick bow, he went off to join the clerk and they left on their errand.

Oliver *had* been kind to her in many respects. He'd kept his word and hired Mr. Pinter. He'd offered to buy her gowns, and he'd treated Freddy with more indulgence than could be expected of any man.

But his actions in the carriage hadn't been a kindness. Because now she knew exactly what she'd be missing if she married Nathan and settled for his mild kisses.

As she went about the shop selecting gowns, she told herself that maybe passion could develop between two people over time. Maybe once she was married to Nathan, it would come out all right in the end.

Deep inside, however, in the naughty part of her that had reveled in Oliver's fervent kisses, she knew she was lying to herself. Because right now, the only man she ever wanted to kiss again was Oliver.

Chapter Thirteen

As Oliver and Freddy pulled away from the Blue Swan, Oliver paid little heed to the lad's chatter about his spectacular meal. All he could hear was Maria calling him *my lord*, as if she hadn't just been trembling in his arms.

And the look on her face! Had she been insulted? Or just ashamed? How the devil had she stayed so collected, when he'd felt ready to explode after seeing her find her pleasure so sweetly in his arms? He'd actually come in his trousers, like a randy lad with no control over his urges. Now he had to keep his cloak buttoned up until he could reach Halstead Hall and change his clothes.

She'd made light of their encounter, damn her. *Though I thank you for the lesson in passion . . .* Had it meant nothing more to her? Apparently not, since she'd said, *It isn't something we should repeat.*

Though the idea grated, she was right. They should stay apart, for his sake as well as hers. He'd actually offered to make her his mistress! *He*, who'd never kept a mistress in his life, who'd joked to his friends that mistresses were more trouble than they were worth since one woman was as good as another.

He'd always been driven by the fear that a mistress might tempt him to let down his guard and reveal his secrets. Then even his family would desert him, and he couldn't bear that.

Even with his friends, he kept the strongbox of his secrets firmly closed. But with Maria . . .

He stared out the window, trying to figure out at what point in their conversation he'd lost all good sense. Had it been when she'd said she didn't believe the gossip about him? Or before that, when she'd chastised Pinter for telling it to her?

No. Astonishing as those things had been, what had prompted his rash offer was the lost look on her face after he'd pointed out that Hyatt might not wish to be found. Even now he could see the fear rising in her eyes, much like the fear he'd seen in Mother's eyes—of being inconsequential, unwanted.

And suddenly he'd desired nothing more than to make Maria feel wanted.

Not that he'd succeeded very well. She could hardly be flattered that he wanted her only for a mistress. He hadn't meant it to insult her—he'd just been utterly swept up in the idea of her and him in a cottage together somewhere, without the rest of the world to muddy their lives.

Marriage meant jointures and pin money and siring an heir to continue the dynasty. A cottage meant just him and Maria.

What a fool he was. Even a woman with Maria's low connections wanted more. And he couldn't give it. The very thought of attempting it made him ill, because he could never make her happy. He would muck it up, and the legacy of misery would go on.

But he'd be damned if he'd watch her throw herself away on that fool Hyatt. She deserved better than an indifferent fiancé who had no clue how to make her eyes darken in passion as she shuddered and trembled and gave her mouth so sweetly . . .

He groaned. He shouldn't have gone so far with her. It had frightened her. Worse yet, his reaction to it bloody well terrified him—because he'd give a great deal to be able to do it again. He'd never felt that way for any other woman.

Freddy was still blathering on, and suddenly a word arrested him.

"What was that you said?" Oliver asked.

"The beefsteak needed a bit more salt—"

"Before that," he ground out.

"Oh. Right. There was a chap in that club claiming he was your cousin. Mr. Desmond Plumtree, I think."

His stomach sank. When had Desmond gained membership at such a selective club? Did it mean the bastard was finally becoming accepted in society?

"Though if you ask me," Freddy went on, "with family like him, who needs enemies? Insulting fellow. Told me a bunch of nonsense about how you'd killed your father and everybody knew it." Freddy sniffed. "I told him he was a scurrilous lout, and if he couldn't see that you were a good sort of chap, then he was as blind as a town crier with a broken lantern. And he didn't belong in the Blue Swan with all those amiable gents, neither."

For a moment, speech utterly failed Oliver. He could only imagine Desmond's reaction to *that* little lecture. "And . . . er . . . what did he say?"

"He looked surprised, then muttered something about playing cards and trotted off to a card room. Good riddance, too—he was eating up all the macaroons."

Oliver gaped at him, then began to laugh.

"What's so funny?"

"You and Maria—don't you Americans ever pay attention to gossip?"

"Well, sure, if it makes sense. But that didn't make sense. If everybody knew you'd killed your father, you'd have been hanged by now. Since you're sitting right here, you can't have done it." Freddy tapped his forehead. "Simple logic is all."

"Right," Oliver said. "Simple logic." A lump caught in his throat. Maria's defending him was one thing; she was a woman and softhearted, though that had certainly never kept any other woman from gossiping about him.

But to have an impressionable pup like Freddy defend him . . . he didn't know whether to scoff at the fellow's naïveté or clap him on the shoulder and pronounce him a "good sort of chap" as well.

"Oh, look," Freddy said, already on to the next subject as they pulled up before the shop. "It appears that Mopsy is done shopping already, thank God."

Oliver's eyes narrowed. Either "Mopsy" chose her clothes with less care than most females, or something was amiss.

After they left the coach, a few short words with the shopkeeper revealed that Maria had traded her mourning gowns to pay for the new ones, which had left her with a decidedly smaller clothing budget than she needed. He understood pride, but this was too much.

"My fiancée isn't finished shopping," he told the shopkeeper. "With a whole trousseau to buy, she needs quite a few more items."

"Oliver, please," Maria hissed under her breath as she drew him aside. "They'll think—"

"That I can afford to outfit my fiancée properly? I hope they do." He used the only argument that might influence her. "Otherwise, they'll assume I'm even more in debt than has been rumored. Of course, if you enjoy watching people heap gossip on me . . ."

"Certainly not!" With a glance at the shopkeeper, she lowered her voice. "But I don't want to bear any greater obligation to you than I already do."

"Now you sound like Pinter."

Her gaze shot to his, full of concern. "I didn't mean—"

"I owe you clothes," he clipped out. "There's no obligation. Especially with Pinter refusing to charge me a fee." Besides, he *wanted* to see her dressed well, with her beautiful blue eyes complemented by a gown of periwinkle silk, and her fine bosom displayed properly so she felt no need to hide it with a stupid pelerine.

Not that he could tell her that. It would only alarm her.

"No one will believe that I would betroth myself to a woman who dresses poorly," he went on. "We must preserve the illusion. I thought Gran would surely relent the first night when I passed you off as a . . . woman of a certain kind, but she didn't.

When she sees me spending money on you, she'll *have* to believe I'm serious."

He could see her wavering, so he pressed his advantage. "If you don't let me do this, I'll assume that I insulted you earlier in the carriage."

Blushing deeply, she dropped her gaze to his chest. "You didn't insult me. I let it go on when I shouldn't have."

"You did nothing wrong," he said sharply. "I'm the one who behaved badly, and to make amends for that, I'm more than willing to buy you a few fripperies." Without waiting for further protests, he turned to the shopkeeper and said, "Miss Butterfield has agreed that she needs a more extensive wardrobe."

"Very good, sir. I have some special items I've been holding in the back. With a few alterations, I believe they would fit your fiancée." As the shopkeeper hurried off to fetch them, Oliver bent close to whisper, "If it will soothe your fears, I withdraw my earlier offer to make you my mistress. I meant no insult, and I wish you to be easy on that score."

"Thank you," she said, though she didn't look as relieved as he'd expected.

He didn't feel as relieved as he'd expected, either.

Now he had to watch her try on respectable gowns more suited to her station. That further muddied the waters, reminding him that no matter how exquisitely she'd come apart in his arms, she was still respectable. Suddenly, the woman he'd felt free to caress most inappropriately had become one of *those* women—the ones he avoided, the untouchable virgins. Something he must not forget again.

Two hours later, they left the dress shop with an abundance

of gowns and other necessities. He'd been able to indulge her in shawls and reticules and shoes, though it irritated him to have to buy them in so mean a place. Mrs. Tweedy's might be the best of the secondhand shops, but it was still secondhand.

He wanted to see her dressed in expensive silks of the latest fashions, with costly jewels about her neck. It was a mad desire he'd never experienced, never having cared how his bed partners dressed. But the wistful look she'd cast at items she'd obviously felt were beyond his purse made something clench in his gut.

Which was precisely why he'd never taken a mistress. Once a woman tugged at your sympathies, you were lost. She could twist you about her fingers like twine in a cat's cradle. From there, it was only a short step to opening up the strongbox and letting her see your secrets . . . and finding yourself hated for them.

Their ride back to Ealing was quiet. She avoided looking at him, while he couldn't seem to *stop* looking at her. He tried to engage her in conversation, but the tart-tongued angel was in hiding, and he didn't know how to get her back. Even Freddy must have realized that something had changed, for he kept his inane chatter to a minimum. By the time they reached Halstead Hall, Oliver's nerves were on edge.

He was relieved that he could excuse himself to go work in his study on the ledgers he'd ignored last night, but he didn't get very far. Even after an hour of turning pages and noting transactions, he kept hearing Maria's sighs of pleasure, kept seeing her teasing smile as she said, "Would you offer to ravish me?"

Damned right he would.

A knock came at the door, jerking him from his disturbing reverie. As he glanced at the clock, shocked to discover that two hours had passed, Jarret entered and strolled over to the desk.

"Amazing," the scapegrace said. "When the servant said you were in here working, I thought surely I'd misheard him."

"Very amusing. If we're to live here even for a few weeks, some matters must be handled." Leaning back, he arched one eyebrow at his brother. "Unless *you* want to take over the task. You're better at numbers than I am."

Jarret turned the ledger so he could glance at it. "I don't know. Appears to me that you know a thing or two." He plopped down in the chair opposite Oliver. "Besides, I'm riding into town tomorrow to spend my Saturday at the Blue Swan. Kirkwood's brother will be there, and you know he always plays deep."

"And badly, too, when he's in his cups—a fact that you take advantage of."

With a shrug, Jarret folded his hands over his midsection. "I thought I should make *some* attempt to add to the family coffers."

"Then you'd be better off playing cards with bankers, not barristers. It will take more than anything Giles Masters can offer to dig us out of this hole."

"Interesting that you should say that. Minerva told me last night about Miss Butterfield's missing fiancé. So I had a little chat with young Freddy this morning, and learned that Miss Butterfield is due to come into a tidy fortune, assuming she doesn't marry her Mr. Hyatt. Were you aware of that?"

Oliver poured himself a glass of brandy from the decanter on the desk. "I don't know how tidy it will be. How much could one small shipping company in America be worth?"

"Have you really never heard of New Bedford Ships?"

"Why should I have?" He drank some brandy. "It's not exactly an industry I'm familiar with."

"Well, it happens to be an industry I invest in when I have extra funds, which isn't often."

Jarret was an excellent gambler and generally won more than he lost, but he had a deplorable habit of risking too much from time to time, which often sank him in the end. Oliver had never understood it; his brother seemed compelled to tempt Fate.

"I rode into town earlier to talk to my sources," Jarret went on, "to see what I could learn about the company. By all accounts, New Bedford Ships is worth a quarter of a million pounds. Assuming that she gets half, she'll come into a cool 125,000 pounds."

Oliver choked on his brandy. "You've got to be joking."

"I never joke about money."

It took Oliver a moment to register that incredible bit of news. "Is she aware that it's so much?"

"I don't think so. Freddy speculated that it might be as much as 'ten thousand dollars,' which the pup seemed to think was an enormous amount. I gather that her father was the frugal sort, and she was kept in the dark about many things concerning his business."

Oliver knew why, too. He'd already figured out that Adam Butterfield had wanted to run his daughter's life even from beyond the grave. The man must have known that if she were aware of the magnitude of her fortune, she might balk at his choice for a husband.

It also explained why Hyatt had agreed to marry her despite showing her no real affection. If she chose to sell her half, he probably couldn't afford to buy it, so marriage was clearly more advantageous to Hyatt. And *less* advantageous to her.

He scowled at the thought.

"So you see, my dear brother," Jarret continued, "the answer to our problems is right before you. You could forget about the pretense and marry her for real. That would solve all our problems."

A cold rage seized Oliver. "It would also make me as bad as Father."

"And that bothers you?"

"Of course it bothers me! He practically drove Mother to the grave." Though Oliver had given the final push. "You can forget my marrying Miss Butterfield for her money." The very idea sickened him.

"Then perhaps you shouldn't be attempting to seduce her in your carriage," Jarret said in a steely voice.

Oliver froze. "I don't know what the devil you're talking about."

"Yes, you do." Jarret's face wore that stiff look he sometimes got whenever people insulted their sisters within his hearing. "John informed me that you and Miss Butterfield were stopped in front of the dress shop for several minutes with the curtains closed and without Freddy in attendance. He also said that when you finally emerged, Miss Butterfield was quite agitated."

Oliver's fury found a new object. "I see I'll have to have a word with my gossiping servant. He's well paid to keep his mouth shut."

"All the money in the world won't keep a good man silent when something offends his conscience. Besides, he seems to like Miss Butterfield." Jarret's tone hardened. "We all do. You know damned well that she isn't one of your opera dancers whom you can toy with and cast aside. She's a respectable woman. If you're so determined not to be like Father, perhaps you should remember that the next time you think to put your hands on her."

The fact that Jarret had a point didn't dim Oliver's fury one bit. "You don't know anything about her."

"Are you saying she's *not* respectable?"

"No, damn it! I'm saying . . ." He strove to contain his temper, which was unreasonably high. "That ass Hyatt wants to marry her for her money, and she's letting herself be coaxed into it out of some sense of duty to her father or some foolish hope that it will turn out well. I have to convince her she's making a mistake."

"I can think of better ways to do that than seducing her," Jarret said dryly. "Try talking to her instead. You might even spend time getting to know her. I realize that's not your usual style, but you might have more success if you treat her like the reasonable female she seems to be, instead of another conquest."

"I'm not treating her like—" He caught himself before he said too much. "Thank you for the advice, but I know how to comport myself with Maria."

"That remains to be seen." Jarret rose, then bent to plant his hands on the desk. "But know this—none of us will stand by and let you ruin a young woman just to provoke Gran."

Oliver shot to his feet. That his brother thought him capable of such a thing infuriated him, as did being lectured by him. It had never happened before, and he wasn't about to allow it now.

Leaning forward until he and Jarret were eye to eye over the desk, he growled, "And what the deuce do you think you can do to stop me from acting as I please?"

A grim smile touched Jarret's lips. "I could attempt to steal her from you."

Somewhere in the recesses of his sanity, Oliver knew he was being baited, yet it made no difference. Just the idea of Jarret seeking to engage Maria's affections crushed his usual control.

"If you lay a hand on her," he ground out, "Gabe won't be the only one wearing a sling in this family."

With an enigmatic look, Jarret pushed back from the desk. "Fine." His eyes turned to ice. "But be warned—the rest of us intend to make sure that *you* never lay a hand on her, either." Without waiting for a response, he strode from the room.

Oliver stood there shaking while anger and some other, indefinable emotion swept through him. The sheer audacity of his brother—to command what he must do! It was laughable. And to think that his most loyal footman had dared—

All the money in the world won't keep a good man silent when something offends his conscience.

He grimaced. John's conscience must have been offended indeed, if he'd gone to Jarret about it. And the very fact that the footman had guessed at what had been going on made Oliver's blood run cold. Why hadn't he realized what his servants would think?

Suddenly he remembered the look on Maria's face when he'd said that the servants understood not to open the door when the curtains were closed.

Dropping into the chair, he stared blindly at the fireplace. What was *wrong* with him? He'd thought himself guilty only of insulting and frightening her, but he'd been guilty of so much more. No wonder she'd behaved so differently after leaving the carriage. No wonder she'd balked at his purchasing gowns for her. He'd practically proclaimed her one of his whores before his servants, and she was damned sensitive about that.

With good reason, of course. She *was* a respectable woman. And an heiress. A very rich heiress.

Damn it all to hell. He hadn't guessed she was worth so much. And if she didn't realize it herself, she was even more susceptible to being taken advantage of by that scoundrel Hyatt.

Oliver downed the rest of his brandy, then set the glass firmly on the desk. He had to save her from the man. He owed her that for her help with Gran.

When this was done, Miss Maria Butterfield would no longer be shackled to some ambitious weasel with an eye on her fortune. Not if he could help it.

HETTY WAS AWAKENED from a doze in a chair by the sound of a door opening. She was about to make herself known to whoever had entered the library when someone else entered, too, and she heard Minerva say, "Well? What do you think? Am I right about Oliver and Miss Butterfield?"

Shrinking into the chair, she prayed she wouldn't be noticed in the corner.

"It certainly looks that way." It was Jarret's voice. "He does seem to have genuine feelings for her. I've never witnessed him act like that over a woman. You should have seen him—ready to strike me when I suggested going after her myself."

"What a brilliant touch!" Minerva cried. "I *told* you he liked her. And I'll hazard a guess that she likes him, too. I went up to her room after they got back, and she blushed furiously when I asked if Oliver had behaved himself."

"That's the problem. Liking her is one thing, but whether he'll act on the attraction honorably is another matter entirely. Oliver isn't used to being around a woman he's not allowed to . . . er . . ."

"Take to bed."

Hetty blinked.

"My God, Minerva, don't say things like that! You're not supposed to know about such matters."

"Pish posh. I could hardly grow up with a rogue for a father and three rogue brothers without hearing a few things."

Hetty had to chomp on the inside of her cheek to stifle her laugh.

"Well, at least *pretend* you don't know, will you?" Jarret grumbled. "One day you'll say something like that in public and give me heart failure."

"We have to find a way to push them together," Minerva said. "You know perfectly well that if Oliver marries, Gran will forget this ridiculous idea of hers about the rest of us marrying. She just wants him to produce an heir."

Hetty's eyebrows shot high. Her granddaughter had a big surprise coming down the road.

"And you're willing to throw him under the wheels of the coach to save yourself, is that it?" Jarret quipped.

"No!" Her voice softened. "You and I both know he needs someone to drag him out of himself. Or he's just going to get scarier as he gets older." She paused. "Did you tell him about Miss Butterfield's being an heiress?"

That certainly arrested Hetty's attention. She hadn't dreamed that the girl had money.

"Yes, but I fear that might have been a mistake—when I suggested that he marry her for her fortune, he got angry."

Of course he got angry, you fool, Hetty thought with a roll of her eyes. Honestly, did her grandson know nothing about his brother?

"For goodness sake, Jarret, you weren't supposed to suggest that. You were supposed to get him concerned that she might fall prey to fortune hunters."

At least Minerva had a brain.

"Damn," Jarret said. "Then I probably shouldn't have exaggerated the amount."

"Oh, Lord." Minerva sighed. "By how much?"

"I kind of . . . tripled it."

Minerva released an unladylike oath. "Why did you do that? Now he won't go *near* her. Haven't you noticed how much he hates talk of marrying for money?"

"Men say things like that, but in the end they're practical."

"Not Oliver! You've just ruined everything!"

"Don't be so dramatic," Jarret said. "Besides, I have a plan—I laid the seeds for it before I even left Oliver's study. Come, let's go talk to the others. It will take all of us working together." His voice receded as the two of them apparently left the room. "If we merely . . ."

Hetty strained to hear, but she lost the thread of the conversation. Not that it mattered.

A smile tugged at her mouth. It appeared she would not have to carry off this match alone. All she need do was sit back and watch Jarret work on Oliver. In the meantime, she would let Minerva go on thinking that finding Oliver a wife would solve their dilemma. That would spur the girl to try harder.

In the end, it didn't matter why or how they managed it, as long as they did. Thank God her grandchildren had inherited her capacity for scheming. It made her proud.

So Oliver thought he was going to get around her this time, did he? Well, he was in for a shock. This time he had more than just *her* to worry about. And with every one of the Sharpe children on Miss Butterfield's side? She laughed.

Poor Oliver didn't stand a chance.

Chapter Fourteen

When Maria left her room, headed for dinner, a deep voice said, "I see you've recovered from our trip to town."

She whirled to find Oliver sitting in a chair near her door. Had he been waiting for her? "Good evening, my lord," she said as he rose. "You look well."

In truth, he looked amazing in dinner dress—it suited him better than any man she knew. The stark white of his shirt and cravat contrasted beautifully with his olive skin, and his black swallowtail coat with its high velvet collar enhanced the velvety black of his eyes. Unfortunately, his figured waistcoat of gold silk also reminded her that he was far above her in station, no matter what his finances, and the tight trousers of black kerseymere molded to his flesh reminded her of . . .

No, she could *not* be thinking about their encounter this afternoon, of all things. That was behind her.

"You look like a goddess," he murmured as he raked his eyes down her form.

And she melted into a puddle.

"Thank you." She tried to sound cool and sophisticated. "I much prefer wearing a gown that's not too tight."

"Except where it should be." He dropped his gaze pointedly to her bosom.

The frank admiration in his eyes made her glad that she'd let Betty guide her choice for tonight. After that other scandalous gown, she'd been reluctant to wear anything low cut, but this one did look beautiful on her, even with its décolletage. Salmon had always been a good color for her, and the satin rouleaux trim made her feel pretty and elegant.

"So it's presentable enough for dinner with your family?" she asked.

"They don't even deserve to see you in it." The low rumble of his voice made her breath catch in her throat. "I only wish that you and I could—"

"You do look lovely," said another voice. Lord Gabriel came up from behind Oliver, dressed all in black as usual. A look of pure mischief crossed his face. "Sorry I'm late, Miss Butterfield, but thank you, brother, for keeping her company until I arrived."

Oliver glared at him. "What the devil do you mean?"

"I'm taking the young lady down to dinner."

"That office should be left to her fiancé, don't you think?" Oliver bit out.

"Pretend fiancé. You have no real claim on her. And since you had her to yourself all day . . ." Lord Gabriel offered his arm. "Shall we, Miss Butterfield?"

Maria hesitated, unsure what to do. But Oliver was a danger to her sanity, and his brother wasn't. So she was better off with Lord Gabriel.

"Thank you, sir," she said, taking his arm.

"Now just wait one blasted minute. You can't—"

"What? Be friendly to our guest?" Lord Gabriel asked, his face a mask of innocence. "Really, old boy, I didn't realize it mattered that much. But if it upsets you to see Miss Butterfield on the arm of another man, I'll certainly yield the field."

Lord Gabriel's words seemed to give Oliver pause. Glancing from Maria to his brother, he smiled, though it didn't nearly reach his eyes. "No, it's fine," he said tightly. "Perfectly fine."

When they headed down the hall with Oliver following behind, Lord Gabriel flashed her a conspiratorial glance. She wasn't sure what the conspiracy was, but since it seemed to irritate Oliver, she went along.

The incident was only the first in a series that continued throughout the week. Whenever she and Oliver found themselves alone, even for a moment, one of his siblings popped up to offer some entertainment—a stroll in the gardens, a ride into Ealing, a game of loo. With each instance, Oliver grew more annoyed, for no reason that she could see.

Unless . . .

No, that was crazy. If his family's blatant attempts to separate them irritated him, it was only because he hated losing the chance to seduce her. After all, he had offered to make her his mistress. It wasn't as if he truly cared for her. There was no point in hoping for anything more from him.

Hoping? That was equally absurd. She wasn't hoping for anything from him—she already had a fiancé.

The trouble was, it was hard to think of Nathan at Halstead Hall. The place's otherworldly antiquity made every day in it seem like something out of a book. One day she would stumble across a Rembrandt hung carelessly in a boudoir, and another day a rat would scurry across her path. The house was rags and riches all in one.

And the servants! Mercy, they buzzed around her like bees serving the queen of the hive. She couldn't understand it—there weren't that many of them. So how was it she was always finding one or two underfoot whenever she carried something, or moved a chair into a patch of light so she could read better, or went to the kitchen for a snack? She didn't know how the Sharpe family could stand it.

Meanwhile, Oliver's siblings talked incessantly about the upcoming St. Valentine's Day ball being held by the Duchess of Foxmoor. The closer it got, the more nervous she became, since Mrs. Plumtree kept speaking of it as the event where Oliver would announce their betrothal. Clearly, she was not backing down as quickly as Oliver had predicted.

So Maria was relieved when, on the day before the ball, a servant informed her that his lordship wished to speak to her in his study. This was her chance to talk to him alone. She hurried there, praying that for once none of his siblings would appear.

As soon as she entered, he closed the door and gestured for her to take a seat. Then he began to pace, clearly uncomfortable. Her heart began to pound. Had he heard from Mr. Pinter? Was there bad news about Nathan?

At last, he stopped behind his desk. "Have my servants displeased you?"

She blinked. *That* was completely unexpected. "Certainly not."

"They're laboring under the impression that they have."

"I can't imagine why."

"They say you make up your own bed in the morning."

"Well, yes, of course."

He raised an eyebrow at that. "And build your own fire in the grate, and fetch your own tea."

"Why wouldn't I?"

His eyes narrowed. "Had you no servants at home?"

"Certainly." She tipped up her chin. "We had a coachman and a groom, and two maids to help me and my aunt with the laundry and the cooking."

A smile tugged at his lips. "Ah, I begin to see the problem."

"I certainly hope you'll explain it to me, since I don't see it at all."

"Servants in England aren't there to help. They're there to *do*."

"What do you mean?"

He propped one hip on his desk. "Whenever you make your own bed, they assume it's because you disapprove of how they do it. The same is true for building the fire and fetching tea. They want to serve you, and when you don't allow them to, they think they've failed you."

"That's absurd. I'm always telling them I don't need any help."

"Precisely. And with those words, you take away their purpose in life, which hurts their pride."

She winced as she thought of the anxious look Betty always wore. "Surely no one's ultimate purpose in life is to be a servant."

"In England, it is." His voice gentled. "I know it's hard for you as an American to understand this, but English servants are very proud of what they do, of the family they serve, of how important their positions are within that family. When you deny them the chance to do their duty, you make them feel as if you don't respect them."

Heat spread over her cheeks. "Oh, dear. Is that why they're always underfoot, trying to do things for me?"

"Yes. The more you take upon yourself, the more they think they've erred."

Heavens alive. "I only wanted to make things easier for them. With your grandmother's servants returned to London, and such a big house needing so much work—"

"I know. It's all right." He took a seat behind the desk. "Just let them do their jobs. They believe that you'll soon be their mistress, so they're eager to please you."

She swallowed. This was the opening she'd been waiting for. "About that—do you really intend to announce our 'engagement' at the ball tomorrow night?"

He shook his head. "It won't go that far. Gran may have been calling my bluff until now, but she'll never carry our battle into the public eye. She's too aware of the family's consequence. In the end, she'll back down, I assure you."

"What if she doesn't? If you make it public, word of it might reach Nathan . . ."

His face hardened. "Word of it won't reach anyone, because the announcement will never happen."

"I hope you're right." Lately her conscience had really begun to plague her about Nathan. She'd agreed to marry him; she'd made a solemn promise. And every time she let Oliver get in the way of it, she behaved dishonorably.

"Trust me, Maria, it'll be fine."

An awkward silence fell. She rose. "Well then, if that's all—"

"Don't go," he murmured as he rose, too.

Her gaze shot to him. His eyes scoured her in a most alarming fashion, yet she seemed powerless to turn away. "Why?"

"We've scarcely had any time to chat of late, what with my brothers and sisters keeping you so well occupied." His voice held an edge. "Sit down. Please. We'll talk."

Talk? That didn't sound like Oliver. "All right." She took her seat again, bemused by his change of mood. "What do you wish to talk about?"

He suddenly looked at a loss, which was unexpectedly endearing. No doubt he spent most of his time with women doing things other than talking.

She spied a book atop his desk, and a mischievous impulse seized her. "I see you're reading Minerva's latest novel."

To her shock, he colored. "I figured I should find out what my sister is up to."

"So is this your first foray into Minerva's world of 'Gothic horrors'?"

"Yes." He looked uncomfortable with the topic, which of course made her only more eager to pursue it.

"You made an excellent first choice. *The Stranger of the Lake* is my favorite."

He scowled. "Why? Because Rockton gets his comeuppance in that damned rapier duel?"

A smile tugged at her lips. "Because Minerva lets him live. She usually kills the villain off in a very gruesome manner."

"Ah, and you hate the gruesome parts."

"Actually, no, I love them. It's too awful, isn't it? She almost can't make it gruesome enough for me." When he blinked at her, she added with a grin, "At home, I had a subscription to *The Newgate Calendar.* Well, Freddy had a subscription. Father didn't approve of my fascination with murder and mayhem."

"I imagine he didn't." He sat back in the chair to stare at her. "So, if you like the gruesome parts, why are you glad she didn't kill off Rockton?"

"She gives just enough hints about him to make you wonder why he became so villainous. And if he dies, I'll never learn the answer."

Oliver eyed her closely. "Perhaps he was born villainous."

"No one is born villainous."

"Oh?" he said with raised eyebrow. "So we're all born good?"

"Neither. We start as animals, with an animal's needs and desires. It takes parents and teachers and other good examples to show us how to restrain those needs and desires, when necessary, for the greater good. But it's still our choice whether to heed that education or to do as we please."

"For a woman who loves murder and mayhem, you're quite the philosopher."

"I like to understand how things work. Why people behave as they do."

He digested that for a moment. "I happen to think that some of us, like Rockton, are born with a wicked bent."

She chose her words carefully. "That certainly provides Rockton with a convenient excuse for his behavior."

His features turned stony. "What do you mean?"

"Being moral and disciplined is hard work. Being wicked requires no effort at all—one merely indulges every desire and impulse, no matter how hurtful or immoral. By claiming to be born wicked, Rockton ensures that he doesn't have to struggle to be good. He can just protest that he can't help himself."

"Perhaps he can't," he clipped out.

"Or maybe he's simply unwilling to fight his impulses. And I want to know the reason for that. That's why I keep reading Minerva's books."

Did Oliver actually believe he'd been born irredeemably wicked? How tragic! It lent a hopelessness to his life that helped to explain his mindless pursuit of pleasure.

"I can tell you the reason for Rockton's villainy." Oliver rose to round the desk. Propping his hip on the edge near her, he reached out to tuck a tendril of hair behind her ear.

A sweet shudder swept over her. Why must he have this effect on her? It simply wasn't fair. "Oh?" she managed.

"Rockton knows he can't have everything he wants," he said hoarsely, his hand drifting to her cheek. "He can't have the heroine, for example. She would never tolerate his . . . wicked impulses. Yet he still wants her. And his wanting consumes him."

Her breath lodged in her throat. It had been days since he'd touched her, and she hadn't forgotten what it was like for one minute. To have him this near, saying such things . . .

She fought for control over her volatile emotions. "His

wanting consumes him precisely *because* he can't have her. If he thought he could, he wouldn't want her at all."

"Not true." His voice deepening, he stroked the line of her jaw with a tenderness that roused an ache in her chest. "Even Rockton recognizes when a woman is unlike any other. Her very goodness in the face of his villainy bewitches him. He thinks if he can just possess that goodness, then the dark cloud lying on his soul will lift, and he'll have something other than villainy to sustain him."

"Then he's mistaken." Her pulse trebled as his finger swept the hollow of her throat. "The only person who can lift the dark cloud on his soul is himself."

He paused in his caress. "So he's doomed, then?"

"No!" Her gaze flew to his. "No one is doomed, and certainly not Rockton. There's still hope for him. There is always hope."

His eyes burned with a feverish light, and before she could look away, he bent to kiss her. It was soft, tender . . . delicious. Someone moaned, she wasn't sure who. All she knew was that his mouth was on hers again, molding it, tasting it, making her hungry in the way that only he seemed able to do.

"Maria . . ." he breathed. Seizing her by the arms, he drew her up into his embrace. "My God, I've thought of nothing but you since that day in the carriage."

His mouth found hers again, sweeping away every objection. Her hands slid inside his coat to hold him at the waist—she hardly knew how. What was wrong with her, that she seemed incapable of resisting him? How easy for her to speak of morality and discipline, yet how hard for her to practice it!

He made her want to throw caution to the winds with just a kiss.

Not *just* a kiss. His mouth devoured hers, taking whatever it wished with bold purpose. His hands swept over her body, as if relearning every curve and bend, every sensitive stretch of skin that ignited at his touch. And she reveled in it. He was so commanding, so unlike the cautious Nathan.

It made her want to touch him, to know every inch of him. As he explored her, she explored him through his shirt, marveling at the muscles that tightened beneath her fingers. It never ceased to amaze her that he was no soft, indolent aristocrat, but a man of fierce strength who clearly had mastery over his body.

So why had he no mastery over his soul? Why did he not see how much more he could be, if only he let himself?

As if to demonstrate just how little he desired to be better, he cupped her bottom, urging her between his thighs until she felt the evidence of his desire imprinted on her soft flesh.

That gave her the strength to tear her lips from his. "We can't do this."

Deprived of her mouth, he trailed warm, sensuous kisses down her neck. "We can do as we please."

She pushed away from him. "*You* can do as you please. I cannot. I'm still bound by a promise to another man. I may have forgotten it the last time we were together, but I shouldn't have."

As she turned for the door, he caught her around the waist, dragging her against his body. "Forget Hyatt," he said harshly, a note of desperation in his voice. "We both know he isn't the man for you."

"It doesn't matter. I made a promise. And I have to keep it."

"I can make you forget your promise," he growled, bringing one hand up to cover her breast, kneading it with a delicate touch that sent pleasure coursing through her veins.

When his other hand slid down to caress her between the legs through her gown, a strangled sigh of need escaped her. He kissed her ear, his breath heavy against it as his teeth tugged at the lobe. The cornucopia of sensations aroused her so deeply that she found herself arching against him like a wanton cat, rubbing her bottom against the hard bulge in his trousers.

With a growl, he turned her in his arms and took her mouth again while he filled his hands with her breasts, thumbing the nipples through her gown, making her insane. She grabbed at his shoulders, reveling in the power of their taut muscles as she pressed herself into his questing hands.

Why was it that he alone could turn her into this creature of fiery desires? That he alone could tempt her to forget every principle of decency?

A knock sounded at the door. They froze.

"What is it?" he snapped, holding tight to her when she would have left his embrace.

"Is Miss Butterfield with you, Oliver?" It was Celia's light voice.

"Yes," Maria called out, seizing her chance to escape him. And her own weakness.

Though he cursed under his breath, he let her leave his arms.

Celia burst in, her inquisitive gaze swinging from Maria to Oliver and back. "Minerva says she's found the perfect shoes to go with your gown for the ball. Do you want to come try them on?"

"I'd be delighted, thank you." It was all Maria could do to quell her frantic breathing; there was no way to quell the thundering pace of her heart.

Walking toward the door, she felt Oliver's heated gaze boring into her back. Just as she reached Celia, he said, "I do hope we can finish our discussion later, Maria."

She whirled to see him holding up Minerva's book, his face wearing as brooding a mask as that worn by any Gothic hero—or villain—she'd ever imagined. But his voice was soft as velvet, the voice of temptation . . . the voice of sin. "We haven't come to an agreement about the reason for Rockton's villainy."

She met the hot intensity of his eyes with a look of sheer desperation. "I doubt we'll ever agree on that, my lord. Our philosophies don't match. So I see little point in discussing it further."

As she left the room arm in arm with his sister, she prayed that he would take no for an answer. Because the more he tried to tempt her, the more her resolve weakened, and she feared that one day all her discipline and morality and lofty talk about promises would fly right out the window.

Then she would be the one who was doomed. And that must never happen.

Chapter Fifteen

Oliver hurled his book across the room. His brothers and sisters were determined to keep her from him. It was not to be borne!

He'd spent the past week in an agony he was unaccustomed to enduring. He'd expected his family to charm her; instead she had charmed *them* with her frank and unusual opinions, and her habit of saying exactly what she meant. He was ignored and relegated to keeping Freddy from harm, while his sisters fawned over her, and his brothers—

A murderous scowl knit his brow. If he saw Jarret flirt with her or Gabe make her laugh even one more time, he was liable to throttle them both. Jarret had probably told Gabe about her fortune, and now the two were competing for her favors, figuring that if one of them secured her for himself, he could solve some of the family's problems. And since Oliver had made it clear that *he* would not marry her . . .

He balled his hands into fists. His brothers couldn't have her. Hyatt couldn't have her. He wouldn't allow it!

And in a flash, he knew why. Because he was jealous. God preserve him, he was jealous of his brothers.

He'd seen his friends suffer jealousy, watched his mother languish away because of it. He'd always thought them mad for letting it affect them so. No woman had ever roused the spurious emotion in *him*; he'd assumed he was immune.

To discover that he wasn't, that Maria held such astounding power over his feelings, terrified him to the bone. He couldn't deny it, for it ate at his gut worse than cheap liquor. He would have to find a way to deal with it. And keep his brothers away from her.

How will you do that? They at least offer her a respectable connection. You offer her only disgrace.

Therein lay his problem. If he offered her more, he would be sentencing her to the same hell his mother had suffered. But if he offered her less and she accepted, then he was sentencing her to an even worse fate.

The only way to win was to let her go unscathed. But that meant he had to stand by and watch her either marry someone else, or inherit her fortune and return to America. He didn't want either one.

He scrubbed his hands over his face, tired beyond words. This mad obsession consumed his energies at a time when he had more important concerns. Like the ever-present worries about money. In town, he'd been able to turn a blind eye and let himself sink into debt without thinking of the consequences.

But here he was constantly reminded that he wasn't sinking alone. His family sank with him, as did the servants and his tenants. It was this damned house—it dragged him down into remembering the life he'd deliberately left behind.

He'd spent his boyhood being schooled by his father in how to run the estate, how to govern his tenants, how to make sure that their money was well invested . . . how to *care*. He'd promised himself that the sacrifice of Mother's happiness so Father could keep Halstead Hall afloat wouldn't be in vain. But then had come that fateful afternoon.

He swore under his breath. He had to escape this place, damn it!

Striding to the door, he jerked it open and called for John. As soon as the footman appeared, he snapped, "Have my carriage brought round. I'm going to town."

John blinked. "So you won't be here for dinner, milord?"

"No. Nor for breakfast, if I can help it."

Color rose in John's cheeks as he realized what that meant. "What shall I tell Mrs. Plumtree, sir? And Miss Butterfield?"

His conscience nagged at him. He ignored it. "Tell them whatever you please," he ground out. "Just get me that goddamned carriage!"

"Yes, milord." John scurried off to do his duty.

This sober life was too much for him. He needed a good night of wenching and drinking to remind him of who he was, *what* he was. Only then could he continue the farce of his betrothal.

Only then could he banish this foolish longing for what he couldn't have.

* * *

MARIA HAD DRESSED carefully for dinner that evening, even knowing that she shouldn't. But she kept hearing the ache in Oliver's voice as he'd murmured, *Her very goodness in the face of his villainy bewitches him.*

Goodness? Hardly. Though she did like the idea of bewitching him. *If* it weren't just another passing fancy for him. From what she'd gathered, beautiful women often captured his interest, but only briefly. How likely was it that a simple American who didn't know how to behave around servants could make it last any longer than any other woman had?

Yet even while telling herself it was unlikely, hope bubbled up inside her as she entered the dining room. Until she saw everyone there except him.

She fought the urge to comment on his absence, but lost the fight as she took her seat. "And where is his lordship this evening?"

The uncomfortable glances his siblings exchanged struck her with foreboding.

"He went to town," Freddy offered cheerily. "You know these English lords. Always like to have a bit of fun."

She stared at Freddy, then glanced at Lord Jarret, who wore a stony expression as he dipped his spoon into the soup the servant had just brought. *A bit of fun.* Surely he was not—

"He's spending the evening at his club," Lord Jarret said, with a furtive glance at his grandmother. "Probably doing a little gambling."

"I thought you told Lord Gabriel this afternoon that he

was going to the broth—" Freddy broke off with a yelp, then scowled at Celia. "What was that for?"

"Oh, I'm sorry, did I step on your toe?" she said sweetly. "I didn't mean to."

Freddy scowled at her as he reached down to rub his sore foot.

The brothel. Of course. Where else would Oliver go for fun? She ducked her head, fighting to control the pain that lanced through her chest. It was sweet of Celia to try to shield her, but everyone at the table except their grandmother knew he had every right to trot off to a brothel. What a ninny she was, to have hoped he might truly care for her! Oliver cared for one thing only—pleasure. If he couldn't have it from her, he would go elsewhere for it.

"I wish I'd known he was going to his club," Freddy went on. "I'd have asked him to take me, too." Freddy slurped a big spoonful of soup. "He promised to introduce me around it."

"I'm sure you'll have another chance for that, Freddy," Maria said, praying her voice sounded nonchalant. Determined to hide her wounded feelings from all of them, she added, "So, about this ball being held tomorrow night by Lord Foxmoor—"

"Just Foxmoor," Gabe said helpfully. When his sister elbowed him, he said, "Do you want her to embarrass herself right there at the ball? That's no kindness."

Mortification spread over Maria's cheeks. She couldn't seem to get any of this right.

"Dukes are not called 'lord,' Miss Butterfield." To Maria's shock, the gentle correction came from none other than Oliver's grandmother.

When her gaze shot to the woman, Mrs. Plumtree seemed to remember herself and hardened her tone. "It is 'your grace,' 'his grace,' just plain Foxmoor, or the duke. Never 'Lord' anything. That is only for the lower tiers of the peerage."

"Thank you." Maria lifted her chin a notch. "Anything else I should know before I make a fool of myself tomorrow evening?"

"You'll be fine," Minerva said with a kind smile. "Everyone will be so focused on drawing lots for their valentines that they won't care one whit if you miss an honorific here and there. Will they, Jarret?"

"God knows I won't." He scowled at Minerva. "It's been so long since I've attended a St. Valentine's Day affair that I forgot all about that lottery business. Is there any way to make sure I don't draw the name of some prune-faced miss with an eye to reform me? My luck always seems to vanish at these gatherings."

"So you draw lots here, too?" Maria asked. "In America, we have the unmarried gentlemen draw from among the names of the unmarried ladies to see who's their valentine for the year."

"That's how it works in England, too," Celia put in, "but the Foxmoors treat it as part of the entertainment. When a man draws a woman's name, he gets to dance the final waltz with her and take her in to supper, that's all."

"At least it's late in the day," Freddy said. "There won't be a bunch of women wandering the place with their eyes closed, bumping into everything."

"Freddy," Maria said in a low voice, "I'm sure the English don't do such a silly thing as that on St. Valentine's Day. That's probably an American custom."

"Actually, no," Minerva said. "Plenty of people here still have that superstition. It's nonsense, of course—the idea that a girl might be yoked to a man for all eternity simply because he was the first person she saw on St. Valentine's Day, but you can't convince some people of that."

Jarret nodded. "You'll definitely find one or two of the maids walking about tomorrow morning with their hands over their eyes for fear they'll see the wrong man before they meet up with their sweethearts." He gestured to Gabe. "That joker there likes to ask them to pick something up, just to see if they can do it with their eyes closed. He's a devil that way."

"It serves them right to be thwarted if they're foolish enough to participate in such a ridiculous superstition," Mrs. Plumtree said with a snort. "I'd never let any of *my* servants do it. It smacks of country ignorance."

"I think it's romantic," Celia said dreamily. "You let Fate choose your mate. The stars align, and suddenly you're confronted with the man of your dreams."

"Or the man of your nightmares," Maria bit out, thinking of how Fate had thrown her into Oliver's power a week ago. "Fate can be rather fickle in that respect, if you ask me. I wouldn't trust Fate with my future."

Minerva eyed her over her glass of wine. "Probably a wise policy."

That began a debate among the Sharpe siblings about love and marriage and how difficult it was to find a mate in society. From the surreptitious glances they cast their grandmother throughout, Maria guessed that most of the discussion was for Mrs. Plumtree's benefit. She wondered if the woman even noticed. She seemed distracted this evening, probably for the same reason Maria was.

Oliver and his curst "bit of fun."

As soon as they'd finished eating and it was acceptable for her to bow out, she excused herself to head upstairs. She had to escape them, to be alone with her thoughts. But before she could reach her room, Freddy came up behind her.

She halted to face him. "What is it?"

He looked worried, an unusual state for him when he was well fed. "You're upset because of what I let slip about Lord Stoneville going off to a brothel."

"Why would that make me upset? He has the right to go where he pleases."

"But I was wrong," he protested. "He went to gamble. Lord Jarret said so."

She arched an eyebrow. "Lord Jarret will say whatever he must to hide his brother's peccadilloes from his grandmother. But there's no need to hide them from me. I know his lordship's faults."

When she started to walk away, Freddy laid his hand on her arm. "I'm sorry, Mopsy. I messed that up. I didn't mean to hurt your feelings."

"You didn't. I'm fine, really I am." Her throat tightened. "You and I both know that Lord Stoneville sees me only as a means to an end."

"That's not true," Freddy said earnestly. "I've seen how he looks at you. It's how I look at the last bit of bacon on the serving plate. He likes you."

"Don't be absurd."

"And you like him, too."

She let out a shuddering breath. "I like Nathan."

"But if Mr. Pinter doesn't find Nathan—"

"Then we'll go home and hope Nathan doesn't take too long in returning."

"You could marry Lord Stoneville," Freddy said.

A hysterical laugh bubbled up in her throat. No. She couldn't, even if Oliver wanted to. But there was no point in telling him that. "I hardly think that a man who runs off to brothels at every opportunity would make a good husband."

Freddy slumped his shoulders. "I suppose not."

"Why don't you join the gentlemen at their port? I promise, I'm right as rain."

With an expression of relief, he nodded, then trotted off down the hall.

She watched him go, her heart in her throat. *And you like him, too.* She did. But it could go no further. She wasn't fool enough to lose her heart to a man who could kiss her passionately one minute and head off to a brothel the next.

No matter how much her heart broke for what he'd suffered.

Chapter Sixteen

Oliver sat in his usual chair drinking brandy, while a succession of Polly's whores paraded in front of him. And he felt . . .

Nothing. No stirring in his cock. No urge to tup. Just a bone-deep disgust with himself.

When had Polly's whores started looking so . . . sad? The madam had done her best to please him, offering her choicest ladies to pique his interest. Yet their soft words and lush bodies and erotic gestures were wasted on him. For the first time, he saw the falseness in their smiles, the boredom they tried hard to hide.

Worse, he kept comparing them to Maria. Her smiles were never false. They might be rare, but when he won one it felt like a real triumph, precisely because it was genuine. Because she gave it to him by choice.

What triumph was there in winning the smile of a whore, when all she wanted was the contents of his purse? Not that he'd ever thought they would clamor to bed him without the money, but he could usually maintain the illusion enough to forget himself in their bodies. Sunk in his own misery, he generally paid no attention to theirs.

Now that was all he could see. Seemingly overnight, they'd transformed from genial companions in wickedness to everyday women living a hard life where they only survived by satisfying men's urges. *His* urges.

Being moral and disciplined is hard work. Being wicked requires no effort at all—one merely indulges every desire and impulse, no matter how hurtful or immoral.

He knocked back the rest of his brandy in a vain hope that the fiery liquor would purge Maria's words from his mind. What did she know about it? And why did he even care what she thought? It was none of her concern how he chose to forget his troubles. He paid for his pleasures, damn it, and he paid well.

While his estate suffered. While his tenants worked their farms from dawn to dusk. While his servants relied on him for their livelihood, and his siblings looked to him to save them all.

A cold chill swept over him that even the brandy couldn't warm.

"Milord," Polly said, perching on the arm of his chair with a salacious smile. "Perhaps you need something a bit more fresh and sweet to tempt your palate."

It wasn't the first time she'd offered him a "virgin." He'd always refused politely but firmly, uninterested in that unsavory part of the trade—country girls who came to the city, eager to see the world, only to find themselves forced onto their backs because of clever women like Polly.

This time, the very idea of it revolted him. He kept seeing Maria landing in such a situation through no fault of her own—sometimes the line between respectable woman and fallen woman could be paper thin. He knew that better than anyone. Why, even his sisters, if taken advantage of . . .

"No," he said hoarsely, pushing himself to his feet as his stomach churned. "God, no."

He stumbled from the brothel to retch in the street. It was the brandy, that's all. The damned cheap brandy, mingling with his morbid mood to make him unable to find pleasure in his usual pursuits.

Deuce take it all, he *would* find pleasure if it killed him! There were other places he could go, places less sordid. That's what he needed.

Reaching the opera house just as the night's performance was ending, he went backstage to where half a dozen dancers were entertaining admirers in their dressing room. They were fun girls, always ready for a night on the town. Fun girls were what he needed right now.

Yet after ten minutes of their flirtations, he'd had enough. He kept thinking that any man of consequence would please them—if he dropped dead in their presence right now, they would mourn him with a drink and a dance, and forget him by next week.

Suddenly, that wasn't enough.

The realization staggered him. Swearing foully, he left there to go to a tavern, then a club, then a party that someone in the club dragged him to, where the demimonde were sporting with their protectors. But all he could rouse himself to do was drink, and even that he was sick of by the end of the evening.

It was no use. Maria had infected him somehow with her morality. He would have to purge her from his mind and body before he could return to his usual pursuits.

If he ever could. The sobering thought plagued him as he ordered his coach around and had the man head for home.

Home? Halstead Hall wasn't home! This was what came of letting a sweet little virgin capture your eye. You started considering the future, letting the weight of responsibility color your actions. You started hoping for the impossible. You started thinking that perhaps you could actually—

A groan escaped him as he settled against the squabs. This obsession with her was mad. He'd spent his entire night on the town without once plunging his cock into a willing whore, without even *wanting* to. It was insanity!

Yet it was Maria who consumed his mind on the journey home, Maria and the light in her eyes as she'd said he wasn't doomed. Maria and her lush, innocent kisses and how they made him feel.

He didn't want to feel, damn it! He'd survived all these years without feeling. Now all the feelings he'd kept in his strongbox were spilling out, no matter how much he held down the lid.

As soon as he reached Halstead Hall, he passed through the courtyards until he came to the staircase that led to the floor where her bedchamber lay. Then he stood hesitating, his obsession making him ache to see her. Did he dare to try, despite the hour?

The debate became moot when male voices drifted down from above. His brothers were up there. What the devil?

Half inebriated, he vaulted up the stairs to find them lolling in chairs in the hall outside Maria's door. Gabe clasped a bunch of violets in his hand while Jarret held a rolled-up piece of parchment in his.

"What are you two louts doing here in the middle of the night?" he growled.

"It's nearly dawn," Gabe said coolly. "Hardly the middle of the night. Not that you would have noticed, in your drunken state."

Scowling, Oliver took a step toward them. "It's still earlier than you, at least, ever rise."

Gabe glanced at Jarret. "Clearly, the old boy doesn't remember what today is."

"I believe you're right," Jarret returned, a hint of condemnation in his tone.

Oliver glared at them both as he sifted through his soggy brain for what they meant. When it came to him, he groaned. St. Valentine's Day. That sobered him right up. "That doesn't explain why you're lurking outside Maria's door."

Jarret cast him a scathing glance as he got to his feet. "Why do you care? You ran off to town to find your entertainment. Seems to me that you're relinquishing the field."

"So you two intend to step in?" he snapped.

"Why not?" Gabe rose to glower at him. "Since your plan to thwart Gran isn't working, and it's looking as if we'll have to marry *someone*, we might as well have a go at Miss Butterfield. She's an heiress and a very nice girl, too, in case you hadn't noticed. If you're stupid enough to throw her over for a bunch of whores and opera dancers, we're more than happy to take your place. We at least appreciate her finer qualities."

The very idea of his brothers appreciating anything of Maria's made his blood boil. "In the first place, I didn't throw her over for anyone. In the second, I am damned well not relinquishing the field. And I'm certainly not giving it over to a couple of fortune hunters like you."

The sound of footsteps coming down the hall from the servants' stairs made them whirl in that direction. Betty walked slowly toward them, one hand shading her eyes.

That's when it hit him. His brothers were here because of that silly superstition about a maiden's heart being joined to that of whoever was the first man she spotted on St. Valentine's Day.

"Good morning, gentlemen," Betty murmured as she approached, carefully avoiding looking at any of them.

A devilish grin lit Gabe's face. "Betty, catch!" he cried and tossed a violet at her.

She didn't even move a finger to stop it from bouncing off her and falling to the floor. "If your lordships will excuse me," she said in a decidedly snippy tone, "my mistress rang the bell for me." With a sniff that conveyed her contempt for them, she slipped inside Maria's room and shut the door firmly behind her.

"That was shameful," Jarret told Gabe. "You know bloody well that Betty and John are sweethearts."

"It's not my fault that John didn't show up this morning so she could see him first," Gabe said with a shrug.

"He couldn't," Oliver ground out. "John was with me."

His brothers turned their gazes on him again. "Right," Jarret said coldly. "At the brothel. We know. We all know. And so does *she*." Eyes glittering, he tipped his head toward Maria's door.

An icy rage swelled in Oliver, directed mostly at himself. Of course she'd heard about his night in town. How could she not? Servants had a tendency to talk, and he'd been a fool to ignore that yet again. But he'd been so desperate to get away from here . . .

Now she would despise him even more.

He stiffened. All right, so he'd have to get past that. And he would, too. He wasn't about to allow his brothers to step in and woo her. *He* was the one who'd discovered her. *He* was the one who'd brought her here and paid for her gowns, and they weren't going to enjoy the benefits of that. The very idea of it made his stomach knot.

A groan escaped him. There he went again—being consumed by jealousy. It was like a pox; it ate at him day and night. There was only one way to cure himself of it—he had to bed her.

Yes, that was the answer. Once he reached his release in her arms, this obsession would surely end, and he could find himself again. He could go back to living his life as he pleased and ignoring the ramifications of his behavior. That's what he must do. Scratch his itch. No matter how much his deuced family tried to interfere.

He'd had quite enough of their shenanigans this week. He'd allowed them to play their games and carry her off wherever they wished, but no more. She was his. All he had to do was convince her of it. And if that meant heeding some stupid superstition on St. Valentine's Day, then by God he'd do it. To hell with them all.

"All right, you two," he announced, "you've been having a grand time at my expense, but that's over now."

With a smirk, Jarret glanced over at Gabe. "I don't know what he's talking about. Do you?"

"Not a clue," Gabe replied.

"Then perhaps I should demonstrate." Oliver grabbed the violets out of Gabe's hand, then knocked on Maria's door, planting himself across the doorway before either of them realized what he was up to. After a second, the door swung open, and she blinked at him. "Oliver! What are you doing here?"

Words utterly failed him. She wore a white cotton wrapper over her linen night rail, both buttoned up to the chin and chaste as a nun's habit. Yet just the sight of her in such attire aroused him as none of Polly's girls had managed to do. All he wanted was to back her into the room and swive her senseless.

Instead, he thrust the violets at her. "For you. For St. Valentine's Day."

Her blue eyes turned to ice. "Take them to your friends at the brothel. I want none of them."

"Please, Maria," he said hoarsely, "let me explain."

"You owe me no explanation." With a glance at Betty, who had her back to them but was clearly listening avidly, she murmured, "I'm only your pretend fiancée, after all. So if you'll excuse me—"

"I won't." If he hadn't caught the glint of tears in her eyes, he might have walked away. But he'd be damned if he'd do it now.

He'd hurt her. He'd sworn never to hurt a woman, which was why he'd kept his relations with women casual. If they became attached, he broke with them before it could turn nasty.

Yet he'd still hurt her, the one woman he'd least wanted to hurt. He didn't like how it made him feel. Right now he would give anything, do anything, to wipe that wounded expression from her face.

"I'm the first man you saw today," he pointed out, "so I'm officially your valentine."

She let out a harsh laugh. "Because of a silly superstition? I think not."

"Because I want to be," he said in a low voice. "And because you want me to be, too."

Her gaze would have skewered a stone. "Want a drunken debaucher fresh from some whore's bed as my valentine? Not if you were the last man on earth."

She slammed the door in his face.

His brothers laughed, but he ignored them. He couldn't blame her for being angry; he'd given her good reason to be so.

But it didn't change a thing. He'd be damned if he let her go now. One way or the other, Maria Butterfield was going to be his. One way or the other, she *would* share his bed.

Chapter Seventeen

Maria managed to avoid Oliver for most of St. Valentine's Day. It wasn't difficult—apparently he spent half of it sleeping off his wild night. Not that she cared one bit. She'd learned her lesson with him. Truly she had. Not even the beautiful bouquet of irises he'd sent up to her room midafternoon changed that.

Now that she was dressing for tonight's ball, she was rather proud of herself for having only thought of him half a dozen times. *Per hour*, her conscience added.

"There, that's the last one," Betty said as she tucked another ostrich feather into Maria's elaborate coiffure.

According to Celia, the new fashion this year involved a multitude of feathers drooping from one's head in languid repose. Maria hoped hers didn't decide to find their repose on the floor. Betty seemed to have used a magical incantation to keep them in place, and Maria wasn't at all sure they would stay put.

"You look lovely, miss," Betty added.

"If I do," Maria said, "it's only because of your efforts, Betty."

Betty ducked her head to hide her blush. "Thank you, miss."

It was amazing how different the servant had been ever since Maria had taken Oliver's advice to heart, letting the girl fuss over her and tidy her room and do myriad things that Maria would have been perfectly happy to do for herself. But he'd proved to be right—Betty practically glowed with pride. Maria wished she'd known sooner how to treat them all, but honestly, how could she have guessed that these mad English would *enjoy* being in service? It boggled her democratic American mind.

Casting an admiring glance down Maria's gown of ivory satin, Betty said, "I daresay his lordship will swallow his tongue when he sees you tonight."

"If he does, I hope he chokes on it," Maria muttered.

With a sly glance, Betty fluffed out the bouffant drapery of white tulle that crossed Maria's bust and was fastened in the center with an ornament of gold mosaic. "John says the master didn't touch a one of those tarts at the brothel last night. He says that his lordship refused every female that the owner of the place brought before him."

"I somehow doubt that."

Paying her no heed, Betty continued her campaign to salvage her master's dubious honor. "Then Lord Stoneville went to the opera house and left without a single dancer on his arm. John says he never done that before."

Maria rolled her eyes, though a part of her desperately wanted to believe it was true—a tiny, silly part of her that she would have to slap senseless.

Betty polished the ornament with the edge of her sleeve.

"John says he drank himself into a stupor, then came home without so much as kissing a single lady. John says—"

"John is inventing stories to excuse his master's actions."

"Oh no, miss! John would never lie. And I can promise you that the master has never come home so early before, and certainly not without . . . that is, at the house in Acton he was wont to bring a tart or two home to . . . well, you know."

"Help him choke on his tongue?" Maria snapped as she picked up her fan.

Betty laughed. "Now that would be a sight, wouldn't it? Two ladies trying to shove his tongue down his throat."

"I'd pay them well to do it." With a sigh, Maria turned for the door. "He only refrained from bringing his tarts home because of his grandmother and sisters. In Acton, he was running a bachelor's house. Here it's different."

Betty's face fell. "I suppose that's true."

"But thank you for trying to cheer me up," Maria said softly. "You've been very good to me, and I appreciate it."

The servant beamed at her. Honestly, it took so little to make Betty happy.

She headed downstairs, relieved to notice that the others were already below her in the great hall. She wouldn't have to be alone with Oliver. If his servants were making excuses for him, she could well imagine the ones he'd start making for himself. Or worse, *wouldn't* start making for himself. She had no claim on him, and whether he went to a brothel should be none of her concern.

She could only blame herself for the fact that she felt like it was.

Especially when he glanced up to follow her descent, his hot, intense gaze burning her body. Lord help her, but he looked splendid—too handsome for his own good, as always. His blend of sin and sophistication made a woman want to sink down with him into any sort of degradation, whatever it took to have him.

He wore an opera cloak of dark blue wool over his usual black evening attire, which made his hair shine blue-black in the candlelight. White silk gloves encased his long, narrow fingers, the same fingers that had stroked her cheek. Mercy, had that only been yesterday? It seemed a lifetime ago. She couldn't stop thinking about the tender way his hand had swept her hair from her forehead.

She scowled at her traitorous memory. No wonder women trailed after him everywhere. How could they not when he did such things? And when he gazed at her as he was now, with a hunger he didn't bother to mask even in front of his scowling grandmother, he fairly took her breath away.

Curse him for that. She was *not* going to lose her breath, her heart, or anything else to him. Not after last night.

He approached her with a smile. "Any gown that looks so perfect on you deserves something extra to set it off." He drew out a velvet box.

When he opened it to reveal a lovely pearl necklace with a diamond-encrusted clasp, she sucked in a breath.

"Clearly this belongs with that gown," he said, and held the box out to her. "The necklace was my mother's."

She glanced at his siblings, who all looked shocked. His grandmother looked fit to be tied.

She lowered her voice. "I don't think this is proper—"

"You're my fiancée. No one will take it amiss if I give you a gift."

A gift? Heavens alive, she'd thought it a loan at best. "It's too expensive." *And you do it only to make me forget last night.*

"Don't you think I would have sold it by now if it were that costly?"

A good point. Still, it had to be worth something. And it was of great sentimental significance, which was farcical under the circumstances. "Surely it should go to Minerva or Celia."

"Oh, it's far too heavy for me," Celia said airily, having recovered with surprising speed from watching her brother offer her mother's necklace to a virtual stranger. "I'd look like a chicken with an anchor around her neck."

"And I don't like pearls," Minerva added.

Maria met Minerva's gaze. "You realize he's only trying to buy my forgiveness for his . . . transgressions."

As Oliver stiffened, Minerva cast her a sly smile. "All the more reason to accept it. He deserves to pay. That doesn't mean you have to forgive him."

"Perhaps you should stay out of it, Minerva," Mrs. Plumtree cut in, her voice frigid. When they looked to her, she added, "They're *my* daughter's pearls, after all. If anyone should say who gets them, it's me. At least Miss Butterfield has the good sense to realize that."

As an awkward silence fell upon the company, Maria felt her cheeks heat with mortification. The arch look Mrs. Plumtree shot her grandson showed that she didn't at all approve of his giving so important a family heirloom to a nobody.

Occasionally during the past week Maria had thought she saw Mrs. Plumtree looking at her with a certain softness in her face, but clearly she'd imagined it.

"They belong to *me*, Gran," Oliver snapped. Removing them from the velvet box, he walked behind Maria and clasped them about her neck. "And I will give them to whomever I wish."

"Please, Oliver," Maria murmured as the heavy weight of them settled about her throat. "I don't want to cause any trouble."

"It's no trouble." He moved up beside her to offer her his arm, with a dark scowl for his grandmother.

Maria stole a glance at Mrs. Plumtree, but the woman wouldn't look at her, obviously still appalled by Oliver's reckless gift. Why did it matter what the woman thought anyway? It wasn't as if Oliver actually meant to marry her. If Mrs. Plumtree despised her, then Oliver was more likely to win his strategy, and Maria would be done with this at last.

Yet it *did* matter. Truth was, Maria had grown to like Mrs. Plumtree. She couldn't say why, except that the lady's acerbic remarks often matched exactly what Maria herself was thinking.

Two carriages pulled up in front. Freddy announced that he wished to ride in the first one with Jarret and Gabe, whom he'd clearly begun to idolize, and Celia said she'd go along. The young woman did always seem more comfortable with the men than the women.

As Freddy climbed up into the carriage, Maria couldn't resist one last bit of advice. "Remember to follow the lead of the other gentlemen at the ball. They may do things differently here than in America."

Freddy thrust out his chin with youthful belligerence. "I'm not a child, Mopsy. I know how to handle myself."

When that carriage left, and the next one pulled up for her, Oliver, Minerva, and Mrs. Plumtree, Oliver patted Maria's hand. "Freddy will be fine," he reassured her in his smooth-as-chocolate voice. "I'll make certain of it."

As Oliver was handing his grandmother up into the carriage, Minerva laughed.

With an arch of one eyebrow, Oliver handed Maria up next. "You find that amusing, Minerva?"

"Given the trouble you and Foxmoor and the others routinely got into when you were Mr. Dunse's age, don't *you* find it amusing?"

It was the first time any of his family had mentioned Oliver in his youth. Maria tried not to be intrigued but failed. "I can only imagine the sort of havoc Oliver must have wreaked as a boy."

Oliver handed Minerva in, then climbed in to sit beside her. "We weren't that bad."

"Don't listen to him," Minerva exclaimed, her eyes twinkling. "One dull evening, he and his friends went to a ball dressed in the livery of the hired footmen. Then they proceeded to drink up the liquor, flirt and wink at the elderly ladies until they were all blushing, and make loud criticisms of the entertainment. After the lady of the house caught on to their scheme and rounded up some stout young men to throw them out, they stole a small stone cupid she had in her garden and sent her a ransom note for it."

"How the devil do you know that?" Oliver asked. "You were, what, eleven?"

"Twelve," Minerva said. "And it was all Gran's servants could talk about. Made quite a stir in society, as I recall. What was the ransom? A kiss for each of you from the lady's daughter?"

A faint smile touched Oliver's lips. "And she never did pay it. Apparently her suitors took issue with it. Not to mention her parents."

"Great heavens," Maria said.

"Come to think of it," Oliver mused aloud, "I believe Kirkwood still has that cupid somewhere. I should ask him."

"You're as bad as Freddy and my cousins," Maria chided. "They put soap on all the windows of the mayor's carriage on the very day he was supposed to lead a procession through Dartmouth. You should have seen him blustering when he discovered it."

"Was he a pompous idiot?" Oliver asked.

"A lecher, actually. He tried to force a kiss on my aunt. And him a married man, too!"

"Then I hope they did more than soap his windows," Oliver drawled.

The comment caught Maria by surprise. "And you, of course, have never kissed a married woman?"

"Not if they didn't ask to be kissed," he said, a strange tension in his voice. "But we weren't speaking of me, we were speaking of Dartmouth's dastardly mayor. Did soaping his windows teach him a lesson?"

"No, but the gift they left for him in the coach did the trick. They got it from the town's largest cow."

Oliver and Minerva both laughed. Mrs. Plumtree did not. She was as silent as death beside Maria, clearly scandalized by the entire conversation.

"Why do boys always feel an urgent need to create a mess others are forced to clean up?" Minerva asked.

"Because they know how much it irritates us," Maria said.

"I don't know how Oliver turned into such a scapegrace." Mrs. Plumtree surprised them all by breaking her silence. "At fourteen he was a perfect gentleman—rode out with his father to visit the tenants, spent hours with the steward learning how to balance the accounts . . ."

"I wasn't *that* perfect, Gran," Oliver said, an edge to his voice. "I had my faults."

"None of real consequence until after your parents—"

"Have you forgotten the trouble I got into at Eton before then?" Oliver said.

"Pish, that was nothing. Boyish shenanigans after you took up with those other rascals. When you came home for the holidays, you behaved like a dutiful son and the future heir to a great estate. You applied yourself to your studies and sought to improve the house. You were a responsible young man."

"You have no idea what I was," he hissed. "You never did."

The harsh words reverberated in the coach. Maria felt Mrs. Plumtree stiffen beside her, and her heart went out to the woman. Oliver's grandmother might be too aware of her own consequence, and she might have some draconian ideas about how her grandchildren's lives should play out, but anyone could see that she cared about them in her own way.

Oliver took a shuddering breath. "Forgive me," he said tightly. "That was uncalled for."

"It certainly was," Maria said. "She was saying nice things about you."

His gaze shot to her. "She was pointing out, yet again, how I've failed my family."

"If you don't like it," Maria countered, "why don't you *stop* failing them?"

"Touché, Maria," Minerva said softly.

Gritting his teeth, Oliver turned his gaze out the window, no doubt wishing he could be well away from them all. And as he retreated into himself, Minerva began to tell one story after another about Oliver as a boy.

Maria didn't want to be enchanted by them, but she couldn't help herself. She laughed at the tale of how he'd fallen into the pond in front of Halstead Hall while trying to "charm" fish into the boat the way Indians charmed snakes out of their baskets. She tried *not* to laugh at the one where he coaxed Gabe into sharing Gabe's piece of cake by claiming that it might have been poisoned, requiring Oliver to "taste it and make sure it was safe."

But the tale about some lad pulling five-year-old Minerva's hair, and Oliver jumping to her rescue by punching Minerva's attacker, made Maria want to cry. The Oliver who'd defended his sister still existed—she glimpsed him from time to time. So where had the other, carefree Oliver gone? His siblings didn't seem nearly as bitter over the tragedy of their parents' deaths as he. Was it simply because he'd been older? Or did something else about it plague him?

A sudden jolt made her glance out the window. They were already in town and she hadn't noticed, too caught up in Minerva's tales. Now they were stopped in a queue of other vehicles on a gaslit street with a row of amazingly lavish houses. This must be the wealthy part of London.

"Ah," Mrs. Plumtree said, "we're nearing Foxmoor's. I should have known there would be a crush." She fixed her gaze on Oliver. "I suppose you mean to scandalize society by announcing your betrothal to Miss Butterfield tonight."

"Of course," Oliver said, without a trace of irritation. "Unless you'd rather do it yourself. I'm more than happy to hand the office over to you, Gran. Maria and I will just nod and smile while you get all the glory for making the match."

Mercy. Talk about throwing down the gauntlet.

Mrs. Plumtree's mouth fell open. Then snapped shut. When she spoke again, her voice sounded strained, though Maria could have sworn she caught a gleam in the elderly lady's eye. "Perhaps I will. God knows you won't do it properly."

"Go ahead." His eyes said, *I dare you.*

There was a trace of smugness on his face now, as if he knew he was on the verge of winning.

A tense quiet fell over the carriage. Clearly Mrs. Plumtree and Oliver were each waiting for the other to back down.

Then the carriage halted before the mansion, and the moment was broken. A footman scurried to put down the step and open the door. Oliver got out to help each of them down.

As Oliver took Maria's arm and led her up the entrance

steps, she whispered, "You're playing with fire. Your grandmother just might go through with it."

"Not on your life," he whispered back. "You don't know Gran like I do." He patted her hand. "She'll never make the announcement. You'll see."

Maria sneaked a glance back at Mrs. Plumtree, and her heart sank. The woman wore a secretive smile, though she wiped it off her face as soon as she caught Maria's eye on her. Uh-oh. That boded ill for Oliver's plans.

"Oliver—" she began.

"Oliver, thank heavens you're here!" Celia exclaimed. She was at the top of the steps, an anxious expression on her face. "You have to go rescue Gabe before he does something foolish. Chetwin is here and they're near to coming to blows over that stupid race. They're in the card room."

"Oh, for God's sake, I can't believe Foxmoor invited that idiot." He hurried off.

As soon as Oliver disappeared into the house, Celia and Minerva tugged Maria inside, grinning. "Hurry, before he gets back."

They were met by Lord Gabriel and Lord Jarret, who strode up with several young men in tow.

"Lord Gabriel!" Maria exclaimed. "Your brother—"

"Yes, I know. And while he's gone . . ."

He and Jarret introduced the other gentlemen to her. By the time Oliver returned, she'd promised dances to all of his brothers' friends.

Oliver's frown deepened as he saw Gabe standing there, blithe as could be. He raised an eyebrow at his sister. "Was running me off in search of Chetwin your idea of a joke?"

"I got confused, that's all," Celia said brightly. "We've been introducing Maria around while you were gone."

"Thank you for making her feel welcome," he said, though he eyed the other gentlemen warily. Then he held out his arm to Maria. "Come, my dear, let me introduce you to our hosts, so we can dance."

"Sorry, old chap," Gabe said, stepping between them, "but she's already promised the first dance to me."

Oliver's gaze swung to her, dark and accusing. "You didn't."

She started to feel guilty, then caught herself. What did she have to feel guilty about? *He* was the one who'd spent last night at a brothel. *He* was the one who'd been so caught up in his battle with his grandmother that he hadn't even bothered to ask her for a dance. He'd just assumed that she would give him one, because he'd "paid" for her services. Well, a pox on him.

Meeting his gaze steadily, she thrust out her chin. "You never mentioned it. I had no idea you wanted the first dance."

A black scowl formed on his brow. "Then I get the second dance."

"I'm afraid that one's mine," Jarret put in. "Indeed, I believe Miss Butterfield is engaged for every single dance. Isn't that right, gentlemen?"

A male swell of assent turned Oliver's scowl into a glower. "The hell she is."

Mrs. Plumtree slapped his arm with her fan. "Really, Oliver, you must watch your language around young ladies. This is a respectable gathering."

"I don't care. She's *my* fi—" He caught himself just in time. "Maria came with me. I deserve at least one dance."

"Then perhaps you should have asked for one before she became otherwise engaged," Celia said with a mischievous smile.

Gabe held out his arm to Maria. "Come, Miss Butterfield," he said in an echo of his older brother's words, "I'll introduce you to our hosts." As she took his arm, he grinned at Oliver. "You'd better start hoping you draw her name in the lottery for the supper waltz, old boy. Because that's the only way you're going to get to dance with her tonight."

Chapter Eighteen

"I'm going to kill him," Oliver muttered under his breath as he watched his brother walk off with Maria. Jarret and the other gentlemen also headed for the ballroom with Celia and Minerva in tow, leaving him standing in the foyer with Gran.

"She is an American," Gran said in a cool voice. "They do not know how to behave themselves anywhere except in some colonial barn. She doesn't realize she ought to have held a dance for you. Although I must say, you did take your time about asking her for one."

He glared at her. "I'm her fiancé."

"Well, you certainly have not been acting like it. Considering where you went last night . . ."

Heat rose in his cheeks. "Damn it, Gran—"

She slapped his arm with her fan again. "I do not know where you learned these horrible manners."

"Would you stop that?" He grabbed her fan. "I swear, sometimes you and Maria are enough to make a man run screaming into the night."

With a sniff, she snatched her fan back. "You need to do some screaming. It would be good for your soul."

He gave a harsh laugh. "You and Maria make quite a pair. *She* thinks to save my soul, too. Someone needs to tell her that it's a lost cause."

"Is it?" Gran said quietly.

There's still hope for him, he could hear Maria saying about his alter ego, Rockton. *There is always hope.*

It sounded so much like something Gran would say that he cast her a sharp glance. Was it possible that she had softened toward Maria?

Gran scowled. "I cannot believe you gave Prudence's pearls to that chit."

He relaxed. Gran would never find Maria suitable to be his wife. "They were mine to give."

In truth, he'd intended merely to offer them as an accessory for the evening. But then he'd seen her in that dress, and felt her embarrassment at Gran's disapproval, and something in him had snapped.

It was just as well, he told himself defensively. How better to convince Gran that he meant to go through with marrying Maria? That was the *only* reason he'd given Maria the pearls.

"Let's go find Foxmoor," he said. "I need to speak to him about something. And you need to talk to his wife about announcing my betrothal."

Gran's eyes narrowed on him. "You know, you do not have to go through with this farce. You could end it now."

"Or you could drop your ultimatum," he shot back.

"Never," she said.

"Your choice." He cast her a hard glance. "But if you don't make the announcement, I will."

Making her see that he wouldn't back down was the only way to make her give in, and he felt certain she would do so. Because if the betrothal was announced before everyone, Gran would feel compelled to let it stand to save the family honor, and she was never going to accept some Catholic American.

They found Foxmoor standing at the entrance to the ballroom receiving guests with the duchess, though he was more than ready to let Oliver pull him aside. Meanwhile, Gran went off to speak to his wife. Of course, Oliver knew better than to believe she was actually asking about making a betrothal announcement. It was all a show for his benefit.

"Why are you here?" Foxmoor asked. "As I recall, last year you swore that the only way you'd attend a ball on St. Valentine's Day was in a casket." He glanced behind Oliver. "So where is it?"

"Plague me if you must, as long as you do me one favor. I need you to help me rig the drawing."

Foxmoor's eyes narrowed. "If you think I'll let you use my wife's favorite social occasion to play a trick on one of your hapless brothers—"

"Not a trick. I want to rig it so a certain female will end up dancing the supper waltz with me."

Clutching his hand dramatically to his chest, Foxmoor staggered backward. "*You?* Wanting to dance with an eligible female?" He eyed Oliver closely. "You do know that the only women who participate in the drawing are young, unattached, and respectable."

Oliver gritted his teeth. "I'm perfectly aware of that."

"And you want to dance with one of them." Laughter erupted from Foxmoor.

"Oh, for God's sake, can you do it?"

"Certainly," his friend said merrily. "Whatever you wish. And while I'm at it, I'll snatch the moon from the sky to be your dinner plate and the stars to light your way to supper."

"I mean it, damn you. I need to dance with her, all right? It's important."

"Then why don't you just ask her?"

"I did, but my brothers played a trick on me." He ran his fingers through his hair distractedly. "By the time I got to her, they'd convinced every one of their friends to claim a dance with her."

"Good God, you're talking about that pretty little chit that Gabe introduced to me and Louisa, aren't you? Miss . . . Butter something? The one who's visiting at Halstead Hall?"

"That's her, yes."

Foxmoor scowled. "Now I know why you want to dance with her. You've got seduction on your mind. She's exactly your preference, so you mean to use my wife's ball—"

"Deuce take it, Foxmoor! For once in your life, could you just do as I ask without making judgments about it? You're as bad as Maria, with all her talk of morality and compassion and saving one's soul. I just want one favor, one dance with the blasted woman, and you won't even help me with that!"

When Foxmoor looked taken aback, Oliver realized he'd expressed himself too forcefully.

Then his friend's expression shifted to a more enigmatic one. "Maria, is it?"

"It's her Christian name."

"Yes. I gathered that." He stared out over the ballroom. "You want the drawing fixed? Very well. When she throws her name into the hat, I'll use a little sleight of hand to snag it, then hand it off to you so you can 'draw' it out of the hat. Very simple."

Oliver's eyes narrowed. "You've done it before."

Foxmoor smiled faintly. "Once or twice. Men in love generally don't like to risk their ladies being chosen by some other man on St. Valentine's Day."

"I'm not in love," Oliver snapped. "So if that's what you're thinking—"

"Of course not." But the duke looked unconvinced.

Oliver was tempted to tell the idiot that he really *did* have seduction on his mind, if only to wipe that suspicious expression away. But he wasn't about to risk losing his chance of having Maria partner him for the supper dance. That might be his only opportunity to speak to her alone, since his siblings were doing their best to "protect" her.

He turned to search the crowd for her. She was dancing with Gabe in that angelic-looking gown that made him feel like the devil just for lusting after her in it.

And God, how he lusted after her. He wanted to kiss her rich, heady mouth while he took down that hair one amber lock at a time. Then he wanted to slip that creamy bodice off the shoulders it barely clung to and lavish her full breasts with caresses, tonguing the nipples into fine little points. He wanted to see her smile warmly at him as he lifted her skirts and buried his mouth between her legs to taste her pungent nectar.

He wanted to see her smile at him, period. He wanted it almost more than he wanted to have her in his bed.

Christ, what was wrong with him? How could he even compare a smile to a good swiving?

Yet his pulse pounded in his veins just remembering her smiles in his study yesterday. He wanted her to talk to him as she had before, to tease him and even chide him. Anything but these aloof glances and her insistence upon avoiding him. But after tonight . . .

It struck him like a thunderbolt. If he won his battle with Gran tonight, Maria would have no more reason to stay. Their arrangement would be done.

A chill crept over him. He wouldn't allow it. He'd renew his offer to make her his mistress, and this time he'd convince her, too. He'd seduce her into it. She couldn't leave—not yet. He couldn't stand even the thought of it.

"Don't you agree?" Foxmoor said beside him.

Oliver blinked. "Of course," he said, praying that was the right answer.

"You're not going to make some snide remark about marriage being the ruin of every man?" Foxmoor pressed. "That's your usual response to any comment on someone's happy union."

"I'm not in the mood for snide remarks tonight."

"You didn't hear a word I said, did you?"

He grimaced. Foxmoor was far too astute for his own good.

The duke smirked at him. "I was talking about Kirkwood.

About how he looks lost without Lady Kirkwood by his side tonight."

"Has the bloom left the rose already?" Oliver said, strangely disappointed by that thought.

"Ah, there's the Stoneville I'm used to. But no; hadn't you heard? She's in her confinement. They expect the arrival of their first child any day now."

Unexpectedly, he felt a blow to his chest. Kirkwood, a father. He'd never thought to see that day. Now every one of his friends would have children . . . and he would not.

He scowled. What did it matter? He didn't want children. He couldn't imagine a worse father than himself.

So why did an image of Maria, heavy with his child, dart into his mind? Why was it he could picture himself sitting in the old rowboat with a blue-eyed lad as he pointed out the best fishing spots on Halstead Hall's pond? Or imagine himself reading a story to a dark-haired girl who kept her thumb tucked in her mouth as Celia used to do?

Deuce take it. All Minerva's talk of his boyish escapades was poisoning his mind, making him yearn for the idyllic childhood she'd thought he'd had. Making him wish he could give it to some child.

But he could not.

"I gather that Kirkwood didn't want to come tonight," Foxmoor said, "but his wife insisted. She said she wanted to hear all the latest gossip, and he would have to gather it." The duke snorted. "As if Kirkwood would know how to glean gossip! The woman is clearly blinded by love."

And *that* was the trouble: love blinded you only until it ensnared you. Once ensnared, you saw everything clearly enough to sink you into misery.

He was too smart for that.

But as the evening wore on and he was forced to watch Maria dance with a succession of young and handsome gentlemen, he began to wonder if he was so smart after all. Because seeing her with them was really chafing him raw.

One of the idiots made her laugh several times—an egregious transgression. Another let his hand linger on her waist after the dance was done—a cardinal sin. And the last one before the drawing had the audacity to whisper something in her ear that made her blush—a crime so unpardonable that Oliver wished he could thrash the man senseless for it. He'd never wanted to thrash so many men at one time in his whole life.

Somehow he managed to remain calm as the gentlemen gathered for the drawing. He watched Maria write her name on a slip of paper and put it into Foxmoor's top hat, but he couldn't tell if Foxmoor succeeded in snagging it. He held his breath through the entire process, only relaxing when the men started drawing names and Foxmoor dropped a slip of paper into the hat with a meaningful smile just as Oliver reached in.

Pulling the slip out, he read aloud, "Miss Maria Butterfield."

Maria didn't say a thing, her expression unreadable.

But she was his for the next dance whether she liked it or not, and his for supper, too. He meant to make the most of it.

* * *

MARIA HAD SPENT the entire night putting a good face on things. Although Gabe's and Jarret's friends were nice, polite men, she felt as if all the other guests were whispering about her. The whispers were at their greatest whenever she was with one of the Sharpes, and this was at a ball held by their friends! She could only imagine what it must be like for them at other affairs.

Then again, maybe they weren't invited to other affairs. It seemed as if Celia and Minerva danced only with their brothers or their brothers' friends, who'd apparently also been called into service for the Sharpe women. Maria had seen Minerva standing alone for more than one dance, though the look on her face had made it clear she refused to be cowed by a bunch of rumormongers.

Between the dances, Maria had heard murmurs of "the poor American girl . . . yes, the Sharpes . . . can you believe it?" One particularly nasty harpy resurrected the old scandal with great relish. Fortunately Maria's partner, one of Gabe's good friends, clipped the woman's wings with a blistering rejoinder.

Throughout it all, Maria had been aware every moment of where Oliver stood and what he was doing. He hadn't danced with a single woman, which she found curious. And flattering, though she knew she shouldn't. Mostly he watched her—though it was more like devouring her with his eyes.

When he wasn't doing that, he was scowling at her dance partners. One fellow had even mentioned that Lord Stoneville appeared to be jealous.

She found that highly unlikely.

Yet as he headed toward her now, she felt disturbingly happy that he'd drawn her name. After spending the whole evening smiling until her face hurt, ignoring spiteful comments and pretending to be in England in search of Freddy's "brother Nathan," she ached to be with someone who knew her for what she was.

Even with Oliver's brothers, she felt compelled to pretend, to be the angelic creature they seemed determined to protect. And though the man they wanted to protect her from was striding toward her with a frightening look of determination on his face, a ridiculous thrill went through her that wouldn't be quelled.

Oliver halted beside her as the drawing continued. Freddy drew the name of a very pretty little maiden, which he fairly preened over. A man named Giles Masters drew Minerva's name. The man seemed pleased; Minerva did not.

Then Oliver bent to whisper in her ear, and Maria stopped noticing who drew what name. "I see you're having a fine time tonight."

"What makes you say that?" she whispered back.

"You smile at every young fool who takes your hand," he grumbled.

"And you glare at them," she pointed out. "Does that mean you're having a terrible time?"

"I'd do more than glare, if I could. Have you forgotten you have a fiancé?"

"A pretend one."

"I was speaking of Hyatt."

She swallowed past the lump of guilt in her throat. Then something occurred to her, and she shot him a curious glance.

"Since when do you care about protecting my fiancé's interests?"

A sullen expression crossed his face. "I just think that a woman who's engaged shouldn't be encouraging the attentions of young pups."

Oh, that *really* took the cake. "And I think that a man who's pretending to be engaged shouldn't be running to brothels under his pretend fiancée's nose," she hissed.

He looked as if he were about to speak, but the drawing had just finished, and everyone was being told to take their partners to the floor.

When they found their spot, he said, "You're absolutely right." His gaze locked with hers, full of regret. "It was appallingly bad form. And it will never happen again."

"Is that supposed to be an apology?" she snapped.

"No," he said in a low, intense voice. "This is. I'm sorry I embarrassed you in front of my servants. I'm sorry I treated your feelings so cavalierly. Most of all, I'm sorry I made you feel as if you were worth so little to me. Because you're not."

She dropped her gaze, afraid that he might see how deeply his words had affected her. "It doesn't matter."

He took her hand and seized her by the waist, drawing her scandalously close. "It matters," he said, echoing her words to him at Mr. Pinter's office.

The music began, and he swept her into the waltz with the expert ease of a man who'd clearly danced it many times. Yet in his arms, she didn't feel like just another of his women. His gaze never left hers, and his hand held her with a possessiveness that made her pulse jump.

"If it's any consolation," he murmured, "I had a miserable time last night."

"Good. You deserved to." She smiled. "Not that I care one way or the other."

"Stop pretending that you don't care," he said hoarsely. "We both care, and you know it. I care more than you can possibly imagine."

She wanted to believe him, but how could she? "You say that only to coax me into your bed."

He smiled mirthlessly. "I don't need to coax women into my bed, my dear. They usually leap there of their own accord." His smile faded. "This is the first time I've apologized to a woman. I've never given a damn what any woman thought of me, though plenty of them tried to make me do so. So please forgive me if I'm not handling this to your satisfaction. It's not a situation I'm accustomed to."

He was holding her so tenderly, it made her want to weep. Every move they made was a seduction—his leg advancing as hers went back, his hand gripping her waist, the waltz beating a rhythm that made her want to whirl around the ballroom with him forever. Her mind told her she should resist him, but her heart didn't want to listen.

Her heart was a fool.

She gazed past his shoulder. "My father used to go to a brothel. He never remarried, so he went there to . . . er . . . feed his needs. I had to go fetch him a few times when my cousins were working and my aunt was looking after my grandmother, who lived nearby."

She didn't know why she was telling him this, but it was a

relief to speak of it to someone. Even her aunt and cousins preferred to pretend it never happened. "It was mortifying. He would . . . forget to come home, and we would need money for something, so I would have to go after him."

"Good God."

Her gaze locked with his. "I swore I'd never let myself be put in such a position again." She tipped up her chin. "That's why I'm happy to have Nathan as my fiancé. He's genteel and proper. He would never frequent a brothel."

Oliver's eyes glittered darkly at her. "No. He would just abandon you to the tender mercies of men who do."

She forced a smile. "There's more than one way to be abandoned. If a woman's husband is forever at a brothel, he might as well be halfway across the sea. The result is the same."

A stricken expression crossed his face as he stared at her. Then he glanced away. "My mother never fetched my father from the brothel," he said in a curiously emotionless voice. "But she knew he went there. In the early years, they would argue over it when he returned. Then she would cry for hours after he stormed off."

"How did she know where he'd gone?" she whispered, her heart breaking for the small boy forced to watch his parents fight over such things. It was the first she'd ever heard him mention his parents' life together.

"Because he came home stinking of cheap perfume and woman. It's a smell you don't forget."

Maria stared at him. Early this morning, when he'd come to her door, he'd reeked of liquor but not perfume. It was a small detail, yet coupled with what Betty had said, it comforted her.

"I used to wish I could make him stop," he went on in a bitter voice. "In the end, she took care of that herself."

Was he implying that his mother had deliberately murdered his father? He'd claimed it was a tragic accident.

"We make quite a pair, don't we?" he said, and glanced at the couples swirling around them. "Here we are, dancing to the silliest music ever written, surrounded by hundreds making small talk, yet all we can speak of is brothels and death."

"It's better than never speaking of it at all, wouldn't you say?"

His gaze darkened on her. "You sound like Gran."

"I don't mind. I'm beginning to like her."

"I like her, too—when she's not plaguing the hell out of me."

Maria eyed him curiously. "Why do you curse so much around me? Other men don't. And you don't curse around other women, as far as I can tell. So why around me?"

"I don't know," he admitted. "I can be myself around you, I suppose. And since I'm a foulmouthed son of a bitch in general—"

She pressed a finger to his lips. "Don't say that. You're not as bad as you're always making out." Then realizing that people were noticing her intimate gesture, she returned her hand to his shoulder.

"That's not what you thought earlier," he said in a rough rasp. His hand swept her waist surreptitiously, as if he couldn't keep from caressing her.

"Let's just say I'm willing to give you the benefit of the doubt."

They finished the waltz in a silence that only increased her agitation. His eyes couldn't seem to leave her face, nor hers his.

Every step together seemed to bring them closer, until she was sure they were dancing far too close for propriety. Yet she didn't care. It was pure bliss.

And it didn't change a thing—there was nothing between them but this inconvenient attraction. But she still found herself memorizing his features, trying to save the sensation of his hand riding her waist, his body moving in time with hers.

His other hand gripped hers tightly, and his gloved thumb began to stroke along the curve between her thumb and forefinger in a carnal caress that stoked her already inflamed senses. When the music stopped, he squeezed her hand before settling it on his arm to lead her in to supper.

With awareness crackling between them, she asked, "Is there anything I should know about supper customs in England? I don't want to embarrass you or your family."

"You could never embarrass me," he said in a deep voice that sent a wanton shiver along her spine. As if realizing how much he'd admitted, he added, "To be embarrassed, I'd have to care what people think of me, and I don't."

She began to believe that wasn't entirely true.

The rest of the guests were surging toward the dining room across the hall, but she felt entirely alone with him, as if they were wrapped in their own little cocoon. Did he feel that way, too, or was she just inventing a deeper connection between them?

When they reached the supper room, Oliver guided them expertly toward a table with two empty chairs. A beautiful woman cut into their path in what seemed like a deliberate attempt to gain the chairs.

"I beg your pardon, Kitty," he said in a cool voice as he grabbed the back of the nearest chair before she could. "But we spotted them first."

"How astonishing to see you here, Stoneville," the woman remarked with condescension, then scanned Maria with a critical eye. "And who is your new 'friend'?"

She said it with such contempt that Maria flushed, fairly sure of what the woman was implying.

Oliver must have been, too, for a muscle ticked in his jaw. "Lady Tarley, Miss Maria Butterfield. Miss Butterfield has lately come from America, and is a guest of my sister's."

Lady Tarley lifted one eyebrow. "What a pleasure to meet you, Miss Butterfield," she said in a tone that belied her words. "And what a lovely gown you're wearing. I enjoyed wearing it myself, before I cast it off. I see you kept the tulle bodice exactly as I had it when it was specially made for me. It looks very well on you."

Heat rose up to flame in Maria's cheeks. Mercy, she should have known something like this might happen.

Oliver's eyes narrowed to slits. "You must be mistaken, Kitty. I was sitting right there when the dressmaker showed Miss Butterfield the design. I'm sure the woman adapted one she'd used before." He offered a thin smile. "Never trust a dressmaker who says she's making something especially for you. Particularly when you're not willing to pay them what they're worth."

Lady Tarley's eyes flashed. "I recognize the ornament. I daresay it has a scratch on the back of it, just as mine did."

When she reached for the ornament on Maria's gown, Oliver caught her hand in an iron grip. "You'll keep your hands off my fiancée's gown, if you know what's good for you."

As Lady Tarley snatched her hand free, her eyes lit up like a tigress's scenting prey. "Your fiancée? Well, now, isn't that interesting news?"

Maria groaned. She couldn't believe Oliver had said that.

Apparently he couldn't, either—his arm had tensed beneath her hand. "We haven't announced it yet, so we'd appreciate it if you keep it quiet."

"Certainly, Stoneville." She pressed a finger to her lips. "Mum's the word."

As she hurried off in a swish of skirts to collar the first female she saw, Maria said, "She's not going to keep it secret, is she?"

"No," Oliver ground out. "Damn it all to hell. I'm sorry, Maria. I don't know what came over me. I can't believe I forgot it wasn't—" He caught himself and pulled out the chair for her. "Stay here, and I'll do my best to nip it in the bud."

As he strode across the room after Lady Tarley, Maria found herself smiling. She ought to be furious with him, knowing that the gossip might make it into the London papers and get back to Nathan. So why wasn't she?

Because he'd done it to save her from embarrassment. And because Oliver rarely said anything on impulse. Considering how he'd fought the idea of marriage, it was astonishing he would let something like that slip. It made her hope . . .

No, she'd be mad to hope for anything more from him—especially given his clear alarm over how he'd misspoken.

The woman Lady Tarley had been talking to hurried to

Mrs. Plumtree, who broke into a cat-in-the-cream smile after the woman said a few words to her. Mrs. Plumtree glanced over at Maria, and to Maria's shock, she winked.

Winked! Maria didn't know what had happened in the past few hours, but somehow Mrs. Plumtree had gone from disapproving of her as a wife for Oliver to approving of her wholeheartedly.

Oh dear. She had a sinking feeling that this evening was about to head in a direction Oliver hadn't anticipated.

And the worst part was that a tiny, ridiculous corner of her heart was glad.

Chapter Nineteen

Oliver headed after Kitty, cursing soundly. How dared that vindictive creature insult Maria? The look of mortification on Maria's face—was it any wonder he'd spoken out of turn? He'd wanted to throttle the woman.

Kitty had hated him ever since he'd refused her overtures while she and his friend Anthony were still involved. Anthony had broken with her shortly after, so she'd assumed that Oliver had scotched things with Anthony. She'd despised him from that day forward.

Little did she know that Anthony had figured out on his own what a bitch she was. Anthony's new wife called her Lady Tartley. Oliver thought that an insult to tarts.

And now, thanks to her, Maria had been dragged even further into his battle with Gran. Kitty zigzagged about the room like lightning, no doubt telling everyone within hearing of the latest *on dit.*

With every stride across the room, someone stopped him to

ask if he was indeed betrothed to "the American girl." After the first few attempts to protest that it wasn't official, he gave up. By then, the story was whisking about the mansion of its own accord; denying it would only give it fuel.

Suddenly he spotted Gran deep in conversation with Kitty's closest friend, and relief coursed through him. Gran would squelch the tale at once. And once she tried to quash the gossip, he would win—because he could then threaten to send notice to the papers of his betrothal if she didn't back down. She'd have no choice but to give up on her scheme.

Except . . . she wasn't acting as if she meant to squelch it. She was talking to the other woman with great animation. And when she met his gaze from across the room, beaming from ear to ear, he realized in a flash that he'd misunderstood everything. *Everything.*

She hadn't been bluffing him. All the rot about trying to buy Maria off, the disapproving looks and snide remarks . . . all along, Gran had been goading him toward what she wanted. God preserve him.

With a sickening sense of inevitability, he saw her go to the duchess's side and whisper a few words, then saw the duchess rise and tap her glass to indicate she had an announcement to make. With a triumphant smile, Gran announced the engagement of her grandson, the Marquess of Stoneville, to Miss Maria Butterfield of Dartmouth, Massachusetts.

All eyes turned to him, and the whispers began anew.

He couldn't believe it. How could he have been so blind? He'd lost the battle, maybe even the war.

And the worst of it was, Maria was caught in the middle.

He'd sworn it wouldn't go this far, that she wouldn't have to worry about word of it reaching Hyatt. She'd tried to warn him that Gran might go through with the announcement, but he'd been so damned sure of himself that he hadn't listened. Now there would be hell to pay.

Within seconds, both he and Maria were surrounded by well-wishers, neither of them able to reach the other. In the background, the gossips already speculated about why he was marrying a nobody of little consequence. It infuriated him that thanks to his blunder, Maria would be subjected to the same nasty gossip his family had endured for years.

It took him half an hour to plow his way back to her, but before he could even speak to her, Minerva tugged on his arm. "Gran wants to leave."

"I'm surprised," he growled. "Now that she's accomplished her purpose, I'd think she'd wish to hang around and gloat."

Minerva's lips thinned in disapproval. "She says she's tired, and she's not lying. I can see it in her face. Celia and I are going to take her home."

"Fine." He glanced over to where Maria was speaking to three women, her face rigidly smiling, and a strange swell of protectiveness swamped him. "Take Maria, too. She's looking overwhelmed. I have to salvage what I can of this situation before I can leave, and that will be easier if I don't have to look after her. It will be in all the papers by tomorrow if I don't do something, and Maria is worried that her real fiancé will hear of it."

Not that he gave a damn if that happened. Hyatt didn't deserve her. But he'd promised her it wouldn't occur, and somehow he must keep his promise.

"How did Lady Tarley even learn that you and Maria—"

"Don't ask," he said with a groan. "You wouldn't believe it, anyway."

"Given Gran's reaction, I'd say your plan hasn't turned out as we hoped."

"Gran has played me for a fool."

"It appears that she's played all of us for fools." She eyed him closely. "What are you going to do?"

"Hell if I know. At the very least, I have to keep it out of the papers. I owe Maria that much."

Fortunately, Maria agreed to leave with the other females in his family, which made his task easier. He spent the next hour hunting down everyone at the ball who had any connection to the press, and explaining that he didn't want the engagement announced until he and Maria could inform her family in America.

By the time he and his brothers and Freddy headed for home, he was too weary to do more than grunt in answer to their questions. Fortunately, Freddy filled in the conversation with an endless stream of inanities about the ball and the gentlemen's fine coats and what a grand supper he'd had.

As soon as they reached Halstead Hall, Oliver bade the others good night and headed to his study to fire off letters to those of the press he'd missed at the ball. It was nearly two a.m. when he decided to retire.

Yet he was restless. He hadn't spoken a word to Maria privately since the fiasco. How had she taken it? He wouldn't blame her for hating him.

He had to talk to her. Though it was late, perhaps she was

still awake. If he let it wait until morning, he'd have to battle his damned family to get near her. Besides, he couldn't rest easy until he'd reassured her that it wouldn't go beyond local gossip—even if he wasn't entirely certain of that.

Seconds later, he was at her room. Relief swamped him when he saw the glow of candlelight beneath the door. She must still be up. Yet when he knocked, there was no answer. He hesitated. He shouldn't go in. He had no business entering her room uninvited at this hour, but it wasn't safe for her to leave candles burning, was it?

He would just make sure she was all right. He opened the door to glance inside. On her bedside table, the candle cast a golden light over her sleeping form. Her amber hair was spread out across the pillow, and she clutched a book to her breast like a little girl holding a favorite doll. Except that the body outlined by the coverlet wasn't that of a girl, but of a full-grown woman—one he desperately desired.

But that had no bearing on this. He wasn't here for that. He would just snuff out her candle to keep her safe.

He went in and closed the door behind him. When he neared the bed, he saw the title of the book—*The Stranger of the Lake*—and sucked in a harsh breath. Did it bode well for him that she'd chosen the book they'd discussed in his study yesterday? Or ill, that she'd chosen the one where Rockton committed some of his worst villainies?

No doubt she was reminding herself of his faults. He still wasn't even sure if she'd forgiven him for going off to the brothel. That had been left in the air.

You could make *her forgive you*, said an insidious voice inside him. *You could climb into that bed and bring her halfway to seduction before she realized what was happening.*

He stared at her a long moment, then shook his head. No, he couldn't.

A mad laugh bubbled up in his throat. Apparently he had scruples. Who would have guessed it?

Perhaps I'm not so much like Father, after all.

The thought came from out of nowhere, stunning him. Was it possible? Ever since Maria had shown up, he'd been at sixes and sevens, utterly unlike himself. Was it her? Or was it them both? Was it possible that with her, he could be . . . better? Different, somehow?

The idea was insane.

Yet he did no more than watch her, memorizing the curve of her cheek, the tangled glory of her hair. As if in a trance, he reached out to smooth away a tendril that was ensnared by her long, delicate lashes.

Her eyes opened, and he caught his breath. She gazed up at him, and as the spell of sleep faded from her eyes, she broke into a smile. A smile! For him.

It was his undoing.

With his blood thundering in his ears, he bent down and kissed her perfect lips, unable to stop himself. Realizing what he was about, he quickly pulled back, but she caught him by the neck and drew his head down to hers once more.

He allowed himself to be seduced by her mouth, feeding on her lips as a starving man who'd been handed a feast. After a moment of bliss, he sat on the bed and she lifted herself onto her elbows. That was all the invitation he needed to pull her close and kiss her even more deeply. She buried her fingers in his hair, and he groaned low in his throat as he drove his tongue over and over inside her warm, soft mouth.

She smelled of roses and spice, and he wondered if he'd ever get enough of her scent . . . her taste . . . the touch of her breast beneath his hand—

Deuce take it!

Breaking free of her, he stood. "Forgive me, Maria. I didn't mean—"

"Why are you here, Oliver?"

Eyes alight with curiosity, she sat up fully. The covers fell, leaving her half exposed in a night rail so thin he could see the dark tips of her breasts through it. With her hair tumbling in gold-red strands over her shoulders and her eyes heavy-lidded from sleep, she looked like every man's erotic dream.

Desire arrowed through him, piercing his self control. Muttering a curse, he turned away from the bed to pace. "I'm here to apologize for what happened tonight at the ball."

The long silence that followed made him uneasy. She finally said in a soft voice, "It's all right. I know you didn't mean to misspeak."

He looked sharply at her. "You're not angry?"

She shrugged. "To be honest, I expected Freddy to let the cat out of the bag before you did. I just wasn't sure whether he'd say we were engaged or were *pretending* to be engaged. At least he didn't say anything to make your grandmother guess that it was a sham."

He gave a bitter laugh. "That hardly matters now. She wanted us betrothed. She, too, has been pretending, pretending to disapprove of you while hoping for this outcome."

"Or maybe she's just willing to settle for what she can get."

"Either way, you tried to warn me." He returned to the bed. "I'm sorry I didn't listen. After you left the ball, I tracked down as many of the press as I could." He explained what he'd told them, then dragged his fingers through his hair. "My story seemed to pass muster, but the press loves printing gossip, and gossip about a marriage is their favorite kind."

"I'm sure you tried to prevent that. For all we know, Nathan may not even be where he can see a London paper. As long as word doesn't reach him, it's fine."

It was always her precious Nathan who concerned her, her damned "genteel and proper" fiancé. "I hope word *does* reach him."

Her clear gaze met his steadily. "Do you?"

"Yes. Despite doing my best to make sure it doesn't, I hope that bloody arse reads it and realizes what he's thrown away. He *deserves* to lose you."

Her expression wary, she slid from the bed and reached for her wrapper. "And what about me? Don't I deserve a good husband?"

He tugged the wrapper from her fingers, then tossed it to the floor. "Hyatt couldn't possibly make you a good husband."

"So I'm to live alone, then?"

"No." Snagging her about the waist, he drew her close. "You're going to marry *me*."

The minute he spoke, he realized it was exactly what he

wanted. Her as his. Forever. Even if that scared the hell out of him.

Apparently it scared her a little, too, for she was staring at him with shock. "Why would I do that?" she whispered. "Why would *you*?"

"It's the only way I can have you, isn't it?" He knew his words weren't the flowery effusions that most women expected in a marriage proposal. But Maria wasn't most women. Maria understood him.

She dropped her gaze. "That's hardly a good reason to marry."

"It's good enough for me," he said, bending his head to kiss her.

With a shuddering sigh, she pulled free. "A week ago I was only suitable to be your mistress, and now I'm suitable to be your wife?"

"Suitability had nothing to do with it."

"I'm beneath you."

"I don't give a damn who your parents were or where you're from. I never did." When she remained silent, he pressed his case. "I want you. I wanted you then, and I want you now. Isn't that the reason any man marries?"

Her expression was hard to read. "Men marry for the same reason women marry. Because they fall in love."

"Love is just a fancy word for lust." It had always been his philosophy, and he'd be damned if he'd lie about that to her. Wasn't it enough that she had him practically begging to be allowed to share her bed?

"I don't believe that," she said stoutly.

"So you're in love with Hyatt?"

She flinched. "That's different."

"How? You were willing to marry *him* for practical reasons. Why not me?"

A shaky laugh escaped her. "In what way is it practical for us to marry?"

"It's been three months since you last had news about your indifferent fiancé. So you can either keep hoping he will remember that he's betrothed in time to save you from destitution, or you can marry me. I'm here, and he's not. I want you for yourself. For him, it's all about the money."

Her eyes glittered. "If you're marrying me because your grandmother won't relent, because it's the only way to ensure that your family inherits her fortune, then it's all about the money for you, too, isn't it?"

The harsh words shattered something inside him. He'd thought she understood what he was saying, that she understood his desire for her. But clearly she didn't know him at all. He'd been building castles out of fog.

"Forgive me," he said stiffly. "I should have realized you would see it that way. In future, I'll take care not to bother you."

He turned on his heel to leave.

Chapter Twenty

Cursing her quick temper, Maria watched Oliver head for the door. She hadn't meant to hurt him. She was just tired of his painting Nathan as a fortune hunter, when he would be one, too, if he married her.

But in her heart, she knew that wasn't why he'd proposed. He'd fought so hard against marriage; he wouldn't have done so if he'd wanted her fortune. She grabbed his arm before he could walk out. "I'm sorry, Oliver. I didn't mean that. Your proposal took me by surprise, that's all."

His arm remained rigid beneath her hand. "You have every right to consider me a fortune hunter." He stared sightlessly at the door. "But what you don't understand is I'm probably the last man who'd ever marry you for your money."

"Why?"

He was silent so long that she feared he wouldn't answer. When he did begin to speak, his voice held a dead quality that alarmed her. "My father married my mother because he needed a rich wife to shore up this damned house and all it stood for." A heavy sigh wracked him. "Unfortunately, Mother didn't realize the nature of the transaction until it was too late. She thought he was in love with her, and she believed herself to be in love with him. She thought she was living a fairy tale. It was quite a coup for her to snag a marquess, you see, and to become mistress to such a place as this."

The muscles of his throat worked convulsively. "But once she was ensconced in her precious fairy-tale palace, she learned the truth. That Father wanted her for her fortune alone. That he would have done anything to gain the right wife for his purposes."

His voice hardened. "That he had no intention of changing his way of life for her. He meant to go on whoring his way through London, wife or no. In the end, that was what destroyed them. If not for his treatment of her and her desperate need to make him love her, she would never have—"

When he broke off, she stared hard at him, knowing he'd been about to say something important. "Would never have what?" she asked softly, almost afraid to hear his answer, yet needing to know.

Pulling free of her hand, he went to stand before the fire, a lonely and dark silhouette against the orange flames. "I lied to you before."

Her breath hitched. "About what?"

"About how my parents died. Gran *did* tell everyone that Mother killed Father when she mistook him for an intruder, but the truth is . . . she murdered him deliberately. And then took her own life."

Her heart pounded. "How can you be sure of that? You said that no one really knows what—"

"I was there."

Her mind reeled. "You saw it?" she said, incredulous.

"No. After. I reached them too late."

"Then you don't know for certain what she intended."

His harsh laugh chilled her to the bone. "Yes, I do. She rode out after him, angry at him over . . . something that had happened. I wanted Gran to go after her, because I knew her mother could calm her down, but Gran thought I was overreacting. When it grew dark and Mother hadn't returned, Gran and I rode to the hunting lodge."

His voice had dropped to a whisper, forcing her to edge closer so she could hear him over the patter of rain now beating on the roof.

"There were no lights burning," he said. "The place was eerily still. Gran told me to wait while she went to see if their horses were in the stable, but I didn't. I couldn't. I rushed inside." A shudder racked him. "I was the one to find them."

"Oh, Oliver," she breathed. Her poor, poor darling. She couldn't even imagine stumbling across such a violent scene, but especially one involving one's own parents. Her stomach churned to think of him there alone and clearly blaming himself for not going after his mother sooner. How had he borne it all these years?

Coming up behind him, she laid her hand on his back, but he didn't seem to notice.

"There was blood spattered from ceiling to floor," he said in a low, awful voice. "I still see it sometimes in my nightmares.

Mother lay on the carpet with a hole in her chest. The pistol lay beside her limp hand. And Father's face . . ."

He trailed off with a shudder, and she stroked his back, knowing it was a feeble comfort.

After a moment he continued, his tone a little more steady. "It was clear I could do nothing for him, but I rushed to Mother, thinking that I saw her move. Of course she hadn't. She was cold when I lifted her in my arms. I got blood all over me. That's how Gran found me, holding Mother, rocking back and forth, weeping. Gran had to pry her from my arms."

Maria was weeping now, weeping for the sad loss of it. And for a boy who'd seen something he never should have.

A choked sigh escaped him. "I don't remember much after that. Gran wrapped me in something, and we rode back to the house as if the hounds of hell were on our heels. Somewhere on the journey I lost whatever she'd wrapped around me, so a couple of the grooms saw me in bloody clothes.

"I didn't give a damn, but Gran knew what people might think. After she sent word to the local constable, she had me strip down to nothing and give her my clothes to burn. Then she paid the grooms for their silence, and drummed up the tale of an intruder. I wouldn't be surprised if she bought off the constable, as well."

His voice went cold. "It didn't do much good. The servants kept silent, but we were in the middle of a house party, and our guests couldn't help noticing the commotion or the fact that I'd been missing. That's how the rumors started."

Indignation swelled in her chest. "People can be so cruel."

"Yes." He faced her, his eyes red-rimmed from unshed tears.

"But now you see why I would never marry for money. And I'm not about to let you do so either. It's a trap—it will destroy you."

His mouth covered hers in a long desperate kiss that stole the soul from her. She clutched at his shoulders, the broad shoulders that had borne so much, and held on for dear life as he dragged her against him, flattening her body against his, kissing her into a state of blessed mindlessness where all that mattered was him.

He tore his mouth from hers only to whisper against her ear, "Say you'll marry me, angel. You *have* to marry me."

With his tale of heartbreak in her mind, she feared that he wanted this for all the wrong reasons. "You just want to save me from Nathan."

"Nothing so unselfish, I assure you." He trailed his mouth down her throat. "I want you. I need you. *God*, how I need you."

He spoke of need, but not of love. Then again, he didn't believe in love. And though that stung, at least he was honest about it. He'd always been perfectly frank about what he wanted.

"You need me in your bed, you mean."

"Not just there, and you know it." He drew back, firm resolve sharpening his features. Cupping her head in his large hands, he met her gaze with an intense look. "I'll prove it. Agree to marry me, and I'll leave you to sleep alone tonight and every night until we're joined in matrimony. I'll behave like a respectable gentleman. And I've never done that for anyone."

Her blood thundered in her ears. She could well believe it. And something beyond desire shone in his face. Or was she just wishing on rainbows?

"I don't know, Oliver. Until I can find Nathan—"

"Nathan!" A change came over him, dark and tempestuous. "Forget about Nathan. I won't let him have you." His eyes smoldered with a passion like the one seething in her own breast. "I won't."

He started backing her toward the bed in an unconscious imitation of his blatantly sensual steps in the waltz earlier, and a thrill shot through her. "You said you would leave me to sleep alone."

"Not so you can think about *him* and what you owe *him.* I'll make love to you before I let that happen. Because one way or the other, I mean to have you as my wife." Raw determination shone in his harsh features. "Even if I have to ruin you to manage it."

That errant thrill made her shiver again, no matter how she tried to suppress it. "Then you won't need to marry me. You'll have everything you desire from me."

A ragged laugh escaped his lips. "It will take a lifetime to have everything I desire from you."

His words gave her pause. Perhaps he really *did* need her. Perhaps he felt something even more.

"Besides," he said with a wry smile as he shucked his coat, then his waistcoat, "my family will roast my ballocks on a spit if I ruin you without making an honest woman of you."

"I haven't agreed to let you ruin me," she pointed out.

His black eyes glittered in the candlelight. "Ah, but you will." And with that, he lowered his head to seize her thinly clad breast in his mouth.

Her eyes closed on a sigh. The arrogant devil was so sure of himself—and with good reason. He offered her the headiest of temptations, the sweetest of sins. How was she supposed to resist such a fixed pursuit?

She couldn't, not when she wanted it so desperately, too.

He scraped her nipple through the fabric, sending her up on her toes to strain closer to his heavenly mouth. Unbuttoning her night rail clear down to her waist, he spread it open to bare her breasts to his eager gaze. Then he dropped to one knee and tongued one nipple erect as he fondled her other breast.

"Ohhhh, Oliver . . ." she breathed.

"I love your breasts," he murmured, nuzzling the one he'd just been tonguing. "Every time I see you, I want to pop them out of your gown and suck them until you beg for more."

"That would certainly . . . give the gossips something . . . to talk about," she choked out.

He lavished the other with bold, endless caresses of his mouth. "I love touching you. I never tire of it." She moaned low in her throat, and he cast her a carnal smile. "I love the sounds you make, the way you throw yourself into passion without restraint."

She blushed. "You love seeing me behave as wickedly as you."

His eyes darkened dangerously. "And I love that you think you're being wicked. You have no idea what wickedness is, sweetheart." His hot gaze locking with hers, he pushed her night rail up. "But I'm happy to show you."

With no more warning than that, he bent his head to kiss her between her legs, inside the slit of her drawers. "Oliver!" she exclaimed, shocked. When his tongue delved into her curls to lick her in a most astonishing spot, she sighed, "Oliver . . . heavens alive . . ."

"I've wanted to do this for the longest time," he told her as he spread the opening of her drawers farther apart, then repeated his scandalous caress.

It tickled, and when she reacted to it by jerking back from his mouth, he caught her thighs and tugged her forward so he could really lash at her with his tongue.

She thought surely she would die. Or scream. Or something equally reckless. His tongue felt like his hand had felt in the carriage, only more intense . . . more embarrassing.

Yet her desire outweighed her embarrassment. So when he drew back to say, "This is better done in a bed," and rose to lead her there, she went willingly.

She didn't want to think about how wrong this was, or how foolish it was to give herself to a known seducer. Because tonight Oliver wasn't that man. Not to her. He was the boy who'd cried over his dead mother, the young man who'd lost himself in drink and women to forget the past, the marquess who'd vowed not to marry for money.

He was the man who would be her lover. And without another qualm, she let him tumble her down upon the bed, let him part her legs and settle himself between them.

After that, he began pleasuring her below with such fierce intent that she could do naught but grab at the covers and enjoy. Who could have dreamed that a man could do such amazing things with his mouth?

Only when he had her squirming and arching and begging him did he bring her to the same glorious heights, the same glorious depths, as he had in his carriage that day. And while she was still shaking from her release, still gasping, her heart pounding like a timpani, his gaze raked her, marking her as his.

"I love how you come," he said in a low, silky tone, yanking off his cravat and shirt. "I love how you find your pleasure so openly."

"Do you?" She sat up and reached for his trouser buttons. "Let me," she murmured, enjoying the sight of him shirtless.

He had a dusting of hair across the hard muscles of his chest. Another patch surrounded his navel, growing thicker as it descended toward the trousers she was unfastening. His nipples were hard little points, like hers, and she couldn't resist stretching up to lick at them as he'd licked hers.

With a groan, he clasped her head against him. "I never guessed you were such a teasing minx," he growled as she tugged at one nipple with her teeth.

"Do you like it?"

He fisted his hands in her hair, his breath thickening. "You know damned well I do."

She smiled against his skin. She'd never dreamed that being wicked could be so much fun, that having a man respond to her caresses could arouse her, too. Testing out her newfound feminine wiles, she moved her lips lower to press openmouthed kisses against the muscles that flexed beneath her touch. She scraped his flesh lightly with her teeth.

"God preserve me," he said hoarsely. He pushed her hands away and finished unfastening his trousers and drawers, then shoved them off in one easy motion.

She stared. How could she not? The huge thing he'd unveiled was practically jutting in her face, darker and thicker and longer than she'd expected. Surrounded by a bed of inky curls, it had two round things hanging below it. His ballocks.

Suddenly his long shaft moved, startling her.

"Touch me," he rasped. "Touch my cock." Then, almost as an afterthought, "Please."

It seemed like such an incongruous bit of etiquette, especially for him, that she laughed.

"You think that's funny?" he muttered. "I daresay you do. The Marquess of Rockton begging—"

"Shush," she said with a mischievous smile as she took his "cock" in her hand. "You're not Rockton. You're you. Though it *is* funny that you're begging."

He groaned as she stroked the length of him, fascinated by how his flesh jumped beneath her hand. His fingers closed over hers, making her squeeze him harder. "Like that. Yes."

She caressed him for what seemed like only a moment before he choked out, "I can't bear much more, sweetheart." He tugged her hand from his shaft and pressed her back onto the bed. "I want to be inside you."

As he slid off her drawers, panic hit. "I've never done this, you know," she reminded him as he dragged her night rail over her head.

A rueful smile hovered on his lips. "I know, angel. I know."

He knelt between her legs, and her panic deepened.

"Have you ever even . . . bedded a virgin?" she squeaked.

"No." Amusement shone in his eyes as his hand found the slick, tender flesh he'd pleasured only a short while before. "But I don't imagine it's much different than usual."

His finger delved inside her, making her gasp.

"A-Aunt Rose said it hurts the first time. And there could be blood, and—"

He cut her off with a kiss, his body hard against hers, though the weight of him was oddly soothing. Holding himself partly off her with one hand, he stroked her below with the other while his mouth fed on hers.

She looped her arms about his neck and threw herself into the kiss. This, she knew. This, she liked. She liked the slow, devouring way he took her mouth, as if she were the first woman he'd ever kissed and he had to eke every drop of pleasure from it.

She was so busy enjoying his kisses that she didn't realize he'd replaced his finger with something bigger, until the something bigger began forging its way inside her.

Pulling her mouth from his, she tensed.

"Relax." He held her gaze with his heated one. "Our bodies are made to do this, strange as it seems. And no matter what you've been told, it's the most natural thing in the world."

"It doesn't feel natural."

"That's because you're resisting it." He nuzzled her cheek, then whispered, "Don't fight it. Let go. I promise I won't hurt you any more than necessary."

"That's not terribly reassuring," she said as he pushed farther inside her.

With a strangled laugh, he pressed his mouth to her ear. "Shall I tell you a joke to keep your mind off it?"

She arched one eyebrow. "A naughty one, I suppose."

"Of course."

When he eased deeper into her, she stiffened, unable to prevent it. It was too strange—having him inside her, so thick, so unwieldy. "A-all right."

"An old man asked his daughter what sort of plant she thought grew the fastest. She said, 'A saddle pommel.' 'How so?' he asked. 'Because,' she said, 'when I was riding behind the footman and I was afraid of falling off, he told me to reach around his waist to grab the pommel. It was no bigger than a finger when I grabbed it, but by the time we reached home it was as big around as my wrist!' "

With the evidence of such thickness now planted inside her, she couldn't help but laugh. And while she was still laughing, he broke through her maidenhead.

Though there was pain, it wasn't nearly as bad as she'd imagined. And the feel of him, so intimately joined to her, was indescribable.

"All right?" he murmured against her ear, his voice strained.

"Yes," she breathed.

"It will get better."

Then he made good on that promise. As he drew out, then thrust in again and again, her pain became a liquid warmth, then an urgent heat that engulfed her senses, searing along her nerves, turning her blood molten.

"My God, angel," he said hoarsely as he drove into her. "You feel like heaven."

When she arched up against him, seeking the same sensation she'd felt before, he growled, "I love the way you respond to me." He pressed a kiss into her hair. "And I love your hair. It smells like spices."

She stared up into his face. "For a man who doesn't believe in love, you certainly throw the word around a lot."

He blinked. A strange alarm flitted over his features. Then he bent to take her mouth again.

She rose to his kiss as a flower rises from the earth to meet the spring. Because when she was in his arms it felt like spring, like the world coming alive after the gray death of winter.

His kiss turned desperate, as if he couldn't get enough of her, and his thrusts became more urgent, driving into her in hard, deep strokes that made her gasp against his mouth. Still kissing her, he tugged her knees up higher so that he was pounding against the very part of her that ached for him so desperately.

Fire flared high inside her, until she couldn't think for the flames. Every nerve burned with it, and heat flooded her like molten lava. "That is . . . ohhh . . . my darling Oliver . . ."

"Yes," he said hoarsely, sweat breaking out on his forehead. "Yes, angel. You're mine now. Mine, do you understand? Mine . . . mine . . . *mine* . . ."

The words rang in her ears as she exploded, a wild conflagration of light and white-hot pleasure so intense that she screamed.

With a groan, he drove in to the hilt and spilled himself inside her. And as his body quivered in time with hers, he caught her gaze and added one last time, "Mine."

Chapter Twenty-One

Oliver lay with Maria in his arms, staring blindly up at the ceiling as panic rose in his chest. Had he really just proposed marriage to a respectable woman? And ruined her, most deliberately, to gain her acceptance of his proposal? How had that happened?

One minute he'd been gazing at her asleep and swearing to leave her alone, and the next he'd been making love to her with a desperation he'd never known. It had been the most profound experience of his life.

That petrified him.

Nor did he understand it. He'd bedded many women, but it had never been like that. Was it her? She *was* different from the others, and not just because of her virginity. It was how she approached things—so practical . . . so fascinated. She'd been naughty and innocent, sweet and deliciously wanton. He never knew which to expect, and the element of surprise had taken him off guard.

For God's sake, he'd even told her about that dreadful night at the hunting lodge! Had he lost his mind? He'd come so dangerously close to revealing all. God only knew what she'd think of him if he told her the rest. She would certainly never again believe that he could be "saved."

He would do whatever he must to prevent her disillusionment. He'd become addicted to her soft, tender sympathy, and it terrified him to think of that sympathy turning into disgust. Deuce take it, he was in over his head.

But it didn't matter. He'd ruined her, and marriage was the only way to fix that.

"Oliver?" she whispered.

He stared down at her delicate features, flushed from their exertions, and felt the same swell of possessiveness that had made him claim her with all the subtlety of an ox. *Mine . . . mine . . . mine.* The words still rang in his ears.

Definitely in over his head. "What is it, sweetheart?"

"Is lovemaking always like that? So all-consuming?"

In typical Maria fashion, she'd put her finger on it. All-consuming: that was what had made it different. He'd never bedded a woman without part of him standing back, aloof and unengaged.

He thought about lying but couldn't, not with her gazing into his face, vulnerability plain on her features. "No, not always. Not for me, anyway."

"So it was special for you, too?"

It was that and more. It worried him how much more. "It was amazing, angel."

"You don't have to exaggerate, you know. I—I understand." She looked away.

Cupping her chin in his hand, he turned her face up to his. "What is it you think you understand?"

She bit her lower lip uncertainly. "Well, you've had so many women . . ."

"I've never had a night like that with *any* woman."

Her expression brightened. "Really?"

"Really." He dropped a kiss onto her nose. He loved her pert little nose, with its dusting of freckles over impossibly alabaster skin. And her peach-tinged lips. He loved how kissable—

For a man who doesn't believe in love, you certainly throw the word around a lot.

He tensed. It meant nothing. It was a figure of speech, that's all.

"This was certainly a fitting end to Valentine's Day." She slanted him a glance. "Tell me, was it really just chance that you drew my name at the ball?"

"What do you think?"

"I don't know. Celia told me on the way home that she thought it was Fate."

He arched one eyebrow. "Only if Fate's helper is the Duke of Foxmoor. He rigged the drawing for me."

To his surprise, she laughed. "You ought to be ashamed of yourself! I thought perhaps you'd spotted my name by chance, but deliberately cheating . . . You have no principles whatsoever, do you?"

"Not where you're concerned," he said.

That answer seemed to please her. Reassured of her ability to bewitch him, she stretched beside him like a cat, her full breasts moving enticingly under the sheet.

It roused him instantly. "I wouldn't do that if I were you, my dear."

"Do what?" Her gaze was full of curiosity.

"Display yourself so deliciously. Or I'm going to make love to you again."

A coy smile tipped up her lips. "Are you really?" She slid up next to him, her hand drawing a line down his bare chest in a motion worthy of the most experienced courtesan.

He caught her hand. "I mean it, minx. Don't tempt me. I'll have you on your back so fast you won't know what happened."

"And what would be wrong with that?"

He entwined his fingers with hers. Why couldn't he stop touching her? "It was your first time. Your body needs to rest."

"Oh." She frowned. "I suppose I *am* a little sore." She cast him a teasing glance. "Who could have known that making love would be so . . . vigorous? Or addictive?"

"You have no idea." Already his cock was rock hard beneath the sheet. "But after we're married, I'll be happy to add to your store of experience."

Her smile faltered. Pulling her hand from his, she turned over onto her side, her back to him. Not a good sign. Worse yet, her withdrawal roused an unfamiliar alarm in his chest. He thought the matter of their marriage had been settled when she let him bed her.

"We *are* getting married, sweetheart," he said. "There's no way around it now." Shifting onto his side to spoon her, he dropped a kiss on her shoulder. "In the morning, I'll ride into town to secure a special license. With any luck, we can marry in a day or so."

"A day or so!" she protested, twisting to face him. "No, Oliver, we can't! Not so soon."

He eyed her warily. "Why not?"

"I have to find Nathan first. He deserves to hear firsthand that I'm breaking off my engagement to him."

Jealous anger swamped him. "But you *are* breaking it off."

"Yes, of course." She dropped her gaze. "Now that I'm no longer chaste, it wouldn't be fair to him to do otherwise."

He snorted. "He'd be damned lucky to have you. And since you're breaking it off, I see no reason to wait. He's the one who left *you* behind, remember?"

Her face coloring, she snatched up her night rail and left the bed. He watched numbly as she pulled it over her head, then slid her hands beneath her hair to draw it outside the garment. The motion was unabashedly female, one he'd witnessed a hundred times, yet she made it somehow lyrical, her hair dropping to her waist like a silky, fire-tinged curtain.

The poetic thought made him roll his eyes at himself. Christ, he was losing his mind. "You're *marrying* me, Maria."

She faced him, now girded for battle. "First, I need to know what sort of marriage you mean for us to have."

Warily, he sat up against the padded headboard. "What exactly are you asking?"

"Last night, you said that going to the brothel was 'appallingly bad form,' and it would never happen again. Did you mean that?"

He tensed. It was a monumental question. "I meant that I would never embarrass you in such a fashion again."

Her eyes darkened. "In other words, your visits to the brothel would be more discreet in the future, is that it?"

"No! Yes . . . God preserve me, I don't know." Panic swelled in him anew. She wanted him to promise to be faithful to her. "When I said that, I wasn't considering that we might marry."

"So," she said, her voice cold, "you mean for us to have a fashionable English marriage like that of your parents."

"Certainly not," he said sharply. "Damn it, Maria, you're asking me something I can't answer." Rising from the bed, he dragged on his drawers. For the first time in his life, being naked made him feel vulnerable. "Why do you think I've never married? It's because I *don't* want to have the same sort of marriage as my parents. And I don't know if I . . . I'm not sure if I'm capable of . . ."

"Fidelity?"

His gaze locked with hers. "Precisely."

She swallowed hard, then went to the bed to retrieve her drawers. "Well, at least you're honest about it."

Stepping over to the bed, he tugged her into his arms. "I'm not saying I can't be faithful—just that I don't know if I can promise it. I've never tried before."

Her eyes were overly bright as she glanced up at him. "That's not good enough for me, I'm afraid."

His blood ran cold. "What do you mean?"

"Oliver, when I heard you'd gone off to the brothel—"

"Where I didn't bed a single whore," he cut in. "I spent the whole night drinking. That's all, I swear."

"Yes, I gathered as much. But I didn't know that at the time. And no matter how much I told myself I had no right to expect fidelity from you, it hurt. Almost more than I could bear. I can't imagine how much it would hurt if we were married, and I don't want to find out."

He stared down at her, scarcely able to believe what he was hearing. "If you're asking me to vow undying love or some such nonsense—"

"I know better than to ask that of you," she said in a pained whisper. "But I deserve more than a husband by half measures. You were the one to teach me that."

The words were like a punch to the gut. "You're refusing me," he said flatly. Incredulously.

She reached up to cup his cheek with a disarming tenderness. "You don't really want to marry—admit it. You never did."

"You don't know what I want." Catching her hand in his, he pressed a hard kiss into the palm. "I want *you.*"

"But on your terms. I can't accept those terms." Tugging her hand from his, she wrapped her arms about her waist. "I think you should leave now. The servants will be stirring soon."

"Good. They'll find us together, and then you'll have no choice."

Mutiny shone in her face. "I always have a choice. But you *did* promise not to embarrass me in the future. Do you now mean to break that promise?"

Shame rose in him, an emotion so foreign to him that he

didn't recognize it at first. It warred with the desperation rising in his chest at the thought that she really might not marry him.

"Maria, please—" he began, then broke off. Deuce take her! This was the second time in one night she had him begging her. He'd never begged a woman for anything.

"You're being foolish," he growled. He strode about the room, picking up his clothes and yanking them on without a care for how they looked. "I'll leave, but I'm not going to ruin you and let you suffer the consequences alone, no matter what you say about it. We're both tired. It's been a long day . . . and night. We'll continue this discussion tomorrow."

"It won't change anything."

"Won't it?" Marching up to her, he pulled her close for a blatantly carnal kiss. When she stood stiff in his arms, he drew back with a scowl. Her resistance wouldn't last. "I can be very persuasive when I want."

Only after he saw that he'd unsettled her did he turn on his heel and leave. But her words tormented him the entire way back to his room: *You mean for us to have a fashionable English marriage like that of your parents.*

Blast it to hell—that was the last thing he wanted.

But could he manage anything different? Because she was right: she did deserve a better husband than that. He just didn't know if he could be that husband.

Yet it made no difference. He'd ruined her and he wasn't about to let her suffer for his rash act, no matter how much the idea of marriage terrified him.

Tomorrow he was getting a special license. Then they would marry. And that was that.

Chapter Twenty-Two

After Oliver left, Maria stood frozen in place. Had she really just refused to marry the man who'd ruined her? Was she out of her mind?

I'm not saying I can't be faithful—just that I don't know if I can promise it.

She lifted her chin. No, she was perfectly sane. Maybe these English ladies could accept such terms so they could live in an amazing house and be called lady of the manor, but not her. Half a marriage wasn't enough.

She wouldn't think about it one more minute. She wouldn't let the idea of marriage to Oliver tempt her.

Determinedly, she set about washing the blood from herself, then tossed the soiled water out of the window, hoping the rain would dilute it. After she changed the sheets on her bed, she threw them into the fire, watching as they burned. Thank heavens she'd made her own bed here in the past and knew where the fresh sheets were kept.

Only after she'd hidden any evidence of her reckless act with Oliver did she feel safe to climb into bed. But it was no use. Once she was still and quiet, she could no longer pretend it hadn't happened. She could still smell him on her shift, still see him looming over her, taking her, shattering her with the intensity of his need.

She began to cry. She lay in her Cinderella bed, surrounded by Halstead Hall's enticing charms, and cried until she could cry no more, until she was sick with it.

Afterward, she stared into the dying fire, remembering how Oliver had done the same while telling her about his parents' disastrous marriage. He'd sounded so desperate then. After everything he'd told her, why would he be willing to settle for a society marriage himself?

That's how Gran found me, holding Mother, rocking back and forth, weeping. Gran had to pry her from my arms.

A shiver wracked her. The whole time he'd been telling her of it, she'd had the distinct impression that he was leaving things out.

She rode out after him, angry at him over . . . something that had happened.

What was the something that had happened? More had occurred that night than he had told her, she was sure of it. She could see how his parents' deaths might send him fleeing into a life of emptiness for a while, but nineteen years?

It made no sense. *He* made no sense. She was tired of trying to figure him out. And worried by her increasing fascination with him. Had she made him into more than he was? At his heart, was he just a seducer and debaucher who could never be anything else?

She didn't want to believe it. But given Nathan's abandonment of her, she clearly had no talent for understanding men. So she wasn't sure she should trust her instincts when it came to Oliver. Especially when he clouded them at every turn with his fierce and soul-destroying seductions.

Sometime near dawn she fell into a fitful sleep. When she awoke, the sun was high in the sky. She was tempted to lie there all day, alone in her misery, but she dared not. The others would notice. Whatever she did, she must keep last night's activities secret from them.

Calling for Betty to dress her, she prayed that her newfound harlotry wasn't emblazoned on her cheeks. She managed to answer Betty's eager questions about the ball and what had happened and how his lordship had reacted to her gown, but after several perfunctory answers, Betty caught on that she was in no mood to talk and left her in a blessed silence.

By the time she looked presentable enough to face the rest of the family, it was early afternoon. As she came down the stairs, she heard Celia say on the floor below her, "What, pray tell, are you doing here, Mr. Pinter?"

Maria's pulse leapt.

"As I told your footman, Lady Celia, I wish to see Miss Butterfield."

"I can't imagine why."

"She hired me to find her fiancé."

"Keep quiet, you fool," Celia hissed as Maria reached the landing. "My grandmother isn't aware of that."

"I don't care." His voice was hard, almost angry. "And I certainly want no part of whatever unsavory scheme you and your brother are involved in. I just want to speak to Miss Butterfield."

"I'm here, Mr. Pinter," Maria called out as she hurried down the steps. She glanced from Celia, who looked unusually flushed, to Mr. Pinter, who seemed stiffer than usual. "I was unaware that you knew each other."

Celia tossed back her head. "A few months ago, Mr. Pinter showed up at a shooting match I was in the process of winning. He was most rude and ended it before I could gain my prize. I've never forgiven him for that."

"You remember the incident quite differently than I, Lady Celia. You were *not* in the process of winning. The match had scarcely begun." He stepped closer to the young woman, temper flaring in his generally controlled features. "And you know perfectly well why I ended it—you and Lord Jarret's friends were holding it in a public park, where you might have injured someone. As a man charged with keeping the peace, I didn't want to find some hapless creature lying dead in the bushes after your impromptu match."

Celia stared him down. "There was no one there. We made sure of it."

"So you said. But I don't allow my actions to be governed by the claims of reckless society misses who have nothing better to do with their time than challenge a lot of idiots to shoot guns willy-nilly."

"That's what annoys you, isn't it," Celia hissed. "That I can shoot a pistol as well as any man. And I am not reckless, I'll have you know!"

When Mr. Pinter looked as if he were about to retort, Maria cut in. "You have news for me, sir?"

Mr. Pinter tensed, then looked chagrined. "I beg your pardon, Miss Butterfield. Yes, I have news. Is there somewhere we can speak privately?"

"You should wait until Oliver returns," Celia broke in.

"He left?" Maria said. "Where has he gone?"

"To town. He won't be back for some time." She glanced furtively at Mr. Pinter. "He went to obtain a special license for your marriage. So I think that any discussion of Mr. Hyatt—"

"I'd thank you to stay out of this, Celia," Maria interrupted. "I'm paying Mr. Pinter's fee myself, so it's my business alone."

Celia looked at her aghast. In the past week, they'd become friends, and Maria had never spoken sharply to her. But the fact that Oliver was pursuing marriage without gaining her consent alarmed her.

"I see," Celia said in a hurt tone. "Then I'll leave the two of you to your discussion." She stalked off toward the dining room.

"This way." Maria gestured toward the library, feeling a twinge of guilt. She'd grown quite fond of the Sharpe siblings in only a week, but they had a tendency to push people around, and she wouldn't be bullied. This affected her life, not just their battle with their grandmother.

As she and Mr. Pinter headed for the library, he asked in a low voice, "Why is Stoneville getting a special license?"

"It's part of our sham engagement," she lied.

"That's going rather far for a sham," he said as they entered the library. "If I were you, Miss Butterfield—"

"But you're not, are you?" Closing the door, she faced him. "I hired you to find Nathan, not give me advice."

His jaw went taut, but he acknowledged the reproof with a dip of his head.

Guilt stabbed her. He was doing this without any payment for now; he deserved better from her. "Forgive me, Mr. Pinter. It's been a difficult day." She squared her shoulders. "Have you found Nathan?"

"Yes."

She caught her breath. Now she could inherit Papa's money. Now she was free of both Oliver and Nathan, if that's what she wanted. She ought to feel relief, yet all she felt was a sense of impending doom.

"He's not dead, is he?" she asked, her first fear coming to the fore.

"No." He suddenly looked uncomfortable. "I don't know how to tell you this, Miss Butterfield, but it appears that your fiancé has been operating independently of your father's company."

"What do you mean?"

"He's in Southampton, where he's been ever since leaving London. I'm sorry it took so long for me to find him, but he was careful to cover his tracks."

"That can't be. He doesn't have a deceitful bone in his body. It must be a mistake. You must have found some other fellow."

"An American named Nate Hyatt, selling clipper ships? That *is* what you said he was in England to do, wasn't it?"

A chill coursed through her. "Yes," she breathed.

"And the trail leads directly to him, I'm afraid." Compassion shone in Mr. Pinter's gray gaze. "In Southampton, he has put himself forward as the owner of an American company called Massachusetts Clippers. He's been approaching Southampton shipping companies with an offer to sell them several ships. The process has been a long one, but he's found a prospective buyer, a Mr. Kinsley. It has taken the man time to have Mr. Hyatt's credentials verified."

"Verified! How could he do that if Nathan invented a new company?"

"Someone in Baltimore supported his tale."

Her heart sank. "That's where his family is from. I suppose he's trading on their name for help in his scheme." That explained why he'd pawned the satchel; it bore her company's name on it.

Pain slashed through her at that small additional betrayal. "His parents are dead, but his father's family was in the shipping business and had numerous connections. He must have coaxed one of them into lying for him."

"I haven't discovered who, but I'll keep investigating if you wish."

"There's no point." Now that she knew where he was, she meant to get her own answers from him.

All this time she'd been worrying about him, and he'd been going behind her back with some devious scheme. How could he?

The irony didn't escape her, that after years of reading with fascination about swindlers and cheats caught by the authorities, she should be the victim of one. Crime lost a great deal of its appeal when it happened to *you.*

"There's something else," Mr. Pinter said.

His grim tone made her heart lurch. She wasn't sure she could take anything else. "Yes?"

"Rumor in Southampton has it that the owner of the company he's been dealing with has a marriageable daughter in whom he has shown some interest. The gossips there predict that an offer of marriage will soon be forthcoming."

With her blood deafening her ears, she wandered over to stare at the mullioned window that fractured the light into bits, much as she felt fractured by Mr. Pinter's news.

It wasn't that she loved Nathan. If she ever had, that emotion hadn't survived his months of silence. It certainly hadn't survived her night with Oliver.

But her pride was sorely wounded, as was her confidence in her ability to read a man's character. All this time she'd thought Nathan honorable, yet he was a deceitful devil. Oliver had been right, curse him.

"I would have approached Hyatt with the news of your father's death," Mr. Pinter went on behind her, "except you hadn't given me permission to do so, and I thought you might wish to perform that office yourself."

"Indeed I do." With righteous anger swelling in her chest, she whirled to face him. "How far is Southampton from here?"

"It's on the southern coast. With a fine rig and good weather, the journey can easily be made in twelve hours, maybe less."

Since she had no funds to travel, it might as well be twelve years. She released a despairing sigh.

"If you'll permit me, Miss Butterfield," Mr. Pinter continued, "I shall be happy to take you there. My carriage is waiting, already prepared for a long trip."

She gaped at him.

He smiled faintly. "I suspected you might want to pursue the matter further."

"Yes, but . . . well, it may be some time before I can repay you for any of this, and travel by coach can be so expensive . . ."

"Think nothing of it. I investigated your background as well, and I'm satisfied that you can be trusted to repay me in your own time."

She wanted to kiss him. "Then we must leave at once. I'll fetch Freddy and pack my trunks."

"Very well. I'll see to the rig and make sure everything is ready for the two of you."

She turned for the door, then halted and came back to shake his hand vigorously. "Thank you, Mr. Pinter. Your help is greatly appreciated."

"You're welcome," he said with a kindly smile. "I dislike watching scoundrels like Mr. Hyatt abuse the trust of young ladies. He deserves to be unmasked for the fraud that he is, and I'm more than happy to help you do it."

Casting him another grateful glance, she rushed off. She hadn't gone far up the stairs when Minerva appeared at her side. "Celia said you have news."

"Mr. Pinter has found my fiancé. We're off to the coast shortly to meet him." She was too embarrassed to admit how deceived she'd been in Nathan's character. And she certainly wasn't going to tell Minerva exactly where they were going; she didn't want it getting back to Oliver.

"What about my brother?"

Maria schooled her features to nonchalance as she continued up to her room. "What about him?"

Minerva hurried to keep up with her. "He said he was going to obtain a special license, so I assumed—"

"You assumed wrong." Her heart might think otherwise, but she wasn't going to listen to it this time. It had steered her wrong in the past. "There's no understanding between us, despite the farce played out last night at the ball."

"But you *know* he cares for you. You can't go off without telling him!"

"Yes, I can." If she stayed until he returned, he would fight her leaving. He might only want a half marriage, but he didn't like the idea of anyone else having her, either. Or her being free to leave England without him.

She was probably being a coward, but she knew if he set the full force of his will against her, she would succumb. And she dared not—he could destroy her. He'd come very near to doing so already.

Grabbing her by the arm, Minerva halted her at the landing. "Maria, you're not being fair!"

"Fair!" She snatched her arm free. "You don't know what's fair! First I'm manipulated into playing out this ridiculous game for the five of you, so I can find my fiancé. And then Nathan, the man I thought to marry, the man I trusted . . ."

As tears rose in her eyes, she realized she'd said too much.

Squelching them as best she could, she struggled to speak calmly. "It doesn't matter. I have to do this, and I can't have Oliver interfering. This is between me and Nathan."

"Are you coming back?"

"There's no reason for me to do so. Your grandmother clearly won't back down, so Oliver's plan didn't work. And I can't . . . I mustn't . . ." Her long night and the bad news caught up with her, and her tears spilled down her cheeks.

Minerva looked stricken. "Oh, dear heart, I don't give a fig about Oliver's plan. I care about *you*. What's wrong? What has happened?"

Maria dashed her tears away. "Nothing that I can't handle."

"Did Oliver do something he shouldn't have?" Minerva asked fiercely. "Because if he did, I swear—"

"No, nothing like that," she lied. "Please, I must go. It's urgent."

Minerva nodded. "Very well. Then I'll help you."

"How?"

"For one thing, I can pack a trunk faster than anyone I know."

"Thank you," Maria breathed. "But what would help me more is if you could help Freddy. He takes forever to pack, and is always forgetting things."

Maria was relieved when Minerva said, "Done," and headed for Freddy's room. If Minerva stayed too close Maria would be tempted to tell her everything, and that would just create a worse mess.

Fortunately, Betty was still tidying up Maria's room. Though the maid did her best to wheedle out of her where she was going and why, Maria remained silent. They'd finished packing one trunk and were nearly done with the second, when a knock came at the door. Thinking it must be Minerva, Maria opened it.

And there stood Mrs. Plumtree.

Chapter Twenty-Three

Maria watched as Mrs. Plumtree bustled past her into the room, then surveyed the open trunks. "The servants tell me you are going on a journey."

Maria couldn't stifle her groan. She'd hoped to escape without having to deal with Oliver's grandmother. "Yes, ma'am. Mr. Pinter has found . . . er . . . Freddy's brother, so we're off to fetch him."

Mrs. Plumtree fixed her with a dark glance. "Then why are you packing all of your clothes?"

Actually, she wasn't packing them all. She'd had Betty box up everything Oliver had bought, and she was taking only the ones she'd traded her mourning gowns for. But she couldn't exactly tell the woman that.

Casting Betty a sharp look, Mrs. Plumtree said, "Leave us, if you please."

With a quick curtsy, Betty fled.

"Mrs. Plumtree, I don't think—" Maria began.

"Let us put our cards on the table, shall we?" the woman said. "I know Oliver has been up to some scheme, which you allowed for your own reasons."

"And which you allowed for *your* own reasons," Maria accused.

"True." Mrs. Plumtree cast her a rueful smile. "I am afraid I played a role with you that first night. I had to be sure, you see, that you did not mean to take advantage of him."

"Take advantage of *him*?" she said bitterly. "What about his taking advantage of me?"

"Is that what he did?" the woman asked, a hint of alarm in her voice. "Is that why you are running away?"

Maria sighed. "No." How could it be taking advantage when she'd thrown herself into their lovemaking like a wanton?

Mrs. Plumtree searched her face. "Beneath all his reckless remarks, he is a good man. And he genuinely wants to marry you—after last night at the ball I am certain of that much. So accept his offer, for God's sake. And give me great-grandchildren. That is all I want."

"And what about what *I* want?"

"You want him. I can see it whenever you look at him, the same way I can see it in his eyes whenever he looks at you."

Maria turned away, her heart flipping over in her chest. "Oliver doesn't know what he wants."

"Perhaps." Mrs. Plumtree came up to lay her hand on Maria's shoulder. "And that is my fault. I have let him wander in the wilderness for too long. But he is finding his way back at last. And if you leave now—"

"He is *not* finding his way back—don't you see?" Maria

cried as she faced the woman. "He's still gripped by guilt over that terrible night at the hunting lodge."

Mrs. Plumtree's eyes went wide. "He told you about that?"

"Yes. He told me how he wanted to go after his mother, but you wanted to wait. He told me he was the one to find his parents dead. He told me he was covered in blood and you paid off the servants."

Mrs. Plumtree trembled. "He has never spoken about that to anyone, my dear. Not even me, and I was there. He has never told his siblings, nor his friends, as near as I can determine it. You are the first person with whom he has ever discussed what happened that night. That proves how much he cares for you."

Maria swallowed. "But not enough to change his ways."

"If you would but give him a chance—"

"And end up in the same nightmare you put your daughter in?" When Mrs. Plumtree paled, she said, "Forgive me. I shouldn't have said that."

Mrs. Plumtree stared down at her hands. "No. You are right. I should have seen that Lewis was not the sort of man to be a good husband. I should never have promoted the marriage, never encouraged Prudence's pursuit of him, or his of her." She let out a shaky breath. "But I thought that Prudence's love would change him."

"Just as you think my love will change Oliver."

Startled, the woman lifted a hopeful gaze to Maria. "You love him?"

Maria stared blankly at her. Heavens alive. She did. She loved him. She could not pretend otherwise, even for his grandmother.

Yet he could never love her. He thought love was "a fancy word for lust."

Tears sprang to her eyes, and she willed them not to fall. Seizing Mrs. Plumtree's hands, she said, "Please do not tell him, I beg of you. He will use it against me to gain what he wants."

"My dear—"

"Swear that you won't tell him! Think of your daughter."

"I *am* thinking of my daughter. She would want better for her son than the life he leads now." Mrs. Plumtree gripped her hands with surprising strength. "You seem to think he is like his father, but he is actually like his mother. I do not know why he has pursued his father's path all these years, but it is not his real character, I swear."

"How can you be sure?" Maria whispered.

Mrs. Plumtree's blue eyes held a wealth of heartache. "Something happened to him that night, *before* we went to the hunting lodge. He said he and his mother quarreled, and that is what sent her in search of Lewis. Oliver wouldn't say what it was about, but I know it wounded him deeply. He has ignored the wound ever since. What he needs is for someone to heal it. And I think you might just do that."

"I don't *want* to do that." She drew her hands from Mrs. Plumtree's. "I want my life back, my ordinary American life where people say what they mean and do what they—" She caught herself. Even her ordinary American life was a lie. Nathan had proved that.

Still, it was better than the ever-present pain of loving Oliver when he couldn't love her in return.

"I see I cannot prevent you from going," Mrs. Plumtree said. "So I will not importune you further. All I can do is urge you not to give up on him yet. Not until all hope is gone. I think he still has the power to surprise you."

"Of course you think that—as well you should; you're his grandmother. But I can't afford to be so blind."

Turning away, she returned to her packing.

Mrs. Plumtree walked over to the dressing table and picked something up. "You *are* taking these, aren't you?"

Maria turned to see her holding the box containing the pearls Oliver had given her. "Of course not. I have no right to them."

"And I say that you do." The woman hobbled toward Maria with the box. "They belonged to my daughter. I want you to have them."

"Forgive me, but under the circumstances, I can't accept them."

Mrs. Plumtree shook her head. "You are as stubborn as he is."

"It's the one thing we have in common."

"It's something we all have in common." A faint smile touched Mrs. Plumtree's lips. "Very well. I will keep them until you return." Her voice softened. "You are always welcome here, my dear. No matter what happens between you and Oliver."

Maria cast her a startled glance.

Mrs. Plumtree's smile broadened. "I would prefer to have you in the family, but failing that, I would be pleased and honored if you would consider me a friend."

A lump caught in Maria's throat. "Thank you. I would like that, too."

"And I will keep your secret, though I am not sure it will

matter. I suspect Oliver will not let you go as easily as you think."

"Trust me, he will congratulate himself on his narrow escape."

"You do not really believe that, do you?"

"I only know that if I stay here, he'll wed me out of necessity. I don't want to be his wife by necessity." *Not when passion is clouding his judgment. And mine.*

Mrs. Plumtree merely looked skeptical as she left the room.

Maria wished she could believe in Oliver as much as his grandmother did, but she feared he was like any man whose plans had been spoiled. His pride was pricked, that's all. Once he saw she was gone and there was nothing to be done about it, he would turn to other schemes, other plans . . . another woman who would marry him for his title and his grandmother's fortune.

She gulped down the pain that surged through her. Then she reminded herself that she would suffer even worse pain if she had to watch him break his marriage vows. It was better to get past it now than have it repeated for the rest of her life.

Even if leaving him broke her heart.

OLIVER ARRIVED AT Halstead Hall near nine in the evening. It had taken him far too long to hunt down the Archbishop of Canterbury and then convince the man to issue him a special license. He could only hope that Maria had not retired early. He wanted to see her with a virulence that surprised him.

Minerva met him in the courtyard as he strode through,

headed for the great hall. She looked furious. "How long does it take to get a special license, anyway?"

"Why? What's happened?"

"Maria has packed up and gone, she and Freddy both."

His heart dropped into his stomach. "Gone where?"

"She wouldn't say. All I know is that Mr. Pinter came this afternoon with news of her fiancé. Then she and Freddy headed off to join the man."

"The hell they did!" He dragged his fingers through his hair. "Without a word to me?"

"She said she had no reason to stay, since your plan to fool Gran wasn't working. I pointed out that your getting a special license implied that the two of you had an understanding, but she denied it."

He stared blindly ahead, his blood slowing to sludge in his veins. *She denied it.* So she'd been sincere last night when she'd refused his offer of marriage. Maria wasn't a fool—she could tell a bad candidate for a husband when she saw one. *He* was the fool, behaving like a green lad with his first sweetheart.

And here he'd spent the day reconciling himself to the idea of marrying her! On the way back to Halstead Hall, he'd been able to think of nothing but holding her, kissing her, convincing her that they could make a marriage work, even though he wasn't at all sure of that. Clearly she was even less sure.

He gritted his teeth. What an idiot he was. One word about her fiancé and off she ran, eager to marry that American bastard who cared only for her money. She obviously preferred a fortune hunter to a known profligate, even one who'd seduced her.

But she had no money—how could she travel?

Then he remembered the pearls. She could easily sell those in Ealing to gain money for fares. The pearls were worth enough to fund a trip anywhere in England.

"And she left no note for me?" he couldn't help asking, though it made him sound like the besotted wretch that he was. "Nothing to say why?"

"No. Something had upset her, but I couldn't get her to talk about it." Minerva eyed him closely. "You didn't do anything to her, did you?"

"Nothing that would provoke her to flee." Except ruin her for any other man. And offer her a marriage of the sort she found appalling. And desire her with an intensity that made his throat close up at the thought of her gone.

In a daze, he headed for his study. He couldn't believe she'd left. He couldn't believe he'd driven her away.

In his study he halted, brought up short by the sight of another of Minerva's books sitting on his desk. It conjured up a flood of memories—Maria teasing him about the other one, Maria debating philosophy with him, Maria staring up at him with eyes clear as blue glass as she said, *There is always hope.*

He scowled. For other men, perhaps. Not for him. He'd lost all hope the day he'd driven Mother into killing Father and herself. Leave it to Maria to recognize the depravity that his family seemed blind to.

Minerva trailed into the study after him. "What are you going to do to get Maria back?"

He uttered a harsh laugh. "Not a damned thing. She doesn't want to be back. If she didn't even leave me a note or stay around to—"

He broke off, the words choking him. He'd tried to force her into marriage and Maria didn't take well to bullying. Was it any wonder that she'd fled?

"You can't just do nothing!" Minerva protested. "You have to go after her and convince her to marry you."

"Why?" He faced her with a frown. "So you and the others can pacify Gran? She's had it with the lot of us. And this . . . madness with Maria is the last straw. You might as well start making plans to live here for all eternity, because Gran is not going to stop until she has us married—and I'm not marrying anyone." Not if he couldn't have Maria.

Turning his back on his sister, he picked up the glass near the brandy decanter on his desk and filled it to the brim. He'd been mad to think his life might change. That somehow Maria could "save" him.

No one could save him.

"I don't care about Gran and her ultimatum," Minerva said. "But I do care about Maria. And she cares about *you.*"

"Then she's a fool," he said hoarsely. "Besides, if she cared, she wouldn't have run off after Hyatt."

"I still say that she—"

"Stay out of it, Minerva." He swallowed a healthy measure of brandy. "She made her choice. It's over."

She snorted and marched off in a huff. He stood there drinking, trying to get to that pleasantly numb state where nothing mattered, where he didn't think about Maria and last night, and the sweet way she'd given him her innocence . . .

He downed the rest of the brandy. She was gone, blast it! He should be elated that he'd escaped the fetters of wedlock.

"Damn it all to hell!" He slammed his empty glass on the desk.

"Oh, that will certainly help the situation," Gran said behind him.

Just what he needed—another female plaguing him. Ignoring her, he poured himself more brandy.

"She said you would behave like this," Gran went on. "That you would not care about her leaving, that you would congratulate yourself on a narrow escape."

He drank his brandy in silence.

"I told her you would not give her up easily. I guess I was wrong."

A bitter laugh roiled up from inside him. "It won't work this time, Gran."

"What won't work?"

He faced her, arching one brow. "Your attempts to manipulate me into doing what you want. I learn from my mistakes." And now he was paying the price for that education—this pain of loss weighting his chest, crushing his heart. "Apparently, so does Maria. That's why she ran off the first chance she got."

"She ran off because she's afraid that she cannot resist you, that she cannot be near you without giving in to you. You of all people ought to recognize when a woman does not trust herself around you."

He fought the effect her words had on him. "Whatever the reason, she *left* me. I'm not going to run after her like some half-wit."

"So you are just going to let her American fiancé have her?"

Playing on his jealousy—another of her tactics. Unfortunately, it was working.

He gritted his teeth. "If Hyatt is the one she wants, then I can't—" His eyes narrowed. "How did you know about her fiancé?"

"Minerva told me."

"Of course she did." Draining the rest of the brandy, he set the glass on the desk. "No one in this whole blasted house can keep a secret."

"Except you."

"Don't start with that again," he growled.

"Why not? It is the reason you are letting her trot off after some fool American. Do you not care at all?"

"No," he lied, though the thought of Maria with that ass Hyatt made his stomach churn. "She made her choice. The least I can do is honor it."

"Does it not bother you that she has no money to travel?"

"I'm sure she had the good sense to sell the pearls I gave her."

"Actually, no. She left them here." Limping up to the desk, Gran set the velvet box next to the decanter. "She said she had no right to them."

He stared at the box. Without money, how had she managed the trip? His siblings must have given her something, but it couldn't have been much. She would have had to take a mail coach. The idea of Maria and Freddy traveling without protection, easy prey for sharpers and pickpockets and unscrupulous innkeepers, not to mention highwaymen, made his heart stop.

"I don't care," he said uneasily, though it was getting harder to convince himself.

"Then you probably do not care that she and Freddy went off with Mr. Pinter. He is taking her to meet her fiancé."

"The hell he is!" When triumph glinted in her eyes, he cursed his quick tongue. "You're lying."

She lifted one silver eyebrow.

Striding out into the hall, he bellowed, "Minerva!"

In a second, he heard her slippered feet on the stairs. "What is it?" she asked as she approached.

"How did Maria leave here?"

She glanced nervously from him to Gran. "She went with Mr. Pinter. He offered to take her and Freddy wherever they needed to travel, though it sounded as if it might be a long trip. It was actually very kind of him—"

"Deuced bastard!"

"He is a gentleman," Gran put in, "so I suppose she is safe enough with him."

"A gentleman. Right." The sort who would spend the trip painting Oliver in the blackest terms, relating his most damning exploits, poisoning her against him—

Why the devil did it matter? She'd left. She wasn't coming back. He shouldn't care what she thought of him now.

But he did.

Worse yet, Pinter enjoyed playing the gallant knight, and behind their noble words, gallant knights were as susceptible to a pretty face as anyone. If Pinter was investing money and time in transporting her God knows where—not to mention waiving his fee for her—he'd surely expect something from her in return.

She was vulnerable right now, confused and upset. Alone

with Maria in a carriage for hours, perhaps days, with only that fool Freddy to stop him, Pinter could easily . . .

He would *throttle* the man if he laid one finger on her!

He stalked down the hall. "How long ago did they leave?"

"Five hours," Minerva said.

"And where were they headed?"

"I don't kn—"

"Southampton," Gran put in as she struggled to keep up with his long strides. When he looked at her, she added, "One of the grooms wheedled it out of Mr. Pinter's coachman."

He could be there by morning, if he posted through the night. Traveling at night in winter wasn't ideal, but the moon was out, and depending on the quality of Pinter's coach and cattle, Oliver might reach there within a few hours of their arrival. Even with money tight, he never skimped on his horses.

Once he reached Southampton he'd have to figure out how to find them, and the town wasn't exactly small. He'd have to wrench her away from Pinter, too, which might be no small feat.

"Minerva," he said, "go tell the coachman to prepare for a trip to Southampton. I mean to leave within the hour."

"Good." She hurried off.

As he headed for the stairs to pack some necessities, Gran grabbed his arm. "You are going to bring her back, aren't you?"

He stared down into his grandmother's anxious features. "Only if she wants to come back. I can't be sure that she does." He was done with trying to force her into marriage.

Gran scowled. "Then why are you making the journey?"

"To keep that pompous bastard Pinter from taking advantage of her. With no money and only Freddy for protection, she's too vulnerable. He's only a man, and what man can resist Maria?"

"That's the only reason you're going after her?"

"Yes."

But even as he said it, he knew it was a lie. He was going after her because the thought of her in Hyatt's arms ate at him like a cancer. Because he couldn't bear the idea of letting her leave without a word between them.

Most of all, he was going after her because he could see the years stretching out before him, lonely and bereft of her company. And that prospect was just too damned hard to face.

Chapter Twenty-Four

Exhausted from her sleepless night after the ball, Maria had fallen into a doze as soon as the carriage left Halstead Hall. But although Mr. Pinter had made sure they were as comfortable as possible in his cold, rickety coach, being beaten half to death by ruts in the road wasn't conducive to good sleep. So once they returned to the coach after their late stop for dinner at an inn, she and Mr. Pinter began discussing the situation regarding Nathan.

Freddy had decided opinions about it. "I have my sword. I'll call him out. If I put a blade through him, there won't be a problem with your inheritance."

"Don't be ridiculous—you're not going to duel with Nathan," she said. Though Freddy was fairly adept with a sword, she'd never forgive herself if he got himself killed.

"You should have told his lordship you were leaving," Freddy said. "You should have let *him* come along and fight Nathan."

She ignored Mr. Pinter's none-too-subtle interest in the conversation. She'd explained at dinner the arrangement between her and Oliver, naturally leaving out the part about Oliver bedding her, then proposing marriage. "This has nothing to do with Lord Stoneville," she said firmly.

"He's your fiancé, isn't he?" Freddy persisted.

"That was a sham for his grandmother's benefit, and you know it. Do be quiet about it, will you?"

"I don't think it was all a sham," he said, surprising her.

"Of course it was."

"Not according to what Lady Celia and the lads told me last night on the way to the ball. They said those pearls he gave you were worth a fortune."

Mr. Pinter sat up straighter on the seat.

She cast Freddy an irritated glance. "Don't be ridiculous. As his lordship said, he would have sold them by now if they were worth so much."

"Lady Celia said he couldn't bear to part with them. He sold the jewels that his father bought. But Mrs. Plumtree gave those pearls to his mother upon her debut, and that made them special."

Maria's breath dried in her throat. "Celia must have been mistaken," she whispered. "You must have misunderstood."

But in her heart, she knew he hadn't. And it increased her growing guilt over having left Halstead Hall so abruptly. She'd been a coward. Oliver deserved to have his proposal properly refused to his face.

Still, she *had* refused him last night. He'd simply chosen to ignore her refusal. Was it cowardice to flee when one lacked the strength to hold fast to one's convictions?

Unfortunately, Freddy's revelation prompted Mr. Pinter to ask her yet again about the special license. When she made it clear she didn't want to discuss Oliver further, the conversation dwindled into nothing.

Mr. Pinter probably considered her a fool for trying to protect a man of Oliver's lofty station. She didn't care. Every time she thought of Oliver suffering all those years over the manner of his parents' deaths, it broke her heart.

By the time they reached Southampton, it was two a.m. Much as she wanted to march right over to Nathan's lodgings, Mr. Pinter advised against it, saying she needed rest before confronting her fiancé. He did have a point; she'd never been so tired in all her life.

Fortunately, one of the coaching inns still had empty rooms, so Mr. Pinter was able to take one for her and one for him and Freddy. Before she parted with them, she drew Mr. Pinter aside and instructed him to leave Freddy sleeping in the morning and to awaken her early. She wasn't about to let Freddy and his sword go with them to see Nathan.

Then Maria went to her room, where she fell onto the bed and into a dreamless sleep without even bothering to take off her clothes.

When a knock at the stout oak door awakened her, it seemed like only moments had passed. But the dull gray of impending dawn and the bitter chill of the room now that the fire had died down proved that not to be the case.

"Miss Butterfield?" said Mr. Pinter through the door. "You said that you wished to be roused by seven. I've brought the maid to assist you."

"Thank you!" she called as she dragged herself from the bed and crossed to the door in stocking feet. She opened it to let a sour-faced girl into the room, and stuck her head around the edge of the door to tell Mr. Pinter, "I'll be downstairs shortly."

No doubt used to attending travelers in a hurry, the inn maid briskly helped Maria change from her traveling clothes into her mourning attire. It made Maria long for her lovely new gowns, not to mention Betty and her chatty sweetness.

Stop that! At least you're no longer living a lie. You're back to being yourself.

But was she herself, when her heart yearned to be elsewhere? At Halstead Hall, she'd be awakening in that glorious fairy-tale bed now, waiting for Betty to bring her a pot of chocolate and some toast to nibble until she went down to breakfast with the family. They'd chat about the estate as Betty helped her dress before the roaring fire. She'd be looking forward to seeing Oliver—

Ohh, it was no use. She couldn't stop thinking about him. But she *had* to keep her mind focused on what she would say to the traitorous Nathan when she saw him.

She left the room, then hastened her steps as she heard a ruckus downstairs. Oh, mercy—Freddy was awake.

"I'm going with you," he was saying to Mr. Pinter. "I see you trying to sneak out without me."

"Nonsense," Maria said as she reached them. "Mr. Pinter and I still need to discuss a few matters about Nathan. Since we haven't had breakfast, I was about to awaken you so you could get some kidney pies for us from that shop we saw on the edge of town as we came in."

Freddy's face lit up at the promise of pies. Then his eyes narrowed. "Why aren't we eating breakfast here?"

Thankful that no one was around to hear her, she said, "The breakfast at this inn is very costly, isn't it, Mr. Pinter?"

"Yes, very costly," he said dryly.

"I figured that we should save money where we can." She fished a few coins from the meager store in her reticule and gave her cousin her most winsome smile. "So if you'd be a dear and fetch us some kidney pies, it would be perfect."

He looked wary, but kidney pies were his favorite. "Oh, all right," he grumbled. "But I'll be back directly. Don't go anywhere without me."

"Of course not."

As soon as he was out of sight, she urged Mr. Pinter out the door and toward the lodging house that thankfully lay in the opposite direction. Since Freddy had no idea where it was, her ploy should keep him and his sword safely away.

When they arrived at the neat little cruckwork cottage, Mr. Pinter asked to see Mr. Hyatt. The owner went to fetch him, leaving them in a country parlor with cupboards displaying pretty crockery.

As they waited, Maria moved so that she stood out of sight of the door, over by the window and away from Mr. Pinter. She wanted to catch Nathan unawares.

When he entered, however, he caught *her* unawares. Nathan looked like an entirely different person as he strode toward Mr. Pinter. He'd grown his side-whiskers down almost to his chin, and his hair fell in loose curls instead of the straight blond mop it usually was. Had he begun curling his hair?

And his clothes! He'd always been dismissive of fashion, having grown up resenting his father's emphasis on it. Yet here he stood, dressed in fine attire that would outshine even that of the Sharpe brothers.

Seeing him looking so well, behaving as if nothing were amiss, brought an anger roaring up inside her that threatened to incinerate everything around her.

And he *still* had not noticed her standing there, the oblivious wretch!

"May I help you, sir?" Nathan asked Mr. Pinter in the cool tone of a man of business.

That was the last straw. Before Mr. Pinter could answer, she said, "Good morning, Nathan."

As he whirled to face her, the blood drained from his features. "Maria! What are you—" He halted as he took in her clothes. "What's happened?"

"Father is dead," she snapped, barely able to remain civil.

"My God!" He looked sincerely stricken. "I'm so sorry. I hadn't heard."

"Yes, I know that perfectly well." The words poured out of her. "I sent you several letters, all of which you failed to answer. Meanwhile, the trustees couldn't settle the estate without you, because of Papa's cursed will."

She marched forward, her fury growing with each step. "I had to use my dwindling resources to travel to England in search of you. Now I can't even afford to pay Mr. Pinter his fee for finding you. And here you are, using the knowledge that *my father* taught you, to start a business that would ruin his company!"

"I can explain," he said in a hoarse voice as he stepped toward her.

But there was no stopping her now. "And all this time, I thought you might be dead somewhere!" Tears welled in her eyes that she ruthlessly fought back. "Freddy and I scoured London, sure that you had met with some dreadful mishap."

"Oh, my darling, I'm—"

"Don't you dare call me that!" she cried. "It was all lies, wasn't it? The marriage proposal, your kisses."

"Maria," he said, glancing at Mr. Pinter, "it is not appropriate for you to mention—"

"Appropriate!" she practically howled. "What about lying to your business partner and stealing from him? Are those 'appropriate'?"

He drew himself up, clearly offended. "I didn't steal from your father. I would never do that."

"Really? So you somehow acquired a fleet of clipper ships that you're offering for sale, even though half of them don't belong to you?"

He flinched. With another glance at Mr. Pinter, he lowered his voice. "Could we please have this conversation privately?"

"Absolutely not." She'd learned a thing or two from her reading about crime. Schemers always used their victims' soft hearts against them. She needed Mr. Pinter's stony good sense to deflect any urge she had to believe Nathan's lies. "I want Mr. Pinter to witness this. I don't trust you."

"It isn't what you think!" He fixed her with an earnest gaze. "I did it for us."

"For *us*?" She was incredulous that he could even claim such a thing.

"Has it never struck you that four years is a long time for a betrothal?"

"Of course, but Papa said—"

"I know." His lip curled in disdain. "He said he had to be sure I could run the company before he entrusted you to me."

"He was only testing you. He always believed in you. Why else would he leave half his company to you in his will?"

"Did he? He said he was going to. But I could never be sure he'd do as he promised." Taking her by surprise, he seized her hands. "He has dangled you before me as a prize for four years, and every time I brought up the possibility of us marrying, he said I wasn't ready."

She gaped at him. "That can't be true!"

"Trust me, it is." He squeezed her hands. "I began to fear he only wanted to get as much work out of me as he could, before selling his half to some other chap."

She snatched her hands from his. "Why would he do that? He had no son to inherit. He needed a strong man like you to run the company after he was gone."

"Yet he refused to let us marry. I couldn't wait. I wanted a wife."

"So you went off to find one in England?"

"No!" He rubbed his side-whiskers nervously. "He told me if I could make the deal in London work, he'd let us marry. But negotiations in London fell through. They kept saying your father was an old man—that they couldn't trust New Bedford Ships to provide the ships when I owned only half the company. If something happened to your father, they would be left in limbo."

As she stared at him uncertainly, he softened his voice. "I explained about our betrothal, but they hesitated to trust such an informal arrangement. They feared you might decide not to marry me and instead sell your half to some other partner. Where would that leave them?"

"You knew I wouldn't do that."

"Yes, but *they* didn't know it. So I thought if I settled a deal for the ships on my own as an independent company, I could return to America in a position of strength. I could threaten to take my half of the business—and my new deal—if your father didn't approve the marriage."

It all sounded very convincing . . . except for one thing. "What about me? While you were off arranging your future—"

"*Our* future," he corrected her.

"I was left not knowing what had happened to you, not knowing if you had changed your mind about the betrothal or if you'd died somewhere."

"I had no choice," he said in the patient tone he'd always taken with her when he discussed business. Why had she never noticed how condescending he was? "If I'd written you, your father would have heard of it. You know he would never have allowed us to correspond privately. I couldn't risk tipping my hand."

"So you decided that my feelings, my worries, didn't matter?"

He let out an exasperated sigh. "Of course they mattered. But I figured you would understand once I achieved the goal we both wanted—a speedy marriage."

"If a speedy marriage was our goal, we could have eloped," she pointed out. Disillusionment crept into her voice. "But you wouldn't have risked that. Papa might have refused to leave his half of the company to you."

"Now, Maria, you know that's got nothing to do with it," he began in the placating voice that had seriously begun to grate on her nerves.

Her temper flared again. "Do you think I'm stupid?" She swallowed the bile rising in her throat. "Or maybe you just thought me so desperate for a husband that I would sit patiently waiting until you remembered you had a fiancée. Clearly you weren't worried I might find someone else during the months when I didn't hear from you."

He blinked.

A bitter smile twisted her lips. "And why should you? After all, who would want to marry the too-forthright daughter of a bastard? I'd be lucky to have a man of your social consequence, right? I'd never risk losing a fellow as lofty as you. I'm sure you thought I would wait for you forever."

"That's not . . . I didn't look at it . . . Dash it all, I knew your character! You'd made a promise to me. I knew you would honor your promise."

She fought to ignore the twinge of guilt his words roused. "Yet you felt no compunction to honor *your* promise."

"What do you mean?" he asked warily.

"You're courting the daughter of Mr. Kinsley, who owns the company that might buy the ships you don't fully own."

A dull flush rose in his face, and his gaze shot to Mr. Pinter, confirming what she'd heard. Her heart sank. How had she not seen this side of him before? How could she have been so blind to the shark in him?

"I suppose *you're* the man spouting these lies in my fiancée's ear?" Nathan snapped at Mr. Pinter.

"I passed on what I heard here, yes," Mr. Pinter said coolly. "That's what she hired me to do. You were seen out walking with Miss Kinsley several times, not to mention accompanying her and her mother to concerts and the like."

Nathan tugged at his cravat, as if it was choking him. "I was merely attempting to be polite. It's not unusual in business."

"Rumor has it that you're on the verge of making an offer," Mr. Pinter said.

Nathan returned his gaze to Maria. "You don't believe these rumors, do you?"

She gazed steadily at him. "Should I?"

"No!" When she merely lifted an eyebrow, his color deepened. "All right, I'll admit I smoothed the way for this deal by cozying up to Mr. Kinsley's family, but—"

"That's what I thought." She turned for the door. "You'll be hearing from my attorney. If you wish to purchase my half of the company—"

"Dash it all, Maria, don't be absurd!" He grabbed her by the arm. "I made no promises to the young woman. She means nothing to me!"

She snatched her arm free. "How odd. Neither do I, apparently."

"That's not true!"

Anger surged up in her again. "I cried for you. I worried about you. When you didn't answer my letters, I came all the way to this curst country to find you—and you hadn't even left word at the company as to where you'd gone! I had little money, and no idea what to do—"

"Then you should have stayed home, where you belonged!"

She stared at him incredulously. *Now* the real Nathan came out. All this time she'd believed him to be her friend, a man who understood why she wasn't like other women. But the truth was, he'd always tried to suppress whatever he saw as improper in her. He'd done it in little ways—an admonition here, a disapproving smile there—but disapproval had always lain beneath their easy relationship.

If she were honest, she'd admit that he'd never approved of her the way she was. Only Oliver had done that.

The thought of Oliver roused a powerful yearning to see him. She could almost hear the cynical remarks he would make about Nathan; then he would tell her she deserved better. She would know he meant every word, because for all Oliver's faults, for all his reticence about his past, he'd never lied to her.

"You have no idea how glad I am that I did *not* stay home," she said softly. "Otherwise I wouldn't have discovered how utterly unsuited we are to marry."

He shook his head. "You're wrong. You're just angry right now." He reached up as if to caress her cheek, but when she recoiled, his expression hardened. "We're still legally betrothed. If you break it off because of some silly petulance over Miss Kinsley, you'll force me to take action."

Her pulse pounding in her ears, she stared at him. "What do you mean?"

Determination glinted in his eyes. "I'll sue you for breach

of promise. The court will be very understanding when I point out that your father wanted us to marry, you agreed to the betrothal, and only a fit of pique has you refusing me. I'll regale them with stories of all I did to enhance the company's worth. I can keep the company's assets tied up in the courts for some time. Is that what you want?"

"How dare you?" she cried, appalled that he would even try such a thing. "And what about *your* fraudulent behavior, making business deals based on a lie? What do you think the courts will say to that?"

"They won't even blink," he said coolly. "There's nothing illegal about a man setting up another company. I had to protect my own interests. I'll say I kept your father out of it for his own good, which is the truth."

"It is not! You operated behind his back. *That's* what you did."

"You can't prove that. He's dead. I could argue that he consented to the subterfuge."

"You know perfectly well he did not," she said, shocked by his utter lack of ethics. "What sort of man are you?"

His eyes glinted with determination. "The sort of man who wants a chance. Who still wants you for his wife."

Oliver's words of a week ago leapt into her memory: *I'm watching you head blithely for a marriage to some fellow who will set you up on a shelf with his other possessions, and take you down only when he has a use for you.*

"You don't want *me* for a wife. You don't even know who I am. You want the daughter of Adam Butterfield, half owner of New Bedford Ships."

"Think what you wish. But if you take this hasty action and bring lawyers into it, you'd better be prepared for a battle."

She glared at him. "Go to hell."

While he was still gaping at her over her scandalous language, she walked out.

But even as she congratulated herself for giving him what for, her practical side pointed out that everything was in his favor. She knew how easily a man could blacken a woman's reputation. And once the court learned of her odd "betrothal" to Oliver, any sympathy for her over Nathan's ignoring her for months would evaporate.

A chill swept through her. She glanced at Mr. Pinter, who walked silently beside her. "Can he really sue me for breach of promise?"

"I'm afraid so. I know of at least one case in America where a man sued and won a large settlement."

"He can't take my half of the company from me, can he?"

"It's possible. He'll argue that he had every expectation of receiving it upon his marriage to you, and that by refusing the marriage you originally contracted for, you deprived him of what was promised to him."

Her stomach twisted into a knot. "But won't his fraud sway the court?"

Mr. Pinter grimaced. "As he said, you can't prove he wasn't acting on your father's behalf."

Despair gripped her. "But surely it would hurt his plans with Mr. Kinsley to have it be known that he had a fiancée the entire time he was courting Miss Kinsley."

"The deal isn't set yet, and he has no chance of it being so without your half of the company, which I daresay he lacks the blunt to buy. So if he can't have your half through marriage, he means to get it through treachery. It's his only choice, if you refuse to marry him. He'll blacken your name to get what he wants."

"And he'll use my public betrothal to Lord Stoneville to bolster his case."

"Most likely. Unfortunately, the court disapproves of jilts."

They walked on in silence.

She wished to God she'd never laid eyes on Nathan Hyatt. If Papa had only realized what the man was. At least she had the satisfaction of knowing that Papa had been just as deceived in his character as she.

Or . . . maybe not. Papa *had* dragged his feet at their marriage. A pity that he had left his will intact.

They reached the inn. She was surprised that Freddy wasn't waiting in the hall for them. He had to be spitting mad by now.

"What we need to do," Mr. Pinter said as they climbed the stairs, "is hurry back to London and engage an attorney as soon as possible. I'm sure that your father's will can be circumvented somehow. Don't give up hope."

She sighed. "Thank you, Mr. Pinter, but I think your generosity has been stretched beyond acceptable limits. I truly cannot afford to pay you any longer."

"Nonsense," he said with a wave of his hand. "It is to my advantage to pursue this to its ultimate conclusion. Think of it this way: if I can extricate you from Mr. Hyatt successfully, you will receive your fortune and be able to pay me, not to mention recommend me to all your friends."

"Of which I have none in England." She thought wistfully

of the Sharpes, but seeking their help was impossible. Not only did they have their own troubles, but she could never face Oliver, considering how she had left.

He patted her shoulder as they halted before the door to his and Freddy's room. "You have one friend, Miss Butterfield. You have a friend in me. Remember that."

She tried to swallow past the lump in her throat. "I don't understand why you're doing this. Surely you have more pressing matters to occupy you in London."

His expression turned serious. "I once knew a woman in a similar situation to yours. She truly had no friends, and it was her undoing. I like to think that by helping you, I'm doing what someone should have done for her." He forced a smile as he unlocked his door. "But that is neither here nor there."

The room was empty.

"That's odd," she said. "Freddy ought to have been back by now."

"I'll go fetch him from the pie shop while you go pack up." Tipping his hat, he hurried back down the stairs.

She walked to her own room, discouragement weighing her steps. She couldn't believe that it had come to this—Nathan threatening to sue her.

Reaching her door, she looked down to see a parcel. When she opened it, she found two kidney pies, still warm. So Freddy had already been here, and recently, too. Where was he now? Shaking her head in bewilderment, she unlocked her door and walked in.

Oliver's voice said from the window, "It's about time you returned."

Startled, she dropped the pies.

Despite the shadows beneath his eyes, she'd never seen a more welcome sight. Even with his cravat badly tied, his black hair sticking out in all directions, and his expression uncertain, he made her breath catch in her throat.

"What are you doing here?" she asked.

"You forgot something when you left Halstead Hall," he said hoarsely.

"What?"

Her heart leapt into her throat as he strode purposefully toward her. "Me."

Chapter Twenty-Five

Before Maria could even answer, he was kissing her, his mouth a feast of excess, his arms crushing her to him as if he wanted to absorb her into his body.

For one heady moment she gave herself up to the embrace, letting herself revel in the joy of it. Then reality sank in. Just because he'd come after her didn't mean anything had changed between them.

She pushed him away. Though his eyes darkened, he let her go.

"How did you find me?" she asked as she edged away from him.

His gaze never left her. "Pinter's coachman let it slip to one of my grooms. When I arrived I saw a pie shop, so I just waited until Freddy showed up. Then I followed him here." He arched one eyebrow. "Your cousin never can resist a good English pie."

A heavy sigh escaped her. "I swear, Freddy will be the death of me one day." Painfully conscious of how dowdy her attire must look to him, she removed her bonnet and tossed it onto a chair. "But where did he go? He's not here."

"*That* I can't help you with."

"So how did you get into my room?"

He shrugged. "Climbed in through the window. It wasn't locked." His eyes gleamed at her. "Through the years, I've gained quite a bit of experience at climbing through women's windows. Though usually I'm climbing out."

That reference reminded her why she'd fled him in the first place. "You shouldn't have come."

She regretted the blunt statement when an expression of pain crossed his face. "Look here, Maria. I made a mistake by trying to push you into marriage. I should have given you more time to consider it, before running off to gain a special license." He fisted his hands at his sides. "But you can't marry Hyatt. You don't believe me when I say it, but he's clearly a fortune hunter—"

"I know."

He blinked. "What?"

She just couldn't tell him the whole story. It was too mortifying to have him know what a fool she'd been, putting her faith in such a man. "I'm not marrying him. You needn't worry about that."

He narrowed his gaze on her. "All the more reason that you should marry me." He strode up to grip her arms. "I know that the only thing I have to commend me as a husband is my title, but—"

"Don't say that," she protested. "It's not true."

"Then why did you leave me without a word?" he asked, his voice so hurt that she cursed herself.

"Because you don't really want to marry me. You're only doing it to assuage your conscience for having taken my innocence."

He uttered a harsh laugh. "You're the first woman ever to accuse me of having a conscience."

"That's only because they don't know you." Her throat raw with feeling, she reached up to stroke his stubbled cheek. "But *I* do. I know that you're a good man."

Bleakness showed on his sharp features as he released her. "Don't lie to yourself about that. I want you as my wife, but not if you're convinced I deserve you. I assure you, I don't."

The flat tone of his voice made her heart ache. "You're wrong," she whispered. "You *are* a good man. You just don't trust yourself to behave like one—and how can I trust you when you don't trust yourself?"

"You can't," he said coldly. "You don't know who I am . . . *what* I am. If you did, you would never even consider marrying me. I long ago proved myself to be—" A low curse erupted from him.

Long ago? Her blood began to race. "This is about what happened to your parents that night at the hunting lodge, isn't it?" She laid her hand on his arm. "You still feel guilt over that. But just because you weren't there in time to stop it doesn't mean you caused it."

"That isn't why I feel guilty!" He snatched his arm free and paced to the window, where he stared out over the inn yard.

"Tell me," she pleaded. Mrs. Plumtree was right—he desperately needed to talk about this cancer that was eating at him.

His only answer was silence.

"I know that you quarreled with your mother," she persisted. "Your grandmother told me that. But she didn't know what you quarreled about."

"Thank God," he muttered.

"It can't be that bad."

He shot her a blistering glance. "You don't know a damned thing about it."

"Which is why you must tell me. So I can understand."

"You can't possibly understand."

"Was your quarrel over your father? Is that it?"

"The quarrel was over . . . I did something so . . . unconscionable that . . ." Dragging his fingers through his hair, he gave a shudder. "I can't tell you. If I do, you won't marry me."

"I won't marry you if you don't," she said softly.

"Damn it all to hell." His voice was desperate.

"I mean it, Oliver."

He faced her, eyes blazing. "My mother caught me in bed with a guest at our house party, all right? She caught me in the act of tupping a married woman."

She stared at him, not sure what to make of that.

He went on in that same awful voice, "It was the last time I saw Mother before she ran off to the hunting lodge to find Father. *That,* my dear, is why she killed him."

Maria could see that he believed it, that he was tormented by it. But she couldn't understand why. Yes, it would be a shock for a mother to find her sixteen-year-old son in bed with a married woman, but would it anger her enough to make her kill her husband? That seemed highly unlikely.

"But why . . ."

He let out a strangled oath. "Lilith Rawdon was an army wife. She and Major Rawdon had been invited to Halstead Hall for my parents' house party. When they arrived, Lilith seemed upset over something. But it didn't stop her from flirting with me when no one was watching.

"I was flattered. At that point I'd never bedded a woman. I'd kissed a tavern maid or two at Eton, but nothing more." His voice hardened. "It didn't take long for Lilith to realize how ripe I was for the plucking. When everyone else was at a picnic on the second day of the house party, I cried off because I always hated watching my parents make cutting remarks to each other in the guise of being witty and sophisticated."

Maria didn't speak, afraid to stop the flow of words.

"Lilith found me in my bedchamber reading some dry tome about farming that Father had assigned me to read. I was bored to tears. So you can imagine my reaction when she walked in, closed the door, and began to remove her clothes."

Though shock at the woman's blatant wickedness coursed through her, Maria fought to keep her expression neutral.

"I couldn't look away. Lilith was remarkably beautiful, and she acted as if she found me attractive." He shook his head. "God, what an idiot I was."

Maria wanted to cry at his self-loathing. The cursed woman probably *had* found him attractive. Maria could easily picture Oliver at sixteen—a lithe, olive-skinned Adonis with the energy and vitality of youth. Having watched her male cousins at that age, she could also see how he would have been dazzled by the attentions of a beautiful older woman.

He went on, his breathing ragged. "She climbed on top of me and . . . well, you can guess the rest. I was happily engaged in losing my virginity to the very talented Mrs. Rawdon when the door swung open and Mother walked in." A dull flush rose in his cheeks.

Poor man. Given how furiously one of her cousins had blushed when Maria had found him merely kissing his future wife, it must have been ten times more awful for Oliver.

But she still didn't see why it would lead to such tragedy.

Oliver stared as if the scene were playing out before him. "Instead of covering herself," he went on, "Lilith rose up to stare boldly at Mother. When a vicious smile crossed her face and the color drained from Mother's features, I knew. Lilith had intended for Mother to find us—to find *me*—in that state all along."

"Why on earth would she want such a thing?"

"Apparently I was part of some sick need she had to strike at Mother. That was confirmed when Mother looked at Lilith and said, 'Isn't it enough that you have *him*? Must you take my son, too?' "

So Lilith Rawdon must have been his father's mistress. Great heavens.

Oliver's face was a mask of revulsion. "I'd always wondered why the Rawdons spent so much time with my parents. Mother didn't seem to like Lilith, and Father made fun of Major Rawdon in sly ways that even I could recognize. But that day, when Mother saw me . . ."

He balled his hands into fists. "Oh, God, there was so much pain in her voice. It has haunted me all my life. Mother told me to get out of her sight, and fairly tossed me from the room. The last thing I saw was Lilith smiling at my mother like a cat in the cream."

"But why did the woman do that? If she and your father were engaged in an affair, why taunt your mother with it?"

"I've spent years trying to figure that out. Several rumors were circulating back then about the Rawdons—that their marriage was in trouble, that there was talk of a separation. Divorce was out of the question, of course, but perhaps Lilith hoped to convince Father to run off with her somewhere they could live together. How better to accomplish her purpose than to make Mother angry enough to ask for a separation herself? She would never have left without a strong impetus."

"Or maybe the whole thing was just how it seemed," Maria pointed out. "Lilith Rawdon, clearly a woman of low character, couldn't resist taking a young man into her bed whom she found attractive. Did she try to see you again after that?"

"No. They left that night. I tried to see her later, to get the truth out of her, but when I went to her home, the servants informed me that she and her husband had gone to India. I wrote to her—she never wrote back. My other letters came back marked as undeliverable, so they'd apparently moved on."

He fixed Maria with a tortured gaze. "But there's no doubt in my mind that Lilith had a purpose in what she did that day. And that I, in my stupidity and my weakness for women, let her use me to hurt my mother, to cause her to—"

"Oh, my darling," she said, fighting back tears as she went to him. "It wasn't your fault!"

"Wasn't it?" he choked out. "Mother's last words to me, while I scrambled to hide my nakedness, were, 'You're a disgrace to this family! You're behaving exactly like your father. And I'll be damned if I let him turn you into the same wicked, selfish creature as he is, sacrificing anyone to his pleasures!' That's why she shot him. To prevent what she saw as his bad influence on me."

Oh, her poor dear. What a curse, for that to be the last memory of his mother. No wonder he had lived all these years trying to forget the past. Who wouldn't?

Anger at his mother for putting that burden on him rose up in her. "She shouldn't have said those things."

"They were true."

"They were not true!"

"Maria, all my life, I watched Mother suffer over Father's affairs. He was rarely discreet and she, having foolishly given her heart to him, became more brittle with the passing years. She always said that we children were her only joy, that we made up for everything. Then, in one careless moment, I drove the dagger in her heart."

The anguish on his face tore at her. She grabbed him by the arms, forcing him to look at her. "You did *not* cause your mother's rash act. She made her own choice. When she said those cruel things to you, I'm sure she didn't mean them. She was just angry at your father and took it out on you—because you were the only one available, and because she couldn't take it out on him."

"Ah, but she *did* take it out on him." His eyes blazed at her.

"Yes. And that is a tragedy. But not one you're responsible for."

"You can't possibly understand," he bit out.

"I understand far better than you think. My mother died in childbirth, remember?" Tears clogged her throat, but she pressed on. "For most of my childhood, I felt responsible for her death. I'm sure you can imagine how it feels to know that one's very existence is owed only to the suffering and death of one's mother."

"It's not the same." The stark anguish in his features tugged at her heart. "You didn't intend—"

"And you did? You knew that this Lilith woman hated your mother? That she was involved with your father? That by sharing her bed, you might set off such an awful chain of events?"

He tried to thrust her from him, but she wouldn't release him. He scowled down at her. "I may not have known about Lilith and Father, but I knew she was married. I knew what I was doing was immoral. I just didn't care."

"You were sixteen! You had a father who daily broke those rules. And you knew that other men of your station behaved that way, as well." Tears streamed down her cheeks, but she paid them no mind. "Tell me this: while you were enjoying yourself with Mrs. Rawdon, did you have any thought about your mother and how she might disapprove of your behavior?"

"Don't be absurd!"

"Exactly. Young men don't think before they act. They're impulsive and selfish and randy as goats. I have four male cousins and when they were that age, all the moral training in the world would have flown right out of their heads if a pretty married woman had undressed in their bedchambers and climbed into bed with them."

"That doesn't excuse it."

"No. But it doesn't make you culpable for the tragedy, either. You have cobbled them together in your mind. It's time that you un-cobble them."

He clasped her head in his large hands, his gaze hot with anger. "You forget that I've spent my life proving Mother right. I'm just like my father."

His grandmother's words leapt into her mind: *You seem to think he is like his father, but he is actually like his mother. I do not know why he has pursued his father's path all these years, but it is not his real character, I swear.*

The truth hit her with sudden clarity.

"No," she said softly. "You've spent your life thumbing your nose at her, furious at her for leaving you and the others, for forcing you into the untenable position of having to hide what really happened that night. You've been striking at her ghost, screaming, 'If you didn't want me to turn out like him, you should have stayed to stop me!' "

As his throat worked convulsively, she covered his hands with hers. "But she can't hear you. So all you're doing is trudging a path that isn't your own, growing more weary of it by the day, wanting more from your existence but believing you're cursed to having less. That is no sort of life for anyone, especially for a man with so much potential."

A shuddering breath escaped him. "How can you have such faith in me?" he asked hoarsely. "How can you believe in me when I've given you no reason?"

"You've given me plenty of reasons, but there's only one that matters. I love you, Oliver. I can't help myself. *That* is my reason."

He began to shake, his eyes glistening with unshed tears.

"I love you," she repeated as she kissed his cheek. "I *love* you." She kissed the other cheek, now damp, though she wasn't sure whether from her tears or his. "I love you so much." She brushed his lips with hers.

He held her back to search her face. "God help you if that is a lie," he said in an aching voice. "Because those words have sealed your fate. I'll never let you go, now."

Chapter Twenty-Six

I love you.

The words pounded in Oliver's ears as he dragged Maria against him. He hadn't realized how desperately he'd wanted to hear her say them until she had, and now they sang through every sweet kiss, through every caress of her hands, every stroke of her tongue inside his hungry mouth.

He'd told her all, he'd laid bare every dark corner of his strongbox, and still she was here in his arms, kissing him, holding him, crying over him. It was unimaginable.

If she could believe he was not truly the devil he'd played all these years, could he learn to believe in himself? Could he even, perhaps, be the man that she wanted? The man that his mother had intended him to be? Might he actually be able to change his life?

"I love you," she whispered against his lips again, and his heart gave a leap of joy.

"My God, Maria," he rasped. "You rip the soul from my body when you say that."

"Don't you believe me?" She pressed her mouth to his throat in a reverent kiss that made his pulse beat in a frenzy.

"I believe you're daft. That's what I believe."

"No more than you. No more than anyone in love."

There was that word again, the word he'd always distrusted when he'd heard it from women before, the word that now poured through him with all the sweetness of warm honey. He desperately wanted to trust it. He wanted to swallow her whole, to lay her down on the bed and fill her with his flesh over and over, until he could convince himself that she truly meant the words.

But when he reached for the buttons of her gown, she pulled away. "No, we can't, not right now."

"Yes, now," he insisted.

"Mr. Pinter will be back any minute, and I can't have him find me in the midst of—"

"You're worried about what *Pinter* thinks?" he interrupted as a surge of possessiveness swept through him. "Sounds like you got rather cozy with the Bow Street runner on the way up here."

A teasing smile curved her lips. "Don't tell me you're jealous of Mr. Pinter."

"Damned right I am," he grumbled, backing her toward the bed. "I'm jealous of Jarret, of Gabe, of every blasted fellow who looks at you and wants you."

"You have no need to be jealous." She looped her arms about his neck. "*You're* the one that I love."

There was that word again, striking a sudden blow to his heart. He had a heart? Apparently he did. "Yet you ran off and left me without a word," he accused.

"Only because you told me you weren't sure you could be faithful to me," she said softly.

He sucked in a breath. "That was my fear speaking. My fear that I might indeed have my father's character. My fear that I couldn't be what you needed."

"And where is that fear now?" When her gaze met his, yearning and earnest, he felt a catch in his chest.

"Gone. One day without you told me that I want only you." He dragged his fingers through her hair, scattering the pins, bringing it tumbling down about her shoulders. "When I walk into a room, sweetheart, I see only you. I might as well have been blind yesterday in London, for all the notice I took of other women."

He couldn't believe he was spouting the same sort of words he'd always laughed at his friends for saying about their wives. But every time he'd laughed, there'd been that tiny, envious part of him that knew how hollow his laughter was. And now he understood how hollow the life that went with it was, as well.

"How could I ever prefer another woman to the one I love?" he said.

She alone lifted the darkness from his soul. She alone saw in him the boy who, long ago, had hoped for something better. And the man who still hoped for something better. Who actually had a chance of it, with her in his life.

Her chin began to tremble as her arms tightened about his neck. "Y-You love me?"

Gazing down at her pert nose and the freckles that made him think of an adorable pixie, he felt his throat constrict. "I want you every hour of the day. I can't imagine a future without you in it. The idea of returning to my empty house alone is so hellish that I'd rather wander the world at your heels than be without you. Tell me, is that love?"

She cast him a blazing smile. "It sounds like it."

"Then I love you, my wonderful, sword-wielding, tart-tongued angel. I want you to be my wife. I want you to preside over my table and accompany me to balls and share my bed." A most uncharacteristic happiness surged through him. "And I want to have children with you, lots of them, filling every room in Halstead Hall."

A sudden understanding lit her face. His clever love didn't miss the fact that he was offering her not just himself, but everything else he'd neglected, as well. Everything that he wanted to put to rights. That he needed to put to rights.

"Not filling *every* room, I hope," she teased, even as tears shone in her eyes. "There are three hundred, after all."

"Then I suppose we'll have to get started right away," he said, matching her light tone. His heart near to bursting, he reached again for the buttons on the back of her gown. "These things should never be left until the last minute."

As a laugh of pure joy bubbled out of her, she began to untie his cravat. "I can see you're going to be quite the lusty husband, aren't you?"

He stripped her gown from her, then turned her around to undo her stays. "You have no idea," he murmured, and filled his hands with the breasts he'd freed.

Moaning, she pressed her bottom against him. "I have *some* idea."

There were no more words as they undressed each other. It was the strangest experience of his life. The part of his brain that generally worked constantly while he was tupping a woman, the part that assessed how to get the most from the experience, seemed to be on holiday.

He felt like a randy lad again, too aroused to be cautious, too swept up in the pleasure of her to think beyond the simple enjoyment of uncovering her silky flesh, the heat of unveiling her magnificent body. In a frenzy of need, he tumbled her onto the bed and joined her there, desperate to be inside her, to show her the intensity of what he felt.

But just as he bent to kiss her throat, she pushed him off her and jumped up from the bed. "I didn't lock the door!"

Grabbing her waist, he pulled her down on top of him. "No one will come in, sweetheart." He clamped his legs about hers to keep her there. "And if they do, it will only hasten our march to the altar—which is just fine by me."

Eyeing him askance, she pushed up from his chest. "Why do you always attempt seducing me when someone might happen in upon us? First, you kiss me when you *know* your grandmother is about to walk in, then you do quite wicked things to me in the carriage a breath away from half of London, and then—"

"What can I say?" He grinned up at her. "Since I intend to have only you in my bed for the rest of my life, I have to teach you everything I know." He filled his hands with her ample breasts. "Here's your first lesson. Make love to me, my darling betrothed."

He thrust his cock up at her to emphasize the point, and she caught her breath. "I'm not sure I understand."

"Now that you're perched so fetchingly atop me, I want you to take me inside you."

A delicious blush touched her cheeks. "I can do that?"

He laughed. "It works just as well in reverse, trust me."

Curiosity swept her features as she sat back on her heels to stare at his jutting cock. "Oh, my."

He reached down to the tender flesh between her legs, exulting to find it hot and wet and welcoming. "Oh my, indeed," he rasped. "Come on, my angel. Make love to me. Before I go mad."

With an uncertain smile, she lifted up and lowered herself onto his cock. "Well," she said when she was fully seated. "That's interesting."

"Isn't it, though?" He thrust against her. "But don't stop there."

She began to move, her luscious body undulating atop his and her hair streaming over her breasts, a silky curtain shimmering golden-red in the midmorning light. As the blood rose in him, he stared up into her glowing face and finally understood why men married.

He'd heard the marriage rites at his friends' weddings many a time, their sonorous words spoken with solemnity by a vicar who looked as if he probably bedded his wife with his eyes closed. When the service had come to the part where the couple each said, "with my body I thee worship," Oliver had always choked down a bitter laugh.

He wasn't laughing now. This *was* worship, this joining of a man with the woman he loved. There was no guile in her face, no manipulation, no secrets. She loved him, pure and simple, without reserve. She'd believed in him when he himself could not. And her belief now transformed her into the angel descending to make him whole, to soothe his hurts, to bring his body alive with her spirit.

Wanting to reciprocate, he thumbed her luscious nipples, brushed kisses on her arms, slid his hand between her legs to fondle her pleasure spot and make her gasp. He reveled in the heat of her smile, the delicacy of her skin as Maria rode him like a glorious goddess, her eyes alight with feeling, her hands sweeping his body with tender caresses that made his throat raw with unshed tears.

Had he actually thought to teach her passion that day in the carriage? He must have been mad. Untutored as she was in its ways, she'd understood what he had not—that passion wasn't about the act. It was about the one who joined you in the act.

The need for release came upon him so quickly that he feared he might not last until she found her own, but just as he felt his erupting, she threw back her head with a cry and convulsed around him. He poured himself into her, praying that they'd made a child. It seemed only right that this moment be captured forever in a gamboling son or a laughing daughter.

She collapsed atop him, naked and sated, and his heart nearly burst from joy. A laugh tumbled out of him. If he didn't watch it, she'd turn him into a maudlin creature spouting romantic verse.

She arched an eyebrow at him. "Why do you laugh, sir?"

"I'm happy." Incredibly, it was true. "I'll be even happier

when we can find a man of the cloth and use that special license."

"And what if I decide to take you up on your offer to make me your mistress instead?" she teased. "What if I prefer to keep hold of my inheritance?"

That brought him up short. What exactly had happened during her meeting with Hyatt? "Is that what you want?"

"No," she said softly. "I want you."

"The feeling is perfectly mutual." Taking her by surprise, he rolled her beneath him and began to kiss her neck. "Indeed, I want you right now. Again."

Then a knock came at the door. With alarm in her face, she touched a finger to his lips. He caught it between his teeth, swirling his tongue over the tip, watching with avid interest as her eyes darkened to molten sapphire.

When the knock came again, he choked back a curse and rolled off her.

"What is it?" she called out.

"Is Freddy in there with you, Maria? I thought I heard voices."

Recognizing Pinter's raspy tones, Oliver scowled.

"No, he's not here." She sat up, but Oliver pulled her back down and threw one leg over hers to hold her in place as he trailed kisses along her collarbone.

"Well, he wasn't at the pie shop," Pinter said through the door. "The innkeeper said he'd been here, but went off again. He didn't know where."

Oliver emitted a soft growl of frustration against her shoulder, and she bit her lip, clearly stifling a laugh.

"He probably went in search of more food," she called out. "Check any other cookshops and inns. I'm sure he hasn't gone far."

"Perhaps you should come with me to look—"

"I can't," she cut in. "I . . . I'm not feeling well."

"Should I fetch the innkeeper's wife?" he queried, his voice a mixture of concern and suspicion.

"No!" she cried. "I'm not dressed."

"Now that's an understatement," Oliver whispered against her ear.

"Just . . . go look for Freddy while I rest," she called to Pinter. "I'm sure I'll be feeling much better by the time you find him."

"I can *promise* you'll be feeling better, sweetheart," Oliver murmured, nipping her ear for good measure.

She gave him a chastening glance even as she fought a smile.

"All right," Pinter said. "But I should like to leave here by noon at the latest. We need to consult a lawyer about building a case against Hyatt before he has time to build one against you."

Maria's smile vanished.

What the devil?

"I'm sure I'll be fine by then," she called to the door. "Just find Freddy."

Only when his footsteps moved down the stairs did Oliver feel free to speak. "What is Pinter talking about? What case against you?"

"It's nothing," she said and began to kiss his chest.

But he could tell she was merely trying to distract him. She was in trouble. That was unacceptable. And a husband's first duty was to get his wife out of trouble. "It damned well isn't nothing if Pinter is itching to talk to you about it. Tell me what has happened."

"I'd rather not."

He pinned her beneath him with a warning glance. "I told you what you wanted to know about me. Now it's your turn."

She worried her lower lip with her teeth. "You must promise not to do anything about it."

"I'm not promising that, angel. You know better."

"Then I'm not telling you," she said with a familiar set of her jaw.

"Then I'll have to ask Pinter to tell me, won't I?" He pushed himself off her and threw his legs over the edge of the bed.

"Wait!"

He turned to stare at her, one eyebrow lifted.

"You are such a curst arrogant—"

"Yes. What happened with Hyatt?"

Muttering an oath, she threw her head back against the pillow and dragged the sheet over her naked body.

As she related a tale of remarkable deception, he could scarcely contain his anger. But when she got to the part about Hyatt threatening a breach of promise suit, his blood roared in his ears. Rising from the bed, he said, "I'll kill him with my bare hands."

"No, you will not!" she cried as she pulled him back down. "This is why I didn't want to tell you. If you get involved, it will only make it worse. I am *not* going to let Nathan steal my half of New Bedford Ships, and I'm *not* going to let you blunder in there in a rage at him, giving him an excuse to do so!"

"So how do *you* propose to handle this?" he clipped out.

"Mr. Pinter is going to hire an attorney, and I propose to let them handle it."

Oliver scowled. "As your husband, I should have a say in it."

"You're not my husband yet," she countered. "And you will not *be* my husband until this matter is resolved. I don't want to see you or your family dragged into it."

"That's our choice, is it not?"

"It's my choice," she said, stubborn as ever. "You've all been very kind to me—I don't wish to embroil you in a potential scandal. You have quite enough attached to your names as it is."

Casting her a searching glance, he said, "Very well." He had no intention of staying out of it. But clearly she would do everything in her power to keep him from confronting Hyatt, and she could be quite persistent when she had the bit between her teeth. So he'd have to change strategies—get her sufficiently relaxed so he could slip out and take care of the bastard on his own.

He bent to kiss her, but she pushed against him, eyeing him with suspicion. "Do you promise to leave it to me and the lawyers?"

With a noncommittal grunt, he began to suck at her breast.

"Oliver—" she began in a warning tone.

"I promise not to throttle him until you give me permission to do so." That he could promise. No more.

As he tugged at her nipple with his teeth, he rubbed his swiftly hardening cock against her soft flesh, and her eyes heated instantly. At the moment, he was grateful for his hard-won prowess with women. It might buy him the time he needed for doing what he must, without having to lie to her and tromp on her delicate sense of morality.

"And do you . . . promise not to interfere in any other way?" she asked, though her body was responding quite eagerly to his attentions.

"All these promises you wish to exact from me," he drawled as he reached down to fondle her, reveling when she gasped. "I will be much more amenable to making them, angel, if you . . . soften me up."

A reluctant smile touched her lips. "Will you, now?"

"Oh, yes." Pulling her knees up, he entered her swift and sure, his hard thrust angled perfectly to rouse her. He was rewarded when she arched her back with a moan, then squirmed beneath him.

Oliver used every sensual technique he knew to satisfy her, and when they both lay spent, he pretended to fall asleep. Before long she dozed. Slipping from the bed, he watched her carefully for any signs of waking as he drew on his clothes. Fortunately, she'd probably had little rest the night before, so by the time he was dressed, she was soundly out.

Fighting a breach of promise case in the courts might take years, not to mention involve Maria and her family in all sorts of nastiness. It was time he proved to her that he could take care of her. That he could be the man she wanted him to be, the man who could be worthy of her love.

He knew how to handle men like Hyatt. Not for nothing had he been raised the grandson of Hetty Plumtree.

Unfortunately, there was only one way to be sure the man stayed out of her life for good. Patting his coat pocket to make sure it still contained the velvet jewel box, he headed off to find Nathan Hyatt.

Chapter Twenty-Seven

Maria was dreaming about her bedchamber in Halstead Hall when something awakened her. She lay there in a half doze, a smile curving her lips. Oliver loved her. He truly loved her. It had been there in every kiss, every caress, every sweet word he'd whispered as they'd made love. Twice. With great enthusiasm, not to mention creative technique.

Heat rose in her cheeks. Apparently there were quite a number of things she didn't know yet about lovemaking. But she was very willing to learn. Oh yes. Now that Oliver had put his past behind him and they were to be married, she was blissfully content.

She turned over to tell him so, but he was gone. Bolting upright, she gazed about the room. Where was Oliver?

A pounding began on the door, and she realized what had awakened her—a knock at the door. "Mopsy! You have to let us in!"

Great heavens, Freddy was outside and Mr. Pinter was probably with him. And she was naked as the day she was born!

"Wait a minute—I'm coming!" Swiftly she threw on her shift and her wrap, then dashed about gathering up her clothes. There was no sign of Oliver's. She tossed her garments behind the dressing screen in the corner and hurried to open the door.

Though Freddy stormed into the room without a thought, Mr. Pinter turned beet red when he saw her state of undress.

"Forgive me, I was napping," Maria darted behind the screen to dress. "Have you seen Lord Stoneville?" She had a sneaking suspicion where he might have gone, which concerned her more than her reputation.

"Stoneville's in Southampton?" Mr. Pinter asked, his voice disapproving.

She glanced at him over the top of the screen. "Yes. He came looking for me. You didn't meet up with him anywhere?"

"I didn't see him," Mr. Pinter said. "Did you, Freddy?"

Freddy shook his head.

He'd undoubtedly gone off to fight with Nathan. "We have to find him. He was not happy about my coming here to see Nathan, and I fear he might try to confront him himself."

"So you decided to take a nap while he did?" Freddy asked.

Leave it to Freddy to pay attention the *one* time that she least needed him to notice. "No, silly. He told me he would wait downstairs for you to return, and I should rest until then. I was so tired that I let him persuade me to do so."

That was nearly the truth, except that his persuasion had taken the form of wearing her out in bed, then waiting until her two days of little sleep overtook her before he snuck out, the devious devil.

Her only solace was that he didn't know where Nathan was. But it wouldn't take him long to find out; he'd found *her* well enough.

"Freddy," she called over the screen, "could you fetch me a maid to help me finish dressing?"

Freddy exchanged a glance with Mr. Pinter. "Actually, Mopsy, there's a lady here I'd like you to meet. I'm sure she wouldn't mind helping you dress."

Stepping into the hall, he ushered in a pretty young woman with strikingly beautiful gold ringlets that she wore in a fringe about her face. Maria couldn't help noticing that Freddy seemed oddly solicitous of her.

"Now, Mopsy," he began, "before I introduce you, I think you should know that the lady had no idea of what was going on, and she was just as much in the dark as you, only—"

"Freddy, get to the point," she snapped, more frantic to find Oliver by the moment.

"This is Miss Jane Kinsley."

Who the dickens . . . ohhh, Miss *Kinsley. Nathan's* Miss Kinsley.

"Miss Kinsley," Freddy said to the woman with the pinkening cheeks, "this is my cousin, Miss Maria Butterfield."

"Nice to meet you," the woman said, bobbing a curtsy. "We don't get many Americans hereabouts. I only know three now. You, Mr. Dunse, and Mr. Hyatt." She didn't seem terribly perturbed to be in the same room with her apparent rival, though perhaps the men hadn't explained that fully to her.

"Miss Kinsley and I met in the pie shop," Freddy offered. "She likes pie as much as I do."

"Especially kidney pie," she offered, "though I do fancy leek pie once in a while."

She and Freddy looked at each other and burst into laughter.

"Leek pie," Freddy said, still chuckling. "That's rich."

Maria cast Mr. Pinter a bewildered glance.

"Trust me, you don't want to know," Mr. Pinter said with a roll of his eyes. "Apparently your cousin and Miss Kinsley struck up quite the conversation in the pie shop after she overheard him asking about Mr. Hyatt."

"It was very fortui- . . . fortui- . . ." Miss Kinsley paused, a tiny frown knitting her brow as she glanced at Mr. Pinter. "What was that word you used?"

"Fortuitous."

Heavens alive. Freddy had stumbled upon a woman as thick-headed as he was. With a love of pie, too. What were the chances?

Maria *almost* felt sorry for Nathan, if Miss Kinsley was his new choice for a wife. Though she could see why he'd chosen the woman. She was young, pretty, oblivious, and had a rich father.

Nathan clearly had a talent for finding that sort of female to prey on. It mortified her that she had been one of them.

Still, much as she'd like to stab Nathan through the heart, she had to deal with him, which meant she had to stop Oliver from dealing with him before he made a mess of things. "Miss Kinsley, if you would be so kind, might you help me dress?" she asked.

Miss Kinsley blinked. "Oh! Yes, of course."

As the young woman helped her, Freddy and Mr. Pinter began to talk. Freddy had apparently been busy during her time with Oliver. Not only had he met Miss Kinsley, but he'd become quite chummy with her. She'd been shocked to learn that her suitor had a fiancée. She'd been even more shocked to learn that he'd lied to her papa about his business.

Freddy had brought her back to the inn, but finding Maria and Mr. Pinter gone, had left the pies there. He'd suggested that they talk to her parents about the dastardly Mr. Hyatt, but neither was home. Mr. Kinsley was at a board meeting out of town, and Mrs. Kinsley was shopping.

She and Freddy had gone off looking for her mother, and that's how Mr. Pinter had found them, wandering the streets, thoroughly engrossed in each other's company. Since time was of the essence, Mr. Pinter had hurried them back to the inn while telling them everything that had transpired so far. Clearly Mr. Pinter realized that Miss Kinsley's parents might not be quite so eager to help them as the young woman seemed to be.

Uncomfortable with how Freddy and Mr. Pinter had commandeered the lady, Maria took Miss Kinsley's hands. "I know this is probably very upsetting, and I'm sorry you had to hear about Mr. Hyatt's character in such a frightful manner."

"It's all right," Miss Kinsley said blithely. "I was already wondering about him, to be honest."

"So you're not in love with Mr. Hyatt?" Maria pressed her, wanting to be very sure about that.

"Lord, no. I hardly know him." She screwed up her face in thought. "Besides, he likes to say things I don't understand.

He's too clever for me. And when I ask him to explain, he treats me like a child. I'm *not* a child. Sometimes I just need things explained to me."

"Perfectly understandable," Freddy put in. "Everybody needs things explained from time to time."

Mr. Pinter looked as if he were struggling to keep a straight face.

"But you haven't heard the best part, Mopsy," Freddy exclaimed, practically dancing. "Tell her, Miss Kinsley. Tell her the best part!"

As the young woman laid out "the best part," Maria gaped at her. Clearly Miss Kinsley wasn't as brainless as Maria had assumed. Her news changed everything.

"If you had to," Maria asked, "would you be willing to repeat that in a court of law?"

"I don't think we need wait for that," Mr. Pinter said. "I daresay we can use the information right now."

Maria met the runner's gaze. "You mean—"

"Yes. It's time we pay Mr. Hyatt another visit."

"Do you mind coming with us, Miss Kinsley?" she asked. "I know it's a great imposition."

"It's no imposition at all." With a fetching blush, Miss Kinsley cut her eyes at Freddy and said, "It's the right thing to do."

"And I'll be there to protect you both," Freddy said, laying his hand on the sword at his side.

"You can only go if you leave the sword here," Maria chided as she swept out from behind the screen. Then she thought a moment. If Oliver had found Nathan . . . "On second thought, we might need it."

She headed for the door, then paused to hug Miss Kinsley. "Thank you."

The young woman beamed. "You're welcome."

Maria glanced to Freddy. "And thank you, too, cousin."

He took a typical male posture, though his ears grew red. "Think nothing of it, Mopsy. A man does what he must to protect his family."

But sometimes a little intervention from Fate didn't hurt either. Now if only Fate would keep Oliver from Nathan. The last thing she wanted was to watch the love of her life be hanged for murder.

Unfortunately, when they arrived at Nathan's lodging house, they learned that Oliver had already arrived. The owner appeared disgruntled by all the attention his American man of business was garnering. He directed them back to the parlor, where the men had repaired only minutes before.

Her heart in her throat, Maria hurried ahead. Before she even reached the open door, she heard Oliver say, "It's the best offer you will get, Mr. Hyatt. I advise you to take it."

She paused to listen, motioning the others to do the same. Peeking around the edge of the doorway, she saw Oliver faced off against Nathan. Nathan's gaze was fixed on the contents of a familiar velvet box held open in his hand.

"And how do I know I can trust you concerning the value of the pearls, sir?" Nathan asked Oliver.

Oliver was going to give up his mother's necklace to that scoundrel? Not if she had anything to say about it!

She started to march in, but Mr. Pinter laid a restraining hand on her arm.

"Any man with an eye for quality can tell their value." Oliver's voice dripped condescension.

A rueful smile touched her lips. Oliver could be very good at that when he wanted to be.

"But if you insist upon it," he continued in that bored tone, "we can go to a jeweler and have him second the appraisal."

"It's worth five thousand pounds, you say? That is quite a nice consideration."

Maria sucked in a breath. Five thousand pounds? Her half of the company was only worth about forty thousand pounds. As a bribe, five thousand pounds was quite a 'nice consideration' indeed.

"It's better than you deserve," Oliver drawled. When Nathan bristled, Oliver added, "I assure you that if you pursue a breach of promise suit against Miss Butterfield, you'll regret it. Lawyers are costly, even in America. They can effectively eat up whatever settlement you might receive."

Then menace filled his voice. "And courts are fickle, too. You might not win your suit, and even if you do, the publicity surrounding it could do irreparable harm to your present deal with Mr. Kinsley. Meanwhile, the pearls should prove enough surety to get you whatever loan you need to purchase Miss Butterfield's half of the company. With the profits you make from your arrangement with Mr. Kinsley, you should be well settled."

His gaze sharpened. "But there are two conditions. One, Miss Butterfield must never know of the financial part of the arrangement between us. You will tell her that while it breaks your heart to let her go, you don't wish to marry a woman who clearly isn't eager for the match."

Nathan thrust out his chin. "Maybe it does break my heart."

"Yes," Oliver said in a tight voice. "I can see how much you suffer." When a flush rose in Nathan's cheeks, he added, "Two, if you choose to purchase her half of the company, you'll offer her a fair price. Is that understood?"

"I wouldn't cheat her," Nathan said resentfully, clearly intimidated. Nathan's family might have status and connections in America, but they were nothing to the connections of a British peer, and he undoubtedly knew it.

But he appeared to have guessed something else, too, for his eyes narrowed. "I think I have the right to ask, my lord, why you show such interest in Maria's situation."

"When she and her cousin were in difficult straits in London, my family took her in. I fell in love with her. I intend to marry her. *If* she will have me."

The words, so quietly and eloquently spoken, caught at her heart.

Unfortunately, they also caught at Nathan's greed. "Ah, now I understand. You want to get your hands on her fortune yourself. And if that happens, it seems to me this little arrangement could be . . . improved a bit."

Though a muscle ticked in Oliver's jaw, he in no other way showed his anger. "First of all, Miss Butterfield has not agreed to marry me, since she was still betrothed to you when I made my proposal. I do this for her because she doesn't deserve to be plagued by your lawsuit or suffer whatever slings you mean to throw at her publicly." Oliver flicked a piece of lint from his well-tailored coat. "And secondly, do I *look* as if I need money?"

Maria choked down a laugh. It was rather fun to watch Oliver out-defraud the defrauder.

That brought an uneasy expression to Nathan's face. "No," he admitted, "but you could have offered me cash. Offering me jewelry smacks of desperation."

"I don't generally carry large amounts of cash with me in these days of highwaymen and thieves," Oliver said with a pointed stare. "The pearls were for her. But if you wish to return to London with me, I could arrange to give you cash. Of course the amount would have to be lower, to compensate me for my trouble. And it would take you away from Southampton at a time when you will be wanting to secure your second pigeon. A Miss Kinsley, I believe?"

When Miss Kinsley stiffened beside her, Maria grabbed her hand and squeezed it hard.

Nathan looked none too happy to have his circumstances so well known. He glanced nervously at Oliver, then at the pearls. Then he snapped the box shut. "Very well, my lord. We have a deal."

"The hell you do!" Maria cried out, dashing into the room. She barely noticed that the others stayed behind in the hall.

Nathan looked disconcerted by her appearance, and Oliver looked alarmed. "Leave this to me, Maria," he said tersely.

"The only way that scoundrel is getting your mother's pearls," she shot back, "is if I strangle him with them." She marched up and snatched the box from Nathan. "Besides, you already gave them to me."

"And you left them behind," Oliver reminded her. "Gran said you refused to keep them."

"Well, I want them now."

"At the risk of being dragged through the courts?" he said, coming to her side. "Of having your name maligned by this vermin?" He lowered his voice. "Do you really want him examining every action you've taken in the past two weeks, having it all laid out before a judge?"

She could tell he was thinking of her appearance at the brothel and the unpleasantness there, not to mention her public betrothal to him. "Let him do his worst." She had an ace in the hole.

She was about to call for Miss Kinsley when Oliver said, "Hyatt won't let go of this matter without some financial consideration. With 125,000 pounds at stake—"

Nathan's bark of laughter cut him off. "Is that what she's told you her half of the company is worth, Lord Stoneville?" Nathan sneered. "Now I understand why a marquess is sniffing around her."

Oliver's eyes turned a dangerous shade of black. He seized the man by the throat and slammed him against the wall. "I don't give a damn what her half of the company is worth, you little worm. She could come to our marriage with nothing but the gown on her back and I wouldn't care. She's worth more to me than any amount of money. If you had an ounce of sense, she'd be worth more to you, too."

As Nathan clawed at Oliver's hands, struggling for air, Maria hurried to lay her hand on Oliver's arm. "You promised not to throttle him," she reminded him, though she was rather enjoying it.

After a second's hesitation, he released Nathan with a look of disgust.

Maria glanced back toward the doorway. "Mr. Pinter? Would you mind?"

As Mr. Pinter, Freddy, and Miss Kinsley entered the room, the blood drained from Nathan's face. When Oliver cast Maria a quizzical glance, she smiled. "Oliver, this is Miss Jane Kinsley. Miss Kinsley, the Marquess of Stoneville."

"Delighted to meet you, my lord," Miss Kinsley said with a pretty curtsy, while Nathan stood there agape.

"Likewise," Oliver said, clearly not sure what to make of her presence there.

"Miss Kinsley," Nathan said, having recovered his equilibrium, "I don't know what these people have been telling you, but—"

"They didn't tell me anything that surprised me, once I thought about it." Miss Kinsley regarded him with the look of disgust girls reserved for snails and frogs. "Any man who would suggest to a young woman that she should elope rather than listen to her papa's advice can only be up to no good."

"Elope?" Oliver queried, his eyes narrowing on Miss Kinsley. "This scoundrel proposed marriage to you?"

"Now, Miss Kinsley," Nathan began in his best placating voice, "we both know it wasn't like—"

"Quiet!" Oliver snapped at him. "Or I swear not even Maria will keep me from throttling you."

Nathan swallowed. Hard.

Miss Kinsley sniffed. "Yesterday Mr. Hyatt snuck into our garden where I was trimming the roses, and told me we should run off together. You see, Papa had ordered him not to come to the house anymore. Papa thought he was getting too chummy, and since I have a very large dowry—"

A smile lit Oliver's face. "And by 'large dowry,' what exactly do you mean?"

"I hardly see how that's pertinent," Nathan cut in.

"Stubble it," Oliver growled. "Miss Kinsley? Do you mind?"

"Twenty thousand pounds."

Oliver fixed Nathan with an amused glance. "I'm sure the court would be very interested to hear this news." He looked at Mr. Pinter. "What do you think, sir? Would a judge pay much attention to a breach of promise suit if the woman changed her mind about the marriage because she discovered that her fiancé had proposed marriage to another woman?"

"I doubt they'd even allow it to go to trial," Mr. Pinter said with a smug smile. "They might even suggest that the woman had grounds for her own breach of promise suit."

A look of panic crossed Nathan's face. "I did not propose marriage to Miss Kinsley! You can't listen to her! She's a complete henwit!"

"Don't you dare insult her!" Freddy put in, brandishing his sword.

"I'd be careful if I were you, Hyatt," Oliver drawled. "Young Freddy here is liable to thrust without thinking."

"But she's turning everything round all wrong," Nathan protested. "Why would I propose marriage to Miss Kinsley when it would ruin my hope of ever owning New Bedford Ships?"

"Perhaps because those hopes were already ruined?" Mr. Pinter offered, a positively nasty look crossing his face. "I understand that Mr. Kinsley had decided not to buy your ships after all."

Nathan was having trouble breathing now. "That's . . . that's not true."

"Papa said it was," Miss Kinsley put in helpfully. "He told Mama he wasn't sure of your ability to follow through. That's why he didn't want you coming around the house anymore."

"And he was your last chance," Mr. Pinter put in. "You didn't know that Mr. Butterfield was dead, and without the deal you'd placed all your hopes in, you saw your future sunk with the Butterfields. He would have refused to allow you to marry his daughter, and you would have been stuck with only half the company, which did you no good since you couldn't afford to purchase the other half.

"So your next best choice was to marry Miss Kinsley and her twenty thousand pounds. Unfortunately for you, Miss Kinsley knew better than to fall for your blandishments, since she had attended Mrs. Harris's School for Young Ladies."

When Oliver burst into laughter, Maria asked, "What's that?"

Miss Kinsley straightened her shoulders. "It's a school that teaches heiresses how to recognize fortune hunters. They warned us about elopements. 'If a fellow can't ask your papa for your hand properly,' Mrs. Harris always said, 'there's a good chance his intentions are suspect.' "

"Aha!" Freddy said, twirling the sword at Nathan. "I should call you out, sir, for imposing upon Miss Kinsley!"

"For God's sake," Nathan mumbled, "you're all mad."

"And when Miss Kinsley didn't agree to run off with you," Mr. Pinter went on, "and Miss Butterfield showed up here to inform you of her father's death, you decided to pick up where you had left off with her."

"Except that I am no fool, either," Maria said.

"So you tried to bully her." Oliver's eyes glittered as he came to her side. "I wouldn't blame her if she *did* decide to bring a breach of promise suit against you. She might even win the other half of her father's company."

When Nathan looked positively weak in the knees, Maria said, "It's not worth my trouble. You may keep that, Nathan, since you actually earned it. Maybe you can even find another heiress to provide you with the blunt to buy the other half."

Her voice hardened. "But whatever your decision, you'd best make it quick. I have waited quite long enough for my money. If I don't hear from you or your attorney by next week, I'll be forced to hire one of my own. You can find me at Halstead Hall in Ealing, where I've been staying."

She looked up at Oliver. "Now, my lord, I should like to go home."

"Certainly, my dear." Giving her his arm, he led her out.

When they all emerged into the street, Freddy offered to walk Miss Kinsley home. As the two walked off, Maria turned to Mr. Pinter. "I don't know how to thank you for everything you've done, sir."

"You can add my thanks to that," Oliver surprised her by saying.

"I merely found the man," Mr. Pinter said. "Freddy discovered all the pertinent information."

The three of them glanced down the street to where Miss Kinsley was clinging to Freddy's arm and gazing up at him adoringly.

"Now there's a match made in heaven," Mr. Pinter added.

"Or in a pie shop," Maria quipped. "Though it doesn't sound as if Mr. Kinsley is the sort of father to approve of Freddy as a suitor."

"You never know," Oliver remarked. "Freddy will be cousin to a marchioness, after all. That might tip the scales in his favor."

Mr. Pinter swung a solemn gaze to Oliver. "So you were sincere about offering marriage to Miss Butterfield."

"Utterly sincere." Oliver covered her hand with his. "If she'll have me. I can offer her little, considering what a wreck I've made of my life until now. But I love her."

The Bow Street runner gave a faint smile. "Well, that's the important thing, isn't it?"

"It certainly is," Maria said. "As soon as I receive my money, Mr. Pinter, I'll happily pay whatever fee you require. I'll recommend you to all my friends, as well."

Oliver squeezed her hand, then glanced at Mr. Pinter. "Actually, I'd like to hire you myself, Pinter. If you'll come out to the estate sometime next week, we can discuss it."

"As you wish, my lord," Mr. Pinter said.

"And now," Oliver said, "if you don't mind, I wish to take my fiancée for a stroll in that park. We'll see you at the inn."

"Certainly," Mr. Pinter said.

Maria and Oliver walked together, her arm in his and her heart filled with love. She still couldn't believe the things he'd said to Nathan about her. She would cherish them always.

As soon as they were under the trees, Oliver said, "I have this special license burning a hole in my pocket, so I was thinking we might go find a vicar and use it. Pinter and Freddy can act as witnesses." He looked anxiously at her. "What do you think?"

"Don't you want your family present when we marry? I thought you lordly sorts had to have grand weddings."

"Is that what you want?"

In truth, she'd never been one to dream of her wedding day as a brilliant spectacle. Clandestine weddings were always what captured her imagination, complete with a dangerous, brooding fellow and mysterious goings-on. In this instance, she had both.

He said, "Let me put it this way: we can spend an untold number of days sneaking around just to steal a kiss, being chaperoned every minute while my sisters and Gran plan the wedding of the century. Or we can marry today and share a bed at the inn tonight like a respectable husband and wife. I'm not keen on waiting, but then, I never am when it comes to you. So what is your opinion in the matter?"

She couldn't resist teasing him a little. "I think you just want to punish your grandmother for her sly tactics by depriving her of the wedding."

He smiled. "Perhaps a little. And God knows my friends are never going to let me live this down. I'm not looking forward to hours of their torment at a wedding breakfast."

He stopped in a little copse where they would be hidden from the street. "But if you want a big wedding, I can endure it." His expression was solemn as he took her hands in his. "I can endure anything, as long as you marry me. And keep loving me for the rest of your life."

Staring into his earnest face, she felt something flip over in her chest. She stretched up to brush his mouth with hers, and he pulled her in for a long, ardent kiss.

"Well?" he said huskily when he was done. "If I had any sense of decency, I would give you a chance to consult with a lawyer about settlements and such, especially since you'll be coming into some money. But—"

"You have no sense of decency, I know," she teased. She tapped her finger against her chin. "Or was that morals you claimed not to have? I can't remember."

"Watch it, minx," he warned with a lift of his brow. "If you intend to taunt me for every foolish statement I've made in my life, you'll force me to play Rockton and lock you up in my dark, forbidding manor while I have my wicked way with you."

"That sounds perfectly awful," she said, gazing at the man she loved. "How soon can we start?"

Chapter Twenty-Eight

A month had passed since Oliver married Maria before a rector in Southampton. They'd taken their time about returning to Halstead Hall, sending Freddy ahead with Pinter to inform the family of their marriage while they enjoyed the seaside on a honeymoon trip.

Hyatt had gone back to America to negotiate with Maria's trustees. A lengthy letter from Oliver detailing the man's deceptions had preceded him. Convinced that the men her father had appointed to oversee her funds were honest, Maria assured Oliver that they would hold Hyatt's feet to the fire regarding the sale.

Though Oliver hoped so, he was taking no chances. He and Maria were to leave for America in a few days so she could consult with the trustees and make sure her aunt was well provided for. Freddy and his new bride, Miss Kinsley, were traveling with them, since he wanted to bring her home to meet his mother. But it was only to be a visit; Freddy had decided to live in England and work for his father-in-law. Oliver rather pitied Mr. Kinsley for that.

Now there was only one thing left to do before Oliver and Maria could depart for Massachusetts. They'd been back at Halstead Hall a week now, and he'd put it off as long as he could.

"Are you ready?" he asked Maria as they stood outside the library.

"As ready as I'll ever be," she answered with an anxious smile.

He knew her anxiety was for him, and he shared it. For half a second, he was tempted to return the way they'd just come—climb upstairs to the master bedchamber and spend the rest of the day forgetting duty to the estate and his family while he made love to his wife. But he doubted Maria would let him. For an American, she had quite a keen sense of aristocratic duty herself. To his surprise, he found it highly arousing.

"They're going to hate us both, you know," he said.

"I doubt that," she replied. "And if they do, it won't be for long."

He wasn't so sure, but he opened the door and ushered her in.

His brothers and sisters were ranged about the table much as they had been on the day Gran gave her ultimatum, but today they were in a more jovial mood.

"So, Oliver, what do you think?" Jarret asked as Oliver held out a chair for Maria. "Now that you're leg-shackled, will Gran relent?"

"Why else would she have called this meeting?" Minerva

said. "She's got what she wanted all along—Oliver married and running the estate."

"Even if she doesn't relent," Gabe pointed out, "we don't need her money, thanks to Maria's fortune. Right, Oliver?" He flashed Maria a grin. "We're most grateful to you for that, Maria."

Time to lower the boom. "Actually, my wife and I have decided that part of her fortune should go to help her family—she has an aunt and four cousins, you know. The other part will go into a trust for our children."

Gabe's grin faltered.

"And I was the one who called this meeting," Oliver added. "Not Gran."

At that moment, his grandmother came in, tapping her cane along the floor. "Sorry I'm late, but I had an emergency at the brewery."

"It's no problem," he said. "We were just getting started."

As he held out a chair for her, the stunned expression on his siblings' faces had him fighting a smile.

"Now, then," he said, returning to the head of the table, "I think you should know that Gran's original requirement is still in place. The four of you must marry or she will disinherit the lot of us. I've done my part. So I suggest that while Maria and I are in America, you four start looking for mates."

It took a second for that to sink in.

Minerva exploded first. "That isn't fair! Gran, I'm sure you'll have your heir from Oliver and Maria in no time, given the hours they spend up there in the master bedchamber. Why in heaven's name must you continue this farce?"

"I asked her to continue it," Oliver said. When his siblings gaped at him, he added, "Gran is right—it's time that we take our place in the world as more than hellions. We've been sleepwalking too long, locked into the past, unable to live fruitful lives. Now that Maria has awakened me, I want to wake you up, too. I want you to stop boxing at shadows and hiding in the dark from the scandal of our parents' deaths. I want you to find what I've found—love."

He gazed at Maria, who cast him an encouraging smile. They'd both agreed that this might be the only way to force his siblings awake.

"Speak for yourself," Minerva answered. "I'm perfectly fine. You're just using that nonsense as an excuse for joining up with Gran to ruin our lives." She glanced resentfully at Maria. "Is this the thanks we get for pushing him into your arms?"

"Pushing me into her arms?" Oliver echoed.

"All that making you jealous and keeping you from her—" Gabe began.

"And lying to you about her inheritance," Jarret added. "Though that didn't work out quite as planned."

"You wouldn't even *be* together if not for us," Celia said.

"I suspect my wife would beg to differ," Oliver drawled. "But that's neither here nor there. Rail at me all you want, but Gran's deadline is still in place. You have ten months to marry." He cast them a thin smile. "Given how difficult that may prove, however, I've hired someone to help you."

He turned to the door. "Mr. Pinter? Would you step inside, please?"

The Bow Street runner walked in, looking uneasy at facing the entire cadre of scandalous Sharpes.

"Mr. Pinter has agreed to help you by researching the backgrounds of your potential spouses. I know it can be difficult, especially for you girls, to sort the legitimate suitors from the fortune hunters." He knew that firsthand. "So Mr. Pinter will investigate anyone who sparks your interest. That should make the entire process move more quickly."

"And cold-bloodedly," Celia muttered under her breath.

Pinter arched an eyebrow but said nothing.

"Thank you, Mr. Pinter," Oliver said. "If you'd be so good as to wait in my study, I need to say a few more things to my siblings."

With a nod, Pinter left.

Now came the worst part. Turning to close the door, Oliver went to stand beside Maria. He needed her strength now. She took his hand and squeezed it.

"I've never told you the truth of what happened the day Mother killed Father. It's time that I did. There have been too many secrets among us for too long."

Shocked silence fell upon the room. He'd gone over the speech in his head twenty times, yet now that it was here, he could hardly say the words. Fortunately Maria was at his side, her forgiveness and understanding bolstering his courage.

He clung to that as he related the events of that horrible day. He'd considered not revealing that he'd slept with Lilith—indeed, Maria had tried to convince him that he need not endure that humiliation. But every time he tried to figure out how to tell the tale by glossing over that part, it came out wrong. He had to say it all.

As he got through it, he couldn't look at them. He'd known it wouldn't be easy to tell his siblings that he was responsible for the deaths of the parents they still mourned, but he'd never guessed it would be *so* hard.

Maria had. Trying to protect him, she'd asked him repeatedly if he was sure this was what he wanted to do. But they deserved to know. It was as simple as that.

When he finished, a deathly hush descended upon the room. Maria squeezed his hand painfully tight, and he still couldn't bring himself to meet their eyes.

Then Jarret spoke. "That cold bitch," he said, his voice filled with venom. "I should have known Mrs. Rawdon was mixed up in it. She and Major Rawdon hustled off after the house party in a big hurry."

Oliver's stunned gaze rose to meet Jarret's, which held no hint of condemnation toward him.

"She flirted with every man there, even me," Jarret went on. "And I was only thirteen. It could just as easily have been my room she walked into that day."

Beside Jarret, Celia was silently weeping, and Gabe was clearing his throat with a vengeance. Minerva regarded Oliver with a look of such compassion that tears stung his own eyes.

He couldn't believe it. Hadn't they understood the point? Hadn't they been paying attention? "I thought you should know that I was the one to blame for—"

"You were not to blame for anything!" Minerva cried as she

leapt to her feet. "You were in the wrong place at the wrong time with the wrong person. That's all."

"If anyone's to blame," Gran said from his other side, "it's me."

He turned to look at her. She, too, was crying, her papery cheeks damp from tears.

She lifted a remorseful gaze to him. "I should have listened to you when you said it was important I go after them. I have always regretted that. If I had only known . . ."

He laid his hand on her shoulder. "It wasn't your fault. I was too embarrassed to tell you what Mother and I fought about."

"Can't say as I blame you, old boy," Gabe put in, his voice hoarse. "*I* would never have told Gran such a thing. I can't even imagine having Mother walk in on me while . . . That's every chap's nightmare."

They all chimed in to agree with Gabe.

"You know," Celia said, dabbing at her eyes with a handkerchief, "Mrs. Rawdon must have told Mother something to make her go into your room at the right time." When everyone looked at her, she blinked. "It just doesn't seem feasible that Mother would have happened to go into Oliver's bedchamber without knocking or anything."

Oliver said, "Unfortunately, we'll never know for sure. Lilith and the major left England long ago, so I wasn't able to ask."

The conversation turned to speculation about Mrs. Rawdon's motives, and then to memories about their mother and how rigid she could be. Before he knew it, they were laughing at some tale Gabe told of Mother paddling him for running naked across the courtyard at five.

Oliver cast Maria a bewildered glance, and she pulled him into the empty chair beside her. "Let them laugh," she said softly. "It makes it easier for them to face. It's a lot to swallow at once—the knowledge that your mother killed your father on purpose. You have to give them time to absorb it, to figure out what it means to them. Right now, all they can do is laugh or keep crying, and they don't want to hurt you more by crying."

"But they should be blaming me. And they don't."

"Because they're not stupid," she said with a loving smile. "They place the blame where it should be placed, on Mrs. Rawdon and your mother. And on your father, for being a heartless rakehell."

Gran laid her hand on his. "Your mother always was a sensitive soul—too sensitive, if you ask me. I would have gone after your father with a poker the first time he even looked at another woman." She patted his hand. "You may not know this, but your grandfather was quite the rogue in his own day. Shaped right up after he married me, though."

Oliver eyed her askance. "I don't imagine you gave him much choice."

"No, indeed." She blotted her eyes with a handkerchief. "I still miss him, bless my soul. You remind me of him sometimes. He cut quite the dashing figure. And what a dancer! Lord, we used to dance all night."

"I told you," Maria said to Oliver. "It's your mother's line you favor. Not your father's."

He began to think she was right. With Maria in his life, he couldn't imagine looking at another woman, much less bedding one. His duties at Halstead Hall kept him so busy he wondered how his father had ever managed to juggle a wife, an estate, and assorted tarts. The man must have been mad.

"Are we done now?" asked Minerva, jerking him from his reverie. "Or do you have other astonishing revelations to drop into our laps? Because if we're done, I have some writing to do."

He looked around to see that the others were awaiting his answer. He'd expected an entirely different outcome to this discussion, and now he was all at sea.

"Yes, we're done," Maria said helpfully. "Thank you all for being so understanding."

"Well then." Minerva rose to her feet. "We'll see you at dinner."

And with that, the rest of them stood and trooped out of the room.

Minerva paused by his chair. "What Mother said to you was dreadful. I know she didn't mean it. And I'm sorry you've suffered for it all these years." She pressed a kiss to his cheek. "But that *doesn't* mean I forgive you for going over to Gran's side, you traitor."

He couldn't help laughing. Minerva had always been a sore loser.

When his siblings were gone, Gran stood. "Thank you for taking my side in this." She flashed Maria a smile. "And thank you for not giving up on him." Then she, too, left.

Now that they had the room to themselves, Oliver turned to Maria. "I have to second Gran's thanks for not giving up on me."

"I did consider it a few times," she teased. "But you can be such an engaging fellow that I never considered it for long."

"And there was all that encouragement from my siblings," he said. "All their little machinations to help our romance along."

He had the satisfaction of watching his wife blush very prettily. "I didn't have anything to do with that. I had no idea they were trying to 'push you' anywhere."

"Of course you didn't. You don't have an ounce of guile in your entire body. But I knew what they were doing."

She blinked at him. "You did?"

"My siblings are as transparent as that fetching night rail you put on every evening."

"If you knew, why didn't you fight them?"

"Because they were pushing me in a direction I wanted to go."

"That's very sweet, but I'm sure you had no desire to marry until—"

"From the moment I met you, sweetheart, I could tell I was in trouble. I didn't acknowledge it, but on some level I sensed it. When a man first sees the thing he never realized he wanted, he knows it instantly. He just doesn't always know how to get it."

She laughed. "Oh, I think you figured out very quickly how to get it. You just kissed me until I stopped kneeing you in the privates, and after that I was putty in your hands."

"So that's the secret, is it?" Reaching over, he hauled her onto his lap. "Now I know how I'll be spending my afternoon."

Her eyes gleamed at him. "Meeting with the tenants?"

"Guess again." He began to unbutton her gown, which very conveniently opened in the front.

"Consulting with the carpenter?"

"Absolutely not." Kissing each swath of flesh revealed with the release of a button, he started dragging up her skirts with his other hand.

"Seducing your wife?" she teased, then caught her breath as he slipped his hand between her legs to find her already ready for him.

"Exactly. But, if you don't mind, I believe I shall skip the part where you knee me in the privates."

And as she burst into laughter, he set about to show her the decided advantages in marrying a rakehell.

Epilogue

Spring in Dartmouth was delightful, with enough warmth in the air and buds on the trees to cheer Maria until the full glory of it sprang upon them in May. It was a pity that she and Oliver would be gone by then, but he felt that he couldn't in good conscience leave the estate in his steward's hands much longer.

Fortunately, her trustees had found a man to buy her half of the business for a lovely price. So now Nathan had a new partner who, by all accounts, was a dour old drudge with nary a daughter to his name. She'd seen Nathan in town once since then. He had not looked happy.

But she was insanely happy, especially after what the doctor had told her yesterday. With only a few days left at home, she and Freddy had dragged Jane and Oliver on a romantic picnic. So far, it wasn't going all that well. Poor Jane darted up at every sound. Freddy's mischievous brothers had convinced her that wild Indians might descend upon them any minute, and no amount of Freddy's posturing with the sword could relieve her fears.

Oliver was no help, either. He kept pretending to see feather headdresses behind every bush, though Maria had told him repeatedly that the only tribes in their area had left long ago. He was every bit as devilish as her cousins, who'd embraced him instantly as a man after their own hearts. Aunt Rose had pronounced Oliver a smooth-tongued rogue the first time he told her how fetching she looked in her peacock bonnet.

Little did she know.

"Are you sure there's a fish pond back there, Freddy?" Jane asked skeptically as Freddy led her around a deserted cabin.

"Quite sure." He puffed out his chest. "I've caught many a fine trout in that pond."

"More like trout *bait*," Maria told Oliver, who was stretched out on the blanket beside her, reading a letter from Jarret. "I've never seen a fish longer than my thumb in that pond."

"Hmm?" Clearly Oliver hadn't heard a word.

She pushed the letter down with her finger. "How goes Jarret's search for a bride?"

"He doesn't say." Oliver's eyes darkened. "But Gran's ill. She hasn't been able to leave her house in town for a week. Jarret is worried."

"Then it's good we're returning soon."

He nodded. "He also says something rather peculiar."

"Oh?"

"He's been thinking about the day our parents died, and he's almost certain that my memory of the events is wrong in one respect." Oliver stared off across the field. "He claims that Mother did not ride out after Father. That it was the other way around."

"What does he base that opinion on?"

"He doesn't say. All he says is that we'll talk about it further when you and I return."

She considered that a moment. "Does it matter who went after whom?"

"For me, it does. It means Mother didn't go tearing off in anger to kill Father. That perhaps I wasn't as much to blame as I'd thought."

"You were never as much to blame as you thought," she told him softly.

A brief smile touched his lips. "That's what *you* say. But you're biased."

She shrugged. "Maybe a little. But I would never have agreed to marry you if I'd thought you capable of real wickedness. I wouldn't have risked having a child of mine suffer the same torments you and your siblings suffered."

Oliver went still. "And does this sudden mention of some future child have anything to do with your sneaking out of the house to consult with a physician this morning?"

She gaped at him. "You knew? How did you find out?"

"Believe me, angel, I know whenever you leave my bed." His eyes gleamed at her. "I feel the loss of it right here." He struck his heart dramatically.

"Aunt Rose spoke the truth about you," she grumbled. "You *are* a smooth-tongued devil. And apparently you read minds, as well."

He chuckled. "Your aunt simply cannot keep secrets. But to be honest, it's not been hard to notice how little interest you show in your breakfast these days, and how often you like to nap. I know the signs of a woman with child. I watched my mother go through them with four children."

"And here I was hoping to surprise you," she said with a pout. "I swear you are impossible to surprise."

"That's only because you used up all your surprises in the first hour of our meeting."

"How so?"

"By boldly threatening me with Freddy's sword. And by agreeing to my insane proposal. Then by showing sympathy for the loss of my parents. Few people ever did that for me."

As a lump caught in her throat, he pulled her into his arms. "But your greatest surprise came long after, on that day in the inn." Laying his hand on her still flat belly, his voice grew husky. "You surprised me by loving me. That was the best surprise of all."

Don't miss the next book in the "sparkling" (*Library Journal*) Hellions of Halstead Hall series

A Hellion in Her Bed

Available from Pocket Books!

"A perfectly matched pair of protagonists and a lively plot blend equal measures of steamy passion and sharp wit."
—*Booklist* (starred review)

Keep reading for a sneak peek . . .

Chapter One

London
March 1825

In the nineteen years since that fateful night, Jarret had grown a foot taller and had learned how to fight, and he was still gambling. Now, for a living.

Today, however, the cards were meant to be only a distraction. Sitting at a table in the study in Gran's town house, he laid out another seven rows.

"How can you play cards at a time like this?" his sister Celia asked from the settee.

"I'm not playing cards," he said calmly. "I'm playing solitaire."

"You know Jarret," his brother Gabe put in. "Never comfortable without a deck in his hand."

"You mean, never comfortable unless he's winning," his other sister, Minerva, remarked.

"Then he must be pretty uncomfortable right now," Gabe said. "Lately, all he does is lose."

Jarret stiffened. That was true. And considering that he supported his lavish lifestyle with his winnings, it was a problem.

So of course Gabe was plaguing him about it. At twenty-six, Gabe was six years Jarret's junior and annoying as hell. Like Minerva, he had gold-streaked brown hair and green eyes the exact shade of their mother's. But that was the only trait Gabe shared with their straitlaced mother.

"You can't consistently win at solitaire unless you cheat," Minerva said.

"I never cheat at cards." It was true, if one ignored his uncanny ability to keep track of every card in a deck. Some people didn't.

"Didn't you just say that solitaire isn't 'cards'?" Gabe quipped.

Bloody arse. And to add insult to injury, Gabe was cracking his knuckles and getting on Jarret's nerves.

"For God's sake, stop that noise," Jarret snapped.

"This, you mean?" Gabe said and deliberately cracked his knuckles again.

"If you don't watch it, little brother, I'll crack my knuckles against your jaw," Jarret warned.

"Stop fighting!" Celia's hazel eyes filled with tears as she glanced at the connecting door to Gran's bedchamber. "How can you fight when Gran might be dying?"

"Gran isn't dying," said the eminently practical Minerva. Four years younger than Jarret, she lacked Celia's flair for the dramatic . . . except in the Gothic fiction she penned.

Besides, like Jarret, Minerva knew their grandmother better than their baby sister did. Hester Plumtree was indestructible. This "illness" was undoubtedly another ploy to make them toe her line.

Gran had already given them an ultimatum—they had to marry within the year or the whole lot of them would be disinherited. Jarret would have thrown the threat back in her face, but he couldn't sentence his siblings to a life with no money.

Oliver had tried to fight her edict, then had surprised them by getting himself leg-shackled to an American woman. But that hadn't satisfied Gran. She still wanted her pound of flesh from the rest of them. And now there were fewer than ten months left.

That was what had put Jarret off his game lately—Gran's attempt to force him into marrying the first female who didn't balk at the Sharpe family reputation for scandal and licentiousness. It made him desperate to win a large score, so he could support his siblings on his winnings and they could all tell her to go to hell.

But desperation was disaster at the gaming tables. His success depended on keeping a cool head and not caring about the outcome. Only then could he play to the cards he was dealt. Desperation made a man take risks based on emotion instead of skill. And that happened to him too much, lately.

What on earth did Gran think she would accomplish by forcing them to marry? She'd merely spawn more miserable marriages to match that of their parents.

But Oliver isn't miserable.

Oliver had been lucky. He'd found the one woman who

would put up with his nonsense and notoriety. The chance of that happening twice in their family was small. And four more times? Abysmally small. Lady Fortune was as fickle in life as in cards.

With a curse, Jarret rose to pace. Unlike the study at Halstead Hall, Gran's was airy and light, with furnishings of the latest fashion and a large-scale model of Plumtree Brewery prominently displayed atop a rosewood table.

He gritted his teeth. That damned brewery—she'd run it successfully for so long that she thought she could run their lives as well. She always had to be in control. One look at the papers stacked high on her desk made it clear that the brewery was becoming too much for her to handle at seventy-one. Yet the obstinate woman refused to hire a manager, no matter how Oliver pressed her.

"Jarret, did you write that letter to Oliver?" Minerva asked.

"Yes, while you were at the apothecary's. The footman has taken it to the post." Although Oliver and his new wife had already left for America to meet her relations, Jarret and Minerva wanted him to know of Gran's illness in case it *was* serious.

"I hope he and Maria are enjoying themselves in Massachusetts," Minerva said. "He seemed very upset that day in the library."

"You'd be upset, too, if you thought you'd caused our parents' deaths," Gabe pointed out.

That had been Oliver's other surprise—his revelation that he and Mother had quarreled the day of the tragedy, which had led to her going off in a rage in search of Father.

"Do you think Oliver was right?" Celia asked. "*Was* it his

fault that Mama shot Papa?" Celia had been only four when it happened, so she had little recollection of it.

That wasn't the case for Jarret. "No."

"Why not?" Minerva asked.

How much should he say? He had a strong memory of . . .

No, he shouldn't make baseless accusations, no matter *who* they concerned. But he should tell them his other concern. "I well remember Father at the picnic, muttering, 'Where the devil is *she* going?' I looked across the field and saw Mother on a horse, headed in the direction of the hunting lodge. That memory has been gnawing at me."

Gabe took up Jarret's line of reasoning. "So if she'd left in search of Father, as Oliver seems certain that she did, she would have found him at the picnic. She wouldn't have gone elsewhere looking for him."

"Precisely," Jarret said.

Minerva pursed her lips. "Which means that Gran's version of events might be correct. Mother rode to the hunting lodge because she was upset and wanted to be away from everyone. Then she fell asleep, was startled by Father, shot him—"

"And shot herself when she saw him dead?" Celia finished. "I don't believe it. It makes no sense."

Gabe cast her an indulgent glance. "Only because you don't want to believe that any woman would be so reckless as to shoot a man without thinking."

"I would certainly never do such a fool thing myself," Celia retorted.

"But you have a passion for shooting and a healthy respect for guns," Minerva pointed out. "Mother had neither."

"Exactly," Celia said. "So she picked up a gun without forethought and shot it for the first time that day? That's ridiculous. For one thing, how did she load it?"

They all stared at her.

"None of you ever thought about that, did you?"

"She could have learned," Gabe put in. "Gran knows how to shoot. Just because Mother never shot a gun around us doesn't mean Gran didn't teach her."

Celia frowned. "On the other hand, if Mother set out to shoot Father deliberately as Oliver claims, someone could have helped her load the pistol—a groom, perhaps. Then she could have lain in wait for Father near the picnic and followed him to the hunting lodge. That makes more sense."

"It's interesting that you should mention the grooms," Jarret said. "They would have had to saddle her horse—they might have known where she was going and when she left. She might even have said why she was riding out. If we could talk to them—"

"Most of them left service at Halstead Hall when Oliver closed the place down," Minerva pointed out.

"That's why I'm thinking of hiring Jackson Pinter to find them."

Celia snorted.

"You may not like him," Jarret told her, "but he's one of the most respected Bow Street runners in London." Although Pinter was supposed to be helping them explore the backgrounds of potential mates, there was no reason the man couldn't take on another mission.

The door to Gran's bedchamber opened, and Dr. Wright entered the study.

"Well?" Jarret asked sharply. "What's the verdict?"

"Can we see her?" Minerva added.

"Actually, she's been asking for Lord Jarret," Dr. Wright said.

Jarret tensed. With Oliver gone, he was the eldest. No telling what Gran had cooked up for him to do, now that she was "ill."

"Is she all right?" Celia asked, alarm plain on her face.

"At the moment, she's only suffering some chest pain. It may come to nothing." Dr. Wright met Jarret's gaze. "But she needs to keep quiet and rest until she feels better. And she refuses to do that until she can speak to you, my lord." When the others rose, he added, "Alone."

With a terse nod, Jarret followed him into Gran's room.

"Don't say anything to upset her," Dr. Wright murmured, then left and closed the door.

At the sight of his grandmother, Jarret caught his breath. He had to admit that Gran didn't look her usual self. She was propped up against the bed pillows, so she wasn't dying, but her color certainly wasn't good.

He ignored the clutch of fear in his chest. Gran was merely a little under the weather. This was just another attempt to control their lives. But she was in for a surprise if she thought that the tactics that had worked on Oliver would work on *him.*

She gestured to a chair by the bed, and Jarret warily took a seat.

"That fool Wright tells me I cannot leave my bed for a month at the very least," she grumbled. "A month! I cannot be away from the brewery for that long."

"You must take as long as necessary to get well," Jarret said, keeping his voice noncommittal until he was sure what she was up to.

"The only way I shall loll about in this bed for a month is if I have someone reliable looking after things at the brewery. Someone I trust. Someone with a vested interest in making sure it runs smoothly."

When her gaze sharpened on him, he froze. So that's what she was plotting.

"Not a chance," he said, jumping to his feet. "Don't even think it." He wasn't about to put himself under Gran's thumb. Bad enough that she was trying to dictate when he married—she wasn't going to run his whole life, too.

She took a labored breath. "You once begged me for this very opportunity."

"That was a long time ago." When he'd been desperate to find a place for himself. Then he'd learned that no matter what place you found, Fate could snatch it from you at a moment's notice. Your hopes for the future could be dashed with a word, your parents taken in the blink of an eye, and your family's good name ruined for spite.

Nothing in life was certain. So a man was better off traveling light, with no attachments and no dreams. It was the only way to prevent disappointment.

"You're going to inherit the brewery one day," she pointed out.

"Only if we all manage to marry within the year," he countered. "But assuming that I inherit, I'll hire a manager. Which you should have done years ago."

That made her frown. "I do not want some stranger running my brewery."

The perennial argument was getting old.

"If you don't want to do it, I'll have to put Desmond in charge," she added.

His temper flared. Desmond Plumtree was Mother's first cousin, a man they all despised—especially him. Gran had threatened before to leave the brewery to the bastard and she *knew* how Jarret felt about that, so she was using his feelings against him.

"Go ahead, put Desmond in charge," he said, though it took every ounce of his will not to fall prey to her manipulation.

"He knows even less about it than you do," she said peevishly. "Besides, he's busy with his latest enterprise."

He hid his relief. "There has to be someone else who knows the business well enough to take over."

She coughed into her handkerchief. "No one I trust."

"And you trust *me* to run it?" He uttered a cynical laugh. "I seem to recall your telling me a few years ago that gamblers are parasites on society. Aren't you worried I'll suck the life out of your precious brewery?"

She had the good grace to color. "I only said that because I couldn't stand watching you waste your keen mind at the gaming tables. That is not a suitable life for a clever man like yourself, especially when I know you are capable of more. You have had some success with your investments. It wouldn't take you long to get your bearings at the brewery. And I will be here for you to consult if you need advice."

The plaintive note in her voice gave him pause. She sounded almost . . . desperate. His eyes narrowed. He might be able to make this work to his advantage, after all.

He sat down once more. “If you really want me to run the brewery for a month, then I want something in return.”

“You will have a salary, and I am sure we could come to terms on—”

“Not money. I want you to rescind your ultimatum.” He leaned forward to stare her down. “No more threats to disinherit us if we don’t marry according to your dictate. Things will return to how they were before.”

She glared at him. “That is not going to happen.”

“Then I suppose you’ll be hiring a manager.” He rose and headed for the door.

“Wait!” she cried.

He paused to glance back at her with eyebrows raised.

“What if I rescind it just for *you*?”

He fought a smile. She must be desperate indeed if she was willing to bargain. “I’m listening.”

“I will have Mr. Bogg change the will so that you inherit the brewery no matter what.” Her voice turned bitter. “You can stay a bachelor until you die.”

It was worth considering. If he owned the brewery, he could help his brother and sisters if they couldn’t meet Gran’s terms by the end of the year. They’d be on their own until Gran died, of course, but then Jarret could support them. It was a better situation than their present one. “I could live with that.”

She dragged in a rasping breath. “But you’ll have to agree to stay on at the brewery until the year is up.”

He tensed. “Why?”

“Too many people depend on it for their livelihood. If I am to leave the place to you, I must be sure you can keep it afloat, even if you hire a manager to run it once I am gone. You need to know enough to be able to hire the right person, and I need assurance that you will not let it rot."

"God forbid you should trust your own grandson to keep it safe." But she did have a point. He hadn't set foot in the place in nineteen years. What did he know about the brewing business anymore?

He could learn. And he would, too, if that's what it took to stop Gran from meddling in their lives for good. But he would do it on his own terms.

"Fine," he said. "I'll stay on until the year is up." When she broke into a smile, he added, "But I want complete control. I'll keep you informed about the business, and you may express your opinions, but my decisions will be final."

That wiped the smile from her face.

"I'll run Plumtree Brewery as I see fit without any interference from you," he went on. "And you will put that in writing."

The steel in her blue eyes told him she wasn't as ill as she pretended. "You can do a great deal of damage in a year."

"Exactly. If you'll recall, this wasn't my idea."

"Then you must promise not to institute any major changes."

He crossed his arms over his chest. "No."

Alarm flared in her features. "At least promise not to make risky investments."

"No. You either let me have full control or find yourself a manager."

It felt good to have the upper hand. He refused to have her coming behind him, second-guessing every decision. If he was going to run the place, he would run it his way. And once the year was up, he'd be free to live his life as he pleased . . . and ensure that his siblings could do so as well.

Not that Gran would accept his terms. She'd never given up control of anything, for even a day. She certainly wouldn't give it to her "parasite" of a grandson for a year.

So it was with some surprise that he heard her say, "Very well, I will meet your demands. I will have it put into writing for you by tomorrow."

The gleam in her eyes gave him pause, but it was gone so fast, he was sure he'd imagined it.

"I do have one caveat," she continued. "You must keep Mr. Croft on as your secretary."

Jarret groaned. Gran's secretary at the brewery was one of the strangest men he'd ever met. "Must I?"

"I know he seems odd, but I promise that in a week or so you will find yourself glad that you kept him on. He's indispensable to the brewery."

Well, it was a small price to pay for gaining his life back. He'd definitely gotten the better end of their bargain.